EVERYMAN,
I WILL GO WITH THEE,
AND BE THY GUIDE,
IN THY MOST NEED
TO GO BY THY SIDE

IVAN TURGENEV

*First Love*

*and Other Stories*

Translated by
Isaiah Berlin and Leonard Schapiro
Introduced by V. S. Pritchett

EVERYMAN'S LIBRARY

*191*

First included in Everyman's Library, 1994

Translation of *First Love* © Isaiah Berlin, 1950
Translation of *Spring Torrents* © Leonard Schapiro, 1972
Translation of *A Fire at Sea* © Isaiah Berlin, 1957
Introduction to *A Fire at Sea* © Isaiah Berlin, 1957
Published by arrangement with Penguin Books Ltd.

The introduction to this volume by V. S. Pritchett is taken from
material originally published in *The Gentle Barbarian*,
© V. S. Pritchett, 1977, and the essay 'The Russian Day', first
collected in *The Living Novel*, © V. S. Pritchett, 1946. Published by
arrangement with V. S. Pritchett and Chatto & Windus Ltd.

Bibliography and Chronology © David Campbell Publishers Ltd.,
1994
Typography by Peter B. Willberg

ISBN 1-85715-191-7

Published by David Campbell Publishers Ltd., 79 Berwick Street,
London W1V 3PF

Distributed by Random House (UK) Ltd.,
20 Vauxhall Bridge Road, London SW1V 2SA

Typeset by MS Filmsetting Limited, Frome, Somerset

Printed and bound in Germany by
Mohndruck Graphische Betriebe GmbH, Gütersloh

# FIRST LOVE AND OTHER STORIES

# CONTENTS

_____

# INTRODUCTION

What is it that attracts us to the Russian novelists of the nineteenth century? The aristocratic culture made more vivid by its twilight? The feeling, so readily understood by English readers, for *ennui*? No. The real attraction of that censored literature is its freedom – the freedom from our kind of didacticism and our plots. The characters of our novels, from Fielding to Forster, get up in the morning, wash, dress and are then drilled for their roles. They are propelled to some practical issue in morality, psychology or Fortune before the book is done. In nineteenth-century Russia, under the simpler feudal division of society, there is more room to breathe, to let the will drift, and the disparate impulses have their ancient solitary reign. In all those Russian novels we seem to hear a voice saying: 'The meaning of life? One day that will be revealed to us – probably on a Thursday.' And the day, not the insistence of the plot or purpose, is the melodic bar. We see life again, as we indeed know it, as something written in days; its dramas not directed by the superior foreknowledge of the writer, but seeming to ebb and flow among the climaxes, the anticlimaxes, the yawnings of the hours. Turgenev, who knew English literature well, used to say that he envied the English novelists their power to make plots; but, of course, he really disdained it. The surprises of life, the sudden shudders of its skin, are fresher and more astonishing than the imposed surprises of literary convention or the teacher's lesson. And in seeing people in terms of their anonymous days, the Russians achieved, by a paradox, a sense of timelessness in their books. Gogol, for example, seems to date far less than Dickens. In the Russians there is a humility before the important fact of human inertia, the half-heartedness of its wish to move and grow, its habit of returning into itself. This is true of Turgenev; obviously true of Chekhov, and I think also of Dostoevsky. His dynamism and complex narratives are the threshings and confusions of a writer who – if we consult his notebooks and letters – could never bind his mind to a settled subject or a fixed plot.

Yet the use of the eventless day could not alone give the Russian novel its curious power; indeed, it can be its weakness. No novelists are easier to parody than the Russians. Those people picking their noses at the windows or trying on their boots while they go through passion and remorse! The day is a convention like any other. What gives those novels their power, and these persons their gift of moving us, is something which comes from a profound sense of a presence haunting the day. There lies on those persons, even on the most trivial, the shadow of a fate more richly definitive than the fate of any individual human being. Their feet stand in time and in history. Their fate is corporate. It is the fate of Russia itself, a fate so often adjured with eloquence and nostalgia, oftener still with that medieval humility which has been unknown to us since the Renaissance, and which the Russians sometimes mystically identify with the fate of humanity itself.

The presence which haunts Turgenev's novels is pre-eminently the power of spring, the sense of movement, change and renewal. He is the novelist of the moments after meetings and the moments before partings. He watches the young heart rise the first time. He watches it fall, winged, to the common distorted lot. Those are the moments we observe in *First Love* and *Spring Torrents*.

*First Love* was written in 1860 after the publication of Turgenev's novel *On The Eve*. The novel had been a critical failure and Turgenev himself was not altogether happy with it. He had taken the idea for his hero, Insarov, from a young neighbour, who told him the story of a girl he had once known who fell in love with a Bulgarian patriot and went with him to Bulgaria where she died. Turgenev's heroine, Yelena, is a real, troubled character whose doubts and courage are clear to us but Insarov refuses to come to life. It is also clear that Turgenev knew nothing about conspiracy, and the ability to create complex plots and exciting action are not among his gifts.

Perhaps it is therefore not surprising that, after the failure of *On The Eve*, he turned to his own past and produced a masterpiece in the art most natural to him, the story that runs to a hundred pages. The story was *First Love*, the tale, which he said was autobiographical, of a father and his sixteen-year-old son who are in love with the same young girl. In it, Turgenev draws a moving portrait of his father and, indeed, told friends that the story came directly from his own early youth. He had never seen, he said, a man more 'elaborately serene'.

He took scarcely any interest in my education but never hurt my feelings; he respected my freedom; he displayed – if one can put it that way – a certain courtesy ... only he never let me come at all close to him. I loved him ... he seemed to me the ideal man – and God knows how passionately attached to him I should have been if I had not felt constantly the presence of his restraining hand. Yet he could, whenever he wished, with a single word, a single gesture, instantly make me feel complete trust in him ... Sometimes a mood of gaiety would come over him and at such moments he was ready to play and romp with me ... like a boy ... Once, and only once, he caressed me with such tenderness that I nearly cried ... I came to the conclusion that he cared nothing for me nor for family life; it was something very different he loved ...

From his father's sayings, Turgenev took these words for his story:

'Take what you can yourself, and don't let others get you into their hands; to belong to oneself, that is the whole thing in life' ... On another occasion, being at that time a youthful democrat, I embarked on a discussion of liberty ... 'Liberty,' he repeated. 'Do you know what really makes a man free?'

'What?'

'Will, your own will, and it gives power which is better than liberty. Know how to want, and you'll be free, and you'll be master too.'

Before and above everything, my father wanted to live ... and did live. Perhaps he had a premonition that he would not have long in which to make use of the 'thing in life'; he died at forty-two.

And at the end of the story when the father is dying, he says to his son, words that Turgenev repeated in many of his stories throughout his life:

'My son,' he wrote, 'beware of the love of women; beware of that ecstasy – that slow poison.'

When the story appeared, Turgenev had to face more severe

criticism, but this time it came from his own circle. The character based on his father attracted particular dislike. Louis Viardot, the husband of Turgenev's adored Pauline, wrote sternly, as friend to friend, that it was nothing but a glorification of adultery à la *Dame aux Camélias* and that Turgenev was drifting into the sewer of the modern novel. The characters of the dirty, snuff-taking Princess and her daughter were odious. And how could the father in the story be charming and adorable when he had cynically married a rich woman in order to spend her fortune on his mistresses? Why not, at the very least, make him a widower – the censor had made a similar complaint years before when he rejected *A Month in the Country*. Worst of all, Viardot said, the narrator is a man of forty who ought to have known better than to expose the vices of his father. This letter gives us one of those rare sights of the remote Louis Viardot who struck people as being an outsider in his own family and who indeed is known to have complained to his wife that the manner in which she left him out of the conversation with her famous friends at Courtavenel was causing gossip. He begged her to restrain herself. The respectable atheist and Republican enjoyed an extremely indecent piece of *gauloiserie* so long as it had the blessing of history and concerned the vices of Kings and Courts, but he held sternly to the morality of the middle class.

The story and its intention are, of course, quite unlike Louis Viardot's caricature of it which can only have sprung from the anger of a good man who had had to endure the insinuations conventionally made about an elderly husband married to a famous young wife. The story is a study of the devastating loss of innocence and the revelation of the nature of adult passion and, as usual in Turgenev's stories, it turns on the growth of knowledge of the heart. Love is not the simple yet tormenting rapture of a touching adolescent; it is a violent, awe-inspiring passion which leaves its trail of jealousies and guilt. There was some truth in the criticism that Turgenev's love stories have something of the emblem or fairy tale in them, but *First Love*, like the later *Spring Torrents* and the love story in *Smoke*, contains one of his rare statements about the nature of physical passion – rare because of his own romantic idealism or the conventions of the time. There is no pressing on the pedal in the powerful scenes: they are quiet. Truth-telling – quite different from the highly coloured naturalism which Louis Viardot had read into the story – rules every turn of feeling. The boy sees his father at night talking to a woman at the open window of a house. She is Zinaida with whom the boy is in love. She is refusing the father something:

My father gave a shrug of his shoulders, and set his hat straight on his head, which with him was always a sign of impatience ... then I could hear the words '*Vous devez vous séparer de cette ...*' Zinaida straightened herself and held out her hand. Then something unbelievable took place before my eyes. My father suddenly lifted his riding-crop, with which he had been flicking the dust off the folds of his coat, and I heard the sound of a sharp blow struck across her arm which was bared to the elbow. It was all I could do to prevent myself from crying out. Zinaida quivered – looked silently at my father – and raising her arm slowly to her lips, kissed the scar which glowed crimson upon it.

And the boy goes home thinking 'this is love ... this is passion ... yet how could one bear to be struck by any hand, however dear – and yet, it seems, one can, if one is in love...'

My father flung away the crop and bounding quickly up the steps to the porch, broke into the house. Zinaida turned round, stretched out her arms, tossed her head back – and also moved away from the window.

That is the climax of a story which has passed through the comic antics of Zinaida's admirers. We have seen various kinds of love. We have seen feelings change into their opposite. The boy's startled jealousy of his father is violent, then absurd, then turns to admiration amounting to worship, and then is quietly dissolved in the events of ordinary life. What is sometimes called leisurely in Turgenev is not so much a sense of timelessness as one of space in which everything will eventually be accounted for or vanish. Life is affirmed not only in its intense moments but in its continuing: the fact that the boy cannot know all, that indeed no one knows all, gives Turgenev's realism its essential truth-telling quality. In this his realism is finer than Tolstoy's assertion of all knowledge. The story goes on:

Two months later, I entered the University, and six months after that my father died (as the result of a stroke) in St. Petersburg, where he had only just moved with my mother and me. Several days before his death he had received a letter from Moscow which upset him greatly. He went to beg some sort of favour of my mother and, so they told me, actually broke down and wept – he, my father! On the morning of the very day on which he had the stroke, he had begun a letter to me, written in French. 'My son,' he wrote, 'beware of the love of women; beware of that ecstasy – that slow poison.' My mother, after his death, sent a considerable sum of money to Moscow.

But, for Turgenev, explanation is not an end. Life is not enclosed reminiscence:

During the past month, I had suddenly grown much older, and my love, with all its violent excitements and its torments, now seemed even to me so very puny and childish and trivial beside that other unknown something which I could hardly begin to guess at, but which struck terror into me like an unfamiliar, beautiful, but awe-inspiring face whose features one strains in vain to discern in the gathering darkness.

And now the story becomes still more spacious than its observed drama. Years ripple on, 'everything within you melts away like wax in the sun . . . like snow', and the writer hears of Zinaida's death in childbirth. 'So that was the final goal towards which this young life, all glitter and ardour and excitement, went hurrying along.' What had he left now, in old age, fresher and dearer than his memory of 'that brief storm that came and went so swiftly one morning in the spring?' Far more than this personal memory of love and death. He recalls that some days after he heard of Zinaida's death, obeying an irresistible impulse he was present at the death of a poor old woman who had known nothing but bitter struggle with daily want and had had no joy or happiness – wouldn't she be glad to die? No, she feared death and fought it and kept whispering 'Lord forgive me my sins.' We are brought back to Zinaida's, his father's and his own desire for life:

by the death-bed of that poor old woman, I grew afraid, afraid for Zinaida, and I wanted to say a prayer for her, for my father – and for myself.

This is Louis Viardot's vulgar story of adultery! A story that begins as a comedy of intrigue and becomes a tragedy that disperses us into the common lot! We recall Turgenev's quotation from Pascal:

*Le dernier acte est sanglant, quelque soit la comédie en tout le reste. On jette enfin de la terre sur la tête.*

*

Turgenev spent most of the decade following the production of *First Love* in the German spa town of Baden where he lived comfortably with the Viardot family – perhaps too comfortably. As he himself wrote to a friend in 1870, a 'Russian writer who had settled in Baden by that very fact condemns his writing to an early end. I have no illusions on that score, but since everything else is impossible, there is no point in talking about it.' But Turgenev was to be proved wrong about the end of his writing career. In 1871 he moved to Paris with the Viardots and in the following year produced *Spring Torrents*, which is the greatest masterpiece among his love stories.

Some Russian critics despised it *because* it was a love story and also because it was set in Germany. It is in fact very Russian if we think of inconsequence in matters of feeling as being Russian, though of course the story is really about honour and this theme has implications far beyond the love story itself. It is also very funny. Comedy can only be written by serious minds and this one brims with the spontaneous and unthinking delight of youth and youth's misreading of the future:

First love is like a revolution: the monotonous routine of life is smashed; youth takes its stand at the barricades.

Not only *first* love: the story can be felt to be true to the passion, especially to its passage from illusion to illusion, at any age. One knows that Sanin is twenty-two or twenty-three, and Gemma about nineteen; but it is a surprise that the second implicated couple, Polozov the sleepy gourmet and Maria, the *femme fatale*, his wife, are only three years older, though the kind of young who are born old and without innocence. The story is a comedy in which the hours of the day smile at the characters as they pass over them, until passion moves them out of real time and into a state where time seems to stop. For Turgenev, love is an accident, contrived by Nature for its own purpose, and when love becomes sexual passion, honour is lost. There is something in Leonard Schapiro's suggestion that Turgenev had been reading the fashionable and pessimistic Schopenhauer. (Tolstoy was affected by him too.) And of course there is something of Turgenev's mysterious attitude to sex in which love and sex are kept in separate compartments. Whatever conclusions we come to about this, they do not alter the fact that a story set in the 1840s in old-fashioned Frankfurt and Wiesbaden but written from the point of view of the 1870s has the tone, the directness and, above all, the economy which bring it near to ourselves.

The comedy is also a crystallization of Turgenev's sense of his personal tragedy. We are discreetly made aware, by his detachment, of a double view: he has caught the evanescence of the surface of experience – as I have said of the hours flowing through the fond yet baffled people and the scene, and yet we are aware of the moral undertow which drags at the swimmers who are living from moment to moment, drawing them out of their depth. To Turgenev the inevitable passing of youth and of its freedom was agonizing and one can see his pose of premature old age or a perpetual Goodbye as a device for preserving the sense of youth untouched. The very naivety and child-like qualities that were hidden behind his perfect manners suggest that his feeling about lost youth was more than the common nostalgia but rather a wonder always awake in his battered, personal life. Youth was a work of art in itself. The double view of love we find in the story, of middle age looking back on a folly that turns into betrayal and shame, gives the comedy of *Spring Torrents* its moral complexities.

As in several earlier stories, notably *A Correspondence* and *Acia*, the ghost of the Turgenev-Viardot situation stands in the shadow of *Spring Torrents*, but the characters have no resem-

blance to them. Sanin, the impulsive young Russian nobleman, travelling in Germany, is a sort of Turgenev without his
convictions or gifts; novelists find it useful to put a derogatory
half-picture of themselves into a story in order to gain perspec-
tive and to free the story from the maudlin or from the blur of
introspection. The tale is said to have started in his mind from
the memory of meeting a beautiful Jewish girl in Frankfurt
when he was twenty-two. She had, like Gemma the Italian girl
in the story, rushed out of the confectioner's shop when he was
passing to ask him to save her brother who was thought to be
dying inside. The young Turgenev himself went on to Russia,
but the image of the beautiful girl remained in his mind: the
rest of the story is invention. Most important is its frame: it
opens with Sanin-Turgenev at the age of fifty-three coming
back at night from a party of brilliant people in which he
himself had been a brilliant talker. He is exhausted physically
and spiritually and is suddenly attacked by the *taedium vitae*,
the disgust with life, as a man who talks too well may easily be:

He reflected on the useless bustle, the vulgar falsity of human
existence ... Everywhere he found the same squandering of time and
effort, the same treading of water, the same self-deception, half
unconscious and half deliberate ... and then – all of a sudden – like a
fall of snow, old age is upon one – and with it the ever-growing fear of
death, all-consuming, gnawing at one's very vitals – and then, the
abyss.

And once more he sees the familiar nightmare image of death
about which Turgenev had written in *Phantoms*. He is in a
boat, looking down into the transparent water, and out of the
slime below he sees huge hideous fishes; one of these monsters
rises to the surface as if to overturn the boat, but sinks once
more. He knows that 'the destined day will come' when it will
rise up again and sink him for good. This is the classic
nightmare of Turgenev's pessimism. Sanin goes to his desk to
rummage among old papers in order to drive the despair away
and to his surprise comes upon a garnet cross. At once he is
back in his youth in Frankfurt and sees the beautiful girl
rushing out of the confectioner's who has now become the
Italian Gemma. The spring of youth begins to flow, Sanin

loses his fifty-three years and standing over his shoulder presents the ingenuous young Sanin. This world-weary, even sentimental conventional gambit is common enough in story-telling but there is something different in Turgenev's handling of it: that opening portrait is a dramatic shadow that will run with the narrative so that the past will be seen running towards an inescapable present. Turgenev is free to mock his youth and to watch the defeat of innocence without abusing it.

He worked for two years on this story. He wrote the fifty thousand words at least three times. His art is the pursuit of truth-telling and balance; he does not allow one character to obscure another; he lets every character do what it is his nature to do. And each one delights because of the gentle but firm manner in which he makes them add unsuspected traits to themselves. All is movement.

The story also owes much of its freshness to its division into forty-three short chapters, most of them only five or six pages long and reading like variations on a deepening melody. The Italian family is delightfully drawn. There are the fond, shrewd mother, Frau Lenore with her headaches and her tears; the dramatizing Pantaleone, who had once been on the operatic stage but is now sunk to the state of half-servant, half-family friend; the beautiful Gemma who is charming but has a mind of her own; her fiancé Herr Klueber, the pompous rising shopkeeper; the rude blustering German officer, Baron von Doenhof whom Sanin challenges to a duel; the handsome Italian son of the family who wants to be an artist and not a shopkeeper – they are all moved into action. Sanin and Gemma are bemused by each other, each is a wonder. In Sanin, Gemma sees an eloquent young hero, free of the pettiness of shopkeeping, a young man of honour, enchantingly free. Sanin sees Gemma as a goddess and his love begins when he is jealous of Herr Klueber and horrified to think of her becoming the wife of a stiff, obsequious shopkeeper. Klueber, as it turns out, is afraid to stand up to a rude German officer who shouts his drunken admiration of Gemma across the tables at a restaurant. Klueber takes his party away, but Sanin stays behind to challenge Von Doenhof to a duel. Already the feet of Sanin and Gemma have left the earth.

What accident will Nature trick them with to make them fall into each other's arms? As Sanin stands near her window he and Gemma are literally blown together.

Suddenly, in the midst of the deep silence, in a completely cloudless sky, there arose such a rush of wind that the very earth seemed to quake beneath their feet. The thin light of the stars shuddered and scattered, and the very air was whirling around them. The onrush of wind, which was not cold but warm and even torrid, struck at the trees, at the roof of the house, at its walls, at the street.

The din lasts only for a minute and in that time the two have grabbed each other for protection.

In no time the whole Italian family are in love with the lovers. Madness seizes them all. Sanin says he will sell his estates in Russia instantly, take a job in the diplomatic service: better still, turn confectioner. Even Frau Lenore starts innocently working out how she will enlarge the shop. They are all living unreal lives.

Sanin leaves the shop to find someone who will buy his estates. Idiotic luck is on his side: he meets a Russian friend, Polozov, who had been at boarding school with him, and tells him what has happened. Polozov says that he cannot offer any money, but says that, very likely, if managed in the right way, his rich wife probably will. The Polozovs are staying in nearby Wiesbaden. This prospect seems quite normal to Sanin. We now see one kind of illusion in love, turning to a darker one.

Sanin goes with Polozov to Wiesbaden to meet his rich wife. Love is not a miracle for the Polozovs: it is a sophisticated arrangement, a tolerated enslavement which takes the form of freedom. Polozov, an idle and impotent gourmet, is married to a sexually ravenous woman, half-gypsy and possibly of a serf background, apt to be vulgar in speech, intelligent, a beautiful animal, who has married in order to be free to take on any lovers she wants. The chaste Gemma has inspired the idealist in Sanin: Maria Polozov is struck by him and settles to drawing out his sensuality, promising him the money but working on him until his love for Gemma is adroitly turned into sexual desire for herself. The scenes in which she negotiates this are wonderfully done and they end with an after-

noon on which Sanin and Maria go riding into the mountains
and the animal exhilaration of the ride ends in her victory.

This is one of the most sustained evocations of sensual love
in Turgenev's writing and may be said to be unique, for in
*First Love* one has only a brief perception from an outside
observer. In *Spring Torrents* one sees the whole of the experience, except the act itself, from the growth of the intrigue,
those exchanges of personal history in the theatre, those
impatient yet cunning insinuations on the woman's side, the
cornering of Sanin's conscience and the dissembling of the
imagination as desire takes him into bewitchment. The ride
into the mountains is long, constantly distracting him with the
excitement of canter and gallop and yet each distraction
heightening the sexual impulse as Sanin follows Maria from
the road, into the woods, across the sudden light of swampy
field, into darker forest and paths which she knows but he does
not, to the woodman's hut where they tie their tired and
shuddering horses – this detail obliquely suggesting the
exhaustion and will-lessness of the mind, helpless before the
act can seize them and passion come out in its full strength.
Turgenev obtrudes no overt symbolism (which usually mars
such episodes in other writers); indeed as an account of a
healthy ride in the country, passing from sun to shade through
the trees, the whole thing has a kind of innocence. What is
exceptional is the sense of two people in love in hostile ways,
hers a determined gamble – she has in fact a bet with her
husband that she will bring off the seduction – and Sanin's
love, helpless and blind. It is as if, as woman and man, they are
fencing opponents yet united by intention. For both of them,
despite the intention, the act of love will relieve them by
seeming to come from the outside, overwhelming her fear of
losing and his of succeeding. Turgenev is superior to most
authors, especially of his period, in showing us this without
giving us the fatal impression that he is vicariously satisfying
his own erotic wishes. Above all he sees the man and the
woman as separate people, as two different histories: and
conveys nothing of what I have just written by his own
analysis. The people exist for themselves, not for him, just as
the groom who they told to leave them half-way through the

ride, exists only for himself on that day. In his way, and even like the horses, he has this day for its own sake. Turgenev, the nature lover, admired the equilibrium of nature; and this sense of balance gives the whole story a quality one can only call innocence that is a veil.

Of course, mountains and forest can be said to exist for themselves too and it is only here that Turgenev shows his own hand. The act of love, like the act of dying, is part of Nature in a different cycle. Gemma may be forgotten. Maria enslaves Sanin. But Nature enslaves even Maria who pursues power and her own freedom, regardless of others. When they leave the woodman's hut, Maria says to Sanin:

'So where are you going? ... To Frankfurt or to Paris?'

He says:

'I am going wherever you are and I will be with you until you drive me away.'

He writes a shabby note to Gemma.

[Maria] seized his hair with all ten fingers. Slowly she handled and twisted his unresponsive hair ... She drew herself up, quite straight. Her lips curled in triumph. Her eyes, so wide and shining that they looked almost white, showed only the pitiless torpor of one sated with victory. A hawk clawing at a bird caught in its talons sometimes has this look in its eyes.

We notice that pull of the hair: Turgenev's own initiation into sexual love came when the serf girl pulled him by the hair at Spasskoye.

Sanin hasn't the courage to travel back to Gemma's shop and collect his things. He sends Polozov's footman. He remembers every shameful detail of the life that followed: how he actually peeled a pear for the greedy, complaisant Polozov as the carriage rolled along the main street of Wiesbaden on the way to Paris, the humiliations there: the hideous tortures of the slave who is not allowed to be jealous or to complain, until in the end, he is cast off.

Turgenev's late stories are profoundly Russian stories of bewitchment and of being possessed. It is a mistake to dismiss them as lesser works simply because they are not directly concerned with the Russian social question: the Russian 'Calypso's isle' has its own native force. Maria is an example of a contemporary Russian type: the girl who is half-peasant, half-aristocrat. Her belief in freedom is Nihilism without the politics. Sanin is uninterested in politics, but he notices for the first time that selling one's estate means selling human beings as well and that love makes him gloss over a fact which is shocking to Gemma and her family. The Italians are comical, but their young son will be a revolutionary: his honour grows, as Sanin's is lost. Such references are oblique. The epilogue which completes the frame of the story is discomforting and, on the whole, one could do without it (as we could also do without the literary references to Virgil and Hoffmann), although, since Turgenev never quite disentangles himself from the influences of shadow-autobiography, these are interesting. In his remorse before the shameful detail of his memories, Sanin at the age of fifty-three sets out to trace Gemma and her history. In Frankfurt, the old shop where in youth he had proposed to stand behind the counter selling sweets has gone. Even the street has gone. Frankfurt has been rebuilt. He does at last get a letter from Gemma. The sweet sentimental Italian girl was practical. She is married to a rich American businessman in New York, happy in her life. It has all turned out well, despite her tears at the time. At least the Sanin affair had made her break with Klueber who in fact went bankrupt and was sent to prison. Easily she forgives and is sorry for the wretchedness of Sanin's life.

The last we hear of Sanin is that he is talking of going to America. The cynical reader suspects that Sanin-Turgenev is going to attach himself once more to Gemma's family as in the 1860s Turgenev had re-attached himself to the Viardots. There is one sentence, buried in the story, that comes back to one with new force:

Weak people never bring anything to an end themselves: they always expect things to come to an end.

Sanin's will was weak in dealing with Maria Polozov: it was strong only in pursuing illusions.

# INTRODUCTION

It is said that Turgenev did not show this story to Pauline Viardot before it was published, though he may have read it to her in French afterwards. If so, her mind probably wandered to what was always more important to her – her own art. She was too extroverted and practical to share his pessimism and may easily have seen herself as the dark-haired Gemma, comfortably married, with her children. A character out of Turgenev, indeed.

V. S. Pritchett

# SELECT BIBLIOGRAPHY

———

The most useful biographies of Turgenev are Avrahm Yarmolinsky, *Turgenev, the Man, His Art and Age*, 1960, and Leonard Schapiro, *Turgenev, His Life and Times*, 1978. A more recent study by another novelist is V. S. Pritchett's *The Gentle Barbarian*, 1977.

April Fitzlyon's *The Price of Genius*, 1964, a life of Pauline Viardot, has much interesting information about the singer's relationship with Turgenev.

D. S. Mirsky's *A History of Russian Literature*, 1927, sets Turgenev alongside his literary contemporaries and Isaiah Berlin's essay 'Fathers and Children' in *Russian Thinkers*, 1978, does the same from a more social and political point of view.

Richard Freeborn's *Turgenev: The Novelist's Novelist*, 1960, is a critical study of the novels, including a bibliography of commentaries in English, Russian, German and French.

Turgenev's own letters and autobiographical writings are often revealing. These have been translated as *Turgenev's Letters*, 1983, edited by A. V. Knowles; *A Friendship in Letters: Flaubert and Turgenev*, 1985, edited by Barbara Beaumont, and *Turgenev's Literary Reminiscences*, 1959, edited by David Magarshack with an introductory essay by Edmund Wilson.

The biography *Constance Garnett, A Heroic Life*, 1991, by Richard Garnett, has some material on the difficulties of translating Turgenev into English.

Henry James' essays on Turgenev reflect his admiration for the Russian. They can be found in *French Poets and Novelists*, 1878, *Partial Portraits*, 1888, and *The Critical Muse*, 1987, edited by Roger Gard.

# CHRONOLOGY

| DATE | AUTHOR'S LIFE | LITERARY CONTEXT |
|------|---------------|------------------|
| 1818 | Born in Oryol, Russia. Childhood spent on family estate at Spasskoye. | Scott: *The Heart of Midlothian*. Keats: *Poems*. Griboedov: *The Student*. Karamzin: *History of the Russian State* (12 vols. until 1826). |
| 1819 | | George Eliot born. Schopenhauer: *The World as Will and Idea*. |
| 1820 | | Pushkin: *Ruslan and Ludmilla*. |
| 1821 | | Pushkin: *The Prisoner of the Caucasus*. Dostoevsky and Flaubert born. |
| 1825 | | Pushkin: *Boris Godunov*. |
| 1827–34 | Attends school and university in Moscow. | |
| 1828 | | Tolstoy born. Mickiewicz: *Konrad Wallenrod*. |
| 1829 | | Balzac: *Les Chouans* – first volume of *La Comédie Humaine*. |
| 1830 | | Stendhal: *Le Rouge et le Noir*. |
| 1831 | | Lermontov: *A Strange Man*. |
| 1832 | | Lermontov: 'The Sail', 'No, I am not Byron'. |
| 1833 | | Pushkin: *Eugene Onegin*. |
| 1834–7 | Attends St Petersburg University. | |
| 1834 | *Steno* (a poetic drama). | Belinsky: *Literary Reveries*. Pushkin: *The Queen of Spades*. |
| 1836 | | Gogol: *The Government Inspector*. Pushkin: *The Captain's Daughter*. Peter Chaadayev's *Philosophical Letter* describes Russia as 'a gap in the intellectual order of things', with no past, present or future. |
| 1837 | | Death of Pushkin in duel. Dickens: *Pickwick Papers*. Carlyle: *History of the French Revolution*. |

Congress of Aix-la-Chapelle.

Decembrist Revolt crushed. Nicholas I succeeds Alexander I.
Nicholas develops system of autocratic government based upon militarism
and bureaucracy. Especially notorious was the Third Section, under Count
Alexander Benckendorff, which acted as the Tsar's main weapon against
subversion and revolution and as the principal agency for controlling the
behaviour of his subjects.

July revolution in France. Accession of Louis Philippe.
Suppression of Polish uprising.
First Reform Act in Britain.

Abolition of slavery within the British Empire.

Accession of Queen Victoria.

| DATE | AUTHOR'S LIFE | LITERARY CONTEXT |
|---|---|---|
| 1838–41 | Studies at Berlin University. Meets Bakunin, Stankevich and Granovsky, Russian liberal and radical political thinkers. | |
| 1839 | | Stendhal: *La Chartreuse de Parme*. |
| 1840 | | Lermontov: *A Hero of Our Time*. |
| 1841 | Returns to St Petersburg. Takes the side of the Westerners in Slavophile v Westerner debate, while remaining on polite terms with such conservative Slavophiles as the Aksakov brothers. | Death of Lermontov in duel. |
| 1842 | Birth of illegitimate daughter by seamstress at Spasskoye. | Gogol: *Dead Souls* and 'The Overcoat'. |
| 1843 | *Parasha* – first of his works to attract attention. Meets the critic Belinsky, and Mme Pauline Viardot, with whom he falls in love. Works briefly as a civil servant. | Carlyle: *Past and Present*. Birth of Henry James. |
| 1845 | Resolves to devote himself full-time to literature. | Mérimée: 'Carmen'. |
| 1847 | Follows Pauline Viardot and her husband to Paris. First visit to England 1847. | Thackeray: *Vanity Fair*. Balzac: *Le Cousin Pons*. Herzen: *Who is to Blame?* Herzen leaves Russia. |
| 1847–50 | Lives in France. Most of the stories which later comprised *A Sportsman's Notebook* published in *The Contemporary*. | |
| 1848 | Witnesses February revolution in Paris. | George Sand: *La Petite Fadette*. Death of Belinsky. Bakunin: 'An Appeal to the Slavs'. |
| 1849 | *The Bachelor* performed (the only one of his plays of this period not to fall foul of the censor). | Dostoevsky arrested as member of socialist Petrashevsky circle. Sentenced to death and reprieved. |
| 1850 | Inherits Spasskoye from his mother. *Diary of a Superfluous Man*. Finishes *A Month in the Country*. | Tennyson: *In Memoriam*. Browning: *Men and Women*. Dickens: *David Copperfield*. Herzen: *From the Other Shore*. Death of Balzac. |

# CHRONOLOGY

1840s and 50s: Slavophile v Westerner debate amongst Russian intellectuals. Westerners advocate progress by assimilating European rationalism and civic freedom. Slavophiles assert spiritual and moral superiority of Russia to the West and argue that future development should be based upon the traditions of the Orthodox Church and the peasant commune or *mir*.

European revolutions. Tsar's manifesto calls upon Russians to arouse themselves for 'faith, Tsar and country'. Russian armies join those of the Hapsburgs in suppressing nationalist rebellion in Hungary under Kossuth. *Communist Manifesto* published. Pan-Slav congress in Prague.

| DATE | AUTHOR'S LIFE | LITERARY CONTEXT |
|------|---------------|------------------|
| 1851 | | Melville: *Moby-Dick*. |
| 1852 | *A Sportsman's Notebook* published in volume form. 1852–3: confined to Spasskoye under police surveillance after publishing a eulogistic obituary of Gogol. | Death of Gogol.<br>Tolstoy: *Childhood*.<br>Harriet Beecher Stowe: *Uncle Tom's Cabin*. |
| 1854 | | George Sand: *Histoire de ma vie*. |
| 1855 | | Trollope: *The Warden*. |
| 1856–63 | Returns to France, dividing his time between Paris and the Viardots' estate at Courtavenel. | |
| 1856 | *Rudin*. | Sergei Aksakov: *Family Chronicles*. |
| 1857 | | Flaubert: *Madame Bovary*.<br>Herzen's radical journal *The Bell* published in London.<br>Conrad born. |
| 1858 | 'Asya'. | |
| 1859 | *A Nest of Gentlefolk*. | Goncharov: *Oblomov*.<br>Tennyson: *Idylls of the King*.<br>Darwin: *The Origin of Species*. |
| 1860 | *On the Eve*. 'First Love'. | George Eliot: *The Mill on the Floss*.<br>Chekhov born. |
| 1861 | Working on *Fathers and Children* (largely written on the Isle of Wight, where well-off Russians often went for sea-bathing). | Dostoevsky: *The House of the Dead*.<br>Herzen publishes *My Past and Thoughts* (to 1867). |
| 1862 | *Fathers and Children*. Quarrels with Tolstoy during a hunting breakfast in the house of the poet Fet. In spite of this, Turgenev took an active part in getting Tolstoy translated into French, and did much for his reputation in the West. | Hugo: *Les Misérables*.<br>Chernyshevsky imprisoned and exiled to Siberia (to 1883). |
| 1863 | Meets Flaubert in Paris. Settles in Baden with the Viardots (to 1871). | Chernyshevsky: *What is to be Done?* |
| 1864 | Charged with aiding London expatriate group headed by Herzen. Cleared by senatorial | Dostoevsky: *Notes from Underground*.<br>Trollope: *Can You Forgive Her?* |

# CHRONOLOGY

HISTORICAL EVENTS

Great Exhibition in London. Opening of St Petersburg to Moscow railway. Louis Napoleon proclaimed Emperor of France.

Outbreak of Crimean War.

Death of Nicholas I. Accession of Alexander II.

End of Crimean War. By the terms of the Treaty of Paris, Russia forced to withdraw from the mouth of the Danube, to cease to protect the Orthodox under Turkish rule and to give up her fleet and fortresses on the Black Sea. Indian Mutiny: siege and relief of Lucknow.

Russian colonial expansion in South-East Asia.

Garibaldi and 'The Thousand' conquer Sicily. Port of Vladivostock founded to serve Russia's recent annexations from China.

Emancipation of the serfs (February), the climax of the Tsar's programme of reform. While his achievement had great moral and symbolic significance, many peasants felt themselves cheated by the terms of the complex emancipation statute. Outbreak of American Civil War. Lincoln becomes President of USA. Victor Emmanuel first King of Italy. Bismarck becomes chief minister of Prussia. Financial reform in Russia; a ministry of finance and a state bank created.
1860s and 70s: 'Nihilism' – rationalist philosophy sceptical of all forms of established authority – becomes widespread amongst young radical intellectuals in Russia.

Polish rebellion. Poland incorporated in Russian Empire.

The first International. Establishment of the Zemstva, organs of rural self-government and a significant liberal influence in Tsarist Russia. Reform of the judiciary; trial by jury instituted and a Russian bar established.

| DATE | AUTHOR'S LIFE | LITERARY CONTEXT |
|---|---|---|
| 1864 *cont.* | committee in St Petersburg. Beginning of long breach with Herzen. | Tolstoy writes and publishes *War and Peace* (to 1869). |
| 1865 | | Dickens: *Our Mutual Friend.* Leskov: *Lady Macbeth of Mtensk.* Swinburne: *Atalanta in Calydon.* |
| 1866 | | Dostoevsky: *Crime and Punishment.* |
| 1867 | *Smoke.* | Marx: *Das Kapital*, vol. 1. Zola: *Thérèse Raquin.* |
| 1868 | | Dostoevsky: *The Idiot.* Browning: *The Ring and the Book.* Lavrov: *Historical Letters.* |
| 1869 | | Flaubert: *L'Education sentimentale.* |
| 1870 | 'King Lear of the Steppes'. Lives briefly in London. | Death of Herzen and Dickens. Rossetti: *Poems.* |
| 1871 | Settles in Paris with the Viardots. | Dostoevsky: *The Devils.* Zola publishes the *Rougon-Macquart* series of novels (to 1893). |
| 1872 | 'Spring Torrents'. | George Eliot: *Middlemarch.* Leskov: *Cathedral Folk.* |
| 1873 | | Bakunin: *Staat en anarchie.* Tolstoy: *Anna Karenina* (to 1877). |
| 1875 | Meets Henry James in Paris. | |
| 1876 | | George Eliot: *Daniel Deronda.* Death of George Sand. |
| 1877 | *Virgin Soil.* 'Klara Milich'. | Zola: *L'Assommoir.* Flaubert: *Trois Contes.* |
| 1878 | Makes up quarrel with Tolstoy and visits him at Yasnaya Polyana. | Hardy: *The Return of the Native.* |
| 1879 | Receives honorary DCL at Oxford for 'advancing the liberation of the Russian serfs'. | Tolstoy: *A Confession* (to 1882). Ibsen: *A Doll's House.* |
| 1880 | | Dostoevsky: *The Brothers Karamazov.* Death of Dostoevsky, Flaubert and George Eliot. |

# CHRONOLOGY

Slavery formally abolished in USA. Russian colonial expansion in Central Asia (to 1881).

Dmitri Karakozov, a young nobleman, tries to assassinate the Tsar; he attributes his action to the influence of the radical journal, *The Contemporary*, which is suppressed by the government.
Second Pan-Slav congress in Moscow. Sale of Alaska to USA. Second Reform Act in Britain.

Late 1860s–1870s: Narodnik (Populist) 'going to the people' campaign gathers momentum. Young intellectuals incite peasantry to rebel against autocracy. Lenin born. Franco-Prussian War. End of Second Empire and foundation of Third Republic in France.
Paris Commune set up and suppressed. Fall of Paris ends war. Count Dmitri Tolstoy's reactionary educational reforms.

Three Emperors' League between Germany, Austria and Russia.

'Bulgarian Atrocities' (Bulgarians massacred by Turks). Founding of Land and Freedom, first Russian political party openly to advocate revolution.
Russia declares war on Turkey (conflict inspired by Pan-Slavist movement). Queen Victoria proclaimed Empress of India.
Russian forces reach gates of Constantinople. By the Treaty of San Stefano the Turks obliged to recognize independence of Slav nations in the Balkans.
Congress of Berlin; with Bismarck acting as 'honest broker' the Great Powers modify the terms of San Stefano, increasing Austrian influence at the expense of Russia. Afghan War. Famous mass trial of Populist agitators ('The Trial of the 193').
Stalin born. Land and Freedom divides into terrorist organization The People's Will, responsible for numerous political assassinations, including that of the Tsar in 1881, and Black Repartition, which continues campaign amongst peasantry and later the urban proletariat.

| DATE | AUTHOR'S LIFE | LITERARY CONTEXT |
| --- | --- | --- |
| 1881 | 'The Song of Triumphant Love'. | Henry James: *The Portrait of a Lady*. Ibsen: *Ghosts*. |
| 1883 | Writes 'Un Incendie en Mer' ('A Fire at Sea'). Sends a letter to Tolstoy from his death-bed, imploring him to return to literary activity from his spiritual writings. Dies in France, 3 September. Buried in St Petersburg. | Maupassant: *Une Vie*. Fet: *Evening Lights*. |

# CHRONOLOGY

Assassination of Alexander II by Ignatius Grinevitsky. Accession of
Alexander III. Severe repression of revolutionary groups. Alexander III is
much influenced by his former tutor, the extreme conservative Pobedonostsev,
who becomes Chief Procurator of the Holy Synod. Loris-Melikov, architect
of the reforms of Alexander II's reign, resigns. Jewish pogroms.
First Russian Marxist revolutionary organization, the Liberation of
Labour, founded in Geneva by Georgi Plekhanov.

# FIRST LOVE

TRANSLATED FROM THE RUSSIAN
BY ISAIAH BERLIN

# Translator's Note

*My thanks are due to Lady Anglesey for her most valuable assistance at every stage in the preparation of this translation, and to Lord David Cecil and Mr M. W. Dick who kindly consented to read the M.S.*

I.B.

# First Love

## * * *

The guests had left long ago. The clock struck half-past twelve. Only the host, Sergey Nicolayevich and Vladimir Petrovich remained in the room.

The host rang the bell and ordered supper to be taken away.

'Well then, that's agreed,' he said, settling himself more deeply into his armchair and lighting a cigar. 'Each of us is to tell the story of his first love. You begin, Sergey Nicolayevich.'

Sergey Nicolayevich, a round little man with a fair, plump face, looked first at his host and then up at the ceiling.

'In my case,' he finally said, 'there was no first love. I began with a second.'

'How do you mean?'

'Oh, it's quite simple. I was eighteen when I first began to court a very charming young girl, but I did this as if it was nothing new to me, exactly as I later flirted with others. Actually I fell in love for the first and last time when I was about six, with my nurse, but that was a very long time ago. I do not now remember the details of our relationship – and even if I did, how could they possibly interest anyone?'

'Well then, what are we to do?' the host began. 'There was nothing very remarkable about my first love either: I didn't fall in love with anyone until I met Anna Ivanovna, my present wife, and then it all went perfectly smoothly. Our fathers arranged the whole thing. We soon grew fond of one

3

another and married shortly after. My tale is soon told. But I must admit, gentlemen, that when I brought up the topic of first love, I was really relying on you old bachelors; not that you are really old – but you're not exactly young, are you? Vladimir Petrovich, won't you regale us with something?'

'My first love was certainly not at all ordinary,' replied Vladimir Petrovich, after a moment's hesitation. He was a man of about forty with dark, slightly greying hair.

'Ah!' said the host and Sergey Nicolayevich with one voice. 'That's much better, tell us the story.'

'Why, certainly ... no; I'd rather not. I'm not good at telling stories. They come out either too bald and dry, or else much too long and quite unreal; but if you'll allow me, I will write down all I can remember and then read it to you.'

At first they would not agree, but Vladimir Petrovich finally had his way. A fortnight later they met again, and Vladimir Petrovich kept his word.

This is what he had written down:

* * *

I

I was sixteen at the time. It happened in the summer of 1833.

I was living in Moscow, with my parents. They used to take a house for the summer near the Kaluga Toll-gate, opposite the Neskootchny Park – I was preparing for the University, but worked little and slowly.

Nobody interfered with my freedom. I did what I liked, particularly after the departure of my last tutor – a Frenchman who had never got used to the idea that he had been dropped 'like a bomb' (so he said) into Russia; he used to lie in bed helplessly for days on end, with an exasperated expression on his face. My father treated me with good-humoured indifference; my mother scarcely noticed me, although she had no other children; she was absorbed by other cares. My father, who was still young and very handsome, had not married her for love. He was ten years younger than my mother; she led a gloomy life, was in a constant state of irritation and always anxious and jealous – though never in my father's presence. She was very frightened of him – his manner was severely cold and aloof ... I have never seen anyone more exquisitely calm, more self-assured or more imperious.

I shall never forget the first weeks I spent in the country. The weather was magnificent – we left Moscow on the ninth of May, St Nicholas' Day. I used to go for walks in our garden, or in the Neskootchny Park, or sometimes beyond the Toll-gate; I would take a book with me – Kaidanov's lectures, for example – though I seldom opened it, and spent most of the time repeating lines of poetry aloud to myself – I knew a great many by heart then. My blood was in a ferment within me, my heart was full of longing, sweetly and foolishly; I was all expectancy and wonder; I was tremulous and waiting; my fancy fluttered and circled about the same images like martins round a bell-tower at dawn; I dreamed and was sad and sometimes cried. But through the tears and the melancholy, inspired by the music of the verse or the beauty of the evening, there always rose upwards, like the grasses of early spring, shoots of happy feeling, of young and surging life.

I had a horse of my own; I used to saddle it myself and go riding to some distant place. At times I would break into a gallop, and imagine myself a knight riding in a tournament (how gaily the wind whistled in my ears!) – or, lifting my face up, receive into myself the whole blue radiance of the sky.

I remember that at that time the image of woman, the shadowy vision of feminine love, scarcely ever took definite shape in my mind: but in every thought, in every sensation, there lay hidden a half-conscious, shy, timid awareness of something new, inexpressibly sweet, feminine ... This presentiment, this sense of expectancy, penetrated my whole being; I breathed it, it was in every drop of blood that flowed through my veins – soon it was to be fulfilled.

The house we had taken was a wooden building with pillars and had two small, low lodges. In the lodge on the left was a tiny factory for the manufacture of cheap wall-paper. Occasionally I used to wander over to it and watch a dozen or so village boys, lean, tousle-headed, with pinched faces, in long greasy smocks, as they jumped on to wooden levers and forced them down on to the square blocks of the presses, and in this way, by the weight of their shrunken bodies, stamped the brightly coloured patterns on the paper. The other lodge was empty and to let. One day, about three weeks after the ninth of May, the shutters of this lodge were opened and women's faces appeared in the windows – a family had evidently moved in. I remember how that day at dinner my mother asked the butler who our neighbours were, and hearing the name of Princess Zasyekin, first said, not disrespectfully, 'Ah, a princess...', but then she added, 'A poor one, I expect.' 'They came in three cabs, ma'am, and the furniture isn't worth mentioning.' 'Well,' replied my mother, 'it might have been worse.' My father gave her a cold look which silenced her.

And indeed Princess Zasyekin could not have been a rich woman; the house she had taken was so decrepit and narrow and low that no one of even moderate means would have been willing to live there. Actually all this meant nothing to me at the time. The princely title had little effect on me. I had just been reading Schiller's *The Robbers*.

## II

I was in the habit of wandering about our garden every evening with a gun looking for crows. I had an inveterate loathing for these wary, cunning and predatory birds. On the day in question I strolled as usual into the garden and, having scoured every walk in vain (the crows knew me and only cawed harshly now and then from afar), I happened to come near the low fence which divided 'our' property from the narrow strip of garden which ran to the right beyond the lodge and belonged to it. I was walking with my head bowed when suddenly I heard the sound of voices. I looked across the fence – and stood transfixed. A strange sight met my gaze.

A few paces from me – on a lawn flanked by green raspberry canes – stood a tall, slender girl in a striped pink dress with a white kerchief on her head. Four young men clustered round her, and she was tapping them one by one on the forehead with those small grey flowers – I do not know their name, but they are well known to children: these flowers form little bags and burst loudly if you strike them against anything hard. The young men offered their foreheads so eagerly, and there was in the girl's movements (I saw her in profile) something so enchanting, imperious and caressing, so mocking and charming, that I nearly cried out with wonder and delight, and should, I suppose, at that moment, have given everything in the world to have those lovely fingers tap my forehead too. My rifle slipped to the grass; I forgot everything; my eyes devoured the graceful figure, the lovely neck, the beautiful arms, the slightly dishevelled fair hair under the white kerchief – and the half-closed, perceptive eyes, the lashes, the soft cheek beneath them . . .

'Young man! Hey, young man!' suddenly cried a voice near me. 'Is it proper to stare at unknown young ladies like that?'

I started violently, and almost fainted: near me, on the other side of the fence, stood a man with close-cropped dark hair, looking at me ironically. At the same moment the girl too turned towards me . . . I saw large grey eyes in a bright, lively face, and suddenly this face began to quiver and laugh. There was a gleam of white teeth, a droll lift of the eyebrows . . . I blushed terribly, snatched up my gun, and pursued by resonant but not unkind laughter, fled to my room, threw myself on the bed and covered my face with my hands. My heart leaped within me. I felt very ashamed and unusually gay. I was extraordinarily excited.

After a rest I combed my hair, brushed myself, and came down to tea. The image of the young girl floated before me. My heart was leaping no longer but felt somehow deliciously constricted. 'What is the matter with you,' my father asked suddenly. 'Shot a crow?' I nearly told him everything, but checked the impulse and only smiled to myself. As I was going to bed, without quite knowing why, I spun round two or three times on one foot; then I put pomade on my hair, lay down, and slept like a top all night. Before morning I woke up for an instant, lifted my head, looked round me in ecstasy and fell asleep again.

## III

'How can I make their acquaintance?' was my first thought when I woke in the morning. I strolled into the garden before breakfast, but did not go too near the fence and saw no one. After breakfast, I walked several times up and down the street in front of our house – and, from a distance, glanced once or twice at the windows ... I fancied I could see her face behind the curtain; this alarmed me. I hurried away. 'Still, I must get to know her,' I kept thinking, as I paced uncertainly up and down the sandy stretch in front of the Neskootchny Park. 'But how? That is the question.' I recalled the smallest details of yesterday's meeting. For some reason I had a particularly clear image of the way in which she had laughed at me. But as I was frantically making one plan after another, fate was already providing for me.

While I was out, my mother had received from her new neighbour a letter on grey paper, sealed with the sort of brown wax which is only used on Post Office forms, or on the corks of bottles of cheap wine. In this letter, illiterate and badly written, the princess begged my mother for her protection: my mother, the princess wrote, enjoyed the intimate acquaintance of important persons, upon whose favour depended the fortunes of herself and of her children, involved as she was in several vital lawsuits: 'I tern to you', she wrote, 'az one gentelwoman to another; moreover, I am delited to make use of this oportunity.' Finally, she begged my mother's permission to call upon her. I found my mother in a disagreeable frame of mind: my father was not at home, and she had no one to consult. Not to reply to 'the gentlewoman' – and she was a princess too – was impossible. But how to reply? That worried my mother. To write in French seemed inappropriate – on the other hand, her own Russian spelling was not too certain; she knew this and was not anxious to take the risk. She welcomed my return, therefore, and at once told me to call on the princess and explain to her by word of

mouth that she would, of course, at all times be ready to offer
any help within her power to her Ladyship, and begged the
princess to do her the honour of calling upon her towards two
o'clock. This swift and sudden fulfilment of my secret desire
at once delighted and alarmed me. I did not, however, show
any sign of my inner turmoil; I went first to my room in order
to put on my new neck-tie and frock-coat: at home I still went
about in a short jacket and turned-down collar – which I
simply hated.

## IV

In the poky and untidy hall of the lodge, which I entered
trembling in every limb, I was met by a grey-haired old
servant with a face the colour of dark copper, surly little pig's
eyes, and the deepest wrinkles on his forehead and temples I
had ever seen in my life. He was carrying a plate on which
there was a half-picked herring bone; shutting the door which
led into the other room with his foot, he snapped: 'What do
you want?'

'Is the Princess Zasyekin at home?' I asked.

'Vonifaty!' a cracked female voice screamed from within.

The servant turned without a word, revealing as he did so
the threadbare back of his livery with a solitary rusty crested
button; he went away, leaving the plate on the floor.

'Have you been to the police station?' said the same female
voice. The servant muttered something in reply. 'Eh? Is there
somebody there?' said the voice again.

'The young gentleman from next door.'

'Well, show him in.'

'Will you step into the drawing-room, sir,' said the servant,
reappearing and picking up the plate from the floor. I
collected myself and went into the drawing-room. I found
myself in a small and not very tidy room. The furniture was
shabby and looked as if no one had bothered to arrange it. By
the window, in an armchair with a broken arm, sat a woman
of about fifty, plain, her hair uncovered, in an old green dress

with a gaudy worsted shawl round her neck; her small, black eyes pierced into me. I went up to her and bowed. 'Have I the honour to address the Princess Zasyekin?'

'I am Princess Zasyekin. And you are the son of Mr V——?'

'That is so, ma'am. I have come to you with a message from my mother.'

'Won't you sit down? Vonifaty, where are my keys? You haven't seen them, have you?'

I conveyed to Mme Zasyekin my mother's reply to her note. She listened to me, drumming upon the window-sill with her fat, red fingers, and when I had finished, once again fixed her eyes upon me.

'Very good. I'll be sure to call,' she remarked at last. 'But how young you are! How old are you if I might ask?'

'Sixteen,' I replied with a slight falter. The princess extracted from her pocket a bundle of greasy papers covered with writing, lifted them to her nose and began going through them.

'A good age,' she suddenly observed, turning and shifting in her chair. 'Please make yourself at home! We are very simple here.'

'Too simple,' I could not help thinking with disgust, as I took in her unsightly figure.

At that instant, another door flew open and in the doorway there appeared the girl I had seen in the garden the evening before. She lifted her hand, and a mocking smile flitted across her face. 'And here's my daughter,' said the princess, indicating her with her elbow, 'Zinochka, the son of our neighbour, Mr V——. What is your name, if I might ask?'

'Vladimir,' I replied, rising, and stuttering from sheer excitement.

'And your patronym?'

'Petrovich.'

'Yes. I once knew a Chief Constable. He was Vladimir Petrovich too. Vonifaty, don't look for the keys. They are in my pocket.'

The young woman continued to look at me with the same mocking smile, narrowing her eyes a little, and inclining her head slightly.

'I have already seen Monsieur Woldemar,' she began (the silver sound of her voice ran through me with a sort of sweet shiver). 'You will let me call you so?'

'Do, please,' I stammered.

'Where was that?' asked the princess. Her daughter did not answer.

'Are you busy at this moment?' the young woman asked, without taking her eyes off me.

'Oh no, no.'

'Would you like to help me wind my wool? Come with me.' She gave me a little nod and left the drawing-room. I followed her.

In the room we entered, the furniture was a little better and arranged with more taste; though actually, at that moment, I was scarcely able to notice anything. I moved as in a dream, and felt through my entire being an intense, almost imbecile, sense of well-being. The young princess sat down, took a skein of red wool, and pointing to a chair beside her, carefully undid the skein and laid it across my hands. All this she did without a word, with a kind of amused deliberation, and with the same bright, sly smile on her slightly parted lips. She began to wind the wool round a bent card, and then suddenly cast a look at me, a look so swift and radiant that I could not help lowering my eyes for an instant. When her eyes, for the most part half closed, opened to their full extent, her face would be utterly transformed, as if flooded with light. 'What did you think of me yesterday, Monsieur Woldemar?' she asked, after a short pause. 'You disapproved of me, I suppose.'

'I . . . Princess . . . I didn't think anything . . . How could I?' I replied in confusion.

'Listen,' she said. 'You don't know me yet. I am very strange. I wish to be told the truth always. You are sixteen, I hear, and I am twenty-one. You see, I am much older than you. That is why you must always tell me the truth ... and do what I tell you,' she added. 'Look at me ... Why don't you look at me?'

I was plunged into even deeper confusion; however, I did raise my eyes and look at her. She smiled, not as before, but as if to encourage me. 'Look at me,' she said, lowering her voice caressingly. 'I do not find it disagreeable. I like your face. I have a feeling that we shall be friends. And do you like me?' she added archly.

'Princess,' I was beginning.

'First of all, you must call me Zinaida Alexandrovna, and secondly, how queer that children' (she corrected herself), 'that young gentlemen do not say straight out what they feel. That is all very well for grown-ups. You do like me, don't you?'

Although I was very pleased that she should be talking so frankly to me, still, I was a little hurt. I wished to show her that she was not dealing with a mere boy, and so, putting on as solemn a manner as I could, I said as casually as I was able: 'Of course I like you very much, Zinaida Alexandrovna. I have no wish to conceal it.'

She shook her head with deliberation. 'Have you a tutor?' she suddenly asked.

'No, I haven't had one for a long time.' This was a lie. Scarcely a month had passed since I had parted with my Frenchman.

'Yes, I see; you are quite grown up.' She rapped me lightly over the fingers.

'Hold your hands straight.' And she busily began to wind the ball of wool.

I took advantage of the fact that her eyes remained lowered, to scrutinize her features, at first stealthily and then more and more boldly. Her face appeared to me even more lovely than on the previous day. Everything in it was so delicate, clever and charming. She was sitting with her back to a window which was shaded by a white blind. A sunbeam filtering through the blind shed a gentle light on her soft golden hair, on her pure throat, on her tranquil breast. I gazed at her, and how dear she already was to me, and how near. It seemed to me that I had known her for a long time, and that before her I had known nothing and had not lived ... She was wearing a dark, rather worn dress with an apron. How gladly would I have caressed every fold of that apron. The tips of her shoes looked out from under her skirt. I could have knelt in adoration to those shoes. 'And here I am sitting opposite her,' I was thinking, 'I have met her; I know her. God, what happiness!' I almost leapt from my chair in ecstasy, but in fact I only swung my legs a little, like a child enjoying a sweet. I was as happy as a fish in water. I could have stayed in that room – I could have remained in it for ever.

Her eyes softly opened, and once more her clear eyes shone sweetly upon me, and again she gave me a gentle little smile.

'How you do stare at me,' she said slowly, and shook her finger.

I blushed. 'She understands everything; she sees everything,' flashed through my brain, and how could she fail to see it all and understand it all? Suddenly there was a sound from the next room – the clank of a sabre.

'Zina!' cried the old princess from the drawing-room. 'Byelovzorov has brought you a kitten.'

'A kitten,' cried Zinaida and, darting from her chair, threw the ball of wool into my lap, and ran out of the room. I, too, got up, left the skein of wool and the ball on the window-sill and stopped in amazement. In the middle of the room a small tabby cat was lying on its back, stretching out its paws. Zinaida was on her knees before it, cautiously lifting up its little face. By the side of the old princess, filling almost the entire space between the windows, stood a blond, curly-haired young officer, a magnificent figure with a pink face and protruding eyes.

'What a funny little thing,' Zinaida kept repeating, 'and its eyes aren't grey, they're green, and what large ears. I do thank you, Victor Yegorych. It is very sweet of you.'

The soldier, whom I recognized as one of the young men I had seen the evening before, smiled and bowed with a clink of his spurs and a jingle of his sabre rings.

'You were kind enough to say yesterday that you wanted a tabby kitten with large ears ... and here, you see, I have procured one. Your word is law.' And he bowed again.

The kitten uttered a feeble squeak and began to sniff the floor.

'It's hungry!' exclaimed Zinaida. 'Vonifaty, Sonia, bring some milk.'

The maid, in a shabby yellow dress, with a faded kerchief round her neck, came in with a saucer of milk in her hands, and set it before the kitten. The kitten started, screwed up its eyes, and began to lap.

'What a pink little tongue,' observed Zinaida, almost touching the floor with her head, and peering at the kitten sideways under its very nose. The kitten drank its fill and began to purr, delicately kneading with its paws. Zinaida rose, and turning to the maid said casually: 'Take it away.'

'In return for the kitten – your hand,' said the soldier with a simper and a great shrug of his powerful body tightly encased in a new uniform.

'Both of them,' Zinaida replied, and held out her hands to him. While he kissed them, she looked at me over his shoulder. I stood stock still and did not know whether to laugh, to say something, or to remain silent. Suddenly I saw through the open door in the hall, the figure of our footman, Fyodor. He was making signs to me. Mechanically I went out to him.

'What is the matter?' I asked.

'Your Mama has sent for you,' he replied in a whisper. 'Madame is annoyed because you haven't come back with the answer.'

'Why, have I been here long?'

'Over an hour.'

'Over an hour!' I repeated automatically, and returning to the drawing-room, I began to take my leave, bowing and clicking my heels.

'Where are you off to?' asked the young princess, glancing at me over the officer's back.

'I am afraid I must go home. So I am to say,' I added, turning to the old princess, 'that you will honour us at about two o'clock?'

'Yes, my dear sir, please say just that,' she said.

The old princess hastily reached for a snuff box and took the snuff so noisily that I almost jumped. 'That's right, say precisely that,' she wheezily repeated, blinking tearfully.

I bowed again, turned and walked out of the room with that uncomfortable sensation in my back which a very young man feels when he knows he is being watched from behind.

'Now, Monsieur Woldemar, mind you come and see us again,' cried Zinaida, and laughed once more.

Why is she always laughing, I thought, as I returned home, accompanied by Fyodor who said nothing to me, but walked behind me with a disapproving air. My mother scolded me and expressed surprise. Whatever could have kept me so long with the princess? I gave no answer and went off to my room. Suddenly, I felt extremely depressed ... I tried hard not to cry ... I was jealous of the soldier!

## V

The old princess, as she had promised, called on my mother who did not take to her. I was not present at their meeting, but at table my mother told my father that this Princess Zasyekin seemed to her '*une femme très vulgaire*', that she had found her very tiresome, with her requests to do something for her with Prince Sergey; that she seemed to have endless lawsuits and affairs, '*des vilaines affaires d'argent*', and that she must be a very troublesome woman. But my mother did add that she had asked her and her daughter to dinner next day (when I heard the words 'and her daughter' I buried my face in my plate) for she was, after all, a neighbour, and a titled one, too.

My father thereupon informed my mother that he now remembered who this lady was: that in his youth he had known the late Prince Zasyekin, a very well-bred, but empty and ridiculous man; he said that he was called '*le Parisien*' in society because he had lived in Paris for a long time; that he had been very rich, but had gambled away all his property, and then, for no known reason – it might even have been for money, though he might, even so, have chosen better, my father, added with a cold smile – he married the daughter of some minor official and, after his marriage, had begun to speculate in a large way, and had finally completely ruined himself.

'I only hope she won't try to borrow money,' put in my mother.

'That is quite possible.' said my father calmly. 'Does she speak French?'

'Very badly.'

'H'mm. Anyway, that does not matter. I think you said you had asked the daughter too? Somebody was telling me that she is a very charming and cultivated girl.'

'Ah, she can't take after her mother, then.'

'No, nor after her father,' my father said. 'He was very cultivated too, but a fool.'

My mother sighed, and returned to her own thoughts. My father said no more. I felt very uncomfortable during this conversation.

After dinner, I went into the garden, but without a gun. I promised myself not to go near the Zasyekins' garden, but an uncontrollable force drew me thither – and not in vain. I had hardly reached the fence when I saw Zinaida. This time she was alone. She was walking slowly along the path, holding a book in her hands. She did not notice me. I very nearly let her pass by, but suddenly collected myself, and coughed. She turned round, but did not stop. With her hand she pushed back the broad blue ribbon of her round straw hat, looked at me, smiled gently, and again turned her gaze to the book.

I took off my cap and after shuffling a little, walked away

with a heavy heart. '*Que suis-je pour elle?*' I thought (goodness knows why) in French.

I heard familiar footsteps behind me. I looked round and saw my father walking towards me with his quick, light step. 'Is that the young princess?' he asked me.

'It is.'

'Why, do you know her?'

'I saw her this morning in her mother's house.'

My father stopped, and, turning sharply on his heel went back. When he drew level with Zinaida, he bowed politely to her. She also bowed, though she looked a trifle surprised, and lowered her book. I saw how she followed him with her eyes. My father always dressed with great distinction, simply, and with a style of his own, but never did his figure seem to me more elegant, never did his grey hat sit more handsomely upon his curly hair that was scarcely touched by time. I made as if to move towards Zinaida, but she did not even glance at me. She raised her book again, and walked away.

## VI

I spent the whole of that evening and the following morning in a kind of dumb and frozen misery. I remember I tried to work and opened Kaidanov, but the broadly spaced lines and pages of the celebrated textbook flitted past my eyes in vain. Ten times over I read to myself the words 'Julius Caesar was distinguished for military valour', understood nothing, and threw the book aside.

Before dinner I carefully pomaded my hair again, and again put on my little frock-coat and neck-tie.

'Why all this?' asked my mother. 'You are not at the university yet, and Heaven knows whether you will get through the examination. And your short jacket wasn't made so very long ago – you can't throw it away yet.'

'Visitors are coming,' I murmured, almost in despair.

'What nonsense! Visitors indeed!'

I had to give in. I replaced the jacket with a short coat, but did not take off the neck-tie.

The old princess and her daughter appeared half an hour before dinner. The old woman had put a yellow shawl over the green dress in which I had seen her before, and wore an old-fashioned bonnet with flame-coloured ribbons. She began talking at once about her debts and bills, moaning and complaining about her poverty; evidently she felt completely at ease. She took snuff as noisily as ever, and fidgeted and turned about on her chair as much as before. It never seemed to have entered her head that she was a princess.

On the other hand, Zinaida was very stiff, almost haughty – a real princess. Her face remained coldly immobile and solemn. I saw no trace of the glances and smile that I knew, although in this new aspect, too, she seemed to me very beautiful. She wore a light *barège* dress with pale blue flowers on it. Her hair fell in long curls down her cheeks in the English fashion. This style went well with the cold expression on her face. My father sat beside her during dinner, and entertained his neighbour with his usual calm and elegant courtesy. Now and then, he glanced at her, and from time to time she looked at him – but so strangely, almost with hostility. Their conversation was in French – I remember that I was surprised by the purity of Zinaida's accent.

During the meal, the old princess behaved as before, without ceremony, eating a great deal and praising the dishes. My mother obviously found her very tedious and replied to her with a kind of sad disdain. Now and then my father frowned a little.

My mother did not like Zinaida either. 'She seems terribly conceited,' she said on the next day. 'And what has she to be so very proud about, *avec sa mine de grisette?*'

'You've evidently never seen grisettes,' observed my father.

'No, thank God.'

'Yes, indeed, thank God; only in that case how can you have views about them?'

To me, Zinaida had pointedly paid not the slightest attention.

Soon after dinner the old princess began to take her leave.

'I shall hope for your kind aid and protection, Maria Nicolayevna and Pyotr Vassilitch,' she said in a sing-song to my mother and father. 'What can one do? Time was ... but it is over, and here I am, a princess' – and she added with a disagreeable laugh, 'a title's no good without any food!'

My father made an elaborate bow and accompanied her to the door of the hall. There I stood, in my short little jacket, staring at the floor like a prisoner condemned to death. Zinaida's treatment of me had utterly killed me. What then was my astonishment when, as she passed by me, her face wearing its former warm expression, she whispered quickly to me, 'Come and see us at eight o'clock, do you hear? Don't fail me.'

I threw up my hands, but already she was gone, flinging a white scarf round her head.


# VII


Punctually at eight o'clock, in my frock-coat, and with my hair brushed into a coxcomb, I walked into the hall of the lodge where the old princess was living. The old servant gave me a sour look, and rose unwillingly from the bench.

The sound of gay voices reached me from the drawing-room. I opened the door and stopped short in amazement. In the middle of the room on a chair stood the young princess, holding out a man's hat. Five young men clustered round the chair. They were trying to put their hands into the hat, but she kept it above their heads, shaking it violently every now and then. On seeing me, she cried, 'Stop, stop, another guest! We must give him a ticket, too!' and, leaping lightly from the chair, took me by the cuff of my coat.

'Come along,' she said, 'why are you all standing about? *Messieurs*, may I introduce you? This is M'sieu Woldemar, our neighbour's son, and these,' she added, turning to me and pointing to the guests as she named them, 'are Count Malevsky, Doctor Looshin, the poet Maidanov, retired Cap-

tain Nirmatsky, and Byelovzorov the hussar, whom you have
seen already – you will all be friends, I hope.'

I was so acutely embarrassed that I did not even bow. In
Dr Looshin I recognized the same swarthy man who had
humiliated me so cruelly in the garden. The others I did not
know.

'Count,' Zinaida continued, 'write out a ticket for M'sieu
Woldemar.'

'That's not fair,' said the count, with a slight Polish accent.
He was very handsome, with dark hair, expressive brown
eyes, a small, narrow white nose and a thin little moustache
over a tiny mouth, and was fashionably dressed. 'This
gentleman did not take part in our game of forfeits.'

'It's not fair,' echoed Byelovzorov and the figure referred to
as the retired captain, a man about forty, hideously pock-
marked, with curly hair like a negro's, slightly bowed bandy
legs, and wearing a military tunic, unbuttoned and without
epaulettes.

'Write out the ticket, I tell you,' repeated the princess.
'What is this? A mutiny? M'sieu Woldemar is here for the
first time, and today the rule does not apply to him. No
grumbling; write out the ticket – that is my wish.'

The count shrugged his shoulders, but bowing his head
obediently, took a pen in his white, beringed fingers, reached
for a piece of paper and began to write.

'At least may I be allowed to explain to M'sieu Woldemar
what this is all about?' Looshin began in a sarcastic voice.
'Otherwise he'll be quite lost. You see, young man, we are
playing a game of forfeits. The princess has had to pay a
forfeit and the winner, whoever draws the lucky ticket, will
have the right to kiss her hand. Do you understand what I
have just said?'

I only looked at him, and continued to stand there in a haze
while the princess again leapt on to the chair, and once more
began to shake the hat. Everyone moved towards her, I with
the others.

'Maidanov,' said the princess to a tall young, man with a

thin face, small, short-sighted eyes and extremely long black hair, 'you, as a poet, should be magnanimous and yield your ticket to M'sieu Woldemar so that he may have two chances instead of one.' But Maidanov shook his head, tossing back his hair.

I was the last to put my hand into the hat, and, taking the ticket, opened it. Heavens! What did I feel when I saw upon it the word, 'Kiss'!

'Kiss!' I could not help crying out.

'Bravo, he wins,' the princess exclaimed. 'I am so pleased.'

She stepped down from the chair and looked into my eyes with a look so sweet and clear that my heart missed a beat. 'And are you pleased?' she asked me.

'I?' I stammered.

'Sell me your ticket,' blurted Byelovzorov suddenly into my ear. 'I will give you a hundred roubles.'

I gave the soldier a look so indignant that Zinaida clapped her hands and Looshin exclaimed, 'Oh, well done! But,' he added, 'I, as master of ceremonies, am obliged to see to it that all the rules are kept. Monsieur Woldemar, go down on one knee. That is the rule.'

Zinaida stood before me, with her head a little on one side, as if to see me better, and solemnly held out her hand to me. Everything became blurred. I meant to go down on one knee, but fell on both, and touched Zinaida's fingers so awkwardly with my lips that I scratched the tip of my nose on her nail.

'Splendid!' shouted Looshin, and helped me to get up.

The game continued. Zinaida put me next to herself, and what forfeits she thought of ! She had, among other things, to represent a statue, and she chose the hideous Nirmatsky as her pedestal, told him to bend down and then to bury his face in his chest. The laughter never stopped for an instant. For me, brought up as I had been, a solitary boy in the sober atmosphere of a staid country house, all this noise and excitement, this uncontrolled gaiety, the queer new terms on which I found myself with these strangers, all went straight to my head: I felt intoxicated – it was like a strong wine.

I began to laugh and chatter more loudly than the others, so that even the old princess, who was sitting in the next room with some official from the Legal Department, who had been called in for consultation, actually came out to have a look at me. But I felt so immensely happy that I didn't care a rap. I really didn't care what mockery, or what cross looks were directed at me. Zinaida continued to favour me, and would not let me leave her side. For one forfeit I had to sit beside her, both of us under the same silk scarf; I was supposed to tell her 'my secret'. I remember how both our heads were suddenly plunged in a close, fragrant, almost transparent darkness, and how close to me in this darkness her eyes shone softly; and I remember the warm breath from her parted lips, the gleam of her teeth, and how her hair tickled and burnt me. I was silent. She smiled mysteriously and slyly, and finally whispered to me, 'Well?' But I only blushed and laughed and turned away, and could scarcely breathe.

We became bored with forfeits, and began playing 'String'. What joy I felt when, my attention wandering, I received a sharp, strong slap on my fingers, and how, afterwards, I tried on purpose to look as if I weren't paying attention and how she teased me and would not touch my outstretched hands! And the things we did that evening! We played the piano, we sang, we danced, we acted a gipsy camp. Nirmatsky was dressed up as a bear and made to drink salt water. Count Malevsky showed us various card tricks, and finished – after shuffling all the cards – by dealing himself a whist hand, all trumps, upon which Looshin 'had the honour to congratulate him'. Maidanov recited fragments from his poem *The Murderer* (this was at the height of the romantic period) which he intended to bring out in a black cover, with the title printed in blood-red letters. We stole the official's cap off his knee and made him, as a ransom, dance a Cossack dance. We dressed up old Vonifaty in a bonnet, and the young princess put on a man's hat ... We went on endlessly.

Byelovzorov alone kept to his corner, scowling and glowering. Sometimes his eyes would become bloodshot, his face would turn red, and then he looked as if he might, at any moment, suddenly hurl himself at us and scatter us like chaff in all directions. But the princess would glance at him now and then, shake her finger, and he would once more retreat to his corner.

At last we were completely worn out. Even the old princess who, to use her own expression, could take anything (no amount of noise seemed to upset her) – even she began to feel a little tired and decided to go and rest. Towards midnight, supper was brought in. It consisted of a piece of stale, dry cheese and some sort of small cold ham patties, which seemed to me more delicious than any pasty. There was only one bottle of wine, and a very queer one at that. The bottle was dark, with a wide neck, and the wine inside was vaguely pink; in point of fact, no one drank it. Exhausted but happy, almost collapsing, I left the lodge. Zinaida pressed my hand as I left, and again smiled mysteriously.

The night air was raw and heavy against my burning face. A storm seemed to be gathering, the black thunder clouds grew and slowly crept across the sky, visibly changing their misty outlines; a light wind shuddered restlessly in the dark trees, and from somewhere far beyond the horizon came the muffled sound of thunder, as if muttering angrily to itself.

I crept to my room by the back stairs. My man was sleeping on the floor, and I had to step over him. He woke up, saw me, and reported that my mother had again been angry with me, and had again wished to send for me, but that my father had restrained her. (I never went to bed without saying goodnight to my mother, and asking her blessing.)

But there was nothing to be done! I told my man that I would undress and get myself to bed, and then I put out the candle. But I did not undress, and did not lie down. I sat down on a chair, and remained so for a long time, as if under a spell. What I felt was so new, so sweet. I sat quite still, hardly looking round, and breathing very slowly; only from time to time I laughed silently at some memory, or grew cold at the thought that I was in love – it was here – this was love. Zinaida's face swam gently before me in the darkness, floated, but did not float away. Her lips wore the same mysterious smile: her eyes looked at me, a little from one side, inquiring, tender, pensive, as she had looked when I left her.

At last I got up, tiptoed to my bed and, without undressing, laid my head carefully on the pillow, as if afraid of upsetting, by some sudden movement, that which filled my entire being.

I lay down, but did not even close my eyes. Soon I noticed feeble gleams of light constantly lighting the room. I sat up and looked at the window. The frame stood out sharply from the mysterious light of the panes. A storm, I thought, and I was right. A storm it was, very far away, so that the thunder could not be heard; only pale, long forks of lightning flashed ceaselessly across the sky; not flashing so much as quivering and twitching, like the wing of a dying bird.

I rose, went to the window, and stood there till morning . . . the lightning did not cease for an instant. It was what the peasants call a Sparrow Night. I looked at the silent, sandy stretch, at the dark mass of the Neskootchny Gardens, at the yellowish façades of distant buildings which seemed to quiver too, with each faint flash. I gazed, and could not tear myself away. This silent lightning, this controlled light, seemed to answer to the mute and secret fires which were blazing within me. Morning began to dawn. The sky was stained crimson. As the sun rose, the lightning became fainter and less frequent; the flashes came more and more seldom, and finally ceased, drowned in the clear and unambiguous light of the rising day. And the flashes within me died down too. I felt weary and at peace, but the image of Zinaida still hovered triumphant over my soul, though even this image seemed more tranquil. Like a swan rising from the grasses of the marsh, it stood out from the unlovely shapes which surrounded it, and I, as I fell asleep, in parting for the last time clung to it, in trusting adoration.

Oh, gentle feelings, soft sounds, the goodness and the

gradual stilling of a soul that has been moved; the melting happiness of the first tender, touching joys of love – where are you? Where are you?

## VIII

Next morning, when I came down to breakfast, my mother scolded me – not as much as I expected – and made me describe how I had spent the previous evening. I replied briefly, leaving out many details, and tried to make everything seem completely innocent.

'All the same, they are not at all *comme il faut*,' remarked my mother, 'and I wish you would not waste your time in such company, instead of doing some work for your examination.'

Knowing as I did that my mother's concern with my studies would be confined to these few words, I did not think it necessary to answer her; but after breakfast, my father put his arm through mine and, taking me into the garden, made me give him a full account of all I had seen at the Zasyekins'.

My father had a curious influence on me, and our relations were curious too. He took scarcely any interest in my education, but never hurt my feelings; he respected my freedom; he displayed – if one can put it that way – a certain courtesy towards me; only he never let me come at all close to him. I loved him, I was full of admiration for him; he seemed to me the ideal man – and God knows how passionately attached to him I should have been if I had not felt constantly the presence of his restraining hand. Yet he could, whenever he wished, with a single word, a single gesture, instantly make me feel complete trust in him. My soul would open; I chattered to him as to a wise friend, an indulgent mentor ... and then, just as suddenly, he would abandon me, his hand would again push me aside – kindly and gently – but, nevertheless, aside.

Sometimes a mood of gaiety would come over him, and at such moments he was ready to play and romp with me, full of high spirits like a boy. He loved all violent physical exercise.

Once, and only once, he caressed me with such tenderness that I nearly cried ... then his gaiety and tenderness vanished without a trace. But when this happened it never gave me any hope for the future – I seemed to have seen it all in a dream. At times I would watch his clear, handsome, clever face ... my heart would tremble, my entire being would yearn towards him ... then, as if he sensed what was going on within me he would casually pat my cheek – and would either leave me, or start doing something, or else would suddenly freeze as only he knew how. Instantly I would shrink into myself, and grow cold. His rare fits of affability towards me were never in answer to my own unspoken but obvious entreaties. They always came unexpectedly. When, later, I used to think about my father's character, I came to the conclusion that he cared nothing for me nor for family life; it was something very different he loved, which wholly satisfied his desire for pleasure. 'Take what you can yourself, and don't let others get you into their hands; to belong to oneself, that is the whole thing in life,' he said to me once. On another occasion, being at that time a youthful democrat, I embarked on a discussion of liberty in his presence (on that day he was what I used to call 'kind'; then one could talk about anything to him).

'Liberty,' he repeated. 'Do you know what really makes a man free?'

'What?'

'Will, your own will, and it gives power which is better than liberty. Know how to want, and you'll be free, and you'll be master too.'

Before and above everything, my father wanted to live ... and did live. Perhaps he had a premonition that he would not have long in which to make use of the 'thing in life'; he died at forty-two.

I gave my father a detailed account of my visit to the Zasyekins. Sitting on a bench he listened to me, half-attentively, half-absently – drawing in the sand with his riding-crop. From time to time he would laugh lightly, glance at me in an odd, bright, gay manner, and egg me on with short questions and rejoinders. At first I scarcely dared to pronounce Zinaida's name, but could not contain myself, and began to sing her praises. My father merely continued to smile; presently he became thoughtful, stretched himself, and rose.

I remembered that as he was leaving the house he had ordered his horse to be saddled. He was a superb rider and could break in the wildest horse long before Monsieur Rarey.

'Shall I come with you, Papa?' I asked.

'No,' he replied, and his face assumed its usual expression of benevolent indifference. 'Go alone, if you want to; and tell the coachman that I shall not be going.'

He turned his back on me, and walked quickly away. I followed him with my eyes. He disappeared behind the gate. I saw his hat moving along the hedge: he went into the Zasyekins' house.

He did not stay there more than an hour. Then he went straight off to the town and stayed away till evening.

After dinner I myself called on the Zasyekins. In the drawing-room I found only the old princess. When she saw me she scratched her head under her bonnet with a knitting needle and suddenly asked me whether I would copy out a petition for her.

'With pleasure,' I replied, and sat down on the edge of a chair.

'.Only mind, make your letters nice and big,' said the princess, handing me a badly scribbled sheet of paper.

'Could you do it today, my dear sir?'

'I will copy it today, ma'am.'

The door into the next room opened slightly. Through the gap Zinaida's face appeared – pale, pensive, her hair carelessly thrown back. She looked at me with large, cold eyes and softly closed the door.

'Zina, I say, Zina,' said the old woman. Zinaida did not respond. I took away the old woman's petition and sat the whole evening over it.

## IX

From that day my 'passion' began. What I experienced then, I remember, was something similar to what a man must feel when first given an official post. I had ceased to be simply a young boy; I was someone in love. I say that my passion began from that day; and I might add that my suffering began on that day too. In Zinaida's absence I pined: I could not concentrate: I could not do the simplest thing. For whole days I did nothing but think intensely about her. I pined away, but her presence brought me no relief. I was jealous and felt conscious of my worthlessness. I was stupidly sulky, and stupidly abject; yet an irresistible force drew me towards her, and it was always with an involuntary shiver of happiness that I went through the door of her room.

Zinaida guessed at once that I had fallen in love with her, but then I wouldn't have thought of concealing it. My passion amused her. She made fun of me, played with me, and tormented me. It is sweet to be the sole source, the arbitrary and irresponsible source of the greatest joys and profoundest miseries to someone else. I was like soft wax in the hands of Zinaida; not that I alone had fallen in love with her. All the men who visited the house were hopelessly infatuated, and she kept them all on leading-strings at her feet. She found it amusing to excite alternate hopes and fears in them; to twist them according to her whim. She called this 'knocking people against each other'; they did not even think of resistance, but gladly submitted to her. In her whole being, vital and beautiful, there was a peculiarly fascinating mixture of cunning and insouciance, artifice and simplicity, gentleness and gaiety. Over everything she did and said, over every movement there hovered a subtle, exquisite enchantment. Everything expressed the unique, peculiar force of the life which played within her. Her face, too, was constantly changing. It, too, was always in play. It seemed at almost the same instant mocking, pensive and passionate. An infinite variety of feelings, light and swift, succeeded each other like shadows of clouds on a windy summer day, in her eyes and on her lips. Every one of her admirers was necessary to her. Byelovzorov, whom she sometimes called 'my wild beast', or sometimes simply 'mine', would gladly have leapt into the fire for her. With no confidence in his own brains or other qualities, he was constantly proposing marriage to her, implying that the others only talked. Maidanov was responsive to the poetic strain in her soul; somewhat cold by nature, like nearly all writers, he assured her fervently, and perhaps himself too, that he adored her. He composed endless verses in her honour, and recited them with an ardour at once affected and sincere. She sympathized with him and, at the same time, faintly mocked him. She did not really trust him, and after listening to his effusions for a while, used to make him read Pushkin, in order, as she used to say, to clear the air.

Looshin, the sarcastic doctor, so cynical in his talk, knew her best of all, and loved her more than the others, although he attacked her, both to her face and behind her back. She respected him, but did not spare him, and sometimes, with a peculiar malicious pleasure, used to make him feel her complete power over him. 'I am a flirt: I have no heart: I have an actor's nature,' she once said to him in my presence. 'All right then. Give me your hand and I will stick a pin into it, and you will feel ashamed in front of this young man. And it will hurt you, and still you will be kind enough to laugh, Mr Truthful.' Looshin flushed, turned away, bit his lip, but in the end stretched out his hand. She pricked it, and he did begin to laugh, and she laughed too, and drove the pin quite deep, and kept glancing into his eyes, which ran helplessly in every direction.

Least of all did I understand the relations which existed between Zinaida and Count Malevsky. He was good-looking, clever and shrewd, but something false in him, something equivocal, was apparent even to me, a boy of sixteen, and I wondered that Zinaida did not notice it. But perhaps she did notice this falseness and was not repelled by it. An irregular

education, odd habits and company, the perpetual presence of
her mother, poverty and disorder in the house – everything,
beginning with the freedom which the young girl enjoyed,
with her consciousness of superiority over her surroundings,
had developed in her a curious, half-contemptuous kind of
carelessness and unfastidiousness. I remember how, no matter what happened – whether Vonifaty announced there was
no sugar left, or perhaps some squalid piece of gossip
suddenly became public, or some quarrel broke out between
the guests – she would only shake her curls and say,
'Fiddlesticks!' and leave it at that.

But my blood, I remember, used to rise when Malevsky
would sidle up to her like a sly fox, lean gracefully over the
back of her chair, and begin to whisper into her ear with a
self-satisfied and wheedling little smile – while she would fold
her arms and glance at him attentively, then smile herself and
shake her head.

'What induces you to receive Monsieur Malevsky?' I once
asked her.

'Ah, but he has such beautiful little moustaches,' she
replied. 'And anyway that is not your province.'

'Perhaps you think that I love him?' she said to me on
another occasion. 'No! I cannot love people whom I find that I
look down on. I need someone who would himself master me,
but then, goodness me, I shall never come across anyone like
that. I will never fall into anybody's clutches, never, never.'

'Does that mean that you will never love anyone?'

'And what about you? Don't I love you?' she said, and
flicked me on the nose with the tip of her glove.

Yes, Zinaida made fearful fun of me. For three weeks I saw
her every day, and there was nothing that she didn't do to me.
She called on us seldom, and about this I was not sorry. In
our house, she became transformed into a young lady, a
princess, and this made me shy of her. I was frightened of
giving myself away to my mother. She did not think at all well
of Zinaida, and watched us with disapproval. I was not so
nervous of my father. He behaved as if he did not notice me,

and did not say much to her. But what he did say seemed somehow specially wise and significant.

I ceased to work, to read, even to walk in the neighbourhood or to ride. Like a beetle tied by the leg, I circled constantly round the adored lodge. I felt I could have stayed there for ever, but this was not possible. My mother grumbled and sometimes Zinaida herself used to drive me away. Then I used to lock myself in my room, or go to the end of the garden, climb on to the ruin of a high stone greenhouse and, dangling my legs from the wall which looked out on the road, would sit for hours, staring and staring, seeing nothing. Near me, over the dusty nettles, white butterflies fluttered lazily. A pert little sparrow would fly down on to a half-broken red brick nearby, and would irritate me with its chirping, ceaselessly turning its whole body with its outspread tail; the crows, still wary, occasionally cawed, sitting high, high on the bare top of a birch – while the sun and wind played gently in its spreading branches; the bells of the Donskoy monastery would sometimes float across – tranquil and sad – and I would sit and gaze and listen, and would be filled with a nameless sensation which had everything in it: sorrow and joy, a premonition of the future, and desire, and fear of life. At the time, I understood none of this, and could not have given a name to any of the feelings which seethed within me; or else I would have called it all by one name – the name of Zinaida.

And Zinaida still played with me like a cat with a mouse. Sometimes she flirted with me – and that would excite me, and I would melt. At other times, she would suddenly push me away – and then I dared not approach her, dared not look at her. I remember once that she was very cold with me for several days. I was completely unnerved – I would hurry timidly into the lodge and then, like a coward, I would stay with the old princess, in spite of the fact that she was particularly noisy and querulous at this time. Her financial affairs were going badly, and she had already had two encounters with the local police.

Once I was in the garden when, passing the well-known hedge, I saw Zinaida; leaning back on both her arms, she was sitting motionless on the grass. I was about to tiptoe away, but she suddenly raised her head and beckoned to me imperiously. I stood transfixed. I did not understand at once. She repeated the gesture. Immediately I leapt over the hedge and ran up to her happily, but she stopped me with a glance and pointed to a path two steps away from her. In confusion and not knowing what to do, I went down on my knees on the edge of the path. She was so pale, every feature betrayed such bitter grief, such utter exhaustion that I felt a pang and murmured involuntarily, 'What is the matter?'

Zinaida stretched out her hand, plucked a blade of grass, bit it, and flung it away from her.

'Do you love me very much?' she asked at last. 'Do you?'

I did not reply – and indeed, what reason had I to reply?

'Yes!' she said, looking at me as before, 'it is so. The same eyes –' she added; then became thoughtful and covered her face with her hands. 'Everything has become horrible to me,' she whispered, 'why don't I go to the other end of the world! I can't bear it, I can't make it come right ... and what is there before me? ... God, I am so wretched!'

'Why?' I asked timidly.

Zinaida did not reply, but only shrugged her shoulders. I went on kneeling and looking at her with infinite distress. Every one of her words pierced my heart like a knife. At that moment I would, I think, gladly have given up my life if only that could end her grief. I looked at her, and still not understanding why she was so unhappy, conjured a vivid image of how, suddenly, in a paroxysm of ungovernable grief, she had walked into the garden and fallen to the ground as though mown down. All round us it was bright and green. The wind murmured in the leaves of the trees, now and then bending the raspberry canes above Zinaida's head. Somewhere doves were cooing and bees were buzzing, flying low from blade to blade over the sparse grass. Overhead, the sky was blue and tender, but I felt terribly sad.

'Read me some poetry,' said Zinaida in a low voice, and raised herself on one elbow. 'I like your reading poetry. You speak it in a sing-song, but I do not mind it, that's youth. Read me *On Georgia's Hills*, only first sit down.'

I sat down, and recited *On Georgia's Hills*.

' "Which it cannot help but love",' Zinaida repeated after me. 'That is what poetry can do. It speaks to us of what does not exist, which is not only better than what exists, but even more like the truth. "Which it cannot help but love" – it would like not to, but cannot help itself!' She was silent again and suddenly started and stood up. 'Let's go. Maidanov is with Mama. He has brought me his poem, but I left him. He is hurt too, now, but what can one do? One day you will discover ... only don't be angry with me.'

She pressed my hand hastily and moved quickly forward. We went back to the lodge.

Maidanov began to recite to us his recently published *Murderer*, but I did not listen. He shouted his four-foot iambics in a kind of sing-song. The rhymes succeeded each other, ringing like sleigh bells, hollow and shrill, while I could only look at Zinaida, trying to grasp the meaning of her last words.

> Or perchance it was some secret rival
> That sudden cast his spell on thee

exclaimed Maidanov suddenly in a nasal tone, and my eyes and Zinaida's met. She lowered hers and blushed slightly. I saw her blush and froze with terror. I was jealous of her before, but only at that instant did the thought that she was in love flash through my mind: 'My God, she has fallen in love!'


# X


From that moment, my real torment began. I racked my brain, I thought of every possibility, and kept a ceaseless though, as far as possible, secret watch on Zinaida. A change had come over her, that was evident. She began to go for long, solitary walks. Sometimes she refused to see her visitors. For hours she sat alone in her room. She had never done this before. I suddenly developed – or it seemed to me that I had developed – tremendous perspicacity.

'Is it he? Or maybe it is not.' I used to ask myself, anxiously running over in my mind one admirer after another. I secretly looked upon Count Malevsky (although it made me ashamed of Zinaida to admit this) as more dangerous than the others.

I could not see further than the end of my nose, and probably my secretiveness deceived no one. At any rate, Dr. Looshin soon saw through me. Incidentally, he too had altered during this time. He had grown thinner, and though he laughed just as much, his laughter had somehow become shorter, more hollow, more malicious. Where previously there had been light irony and an affectation of cynicism, there was now a nervous irritability which he could not control.

'Why are you always trailing in and out of here, young man?' he once said to me when we were alone in the Zasyekins' drawing-room. The young princess had not returned from her walk. The shrill voice of the old lady resounded on the first floor. She was squabbling with her maid. 'You should be studying, working – while you are young – instead of which, you are doing what?'

'You can't tell whether I work at home or not,' I replied not without arrogance, but also in some confusion.

'A lot of work you do! You've something else on your mind. Oh, well, I won't argue . . . at your age that is natural enough, but your choice isn't very fortunate. Can't you see what sort of house this is?'

'I don't quite understand,' I said.

'Don't understand? So much the worse for you. I consider it my duty to warn you. It is all very well for people like me – for old bachelors – to go on coming here. What could possibly happen to us? We are a hard-boiled lot; you cannot do much to us. But you have a tender skin. The atmosphere isn't healthy for you here. Believe me, you might become infected.'

'What do you mean?'

'What I say. Are you well now? Are you in a normal condition? Do you consider that what you feel now is healthy, is good for you?'

'Why, what am I feeling?' I said, knowing in my heart that the doctor was right.

'Ah, young man, young man,' the doctor went on, looking as if these two words contained something very insulting to me, 'it is no good trying that kind of thing on me. Why, bless you, whatever is in your heart is still written all over your face. But anyway, what is the good of talking? I shouldn't be coming here myself if –' the doctor clenched his teeth, 'if I were not just as mad myself. Only what does astonish me is this; how can you with your intelligence not see what is going on round you?'

'Why, what *is* going on?' I rejoined, all on edge.

The doctor looked at me with a kind of mocking pity.

'But there's not much to be said for me either,' he said, as if to himself. 'In a word,' he added, raising his voice, 'I repeat, the atmosphere here is bad for you. You like it here – well, what of it? Hothouses smell sweet too, but one can't live in them. Take my advice and go back to Kaidanov again.'

The old princess came in and began to complain to the doctor about her toothache. Then Zinaida appeared.

'There,' finished the old princess. 'You must tell her off. She drinks iced water the whole day long. Now can that be good for her, with her weak chest?'

'Why do you do this?' asked Looshin.

"Why, what can it do to me?"

'Do to you? You could catch cold and die.'

'Really? Well, then that would be that.'

'Really? I see, so that's how it is,' grunted the doctor. The old princess left the room.

'Yes, that's how it is,' repeated Zinaida. 'Is life so gay then? Why, if you look round you ... well, is it so very attractive?

Do you think that I don't understand, don't feel it? I get pleasure from drinking water with ice, and can you seriously maintain to me that this kind of life is not worth risking for a moment's pleasure? I don't speak of happiness.'

'Yes, I see,' said Looshin. 'Caprice and independence, the whole of you is contained in these two words. Your entire nature is conveyed by them.'

Zinaida gave a nervous laugh. 'You've missed the post, my dear doctor. You're not a good observer. You're too late. Put on your spectacles. This is no time for whims. Make a fool of yourself, make a fool of me ... the more the merrier. As for being independent – Monsieur Woldemar,' Zinaida added suddenly, stamping her foot, 'don't try to look so sad. I cannot bear to be pitied,' and she left us quickly.

'It is bad, bad for you, the atmosphere here, young man,' said Looshin again.

# XI

That same evening there were the usual guests at the Zasyekins'. I was among them. Maidanov's poem was discussed. Zinaida praised it with complete sincerity.

'But I will tell you something,' she said to him. 'If I were a poet, I would take quite different subjects. Perhaps this is all nonsense, but strange thoughts sometimes come into my head, particularly when I cannot sleep just before morning, when the sky begins to grow pink and grey. I should, for example – you won't laugh at me?'

'No, no,' we all cried with one voice.

'I would,' she continued, crossing her arms and gazing away, 'I would depict a whole company of young girls in a large boat on a quiet river at night. The moon is shining; they are all in white with wreaths of white flowers, and they are singing – you know, something like a hymn.'

'I understand, I understand; continue,' said Maidanov, in a meaningful and dreamy tone.

'Suddenly there is noise, loud laughter, torches, timbrels

on the bank. It is a Bacchic rout singing and shouting along the riverside. Now it is your business to paint the picture, Sir Poet, only I want the torches to be red and very smoky, and I want the eyes of the Bacchantes to gleam under their wreaths, and the wreaths of flowers must be dark, and don't forget the tiger skins and the goblets and the gold – lots of gold.'

'Where is the gold to be?' asked Maidanov, throwing back his long hair and dilating his nostrils.

'Where? On their shoulders, arms, legs, everywhere. They say that in the ancient world women wore gold rings on their ankles. The Bacchantes call to the girls in the boat. The girls have ceased to sing their hymn. They cannot continue it, but they do not stir. The river is carrying them towards the bank. And then suddenly, one of them softly rises. This must be beautifully described. How she rises softly in the moonlight and how frightened her friends are. She has stepped over the edge of the boat. The Bacchantes have surrounded her, and whirled her off into the night, into the dark. Here you must paint the swirling clouds of smoke and everything in chaos. Only their cries can be heard and her wreath is left lying on the bank.'

Zinaida ceased. (Ah, she is in love, I thought again.)

'And is that all?' asked Maidanov.

'All!' she replied.

'That cannot be the subject for an entire poem,' he said pompously, 'but I shall make use of your idea for a lyric.'

'In the romantic style?' asked Malevsky.

'Yes, of course in the romantic style. The Byronic.'

'In my opinion Hugo is better than Byron,' carelessly threw out the young count. 'More interesting.'

'Hugo is a first-rate writer,' replied Maidanov, 'and my friend Tonkosheyev, in his Spanish novel *El Trovador* ...'

'Oh, is that the book with the question marks upside down?' Zinaida interrupted.

'Yes, that is the rule in Spanish. I was going to say that Tonkosheyev ...'

'Oh, you are going to have another argument about classicism and romanticism,' Zinaida interrupted him again. 'Let's play a game instead.'

'Forfeits?' said Looshin.

'No, forfeits are boring. Let's play analogies.' (Zinaida had invented this game herself. An object would be named, and everyone tried to compare it with something else. The person who thought of the best analogy won the prize.) She walked to the window. The sun had just set. Long red clouds stood high in the sky.

'What are those clouds like?' asked Zinaida, and without waiting for our answer said: 'I think they are like those purple sails on the golden ship in which Cleopatra sailed to meet Antony. Do you remember, Maidanov? You were telling me about it not long ago.'

All of us, like Polonius in *Hamlet*, decided that the clouds reminded us of precisely those sails, and that none of us could find a better analogy.

'How old was Antony then?' asked Zinaida.

'Oh, he must surely have been young,' observed Malevsky.

'Yes, young,' Maidanov agreed confidently.

'I beg your pardon,' exclaimed Looshin, 'he was over forty.'

'Over forty,' repeated Zinaida, giving him a quick glance.

I went home soon after. 'She is in love,' my lips whispered involuntarily, 'but with whom?'


# XII

The days were passing. Zinaida grew stranger and stranger, more and more unaccountable. One day, I went to see her and found her sitting on a wicker chair with her head pressed against the sharp edge of the table. She drew herself up ... her whole face was wet with tears.

'Ah! You!' she said with a cruel smile. 'Come here.'

I went up to her. She placed her hand on my head, suddenly seized me by the hair, and began to twist it.

'It hurts,' I said at last.

'Ah, it hurts, does it? And do you think it doesn't hurt me? Doesn't hurt me?' she repeated.

'Ai!' she cried suddenly, when she saw she had pulled out a small lock of my hair. 'What *have* I done? Poor M'sieu Woldemar.'

She carefully straightened the torn lock, curled it round her finger and twisted it into a little ring.

'I shall put your hair in my locket and I shall wear it,' she said, and her eyes were still full of tears. 'This will perhaps comfort you a little ... And now, good-bye.'

I returned home to find a disagreeable state of affairs. My mother was trying to 'have things out' with my father. She was reproaching him for something, and he, as was his habit, answered with polite and frigid silences, and soon went away. I could not hear what my mother was saying, nor was I in a mood to listen. I remember only that when the scene was over, she sent for me to the study, and spoke with great disapproval about my frequent visits to the old princess who, in her words, was *une femme capable de tout*. I bowed to kiss her hand (I always did this when I wanted to end a conversation) and went up to my room.

Zinaida's tears were altogether too much for me. I simply didn't know what to think, and was on the point of tears myself. I was after all still a child, in spite of my sixteen years. I no longer thought about Malevsky, though Byelovzorov every day glared more and more savagely at the wily count, like a wolf at a sheep. But then, I had no thought for anything or anybody. I gave myself up to fruitless speculation, and was always looking for secluded places. I became particularly fond of the ruined greenhouse. I used to climb, I remember, on to the high wall, settle myself on it and sit there, a youth afflicted by such misery, solitude and grief that I would be overcome with self-pity. How I revelled in these melancholy feelings – how I adored them.

One day I was sitting on the wall staring into space, and listening to the bells chiming. Suddenly something went through me, softer than the gentlest puff of wind, scarcely a shiver, like a scarcely perceptible breath, the sense of someone's presence. I looked down. Below – on the road – in a light grey dress, with a pink parasol resting on her shoulder, Zinaida was walking quickly. She saw me, stopped, and turning back the brim of her straw hat, she lifted her velvet eyes towards me.

'What are you doing so high up there?' she asked me with an odd smile. 'Now you always declare,' she went on, 'that you love me. Well, then, jump down into the road to me, if you truly love me.'

Hardly had Zinaida spoken these words when I was falling through the air, just as if someone had pushed me from behind. The wall was about fourteen feet high. I touched the ground with my feet, but the impact was so strong that I could not keep my balance. I fell flat and for an instant lost consciousness. When I came to, still without opening my eyes, I felt Zinaida near me.

'My darling boy,' she was saying, bending over me, and her voice was full of tender anxiety. 'How could you do it? How could you listen to me? When you know I love you ... Oh, please stand up.'

Her bosom rose and fell beside me; her hands were touching my head and suddenly – oh, what became of me then? – her soft fresh lips began to cover my face with kisses. She touched my lips, but then Zinaida probably realized from the expression on my face that I had regained consciousness, although I still kept my eyes closed, and rising quickly, she said: 'Come, get up, you naughty boy, you idiot. Why are you lying in the dust?'

I got up.

'Give me my parasol,' said Zinaida. 'See where I have thrown it. Don't look at me like that – it is too ridiculous. You aren't hurt, are you? Stung by the nettles, I expect ... I tell you, don't look at me ... why, he doesn't understand a word, he doesn't answer,' she said, as if to herself. 'Go home, Monsieur Woldemar, and tidy yourself up, and don't you dare follow me, or I shall be furious, and will never again . . .'

She did not finish her sentence, and moved quickly away. I sank down on the road. My legs would not carry me. My arms were smarting from the nettles, my back ached, my head swam, but at that moment I experienced a sense of bliss such as I never again felt in the whole of my life. It flowed like a delicious pain through all my limbs and finally resolved itself in rapturous leaps and cries. Yes, indeed, I was still a child.

## XIII

I felt so gay and proud all that day. I retained so vividly the sensation of Zinaida's kisses on my face – I recollected her every word with such ecstasy of delight, I nursed my unexpected happiness so tenderly, that I even suffered moments of anxiety in which I would actually have preferred never to see again the author of these new sensations. It seemed to me that there was nothing more I could ask of fate, that one might now 'go, take a deep, sweet, final breath and die'. And yet, on the next day, when I made my way to the lodge, I felt great embarrassment which I tried vainly to conceal by putting on the kind of modest yet quietly self-assured expression of someone who wished to convey that he can keep a secret. Zinaida received me very simply, without the slightest emotion. She merely shook her finger at me and asked whether I wasn't black and blue all over. All my modest self-assurance and air of mystery instantly dissolved, and with them my embarrassment. I did not, of course, expect anything extraordinary, but Zinaida's calm was like a cold douche. I realized that I was a child in her eyes, and my heart sank. Zinaida walked up and down in the room, giving me a quick smile every time she glanced at me; but her thoughts were far away – that I saw clearly.

Shall I begin about yesterday myself, I thought, and ask her where she was hurrying, and find out once and for all? . . . But I couldn't; I let it pass, and humbly sat down in a corner.

Byelovzorov came in; I felt glad to see him.

'I've not managed to find you a quiet horse,' he said gruffly. 'Freitag says he absolutely guarantees one, but I don't feel safe – I feel afraid.'

'Afraid of what, may I ask?' said Zinaida.

'Of what? Why, you don't know how to ride. I dare not think of what might happen. What is this whim that's come into your head suddenly?'

'Ah, that's my own affair, Sir Beast. In that case I will ask Pyotr Vassilievich ...' (My father's name was Pyotr Vassilievich. I was astonished by her light, easy way of using his name – as if she were very certain of his readiness to do her a service.)

'I see,' retorted Byelovzorov, 'it's him you mean to go riding with?'

'With him – or someone else – that can't make any difference to you. Not with you, anyway.'

'Not with me,' Byelovzorov repeated, 'as you wish. Oh, well, I shall find a horse for you.'

'Very well. But don't go and get me an old cow: I warn you, I want to gallop.'

'Gallop as much as you want ... Who is it then, is it Malevsky you want to go riding with?'

'And why not he, Sir Warrior? Now, now, calm yourself,' she added, 'and don't glare so. I'll take you too. You know that for me Malevsky is now – fie –' and she shook her head.

'You only say that to console me,' growled Byelovzorov.

Zinaida puckered her brow. 'Does that console you? Oh ... oh ... oh ... The Warrior!' she said finally, as if unable to find another word – 'and you, M'sieur Woldemar, would you come with us?'

'I am not fond ... a large company ...' I muttered without raising my eyes.

'Oh, you prefer a *tête-à-tête*? Well, freedom to the free, heaven for the holy,' she uttered with a sigh. 'Off you go, Byelovzorov, and do something. I must have a horse for tomorrow.'

'And where's the money to come from?' the old princess broke in.

Zinaida frowned. 'I am not asking you for it; Byelovzorov will trust me.'

'Trust you, trust you,' growled the old woman, and then suddenly screamed at the top of her voice, 'Doonyashka!'

'Maman, I have given you a little bell,' Zinaida put in.

'Doonyashka!' cried the old woman again.

Byelovzorov took his leave; I left with him ... Zinaida made no attempt to detain me.

## XIV

Next day I rose early, cut myself a stick, and went off beyond the town gate. Perhaps a walk would dissipate my sorrows. It was a beautiful day, bright and not too hot, a gay, fresh wind wasgently wandering over the earth; playing and softly murmuring, it touched everything lightly, disturbing nothing.

For a long time I wandered over the hills and in the woods. I did not feel happy – I had started with the set purpose of giving myself up to gloomy reflections. But youth, the beauty of the day, the freshness of the air, the pleasure which comes from rapid walking, the delicious sensation of lying on thick grass far away from everyone, alone – these proved too strong. The memory of those unforgettable words, of those kisses, once more pierced into my soul. I thought with a certain pleasure that Zinaida could not, after all, fail to recognize my resolution, my heroism ... Others please her better than I, I thought; let them! But then others only speak of what they will do – whereas I have done it ... And that's nothing to what I can still do for her.

I saw a vision of myself saving her from the hands of her enemies; I imagined how, covered with blood, I tore her from the very jaws of some dark dungeon and then died at her feet. I remembered the picture which used to hang in our drawing-room: Malek-Adel carrying off Matilda ... and then my attention was absorbed by the appearance of a large, brightly coloured woodpecker, busily climbing up the slender stem of a birch tree, and peering nervously from behind it, alternately to the right and to the left, like a double bass player from behind the neck of his instrument.

After this I sang *Not white the snows* which presently turned into the song well known at that time *For thee I wait when Zephyrs wanton*; then I began to declaim Yermak's apostrophe to the stars from Khomyakov's tragedy; tried to compose something myself in the sentimental style – even getting so far as to think of the concluding line of the entire poem: '... Oh Zinaida! Zinaida!' but in the end made nothing of it.

In the meanwhile dinner-time was approaching, and I wandered down into the valley; a narrow sandy path wound its way through it towards the town. I walked along this path ... The dull thud of horses' hooves sounded behind me. I looked round, stopped almost automatically, and took off my cap. I saw my father and Zinaida. They were riding side by side. My father was saying something to her; he was bending across towards her from the waist, with his hand propped on the neck of his horse; he was smiling. Zinaida listened to him in silence, her eyes firmly lowered, her lips pursed tightly. At first I saw only them; a few seconds later Byelovzorov came into view, in a hussar's uniform with a pelisse, on a foaming black horse. The noble animal tossed its head, pranced, snorted, while the rider at the same time held it back and spurred it on. I moved to one side, out of their way. My father gathered up the reins, and leant back away from Zinaida; she slowly lifted her eyes towards him, and they galloped off.

Byelovzorov raced after them, his sabre rattling. He is red as a lobster, I thought, she – why is she so pale? Out riding the whole morning – and yet so pale?

I walked twice as fast and got home just before dinner. My father was already sitting beside my mother's chair, washed and fresh and dressed for dinner, and was reading aloud to her, in his even, musical voice, the feuilleton from the *Journal des Débats*. But my mother listened to him without attention, and when she saw me asked what I had been doing with myself all day long, adding that she didn't like it when people went off God knows where and with God knows whom. 'But I was out for a walk, quite alone,' I was about to say, but glanced at my father, and for some reason remained silent.

## XV

During the next five or six days I hardly saw Zinaida at all; she declared herself unwell which, however, did not prevent the *habitués* of the lodge from dancing attendance upon her, as they put it; all except Maidanov, who instantly became bored and gloomy whenever there was no excuse for rapture. Byelovzorov sulked in a corner, all buttoned up and red-faced; over the delicate features of Count Malevsky there often hovered a malignant little smile; he really had fallen out of favour with Zinaida and was now waiting upon the old princess with exceptional assiduity; he accompanied her in a hired carriage when she paid a visit to the Governor-General. Actually this expedition turned out to be a failure and involved a disagreeable experience for Malevsky: an old scandal involving some sapper officers was brought up against him, and he had to explain it away by pleading his inexperience at the time. Looshin used to come once or twice a day but did not stay long; I was a little frightened of him after our last open conversation – yet at the same time I felt genuinely attracted to him. One day he went for a walk with me in the Neskootchny, was very amiable and agreeable, told me about the names and properties of various plants and flowers, when suddenly – it was really neither here nor there – he struck himself on the forehead and cried, 'And I, like a fool, thought that she was a flirt! Evidently to sacrifice oneself is the height of bliss – for some people!'

'What are you trying to say?' I asked.

'To you I am not trying to say anything,' Looshin brusquely replied.

Zinaida avoided me: my presence – I could not help

noticing it – was disagreeable to her. Involuntarily she turned away from me ... involuntarily; it was that which was so bitter, so crushing – but there was nothing I could do. I did my best to keep out of her sight, and would try to watch her from a distance, which was not always possible.

As before, something was happening to her which I could not fathom: her face had altered: she became an entirely different being. The change which had taken place in her struck me with peculiar force one warm, still evening, as I was sitting on a low seat under a spreading elder bush. I loved this corner of the garden: from it I could see the window of Zinaida's room. I sat there: in the dark mass of leaves over my head a small bird was rummaging about busily; a grey cat, its back stretched out, was creeping cautiously into the garden; the air, still clear but bright no longer, was heavy with the droning of the early beetles. I sat there, and looked at her window and waited in case it opened – and it did open, and Zinaida stood before me. She was wearing a white dress – and she was pale herself, her face, her shoulders, her arms were pale, almost white. She stood for a long time motionless, gazing straight before her with unmoving eyes, from under heavily knitted brows. Such a look I had never known upon her face. Then she clasped her hands tight, very tight, raised them to her lips – her forehead – then suddenly wrenched her fingers apart and thrust back her hair from her temples, tossed it; then with an air of resolution nodded, and shut the window with a slam.

Three days later she met me in the garden. I was on the point of moving away when she stopped me herself.

'Give me your hand,' she said, in the old caressing manner. 'We haven't had a gossip for a long time.'

I looked up at her: her eyes shone with a soft radiance, her face was smiling as if through a mist.

'Are you still unwell?' I asked her.

'No – it's all over now,' she answered and plucked a small red rose, 'I am a little tired, but that will pass.'

'And you will be the same as you were before?' I asked.

Zinaida lifted the rose to her face and it seemed to me as if her cheeks caught the reflection of its bright petals.

'Why, am I changed then?' she asked.

'Yes, you are,' I answered in a low voice.

'I have been cold to you, I know,' began Zinaida, 'but you should not have taken any notice of it. I couldn't help it ... but then, why talk about it?'

'You don't want me to love you – that's what it is!' I burst out gloomily, against my will.

'No. Love me, yes, but not as before.'

'Why, what am I to do?'

'Let us be friends – that's what,' Zinaida gave me the rose to smell. 'Listen, I am, after all, much older than you, I really might be your aunt – oh, well, perhaps not aunt, but elder sister. And you ...'

'I am a child to you,' I interrupted.

'Well, yes, a child, but a sweet, good, clever child, whom I love very much. I'll tell you what. As from today you are appointed to be my page: and always remember that pages must never leave their mistress's side. And here is the token of your new dignity,' she added, putting the rose in the button-hole of my jacket, 'a sign of our gracious favour.'

'I have received other favours from you before,' I murmured.

'Ah,' said Zinaida, and gave me a sidelong look. 'What a memory he has. Oh, well, I am just as ready now ...' and bent down towards me and placed on my forehead a pure, calm kiss.

I did not look at her – she turned away and, saying 'Follow me, my page,' went towards the lodge. I walked behind her – and could not understand it. Can this gentle, sensible girl, I kept thinking, be the Zinaida whom I used to know?

Her very walk seemed gentler, her whole figure more stately and more, graceful. Great Heavens! With what fresh force my love flamed up within me!

## XVI

After dinner the party gathered again at the lodge – and the young princess came down to them. The party was there in full force, as on that first, to me unforgettable, evening. Even Nirmatsky brought himself to attend: this time Maidanov arrived before anyone else – with some new verses. They played forfeits again, but this time, without the eccentricities and the foolery and noise of the earlier occasion; the gipsy element had gone.

Zinaida gave the evening a different mood. I sat beside her, as her page. In the course of the evening she proposed that whoever had to pay a forfeit should tell his dream; but this was not a success. The dreams were either boring (Byelov-zorov had dreamt that he had fed carp to his mare and that she had a wooden head), or were unnatural and too obviously made up. Maidanov treated us to a full-blown romantic tale, complete with sepulchres, angels with lyres, talking flowers, and sounds of music floating from afar. Zinaida did not let him finish.

'If we are to have made-up stories,' she said, 'then let everyone quite definitely invent something and tell us that.'

Byelovzorov again was obliged to begin. The young hussar was acutely embarrassed. 'I can't think of anything to say,' he cried.

'What nonsense!' Zinaida caught him up. 'Can't you imagine, let us say, that you are married, and tell us how you would arrange your life with your bride. Would you lock her up?'

'I should.'

'And you would remain with her yourself?'

'Certainly. I should certainly stay with her all the time.'

'Admirable. And if this happened to bore her, and she deceived you?'

'I should kill her.'

'And if she ran away?'

'I should pursue and catch her and still kill her.'

'I see. And supposing that I were your wife, what would you do then?'

Byelovzorov, after a silence, said, 'I should kill myself.'

Zinaida begin to laugh. 'I see your tale is quickly told.'

The next forfeit was Zinaida's.

She looked up at the ceiling and sat thinking.

'Listen,' she began at last, 'this is what I have thought of. Imagine a magnificent palace, a summer night, and a wonderful ball. The ball is being given by a young queen. Everywhere, gold, marble, crystal, silk, lights, jewels, flowers, burning incense, every extravagance of luxury.'

'You like luxury?' Looshin interjected.

'Luxury is full of loveliness,' she rejoined. 'I adore all that is lovely.'

'More than the beautiful?' he asked.

'That sounds too clever – I don't understand it. Don't interrupt. Well then, the ball is magnificent. There are many guests. They are all young, beautiful, brave, and all are madly in love with the queen.'

'Are there no women among the guests?' asked Malevsky.

'No, or wait – there are.'

'All ugly?'

'No, ravishing – but the men are all in love with the queen. She is tall and graceful; upon her dark locks is set a small diadem of gold.'

I looked at Zinaida; and at that moment she seemed so high above us all; such luminous intelligence, such power shone from her calm white brow that I thought, 'You are your own story-queen.'

'They all throng about her,' Zinaida continued, 'they make speeches of fulsome flattery to her.'

'And she likes flattery?' Looshin asked.

'How insufferable he is; he will interrupt all the time ... And who doesn't like flattery?'

'Just one last question,' put in Malevsky, 'has the queen a husband?'

'Why, I hadn't thought about that. No, why a husband?'

'Of course,' echoed Malevsky, 'why indeed?'

'*Silence!*' exclaimed Maidanov in French, which he spoke badly.

'*Merci,*' said Zinaida to him.

'And so the queen listens to their speeches, hears the music, but does not glance at any of the guests. Six windows are open from floor to ceiling and beyond them a dark sky with large stars and a dark garden with huge trees. The queen gazes into the garden. There, near the trees, is a fountain; it is white in the darkness and tall, tall as a ghost. The queen hears, through the talk and the music, the soft plashing of its waters. She looks and thinks, You, Sirs, you are all noble, clever, rich, you throng round me, every one of my words is precious to you, you are all ready to die at my feet, you are my slaves ... But there, by the fountain, by the plashing water, he whose slave I am awaits me. He wears neither gorgeous raiment nor precious stones, no one knows him, but he awaits me, sure that I shall come – and I *shall* come – and there is no power in the world that can stop me when I want to go to him, to be with him, to lose myself with him there in the darkness of the garden, with the rustling of the trees and the murmur of the fountain...' Zinaida was silent.

'And is this – fiction?' Malevsky asked craftily.

Zinaida did not even look at him.

'And what should we have done, gentlemen,' began Looshin suddenly, 'if we had been among the guests and had known about this fortunate man by the fountain?'

'Wait, wait,' Zinaida intervened, 'I will myself tell you how you would each have behaved. You, Byelovzorov, would have challenged him to a duel: you, Maidanov, would have perpetrated an epigram against him – or no, you don't know how to write epigrams, you would have written a long poem in iambics in the style of Barbier and would have got it into the *Telegraph*. You, Nirmatsky, would have borrowed – no, you would have lent him money at interest; you, doctor ...' she stopped. 'Now about you, I don't know what you would have done ...'

'Acting in my capacity of court physician,' answered Looshin, 'I should have advised the queen not to give balls when she was not in the mood for guests.'

'Perhaps you would have been right. And you, Count?'

'And I?' echoed Malevsky with his malevolent little smile.

'You would have offered him a poisoned sweet.'

Malevsky's face gave a little quiver and for an instant took on a Jewish expression, but he at once let out a loud laugh.

'As for you, Woldemar,' Zinaida continued. 'However, that's enough; let's play another game.'

'M'sieu Woldemar, as the queen's page, would have carried her train as she ran into the garden,' Malevsky observed with venom.

The blood rushed to my face – but Zinaida quickly put her hand on my shoulder, and rising, said in a voice which trembled a little, 'I never gave your Excellency the right to be insolent and, therefore, I must ask you to leave.' She pointed to the door.

'But Princess, I beg you,' muttered Malevsky, turning quite pale.

'The Princess is right,' cried Byelovzorov, and also rose.

'I do assure you, I never imagined . . .' Malevsky went on. 'Surely there was nothing in my words that . . . I hadn't the remotest intention of insulting you . . . Please forgive me.'

Zinaida looked at him coldly, and coldly smiled. 'Very well, then, stay,' she said, with a careless gesture of the hand. 'There was no reason for me and M'sieu Woldemar to be so angry. You find it amusing to sting . . . I hope you enjoy it.'

'Forgive me,' said Malevsky once again. While I, thinking of Zinaida's gesture, reflected again that no real queen could have shown a presumptuous mortal the door with greater dignity.

The game of forfeits continued for a short time after this little incident. Everyone was slightly embarrassed, not so much on account of the scene itself, but because of another undefined but oppressive feeling. No one mentioned it, yet everyone was conscious of it in himself and in his neighbour.

Maidanov read us his verses – and Malevsky praised them
with exaggerated warmth.

'How kind he is trying to seem now,' Looshin whispered
to me.

We soon dispersed. Zinaida suddenly became pensive. The
princess sent word that she had a headache; Nirmatsky began
to complain of his rheumatism.

For a long time I could not sleep. I was deeply affected by
Zinaida's story. Can there have been some hidden meaning in
it? I kept asking myself. At whom, at what, could she have
been hinting? And if there really was something to hint at –
how could one be sure . . .

'No, no, it cannot be,' I kept whispering, turning from one
hot cheek to the other . . . but I would recall the expression on
Zinaida's face as she told her story, and I remembered the
remark with which Looshin had burst out in the Neskootchny
Gardens, the sudden changes in her behaviour to me, and
could find no answer. 'Who is he?' These three words seemed
to stand before my eyes in the darkness. It was as if a low,
malignant cloud were suspended over me – I felt its weight
and waited from moment to moment for it to burst. I had
become used to a great deal of late, had seen too much at the
Zasyekins'; their untidy lives, the greasy candle-ends, the
broken knives and forks, the gloomy Vonifaty, the shabby
maids, the manners of the old princess herself; this queer
form of life no longer surprised me.

But there was something which I now fancied I dimly
perceived in Zinaida, something to which I could not reconcile myself . . . An adventuress my mother had once called her.
An adventuress – she, my idol, my goddess! The word seared
me like a flame, I tried to escape from it into my pillow. I
burned with indignation, yet at the same time what would I
not have done, what would I not have given, to be that darling
of fortune, the man by the fountain!

My blood was on fire and whirling within me. 'The garden
– the fountain,' I thought. 'I will go to the garden.' I dressed
swiftly and slipped out of the house. The night was dark,

the trees scarcely murmured; a soft chill fell from the sky; the scent of herbs came floating across from the kitchen garden.

I went round every walk; the soft sound of my own footsteps increased my nervousness and yet gave me confidence; I would stand still, wait and listen to my heart beating fast and heavily. At last I went up to the fence and leant on a thin post. Suddenly – or was it my fancy? – a woman's figure glimmered past, a few paces away. I peered intently into the darkness – I held my breath ... What was that? Did I hear steps or was this again the beating of my heart? 'Who is it?' I faltered almost inaudibly. What was that again? A smothered laugh? Or the rustling of leaves? Or a sigh close by my ear? I grew frightened ... 'Who is it?' I repeated, still more softly.

For an instant the air stirred round me. A streak of fire flashed across the sky – a falling star. 'Zinaida?' I wanted to ask, but the sound died on my lips. All at once everything became profoundly quiet round me, as often happens in the middle of the night ... Even the grasshoppers ceased chirruping in the trees – only somewhere a window squeaked. I stood still for a time, and then went back to my bed, now grown quite cold. I felt a strange excitement as if I had gone to a rendezvous, but had not myself met with anyone, passing close by another's happiness.

## XVII

On the following day I caught only a brief glimpse of Zinaida. She was going somewhere in a cab with the old princess. On the other hand, I saw Looshin – who barely greeted me – and Malevsky. The young count smiled and began talking to me with great affability. Of all the visitors to the lodge he alone had managed to insinuate himself into our house, and succeeded in making himself very agreeable to my mother. My father did not care for him and treated him with an almost offensive politeness.

'Ah, *Monsieur le page*,' Malevsky began, 'delighted to see you; and what is your lovely queen doing?'

His fresh, handsome face was so repulsive to me at that moment, and he was looking at me with such an expression of disdainful amusement, that I did not reply at all.

'Are you still annoyed?' he went on. 'You really shouldn't be. After all, it wasn't I who called you a page – they're usually to be found with queens. But let me tell you that you are not carrying out your duties at all well.'

'Oh, and why not?'

'Pages ought never to leave their mistresses' side: pages should know everything their mistresses do; indeed they should watch them,' he added, lowering his voice, 'day and night.'

'What do you mean by that?'

'Mean by it? I should have thought I had made myself clear enough. Day – and night. In the daytime it doesn't perhaps matter quite so much: it is light and there are lots of people about. But night – that's when anything may happen. My advice to you is not to sleep at night, but keep watch – watch with all your might: remember the garden – at night – near the fountain – that is where you must watch. You'll thank me for this yet.'

Malevsky laughed and turned his back on me. Probably he attached no great importance to the words he had just spoken to me. He was a notoriously successful practical joker, celebrated for his skill in bamboozling people at fancy dress parties – an art greatly enhanced by the almost unconscious mendacity which permeated his whole being. He only wanted to tease me a little; but every word he uttered ran like poison through my veins – the blood rushed to my head. 'Aha! so that's it!' I said to myself. 'I see! So it wasn't for nothing that I felt drawn into the garden! But no! It shall not be!' I cried loudly, striking myself on the chest with my fist, although I was not quite clear about what it was precisely that was not to be. 'Whether it is Malevsky himself who will appear in the garden (he might well have let it slip out about himself – he was certainly impudent enough), or whether it is someone else (the fence round our garden was very low, and there was no difficulty about getting over it), whoever he is, he'll be sorry when he falls into my hands – I wouldn't advise anybody to cross my path. I shall show the whole world and her, the traitor (I actually used the word "traitor"), that I know the meaning of revenge!'

I returned to my room, took out of the writing table an English penknife I had recently purchased, felt the sharp edge, and with a frown of cold and concentrated resolution, thrust it into my pocket as if this kind of thing was nothing new or strange to me. My heart rose angrily within me and turned to stone.

All day I wore a stern scowl, and from time to time, with my lips tightly pressed, I would walk up and down, my hand in my pocket clutching the knife grown warm in my grasp, preparing myself long in advance for something terrible. These new unfamiliar sensations proved so absorbing and even exhilarating, that I scarcely thought about Zinaida herself. I saw constant visions of Aleko, the young gipsy – 'Whither, O handsome youth, lie still'; then 'Bespattered art with blood! ... What hast thou done? – Nothing.' With what a cruel smile I kept repeating this 'Nothing' again and again to myself! My father was not at home; but my mother, who had for some time been in a state of almost continuous dull exasperation, noticed my look of doom and said to me at supper:

'Why are you sulking like a mouse in a grain-bin?'

At which I merely gave a condescending smile and thought 'If they only knew!'

It struck eleven; I went up to my room but did not undress; I was waiting for midnight; at last it struck. 'Time!' I muttered through my teeth, and buttoning myself up to the throat, and even rolling up my sleeves, I went into the garden.

I had already selected the exact spot for my vigil: at the end of the garden, at the point where the fence which separated our possessions from the Zasyekins' ran into the common wall, grew a solitary pine tree. Standing under its low thick branches, I could observe, as far as the darkness of the night permitted, all that went on round me: at the foot of the tree ran a path which had always been full of mystery for me. Like a snake it wound its way under the fence, which bore the marks of climbing feet, and led up to a round arbour made of thick acacias. I made my way to the pine tree, leant back against its trunk, and began my watch.

The night was quiet and still, like the night before, but there were fewer clouds in the sky, and the outlines of the bushes – even of the taller flowers – stood out more distinctly. The first moments of waiting filled me with agonizing suspense, and almost with terror. I had resolved to stop at nothing, but I was still trying to decide what to do. Should I thunder forth, 'Where are you going? Stop! Tell me – or die!' Or should I simply strike ... Every sound, every rustle and whisper seemed oddly significant and strange. I was ready, I was all alert. I leant forward ... but half an hour passed, then an hour; my blood grew quieter, colder; the thought began to steal into my brain that it had all been quite pointless, that I was actually making myself a little ridiculous – that it was only a practical joke on Malevsky's part. I left my ambush and wandered round the entire garden. All was quiet: not a sound could be heard anywhere: everything was at peace, even our dog slept curled up by the gate.

I climbed up on to the ruined greenhouse and saw the long open prospect of the fields before me, remembered the meeting with Zinaida, and lost myself in thought.

I started ... I thought I heard the creak of a door opening, then the faint sound of a snapping twig ... In two leaps I got down from the ruin ... I stood frozen to the spot. There was a sound – quite distinct – of footsteps, rapid, light, but cautious, in the garden ... They were coming towards me ... 'Here he is ... here he is at last', raced through my heart. Convulsively I whipped the knife out of my pocket and frantically I forced it open. Queer red spots danced before my eyes, and my hair stood on end in an agony of fury and terror

– the footsteps were coming straight towards me. I stooped and crouched forward to meet them – a man appeared – O God, it was my father!

I recognized him at once, although he was completely muffled in a dark cloak, and his hat was pulled down over his face. He tiptoed past without noticing me, although nothing concealed me, shrunk, huddled and crouched so low that I was almost level with the ground. Jealous Othello, ready for murder, was suddenly transformed into a schoolboy ... I was so terribly startled by my father's unexpected appearance that in the first instant I did not even notice where he had come from and where he had vanished. It took me a moment to get up and to ask myself, 'Why should my father be wandering about at night in the garden,' when all grew silent round me again. In my terror I dropped the knife in the grass – but did not even look for it: I felt dreadfully ashamed.

All at once I was quite sober again; on my way back to our house I did, however, go up to my seat under the elder tree and glance up at the window of Zinaida's bedroom. The small, slightly curved window panes gleamed with a dim blue light under the pale radiance of the night sky. All of a sudden their colour began to change. Beyond them I saw – saw quite distinctly – a whitish blind pulled down cautiously and gently to the window sill, and it stayed down, like that, quite still.

'What is all this?' I said aloud, almost against my will, when I was back again in my room, 'A dream, a chance coincidence, or...?' the ideas which suddenly entered my head were so new and strange that I did not dare let myself dwell on them.

## XVIII

I rose in the morning with a headache. The tense excitement of the previous day had gone. I was depressed, frustrated and overcome by a new, quite unfamiliar kind of sadness, as if something in me were dying.

'Why are you looking like a rabbit who's had half his brain removed?' said Looshin when he met me.

At luncheon I kept glancing at both my parents in turn: my father was, as usual, calm: my mother, as always, secretly irritated. I sat there and wondered whether my father would presently say something friendly to me, as he sometimes did ... but he showed no sign even of his normal, cold affection.

Shall I tell Zinaida everything? I reflected. After all, it can't make any difference now – it is all over between us.

I went to see her, but not only told her nothing – I did not even get an opportunity for a talk which I longed for. The old princess's son, a cadet about twelve years old, had arrived from St Petersburg for his holidays. He was immediately handed over to me by Zinaida: 'Here,' she said, 'my dear Volodya,' (she had never called me this before) 'is a friend for you. He is called Volodya too. Please get to like him; he is still a wild, shy little thing, but he has a kind heart. Show him the Neskootchny Gardens, take him for walks, take him under your wing. You will do it, won't you? You will. You, too, are so very kind.' She laid both her hands affectionately on my shoulders – I felt utterly lost; the appearance of this boy turned me into a boy too. I said nothing and glared at the cadet, who in his turn stood staring dumbly at me. Zinaida burst out laughing and pushed us at each other: 'Go on, children, give one another a hug!' We did so.

'I'll take you to the garden, if you like,' I said to the cadet.

'Very kind of you, I am sure,' he replied in a husky cadet voice.

Zinaida laughed again – and I saw then that the colour in her face was lovelier than ever before.

There was an old swing in our garden: I sat the cadet on the edge of the thin plank and swung him gently. He sat very stiffly in his small, brand-new uniform of thick cloth, with a wide gold braid, and held on tightly to the cords.

'Hadn't you better unbutton your collar?' I said.

'No, thanks – we're quite used to it,' he said, and gave a short cough.

He was like his sister – his eyes especially recalled her. Looking after him gave me pleasure – and at the same time I felt a dull pain quietly gnawing at my heart: 'Today I really am only a little boy,' I thought, 'whereas yesterday . . .'

I remembered where I had dropped my knife the night before, and found it. The cadet asked for it, broke off a thick stem of cow-parsley, cut himself a whistle out of it, and started playing. Othello whistled a little, too.

But the same evening, how he cried, this Othello, in Zinaida's arms when, having discovered him in a distant corner of the garden, she asked him why he was so sad. I burst into tears so violently that she was frightened.

'What is the matter with you, what is it, Volodya?' she kept saying, and when I neither replied nor ceased crying, she made an attempt to kiss my wet cheek. But I turned my face from her and whispered through my sobs, 'I know everything; why did you play with me? What need had you of my love?'

'I am guilty before you, Volodya,' said Zinaida. 'Oh, I am terribly guilty,' she said, clasping her hands tightly. 'There is so much in me that is dark, evil, wicked . . . but now I am not playing with you – I love you – and you haven't an inkling why and how much I love you . . . but anyhow, what is it that you know?'

What could I tell her? She stood before me and gazed at me, and I was hers, utterly hers from head to foot, whenever she looked at me. Only a quarter of an hour later I was running races with the cadet and Zinaida, I was playing tag, and no longer crying; I was laughing, though a tear or two filled my swollen eyelids even as I laughed. Round my neck, instead of a tie, I wore Zinaida's ribbon, and I screamed with joy when I managed to catch her by the waist. She did exactly what she liked with me.

## XIX

I should find it difficult if someone asked me to give a detailed account of what went on within me during the week which followed my unlucky venture into the garden. It was a queer, feverish period; the most violently conflicting feelings, thoughts, suspicions, hopes, joys, pains, tossed and whirled within me in a kind of mad chaos: I was afraid of looking into myself, if a boy of sixteen can be said to do such a thing; I was afraid to face anything – whatever it might be – consciously. I simply tried to get through the day as fast as I could, from morning till night: but then, at night, I slept ... the light-heartedness of childhood came to my aid.

I didn't want to know whether I was loved, and I didn't want to admit to myself that I was not. I avoided my father – but avoid Zinaida I could not. Her presence seared me like a flame ... but what did I care what kind of fire this was in which I burned and melted, when it was bliss to burn and to melt? I gave myself freely to my sensations as they came, telling myself lies and hiding from my own memories, and closed my eyes to what I sensed was coming. This sick, sweet longing would probably anyhow not have lasted long; but suddenly a thunderbolt blasted it, and flung me on to a new and altogether different path.

One day when I came home to dinner from a longish walk, I learned, to my surprise, that I was to dine alone; my father had gone away, my mother felt unwell and had shut herself in her room, saying she did not want any food. I could see by the faces of the footmen that something very unusual had taken place. I did not dare to question them, but one of the pantry boys, called Philip, who was passionately fond of poetry and a beautiful guitar player, was a particular friend of mine, and to him I turned. From him I discovered that a terrible scene had taken place between my parents. (Every word of it could be heard in the maids' room; much of it was in French, but Masha, the lady's maid, had lived for five years with a seam-stress from Paris and understood every word.) Apparently my

mother had accused my father of being unfaithful to her and
of having relations with the young lady next door; my father
had at first defended himself but then flared up and said
something brutal – 'something to do with Madame's age' –
which had made my mother cry; my mother had also alluded
to a loan supposed to have been made to the old princess, and
then made disagreeable remarks about her and about her
daughter too, whereupon my father began to threaten her.

'And what's done all the mischief,' Philip continued, 'is an
anonymous letter, and nobody knows who wrote it; there is no
other sort of reason why these things should ever come out
into the open.'

'Why, was there really something?' I brought out with
difficulty, while my hands and feet grew cold, and deep down
in my breast something began to quiver.

Philip gave a knowing wink. 'There was. There's no hiding
these things. Not but what your father was as careful as could
be – but then there is always something you can't do without;
you have to hire a carriage or something like that ... and you
can't do it without servants, either.'

I sent Philip away and flung myself on my bed. I did not
sob; I did not give myself up to despair; I did not ask myself
where and how all this had happened; I did not wonder how it
was that I had not guessed it earlier – guessed it long ago. I
did not even harbour bitter thoughts about my father ... what
I had learned was too much for me to manage. The sudden
revelation crushed me; all was ended. In one swoop all my
flowers were torn up by the roots and lay about me –
scattered, broken, trampled underfoot.

## XX

Next day my mother announced that she was moving back to
the town. In the morning my father went into her bedroom
and stayed with her for a long time alone. No one heard what
he said to her, but afterwards my mother wept no longer; she

grew calm, and asked for food, but did not herself appear, nor did she change her plans. I remember that I wandered about the whole day, but did not go into the garden and did not once glance at the lodge.

In the evening I witnessed an astonishing scene; my father took Count Malevsky by the arm through the drawing-room, into the hall, and in the presence of the footman, said to him coldly, 'Some days ago, Your Excellency was shown the door in a certain house; I do not now wish to enter into any kind of explanation with you, but should Your Excellency ever again be good enough to deign to pay me a visit, I shall throw you out of the window. I do not like your handwriting.'

The count bowed slightly, clenched his teeth, seemed to shrink into himself, and vanished.

Preparations began for our return to town, to the Arbat, where we had a house. My father himself probably did not want to stay in the country any longer, but apparently he had managed to talk my mother into not starting a public scandal. Everything was done quietly, without haste. My mother even sent her compliments to the old princess, expressing regret that she was prevented by ill health from seeing her before she left.

I walked about in a daze, as if I had lost my wits, longing only for it all to end as soon as possible. One thought kept running in my head: How could she – a young girl and a princess – have brought herself to do such a thing, when she knew that my father was not free, and she could after all have married, say, Byelovzorov? What did she hope for, was she not frightened of ruining her whole future? Yes, I thought, this is it – this is love; this is passion; this is devotion. And I remembered Looshin's words: 'To sacrifice oneself is the height of bliss – for some people.'

Some time later, I happened to catch sight of a pale patch outlined in one of the windows of the lodge. 'Can this possibly be Zinaida's face?' I thought. Indeed, it was. I could bear it no longer. I could not leave without a final good-bye. I seized a favourable moment and went to the lodge.

In the drawing-room, the old princess greeted me with her usual slovenly disregard.

'Your people seem to be getting off in a terrible hurry. Why is that, my dear sir?' she remarked, thrusting snuff into both nostrils.

I looked at her, and a load was lifted from my heart. The word 'loan', which Philip had let drop, had been torturing me. She suspected nothing, or at least I thought so at the time. Zinaida came in from the next room, in a black dress, pale, with her hair let down. Without a word she took me by the hand and drew me out of the room.

'I heard your voice and came out at once. You find it, then, so easy to desert us, you wicked boy?'

'I have come to say good-bye to you, Princess,' I replied, 'probably for ever. You have heard, perhaps, we are leaving?'

Zinaida looked intently at me. 'Yes, I've heard. Thank you for coming. I had begun to think I would not see you again. You must not think too ill of me. I have sometimes tortured you; but still I am not what you imagine me to be.' She turned away and leaned against the window. 'Really, I am not like that. I know that you have a low view of me.'

'I?'

'Yes, you, you . . .'

'I?' I repeated painfully, and my heart began to quiver, as it always did under the spell of her irresistible, inexpressible fascination. 'I? Believe me, Zinaida Alexandrovna, that whatever you did, however much you make me suffer, I shall love you and adore you to the end of my days.'

She quickly turned towards me, and opening her arms wide, put them round my head, and gave me a strong, warm kiss. God only knows for whom that long farewell kiss was seeking, but I tasted its sweetness avidly. I knew that it would never come again.

'Good-bye, good-bye,' I kept repeating.

She tore herself from my embrace, and was gone. I went too. I cannot even begin to convey the feelings with which I left her. I never wish to experience them again, but I should count it a misfortune never to have had them at all.

We moved back to the town. It was a long time before I could shake off the past; long before I could begin to work again. My wound healed slowly, but towards my father I actually bore no ill feeling. On the contrary, he somehow seemed even to have grown in my eyes. Let psychologists explain this contradiction if they can.

One day I was walking in the street and to my indescribable joy, ran into Looshin. I liked him for his straightforward, and candid nature; besides, he was dear to me because of the memories he awoke in me. I rushed up to him.

'Oho,' said he, and knitted his brow. 'So it is you, young man. Let's have a look at you – still pretty yellow; however, the old nonsense seems to have left your eyes. You look like a man and not a lap-dog. That's good. Well, what are you doing? Working?'

I gave a sigh. I did not want to tell a lie and was ashamed to tell the truth. 'Well, never mind,' Looshin continued, 'don't be discouraged. The main thing is to live a normal life and not to be carried away. Otherwise, what's the use? Wherever the wave may carry you, it will always turn out badly. Better a rock to stand on, so long as it's on one's own feet. Now I, you see I've got a cough ... And Byelovzorov, have you heard?'

'No, what?'

'No trace of him. They say he went off to the Caucasus. A lesson to you, young man; and it all comes from not knowing how to break off in time – to break out of the net. Though you seem to have got away quite unscathed. Now mind you don't get caught again. Good-bye.'

I shan't be caught, I thought ... I shall never see her again. But I was destined to see Zinaida once more.


## XXI


My father used to go riding every day. He had an excellent English mare, a chestnut roan, with a long slender neck and

long legs. She was called 'Electric'; no one could ride her
except my father; she was a vicious and tireless animal. One
day he came in to me; he was in an excellent temper,
something which had not happened for a long time. He was
dressed for riding, and was wearing spurs. I begged him to
take me with him.

'We'd better have a game of leap frog,' said my father.
'You'll never keep up with me on your cob.'

'Oh, yes, I will, I'll wear spurs too.'

'Well, all right.'

We set off. I was on a black, shaggy, frisky little horse, with
strong legs; he did, it is true, have to gallop pretty hard when
Electric was in full trot, but still we did not lag behind. I have
never seen a horseman to equal my father. He looked so fine
on his mount, sitting apparently with such effortless ease that
the horse itself – as if conscious of it – seemed to take pride in
the rider.

We rode through all the avenues, visited the Maidens'
Field, took several fences (I used to be scared of the jumps,
but my father despised timidity and I ceased to be afraid).
Twice we crossed the Moscow river, and I had begun to think
that we were going home, particularly as my father had
himself noticed that my horse was getting tired, when
suddenly he veered away from me at the Crimean Ford and
broke into a gallop along the bank. I followed him. Presently
he came up to a tall stack of old logs. Here he stopped, leaped
nimbly off Electric, ordered me to dismount, gave me his
bridle to hold, and telling me to wait for him there, near the
stack, turned into a little side street and disappeared. I began
to walk up and down beside the river, leading the horses, and
scolding Electric, who kept tossing her head and shaking
herself, snorting and neighing, and, when I stopped, would
start ploughing up the earth with her hooves, or whinnied,
and bit my cob in the neck – in a word, behaved in every way
like the spoilt thoroughbred she was.

There was no sign of my father. An unpleasant raw
dampness came drifting from the river. A thin drizzle began

to fall softly, tracing a criss-cross pattern of tiny brown spots on the grey timber. I was thoroughly sick of seeing those wretched logs, as I wandered up and down beside them. I was becoming more and more deeply depressed, and still my father did not return.

A night watchman, who looked like some sort of Finn, grey all over, with an enormous helmet like a kettle and a halbert (what was a night watchman doing, of all places, on the banks of the Moscow river?) loomed up near me, and turning his face, wrinkled like an old woman's, towards me, said:

'What are you doing here with these horses, sir? I'll hold them for you, shall I?'

I did not answer him. He began to beg tobacco from me. In order to get rid of him (moreover, I was consumed with impatience) I took a few steps in the direction in which my father had vanished, walked down to the end of the little street, turned the corner, and stopped. In the street, about forty paces from me, before the open window of a small wooden house, with his back to me, stood my father. He was leaning with his chest over the window sill; inside the house, half concealed by a curtain, sat a woman in a dark dress, talking with my father; it was Zinaida.

I was utterly stunned. This, I admit, I did not expect. My first impulse was to run away. 'My father will look round,' I thought – 'I shall be lost.' But an odd feeling, a feeling stronger than curiosity, stronger even than jealousy, stronger than fear, gripped me. I stood still and looked. I strained my ears to hear. My father seemed to be insisting on something. Zinaida would not consent. Her face is before my eyes now, sad and serious and beautiful, and upon it the imprint – impossible to convey – of grief, devotion, love, and a kind of despair – I can find no other word for it. She spoke in monosyllables, without lifting her eyes, and only smiled, submissively and stubbornly. By this smile alone I recognized my Zinaida, as she once was. My father gave a shrug of his shoulders, and set his hat straight on his head, which with

him was always a sign of impatience ... then I could hear the
words '*Vous devez vous séparer de cette* ...' Zinaida straightened
herself and held out her hand. Then something unbelievable
took place before my eyes. My father suddenly lifted his
riding-crop, with which he had been flicking the dust off the
folds of his coat, and I heard the sound of a sharp blow struck
across her arm which was bared to the elbow. It was all I
could do to prevent myself from crying out. Zinaida quivered
– looked silently at my father – and raising her arm slowly to
her lips, kissed the scar which glowed crimson upon it.

My father flung away the crop and bounding quickly up
the steps to the porch, broke into the house. Zinaida turned
round, stretched out her arms, tossed her head back – and
also moved away from the window.

Faint with horror, aghast, almost out of my wits, I turned
and ran all the way back down the turning, and almost letting
go of Electric, I made my way back to the bank of the river.
My thoughts were in a dreadful whirl. I knew that my cold
and reserved father was liable to occasional fits of fury, but yet
I could not begin to grasp what it was that I had witnessed ...
and in the same instant I realized that however long I lived, I
should always remember Zinaida's particular movement – her
look, her smile at that moment. I realized that this image of
her, this new image which had so suddenly arisen before me,
would live in my memory for ever. Unseeingly I stared
at the river, unconscious of the tears which were streaming
from my eyes. They are beating her, I thought, beating,
beating ...

'What are you doing? Give me the mare.' I heard my
father's voice behind me. Mechanically, I gave him the bridle.
He leapt on Electric's back. The horse, chilled to the marrow,
reared and bounded about six feet forward. But my father
soon had her under control. He plunged his spurs into her
sides, and hit her over the neck with his fist.

'Bah! The whip's gone,' he muttered.

I remembered the swish and the blow of his whip a short
while before, and shuddered.

'Where have you put it?' I asked my father after a short pause.

He did not answer and galloped on. I overtook him. I was determined to see his face.

'Did you get bored waiting for me?' he muttered, through his teeth.

'A little – but where did you drop your whip?' I asked him again.

He gave me a quick glance. 'I didn't drop it,' he said slowly. 'I threw it away.'

He grew pensive and his head fell, and it was then that I saw for the first – and it may be the last – time how much tenderness and passion his stern features could express. He galloped away again, but this time I was unable to catch up with him; I arrived home about a quarter of an hour after him.

'Yes, this is love,' I again said to myself, as I sat that night at my writing desk, on which exercise books and notebooks had begun to make their appearance. 'This is passion.' And yet how could one fail to feel the most furious resentment, how could one bear to be struck by any hand, however dear – and yet, it seems, one can, if one is in love, and I – I imagined ...

During the past month, I had suddenly grown much older, and my love, with all its violent excitements and its torments, now seemed even to me so very puny and childish and trivial beside that other unknown something which I could hardly begin to guess at, but which struck terror into me like an unfamiliar, beautiful, but awe-inspiring face whose features one strains in vain to discern in the gathering darkness.

That night I dreamt a strange and frightening dream. I fancied that I entered a low, dark room. My father was standing there, holding a riding-crop in his hand, and stamping with his feet. Zinaida was cowering in the corner, and there was a crimson mark, not upon her arm, but upon her forehead ... and behind them both rose Byelovzorov, covered with blood. His pale lips parted, and he made angry, menacing gestures at my father.

Two months later, I entered the University, and six months after that my father died (as the result of a stroke) in St Petersburg, where he had only just moved with my mother and me. Several days before his death he had received a letter from Moscow which upset him greatly. He went to beg some sort of favour of my mother and, so they told me, actually broke down and wept – he, my father! On the morning of the very day on which he had the stroke, he had begun a letter to me, written in French. 'My son,' he wrote, 'beware of the love of women; beware of that ecstasy – that slow poison.'

My mother, after his death, sent a considerable sum of money to Moscow.

## XXII

Three or four years passed. I had just left the University, and was not quite sure what I ought to be doing – which door to knock at; and in the meantime wasted my time in complete idleness.

One fine evening, I met Maidanov in the theatre. He had contrived to get married and enter government service, but I found him quite unchanged. He still alternated between the same foolish transports followed by equally sudden fits of depression.

'You know,' he said to me incidentally, 'that Madame Dolsky is here?'

'What Madame Dolsky?'

'Surely you've not forgotten? The former Princess Zasyekin, you remember we were all in love with her. Yes, and you too. You remember, in the country, near the Neskootchny.'

'Is she married to Dolsky?'

'Yes.'

'And she is here, in the theatre?'

'No, in Petersburg. She came here a day or two ago; she is going abroad.'

'What is her husband like?' I asked.

'Oh, a very nice fellow and quite well off. Colleague of mine in Moscow. You understand after that episode ... you must know all about that' (Maidanov gave a meaning smile) 'it was not easy for her to find herself a suitable *parti*. And it did not end there ... but with her brains nothing is impossible. Do go and see her; she will be very pleased to see you. She is more lovely than ever.'

Maidanov gave me Zinaida's address. She was staying in the Hotel Demuth. Old memories began to stir within me ... I promised myself to pay a visit to my 'flame' on the very next day. But various things turned up. A week passed, and then another, and when I made my way to the Demuth, and asked for Madame Dolsky, I was told that she had died four days before, quite suddenly, in childbirth.

I felt a sudden stab at my heart. The thought that I could have seen her, and did not, and would never see her again – this bitter thought buried itself in me with all the force of an unanswerable reproach.

'She is dead,' I repeated, staring dully at the porter, and making my way noiselessly into the street, wandered off without knowing where I was going. The past suddenly rose and stood before me. So that was to be the final answer to it all. So that was the final goal towards which this young life, all glitter and ardour and excitement, went hurrying along. Those were my thoughts as I conjured up those beloved features, those eyes, those curls – in the narrow box, in the dank underground darkness – here, not far from me who was still living, and perhaps only a few steps from where my father lay.

And as those thoughts poured in upon me, and my imagination was busily at work,

Tidings of death heard I from lips unfeeling,
Unmoved, I listened,

ran in my head. O youth! youth! you go your way heedless, uncaring – as if you owned all the treasures of the world; even grief elates you, even sorrow sits well upon your brow. You are self-confident and insolent and you say, 'I alone am alive – behold!' even while your own days fly past and vanish without trace and without number, and everything within you melts away like wax in the sun ... like snow ... and perhaps the whole secret of your enchantment lies not, indeed, in your power to do whatever you may will, but in your power to think that there is nothing you will not do: it is this that you scatter to the winds – gifts which you could never have used to any other purpose. Each of us feels most deeply convinced that he has been too prodigal of his gifts – that he has a right to cry 'Oh, what could I not have done, if only I had not wasted my time.'

And here am I ... what did I hope – what did I expect? What rich promise did the future seem to hold out to me, when with scarcely a sigh – only a bleak sense of utter desolation – I took my leave from the brief phantom, risen for a fleeting instant, of my first love?

What has come of it all – of all that I had hoped for? And now when the shades of evening are beginning to close in upon my life, what have I left that is fresher, dearer to me, than the memories of that brief storm that came and went so swiftly one morning in the spring?

But I do myself an injustice. Even then, in those light-hearted days of youth, I did not close my eyes to the mournful voice which called to me, to the solemn sound which came to me from beyond the grave.

I remember how several days after that on which I had learnt of Zinaida's death, I myself, obeying an irresistible impulse, was present at the death of a poor old woman who lived in the same house with us. Covered with rags, lying on bare boards, with a sack for a pillow, her end was hard and painful. Her whole life was spent in a bitter struggle with daily want, she had had no joy, had never tasted the sweets of happiness – surely she would welcome death with gladness – its deliverance – its peace? Yet so long as her frail body resisted obstinately, her breast rose and fell in agony under the icy hand that was laid upon it, so long as any strength was left within her, the little old woman kept crossing herself, kept whispering 'Lord forgive me my sins . . .' and not until the last spark of consciousness had gone, did the look of fear, of the terror of death, vanish from her eyes . . . and I remember that there, by the death-bed of that poor old woman, I grew afraid, afraid for Zinaida, and I wanted to say a prayer for her, for my father – and for myself.

# SPRING TORRENTS

TRANSLATED FROM THE RUSSIAN
BY LEONARD SCHAPIRO

# *Translator's Note*

\*

Although the action of *Spring Torrents* takes place some thirty years before the date of composition and publication, the author's style is in no possible sense archaic or dated, but contemporary in character. I have therefore made no attempt, in turn, to suggest the style of the seventies of the past century, but have aimed at a contemporary style, which, to the best of my ability, reproduces the style and mood of the author. I hope that the usual difficulties which arise in translation from the Russian will not obtrude themselves too much. I have been sparing in the use of patronymics – but they are to a certain extent unavoidable, and I hope the reader will not find them too bizarre. The other difficulty – the use of 'you' and 'thou', so hard to reproduce in English – has not proved very serious. In some cases the form of address is not so material as to make it important for the reader to know which form is being used. In other cases, where it is important, the situation has been saved by the fact that the vital conversations take place in French, which is a language in which the different forms of address are easily indicated by the use of *tu* or *vous*.

But, it will be asked, why translate at all what has already been translated several times before? I suppose any translator (even so amateur a one as I am) persuades himself that he can do it better than it has been done before. (And I must confess here that I have never read any translation of *Spring Torrents* – perhaps if I did I would scrap this one. But it is too late.) I started to translate *Spring Torrents* for a friend who is a writer, and herself no mean stylist, because I felt that I could reveal Turgenev's art to her in this way better than others had done in the past. It is, of course, not possible for me to judge whether I have succeeded or failed: I merely record what set me upon the translator's path. As I proceeded with the translation I became increasingly aware, to an extent that I had never realized before (though I have read *Spring Torrents* many times since my boyhood), of the superb mastery of his craft that Turgenev exhibits. And so, the work of translation grew into a tribute, a small and humble tribute to a great master from one by whom the craft of writing has never been pursued for its own sake so much as for the utilitarian purposes of the record and analysis of facts.

I must record my gratitude to friends who have been kind enough to help me. Victor Frank generously went through the translation and saved me from a number of errors. Roma Thewes has also critically worked through the text on several occasions, and made innumerable and valuable suggestions for improvement. To both these friends I owe a great debt of thanks. But I am an obstinate and headstrong man, and they are in no way to blame for the many errors or roughnesses which no doubt still remain.

# Spring Torrents

*Those happy years,*
*Those days so gay,*
*Like the rush of spring torrents*
*Have vanished away.*

[From a very old song]

\* \* \*

... About two in the morning he returned to his study. He dismissed the servant who had come in and had lit the candles, then flung himself onto the armchair by the fireplace, and buried his face in his hands.

He had never before felt so tired – in body and in spirit. He had spent the whole evening in the company of agreeable women and educated men. There had been some beautiful women among them too, and nearly all the men had been witty and accomplished. His own conversation had come off very well, brilliantly even ... and yet, and yet ... never before had he felt such disgust for life, such *taedium vitae*, which the Romans talked about in their time. It overwhelmed him like some irresistible force; he felt it choking him. Had he been somewhat younger he would have burst into tears of frustration, boredom and irritation. He felt as if his soul were filled with hot and acrid smoke, like the smoke of wormwood. Like a dark autumn night, a sense of disgust enveloped him; something repulsive and insufferable engulfed him. Try as he would he could not shake it off, could not dispel all this darkness and the pungent smoke. There was no escape for him in sleep; he knew it would not come. So he began to let his thoughts run – slowly, listlessly, and rather angrily.

He reflected on the useless bustle, the vulgar falsity of human existence. One after another he mentally reviewed each age of life (he himself had recently turned fifty-three). He had no good word for any of them. Everywhere he found the same squandering of time and effort, the same treading of water, the same self-deception, half unconscious and half deliberate – anything to keep the child quiet; and then – all of a sudden – like a fall of snow, old age is upon one – and with it the ever-growing fear of death, all-consuming, gnawing at one's very vitals – and then, the abyss. Come to that, it would not be so bad if that were the way life worked out. But there could also be disability and suffering, spreading like rust over iron, before the end came ...

He did not picture life's ocean, as do the poets, all astir with stormy waves. No, he saw it in his mind's eye as smooth, without a ripple, motionless and translucent right down to the dark sea bed. He saw himself sitting in a small unsteady boat, staring at the dark silt of the sea bottom, where he could just discern shapeless monsters, like enormous fish. These were life's hazards – the illnesses, the griefs, madness, poverty, blindness ... Here he is, looking at them – and then one of the monsters begins to emerge from the murk, rising higher and higher, becoming ever more clearly, more repellently clearly, discernible ... Another minute and its impact will overturn the boat. And then, once again, its outlines grow dimmer, it recedes into the distance, to the sea bed, and there it lies motionless, but for a slight movement of its tail ... But the destined day will come, and then the boat will capsize.

He tossed his head, jumped up, paced up and down the room once or twice, and then sat at his desk. He began to pull open one drawer after another and to rummage around among his papers and old letters, which were mostly from women. He had no idea why he was doing this, he was not looking for anything in particular; his only desire was to find some occupation to drive away the thoughts which were exhausting him. He unfolded a few letters at random (one of them disclosed a pressed flower with a faded ribbon tied around it) and shrugged his shoulders. He threw them all aside, with a glance at the fireplace, probably intending to burn this useless rubbish.

Suddenly, as he was rapidly thrusting his hands into one drawer after another, his eyes started from his head. Slowly he pulled out a small octagonal box of old-fashioned design, and slowly lifted the lid. Inside the box, under a double layer of yellowed cotton-wool, lay a tiny garnet cross.

He examined the cross for a few moments without any sign of recognition, and then uttered a faint cry. His features showed something that was neither compassion nor joy, and yet had elements of each. It was the expression of a man suddenly confronted by someone he once loved tenderly, but has long lost sight of; someone who appears unexpectedly before him, looking exactly the same – and completely changed with the passage of time.

He got up and returned to the fireplace. Once again he sat down in the armchair, and once again buried his face in his hands ... Why today? Why today in particular? he kept wondering, and he remembered many things from the distant past ...

This is what he remembered ...

But first I must tell you his name, his patronymic and his surname. He was called Sanin – Dmitry Pavlovich Sanin.

This is what he remembered:

# I

It was the summer of 1840. Sanin was just twenty-three years old, and was in Frankfurt on his way back to Russia from Italy. He was not a rich man, but he had a small private income and almost no family. He had inherited a few thousand roubles from a distant relation and had decided to

spend the money on foreign travel before entering the public
service – before putting on the harness of employment in a
government department, without which it was impossible for
him to envisage any kind of assured existence. Sanin had
carried out to the letter his plan of spending his legacy, and
had managed his affairs so skilfully that on the day of his
arrival in Frankfurt, he had precisely enough money left to
pay for his journey back to St Petersburg.

In 1840, railways scarcely existed: your gentleman on his
tour had to be content with the stagecoach. Sanin had
reserved his seat in the extra coach (*Beiwagen*) which was not
due to leave until after ten o'clock that night. There was still
plenty of time. Fortunately, the weather was superb, and so
Sanin, after lunching at the White Swan Inn (which was
renowned at that date) set off to explore the town. He took a
look at Danneker's Ariadne, which he did not much like, and
visited Goethe's house – he had, incidentally, read nothing of
Goethe except for *Werther*, and in a French translation at that.
Then he went for a walk along the bank of the Main, and felt a
bit bored, as every self-respecting traveller should. At last,
some time after five, tired out and with his boots covered with
dust, he found himself in one of Frankfurt's most insignificant streets. It was a street that he was destined not to forget
for a long time.

On one of the few houses in the street he observed a
signboard: Giovanni Roselli's Italian Patisserie made its
existence known to passers-by. Sanin went into this establishment intending to drink a glass of lemonade. But when he
entered the front shop, there was not a soul inside. It looked a
little like a chemist's. Behind the simple counter stood a
painted cupboard, with a few gold-labelled bottles on its
shelves, and some glass jars, containing rusks, chocolate drops
and boiled sweets. A grey tomcat was blinking and purring,
kneading with its paws the seat of a high cane chair which
stood near the window. A large ball of red wool, glowing
brilliantly in the slanting rays of the evening sun, lay on the
floor beside an overturned carved wooden basket. A confused

noise could be heard coming from the adjoining inner room. Sanin stood for a moment, waiting for the little bell attached to the shop door to stop jangling. Then he raised his voice and called out 'Is anyone there?' At that very moment the door leading to the inner room opened – and Sanin was taken completely by surprise.

## II

A girl of about nineteen, her dark hair falling about her bare shoulders, her bare arms outstretched, burst into the shop. Seeing Sanin, she rushed straight at him, seized his hand, and tugged at him, exclaiming breathlessly: 'Hurry, come here, save him!' Sanin did not follow the girl at once – it was not that he did not wish to obey her, but that he was simply too amazed to move. He was almost rooted to the spot: he had never seen so beautiful a girl in his life. But she turned towards him, with a tone of such despair in her voice, in her look, in the motion of her clenched hand as she lifted it, trembling, to her pale cheek and murmured, 'Oh, come on, why don't you come?' that he rushed after her through the open door.

In the inner room, on an old-fashioned horsehair divan, lay a boy of about fourteen, his white face tinged with yellow, like wax or ancient marble. He was strikingly like the girl, and was evidently her brother. His eyes were closed. His hair, which was black and thick, cast a shadow like a stain on his forehead, which seemed frozen to stone, and on his thin and motionless eyebrows. His clenched teeth were visible under his bluish lips. He did not appear to be breathing. One arm had dropped to the floor, the other was flung above his head. The boy was fully dressed and buttoned up. His throat was constrained by a tight necktie.

The girl flung herself at him with a cry of despair.

'He's dead, he's dead! Only a moment ago he was sitting here talking to me – and then suddenly he fell down and went completely rigid. Oh, God, can nobody help him? And

Mother isn't here! Pantaleone, Pantaleone, what about the doctor?' she added, suddenly switching to Italian. 'Have you been to fetch the doctor?'

'Signora, I haven't been to the doctor, I sent Luisa,' a hoarse voice replied from behind the door, and a little old man came into the room, hobbling on a pair of short bandy legs. He was attired in a lilac-coloured dress coat, with black buttons and a high white stock, short nankeen breeches and blue woollen stockings. His tiny face was all but invisible beneath an enormous shock of iron-grey hair, which sprouted upwards round his head and then fell down in untidy little wisps. This made the old man look rather like a broody hen, and the likeness was made more striking still by the fact that all that could be discerned under the dark grey mass of hair were a pointed nose and a pair of round yellow eyes.

'Luisa will get there faster, and in any case I can't run,' the old man went on in Italian, lifting alternately each of his flat, gouty feet which were encased in high-cut shoes with bows. 'But I have brought some water.'

His dried-up, gnarled fingers were grasping the long, thin neck of a bottle.

'But Emil will die meanwhile,' cried the girl and stretched out her hands to Sanin. 'Oh, sir, please, *Oh mein Herr*, is there nothing you can do to help?'

'It's a stroke, he must be bled,' observed the old man who answered to the name of Pantaleone.

Although Sanin knew absolutely nothing about medical matters, he was quite certain of one thing: fourteen-year-old boys do not have strokes.

'It's a fainting fit, and not a stroke,' he said, turning to Pantaleone. 'Have you some brushes?'

The old man raised his little face.

'What?'

'Brushes, brushes,' Sanin repeated in German and in French. 'Brushes,' he added, going through the motions of cleaning his clothes.

The old man understood at last.

'Ah, brushes! *Spazzette!* Of course we have brushes!'

'Bring them here. We will take off his coat and start rubbing him.'

'Good ... *Benone!* But shouldn't I pour water over his head?'

'No ... Later. Hurry up now and fetch the brushes.'

Pantaleone put the bottle on the floor, ran off, and returned at once with a hair-brush and a clothes-brush. He was accompanied by a curly-haired poodle who wagged his tail vigorously, and stared inquisitively at the old man, the girl and even Sanin, as if anxious to discover what all the excitement was about.

Sanin quickly removed the boy's coat, undid the collar of his shirt, rolled up the shirt-sleeves and, seizing one of the brushes, began to rub the boy's chest and arms with all his might. At the same time Pantaleone wielded the other brush – the hair-brush – over the boy's boots and trousers. The girl threw herself down on her knees by the divan, seized her brother's head with both hands and gazed at him so intensely that she did not even blink her eyes.

Sanin rubbed away, and at the same time kept stealing a glance at her. Dear God! What a lovely girl she was!

# III

Her nose was slightly large, but of a beautiful aquiline shape. There was a faint trace of down on her upper lip. Her skin was smooth and without lustre, for all the world as if she were made of ivory or of meerschaum, and her hair fell in a wave like that of Allori's Judith in the Palazzo Pitti. Most striking of all were her eyes – dark grey, with a black border round the iris – superb, triumphant eyes, even now when their light was dimmed by fear and grief ... Sanin could not help thinking of the wonderful land from which he was returning home ... But even in Italy he had never seen anything to equal this! The girl's breathing was interrupted and uneven: it seemed as

if every time she drew breath she was waiting for her brother
to start breathing too.

Sanin continued to brush the boy, but his eyes were not for
the girl alone. The remarkable figure of Pantaleone also
attracted his attention. The old man was quite weak from the
effort, and was panting: every time he applied the brush, he
gave a little jump and emitted something between a groan and
a squeak. His enormous mane of hair was damp with sweat,
and swayed heavily from side to side, like the roots of some
large plant washed by a rising flood.

Sanin was just about to say to him, 'You might at least take
off his boots...' when the poodle, no doubt excited by the
unusual nature of what was going on, dug in his front paws
and began to bark.

'Tartaglia! Canaglia!' the old man hissed at him.

But at this moment, the girl's face was transfigured. Her
eyebrows lifted, her eyes became even larger and suddenly
alight with joy ... Sanin looked round ... The colour had
reappeared in the young man's face ... There was a movement of his eyelids ... His nostrils quivered. He drew the
air in through his teeth which were still clenched, and gave a
sigh ...

'Emil!' cried the girl. '*Emilio mio!*'

The boy's large, black eyes opened slowly. They were still
dull, but they were smiling weakly. The same weak smile
spread downwards to his pale lips. Then he moved the arm
which was hanging by his side and suddenly and swiftly
raised it to his chest.

'Emilio!' repeated the girl and rose to her feet. The
expression on her face was so strong and vivid that she looked
as if she was near to tears or about to burst out laughing.

'Emil! What is all this? Emil!' came a voice from behind the
door. A neatly dressed woman with silver-grey hair and a dark
complexion walked briskly into the room. An elderly man
followed close behind her. Sanin caught a glimpse of the head
of a maidservant behind the man's shoulders.

The girl ran towards them.

'He has been saved, Mother; he's alive!' she exclaimed, trembling as she embraced the woman who had just come in.

'But what is it all about?' repeated the woman. 'I come back to the house ... and suddenly I meet the doctor, and Luisa.'

The girl began to recount what had happened. The doctor went up to the invalid who was rapidly becoming more conscious and still continued to smile. He looked as if he was beginning to feel ashamed of the alarm which he had caused.

'I see you have been rubbing him with brushes,' said the doctor, turning to Sanin and Pantaleone, 'and you did very well. A most excellent idea ... Now let us see what else we can think of ...' He felt the young man's pulse. 'Hm! Now, let's see your tongue!'

The woman bent over the boy with an expression of concern. He smiled even more openly – and then turned his eyes on her and blushed ...

It occurred to Sanin that he was in the way. He went out into the shop. He had hardly had time to grasp the handle of the street door, when the girl appeared in front of him and stopped him.

'I see you are going,' she said, with a friendly look. 'I won't detain you, but you simply must come and see us this evening. We owe you so much – you may have saved my brother's life. We want to thank you – my mother too. You must tell us who you are, you must join us in our happiness.'

'But I am leaving for Berlin tonight ...' Sanin said hesitantly.

'There is plenty of time,' the girl replied with alacrity. 'Come here in an hour's time for a cup of chocolate. Do you promise? I must get back to him. You will come, won't you?'

What was Sanin to do?

'I'll come,' he promised.

The lovely creature quickly shook him by the hand and was gone like a bird, and he found himself in the street.

## IV

An hour and a half later, when Sanin returned to the
Patisserie Roselli, he was received like a member of the
family. Emilio was sitting on the very same divan where the
rubbing with the brushes had taken place. The doctor had
prescribed some medicine and had advised great care in
avoiding stress, since the patient was of a nervous disposition
and prone to heart trouble. He had had fainting fits before:
but never so prolonged or so deep as on this occasion.
However, the doctor declared that all danger was now passed.
Emil was dressed, as befitted a convalescent, in an ample
dressing-gown, and his mother had wound a pale blue
woollen scarf around his neck. But he looked gay, almost
festive – indeed the whole scene had a festive air. In front of
the divan stood a round table covered with a clean cloth. An
enormous china coffee-pot filled with fragrant chocolate
dominated the table. It was surrounded by cups, little
decanters of syrup, sponge cakes, buns, even flowers. Six thin
wax candles were burning in a pair of antique silver candela-
bras. On one side of the door a great wing chair offered its
soft and comfortable embrace – Sanin was made to sit there.
All the inmates of the Patisserie with whom he had had
occasion to become acquainted that day were present, including the poodle Tartaglia, and the tomcat. There was an
atmosphere of untold happiness. The poodle was actually
sneezing from sheer delight – only the tomcat was still
blinking his eyes and screwing up his face.

Sanin was made to explain who he was, where he came
from and what he was called. When he told them that he was a
Russian, the two ladies were somewhat surprised, and even
exclaimed a little. Both declared in unison that his German
accent was excellent, but that if he preferred to speak French,
he was welcome to do so, since both of them understood
French well and could express themselves freely in that
language. Sanin immediately took advantage of this sugges-

tion. 'Sanin, Sanin?' The ladies had never imagined that a
Russian surname could be so simple to pronounce. His
Christian name, Dmitry, was also much admired. The older
lady observed that she had heard in her youth a beautiful
opera '*Demetrio e Polibio*' but that 'Dmitry' sounded much
better than 'Demetrio'. This kind of conversation continued
for about an hour. The ladies, for their part, initiated him into
all the details of their own lives.

The mother, the woman with the grey hair, did most of the
talking. Sanin learned that her name was Leonora Roselli and
that she had been left a widow after the death of her husband,
Giovanni Battista Roselli, who had settled in Frankfurt as a
pastry-cook about twenty-five years ago. Giovanni Battista
had come from Vicenza, and had been a very good man,
although rather hot-tempered and overbearing, and a republican at that. As she said this, Madame Roselli pointed to his
portrait in oils which hung above the divan. Sanin could only
suppose that the painter – 'also a republican', as Madame
Roselli observed with a sigh – had failed to catch the likeness
of his sitter, since, to judge by the portrait, the late Giovanni
Battista had resembled a grim and severe brigand, for all the
world like Rinaldo Rinaldini!

Signora Roselli herself had been born in the 'ancient and
beautiful city of Parma, where there is such a superb cupola
painted by the immortal Correggio'. But she had become
quite a German through long sojourn in the country. Then,
shaking her head sadly, she added that all that remained for
her now were *this* daughter and *this* son (she pointed to each in
turn), that the daughter was called Gemma and the son
Emilio, and that both were good and obedient children,
especially Emilio ('Am I not obedient then?' interposed the
daughter at this point. 'Oh, you're a republican too,' replied
her mother); that business was, of course, much worse now
than it had been while her husband was alive, for he had been
a great artist in the pastry-cook line. ('*Un grand'uomo,*'
Pantaleone remarked at this point looking stern); but that
thank God, it was still possible to manage.

V

Gemma listened to her mother. She was laughing one moment, sighing the next, now stroking her mother's shoulder, now wagging an admonitory finger at her, and sometimes glancing at Sanin. At last she stood up, put her arms around her mother and kissed her in the hollow of the throat – all of which produced a great deal of laughter from Signora Roselli, and even a few squeals.

Pantaleone was also presented to Sanin. It appeared that he had once sung baritone parts in opera, but had long given up his theatrical life and occupied a position in the Roselli household that was something between that of a family friend and a servant. Although he had lived in Germany for a considerable number of years, he had succeeded in acquiring only a very little of the language, and could really do no more than curse in German, and that mainly by dint of unmercifully murdering the words of abuse. Almost any German was a *'ferroflucto spizzebubbio'* to Pantaleone. But his accent in Italian was perfect, because he came from Sinigaglia where one can hear *'lingua toscana in bocca romana'*.

Emilio was clearly enjoying himself and basking in the pleasurable mood which comes upon one who has escaped imminent danger or is convalescing from an illness. Besides, everything pointed to the fact that the whole family was in the habit of spoiling him. He uttered some shy words of thanks to Sanin, but mostly concentrated on the syrups and the sweets. Sanin was forced to drink two large cups of excellent chocolate and to devour a remarkable number of cakes: no sooner had he swallowed one, than Gemma would be offering another – and it was impossible to refuse.

He very soon began to feel quite at home. It was incredible how swiftly the time passed. There were so many things he had to tell them: about Russia in general, about the Russian climate, Russian society, about the Russian peasants and especially about the Cossacks; about the war of 1812 and

Peter the Great, about the Kremlin, about Russian songs and Russian church bells. Both the ladies had only the vaguest notion of our far-flung and remote country: Signora Roselli, or, as she was more usually called, Frau Lenore, even astounded Sanin by asking him if the famous Ice Palace, built in St Petersburg in the previous century, was still standing: she had recently read such an interesting article about it in a book that had belonged to her late husband, *Bellezze delle arti*. When Sanin exclaimed, 'Do you really think that we never have any summer in Russia?' Frau Lenore replied that hitherto her picture of Russia had been of a country where the snow lay permanently and everyone went around in a fur coat and served in the army – but that the hospitality was quite extraordinary, and all the peasants were very obedient. Sanin did his best to provide her and her daughter with some rather more exact intelligence.

When the conversation touched on Russian music, he was at once requested to sing some Russian air and was shown to a small pianoforte which stood in the room, and which had black keys instead of white, and white ones instead of black. Sanin immediately complied with their wishes without making excuses, and sang, in a small, nasal tenor voice, first 'The Red Sarafan' and then 'Along the Highway', accompanying himself with two fingers of the right hand and three of the left – the thumb, the middle and the little fingers. The ladies praised both his voice and the tunes, but were even more enthusiastic about the soft melodiousness of the Russian language and demanded a translation of the words. Sanin acceded to their wishes, but in view of the fact that the words of 'The Red Sarafan' and 'Along the Highway' (*Sur une rue pavée une jeune fille allait à l'eau*, in his rendering of the original) could scarcely provide his listeners with any very exalted idea of Russian poetry, he turned to Pushkin. He first recited, then translated and then sang, Pushkin's 'I Recall a Wondrous Moment' in Glinka's setting, getting some of the melancholy couplets slightly wrong in the process. The ladies were now absolutely delighted – Frau Lenore even discovered a remarkable similarity between the Russian and Italian languages – the Russian for 'moment', *mgnovenie*, was just like '*o vieni*', 'with me', *so mnoi*, like '*siam noi*', and so on. Even the names Pushkin (which she pronounced Pussekin) and Glinka somehow seemed natural to her. Sanin in his turn asked the ladies to sing something and they did not stand on ceremony either. Frau Lenore sat down at the pianoforte and sang a few *duettini* and *stornelli* with Gemma. The mother had once had a good contralto voice: the daughter's voice was slight but agreeable.

## VI

But Sanin was admiring Gemma herself, not her voice. He was sitting a little behind and to one side of her and thinking to himself that no palm tree – not even in the verses of Benediktov, who was at that time the fashionable poet – could rival the elegant grace of her figure. And when she came to some particularly emotional point in the song and raised her eyes to the heavens, it seemed impossible to imagine any skies that would not open before so beautiful a glance. Even old Pantaleone, leaning against the doorpost, with his chin and mouth tucked into his ample cravat and listening gravely with the look of an expert, even Pantaleone was admiring the face of this lovely girl and marvelling at it – and, after all, he should have become used to it by now. When the *duettino* was finished, Frau Lenore remarked that Emilio *also* sang excellently – a real silver-toned voice. But he had just reached the age when the voice begins to change (he did, in fact, talk in a kind of bass that was constantly breaking) and for this reason he was forbidden to sing. However, Pantaleone – now he might, for old times' sake, honour the guest with a song. Pantaleone immediately looked very displeased. He frowned, ruffled his hair and declared that he had given up all that long ago. Certainly, as a young man, he had been able to give a good account of himself. Indeed, he belonged to that great age when there were real, classical singers – not like the present screechers – and a real school of *bel canto*. He, Pantaleone Cippatola of Varese, was once presented with a laurel wreath in Modena, and on that occasion several white doves were released in the theatre, and incidentally, a certain Russian Prince, Il Principe Tarbusski, with whom he had been on terms of most intimate friendship, was always urging him at supper-time to come to Russia and promised him mountains of gold, literally mountains! But that he, Pantaleone, would not be parted from Italy, the country of Dante, *il paese del Dante*. After that, of course, certain unfortunate things happened, he had himself been somewhat incautious ... Here the old man stopped abruptly, gave a deep sigh, then sighed again and looked at the floor ... Then he began once again to talk of the classical age of singing, about the famous tenor Garcia for whom he had boundless veneration and respect.

'There was a man!' he exclaimed. 'The great Garcia – *il gran Garcia* – never demeaned himself so far as to sing *falzetto* like the present-day miserable little tenors – *tenoracci*. No sir, he sang with a full chest, the full chest, *voce di petto, si*!'

The old man struck his shirt-front hard with his little withered fist.

'And what an actor! A volcano, *signori miei*, a volcano, *un Vesuvio*! I had the honour and good fortune to appear with him in an opera *dell' illustrissimo maestro Rossini* – in *Otello*. Garcia was Othello, I was Iago, and when he pronounced the phrase ...'

Here Pantaleone took up a theatrical stance and sang in a voice which was tremulous and hoarse, but still full of passion.

> '*L'i ... ra da ver ... so da ver ... so il fato*
> *Io più no ... no ... no ... non temerò*

'The whole theatre was in a fever, *signori miei*. But I was not too bad either, and followed on with,

> '*L'i ... ra da ver ... so da ver ... so il fato*
> *Temer più non dovrò!*

'And then he came in suddenly, like a flash of lightning, like a tiger,

'*Morrò! … ma vendicato …*

'Or again, listen to this. When he sang … when he sang the famous aria from 'Matrimonio Segreto': *Pra che Spunti …* now here *il gran Garcia*, after the words *I Cavalli di Galoppo*, used to do this when he came to the words *senza posa caccerà* – just listen how wonderful this is, *com'è stupendo*! This is what he used to do …'

The old man began to sing some kind of extraordinary *fioritura*, but on the tenth note he broke down, and was seized with a coughing fit. He turned away with a gesture of his hands, muttering, 'Why do you torment me?' Gemma immediately jumped up from her chair, clapped her hands loudly, crying 'Bravo! … Bravo! …' ran up to poor retired Iago and gave him a few affectionate pats on both shoulders. Only Emil was laughing without any trace of pity. *Cet âge est sans pitié* – this age knows no compassion – as Lafontaine remarked in his time.

Sanin tried to comfort the old baritone and began to talk Italian to him (he had picked up a little of the language on his recent trip). He spoke of '*paese del Dante dove il sì suona*'. This phrase, together with '*lasciate ogni speranza*', made up the entire Italian poetic equipment of our young tourist. But Pantaleone was not to be distracted by these efforts. With his chin tucked deeper than ever into his cravat, and his eyes staring grimly out of his head, he once again looked like a bird, and an angry bird at that – a raven, or a kite, perhaps. Then Emil, blushing momentarily, as spoiled children usually do, turned to his sister, and said that if she wished to entertain their guest, she could do nothing better than read aloud one of the comedy sketches by Malz, which she did so well. Gemma laughed and rapped her brother's hand, exclaiming, 'He would think of something like that!' However, she went straight to her room and returned, carrying a small book. She sat down at the table beside the lamp, glanced around her, raised her forefinger – meaning 'Quiet, please', a pure Italian gesture – and began to read.

## VII

Malz was a Frankfurt littérateur of the 'thirties. His short, slight comedy sketches, written in the local dialect, portrayed Frankfurt types without any profound wit, but brightly and amusingly. It turned out that Gemma did indeed read superbly well, quite like an actress. She would bring the character to life and sustain it throughout, making good use of the gift for mimicry which she had inherited with her Italian blood. She spared neither her gentle voice nor her lovely face. When it was necessary to portray an old woman who had lost her wits, or a stupid town mayor, she twisted her features into the funniest of grimaces, screwed up her eyes, wrinkled her nose, her voice meanwhile ranging from a high-pitched squeak to a guttural bass ... She did not laugh herself during the reading. But whenever her audience (with the exception, it is true, of Pantaleone, who had left with a show of indignation the moment the subject of *quel ferroflucto tedesco* had been raised) interrupted her with a roar of happy laughter, she would let the book fall on her lap and burst out laughing, throwing back her head, while her black curls cascaded softly about her neck and shaking shoulders. Then the laughter would cease. Gemma would immediately raise the book from her lap, compose her features appropriately and once again resume the serious business of reading.

Sanin could hardly contain his admiration. Most especially striking was the miraculous way in which a face of such ideal beauty could suddenly take on so comical, even common, a look. Gemma was much less successful in the parts of young women, *les jeunes premières* as they were called, and her portrayal of love scenes was not successful. She felt this herself, and tended to read them with a slight trace of mockery, as if to underline her lack of conviction in the enthusiastic protestations of love and fidelity, and the stilted speeches – actually, the author himself avoided such passages so far as possible.

Sanin did not notice how swiftly the evening passed, and only remembered about his imminent journey when the clock struck ten. He jumped up from his chair as if he had been stung.

'What is the matter?' asked Frau Lenore.

'I was supposed to be leaving for Berlin tonight: I had my seat reserved on the stagecoach.'

'When does it leave?'

'At half past ten.'

'Well,' said Gemma, 'that means you have missed it anyway ...You had better stay and I will read some more.'

'Have you paid the full price for the ticket, or just a deposit?' asked Frau Lenore.

'The lot!' Sanin lamented with a gesture of mock despair.

Gemma looked at him with narrowed eyes – and burst out laughing. Her mother scolded her.

'This poor young man has wasted his money, and here you are laughing!'

'That's all right,' said Gemma. 'It won't ruin him, and we must try to console him. Would you like some lemonade?'

Sanin drank a glass of lemonade. Gemma continued with Malz and everything went with a swing.

The clock struck twelve. Sanin began to take his leave.

'You will have to stay a few more days in Frankfurt now,' Gemma told him. 'What is the hurry? You won't find a more entertaining town.' She was silent for a moment. 'Really, that is so,' she added with a smile.

Sanin did not reply, and reflected that in view of the empty state of his purse he would have to stay in Frankfurt, whether he wished or no, until he had received a reply from a friend in Berlin to whom he now intended to write and ask for a loan.

'Yes, do stay,' Frau Lenore said in her turn. 'We will introduce you to Gemma's future husband, Herr Karl Klueber. He could not come this evening because he was very busy in his shop. I expect you noticed when you were in the Zeile, the largest store for silks and woollen cloth ? Well, he is the chief man there. But he will be delighted to pay his respects to you.'

Heaven alone knows why, but Sanin was slightly taken aback by this piece of information. What a lucky fellow he is, flashed through his mind. He glanced at Gemma – and he thought he noticed a slight look of mockery in her eyes. He began to say goodbye.

'So it is till tomorrow? Is that so – until tomorrow?' asked Frau Lenore.

'Till tomorrow,' Gemma pronounced, but as a statement, not a question, taking for granted that it could not be otherwise.

'Till tomorrow,' Sanin replied.

Emil, Pantaleone and the poodle Tartaglia accompanied him to the street corner. Pantaleone could not resist expressing his displeasure on the subject of Gemma's reading.

'She ought to be ashamed of herself! All those grimaces and that squawking! *Una carricatura*. She ought to act noble parts, Merope or Clytemnaestra, some great tragic role. And here she is screwing herself up to sound like some dreadful German woman. Why, I can do that – *mertz, kertz, smertz,*' added the old man in his hoarse voice, poking his face forward and splaying his fingers. Tartaglia started barking at him, and Emil burst out laughing. The old man turned sharply on his heels, and strode back.

Sanin returned to the White Swan Inn (where he had left his belongings in the hall) in a state of some confusion. All those conversations in German, French and Italian were ringing in his ears.

'Engaged,' he whispered to himself, lying in bed in the modest room which had been allotted to him. 'And what a beautiful girl she is! But why on earth have I stayed here?'

However, next day he sent off the letter to his friend in Berlin.

# VIII

He had not yet had time to dress when a waiter came in to announce the arrival of two gentlemen. One of them turned out to be Emil. The other, a tall and impressive young man with a most handsome face, was Herr Karl Klueber, to whom the lovely Gemma was engaged.

It may well be supposed that, at that time, in all the shops in all Frankfurt there was not to be found another such courteous, well-mannered, grave and polite chief assistant as Herr Klueber. His immaculate dress was of the same high level as the dignity of his demeanour and the elegance of his manners – a little prim and stiff, it is true, in the English fashion (he had spent two years in England) – but beguiling elegance for all that. It was evident at a glance that this good-looking, somewhat stern, exceedingly well brought-up and superlatively well-washed young man was in the habit of obeying his superiors and of issuing orders to his inferiors. The sight of such a man behind his counter was indeed bound to inspire respect even in the customers. There could not be the slightest doubt that his honesty surpassed all natural limits – why, one only had to look at the points of his stiffly starched collar. His voice too turned out to be exactly what one was led to expect – deep, self-confident and rather rich in tone; yet not too loud, and even with some notes of a certain kindliness. This is the sort of voice which is particularly well-adapted to giving orders to subordinate shop assistants. 'Bring that length of purple Lyons velvet, will you?' or, 'A chair for the lady!'

Herr Klueber began by introducing himself. In the process, he bowed from the waist with such nobility of manner, while at the same time bringing one leg close to the other in so agreeable a fashion, and touching his heels together with such courtesy, that everyone was bound to think: 'This man's linen and spiritual virtues are both of the first quality.' The grooming of his exposed right hand, which he offered to Sanin modestly but firmly, exceeded the bounds of all probability: each single fingernail was a model of perfection. (In his left hand, which was clad in a suede glove, he held his hat which shone like a looking-glass: in the depths of the hat lay the other glove.) He then declared, in the choicest German phrases, that he desired to express his respect and his gratitude to the *Herr Auslaender* who had rendered so important a service to his future kinsman, the brother of his betrothed. At this point, he gestured with his left hand, which held the hat, in the direction of Emil. The boy was evidently embarrassed, and turned away towards the window, putting his finger in his mouth. Herr Klueber added that he would count himself happy if he ever found it in his power to do something on his part that might be agreeable to the *Herr Auslaender*.

Sanin replied, in German, not without some difficulty, that he was most gratified ... that his services had been of the most trivial nature ... and invited his guests to be seated. Herr Klueber thanked him, and in an instant flung asunder his coat tails and let himself down in a chair, but let himself down so lightly, and adhered to the chair so insecurely, that the inference was clear to all: This man has only sat down out of politeness, and will immediately take wing once again. And indeed he leapt up instantly and executed a few modest movements with his legs, rather like some dance sequence. He then declared that, much to his regret, he could stay no longer since he was in a hurry to return to his shop – business before pleasure! But tomorrow was Sunday, and with the consent of Frau Lenore and Fräulein Gemma he had arranged a pleasurable excursion to Soden, to which he had the honour of inviting the *Herr Auslaender*. He expressed the hope that the distinguished foreigner would not refuse to grace the party with his presence. Sanin consented to grace the excursion with his presence. Thereupon Herr Klueber once again took his leave and departed – displaying a most agreeable glimpse of pea-green trousers of a most delicate hue, and emitting an equally delectable squeak from the soles of his brand-new boots.

## IX

Emil, who had remained standing, looking out of the window, even after Sanin had issued the invitation to his guests to be seated, made a left turn as soon as his future kinsman had departed. Blushing and grimacing in a somewhat childish way, he asked Sanin if it was in order for him to stay a little longer. 'I am much better today,' he added, 'but the doctor has told me not to do any work.'

'Yes, please stay, you are not in the least in the way,' Sanin exclaimed at once: like every true Russian, he was delighted to seize on the first excuse which would relieve him of the obligation to do anything whatsoever.

Emil thanked him, and in no time had made himself at home in Sanin's quarters. He examined all his belongings and questioned him closely about nearly every article – where he had bought it and what its particular qualities were. Then he helped him to shave, observing in passing that he ought to grow a moustache. He told him in the end innumerable details about his mother, his sister, about Pantaleone and even about the poodle Tartaglia, going into minute particulars of their daily life. Emil had lost every trace of shyness. He suddenly felt extraordinarily attracted to Sanin, and not because he thought Sanin had saved his life the day before, but simply because he was such a nice man.

Emil lost no time in confiding all his secret thoughts. He spoke with most heat about the fact that his mother was determined that he should go into business, while he himself *knew*, knew beyond doubt, that he was born to be an artist, a musician, a singer. He knew that the theatre was his true calling. Even Pantaleone encouraged him in this, but Herr Klueber supported his mother, over whom he had a great deal of influence. Indeed, the idea that he should become a tradesman had originated with Herr Klueber, according to whose ideas nothing in the world could compare with the businessman's calling. To sell cloth and velvet and cheat the public by making them pay *Narren- oder*

*Russenpreise** (fools' or Russian prices) – that was his loftiest aspiration.

'Well, then. Now we must go home,' the boy exclaimed as soon as Sanin had finished dressing and had written his letter to Berlin.

'It's too early yet,' remarked Sanin.

'That doesn't matter,' said Emil, coming up to him affectionately. 'Let's go! We'll call in at the post office and then go on to our house. Gemma will be so pleased to see you. You must have breakfast with us ... You can say something to my mother about me, about my future career ...'

'Well, come along then,' Sanin said, and they set off.


## X

Gemma was indeed pleased to see him and Frau Lenore greeted him in the friendliest manner. It was apparent that he had made a good impression on them the night before. Emil ran off to make the arrangements for breakfast, having first whispered in Sanin's ear, 'Don't forget!' 'I won't,' Sanin promised.

Frau Lenore was a trifle indisposed. She was suffering from migraine, and reclining in an armchair, trying not to move. Gemma was wearing a wide-cut yellow blouse, gathered in with a black leather belt. She also seemed exhausted and somewhat pale. There were dark circles round her eyes, but this did not make them shine the less and her pallor added a mysterious appeal to her strictly classical features. That day Sanin was particularly impressed by the elegant beauty of her hands. Every time she raised them to smooth or re-arrange the dark, gleaming waves of her hair he could not take his eyes off these long, pliant, well-separated fingers, like those of Raphael's Fornarina.

* In times gone by – and it may perhaps still be going on – when from May onwards a multitude of Russians began to appear in Frankfurt, prices went up in all the shops and acquired the name of 'Russen', or alas! 'Narrenpreise'.

It was very hot out of doors. Sanin was of a mind to leave after breakfast, but when it was pointed out that the best plan on such a day was to stay quietly in one spot, he agreed – and so he stayed on. It was cool in the back room where he sat with his hostesses: the windows gave out on to a small garden, overgrown with acacia trees. A multitude of bees, wasps and bumblebees droned eagerly and good-humouredly in the thick branches which were strewn with golden flowers. The never-ceasing sound penetrated the room through the half-open shutters and the lowered blinds. It was a sound which sang of the scorching heat which charged the outside air, and made the cool atmosphere of the enclosing, comfortable room seem all the sweeter.

Sanin talked much as he had done the previous day. But not about Russia or Russian life. He wanted to be of help to his young friend, who had been sent off immediately after breakfast to Herr Klueber to get some practice with the account books. So he brought the conversation round to the comparative advantages and disadvantages of art and commerce. He was not surprised to discover that Frau Lenore was on the side of commerce – he had expected that. But Gemma too shared her mother's opinion.

'If one is an artist, and especially a singer,' she asserted, with a vigorous up-and-down movement of her hand, 'one must be at the top. Anything less than that is worth nothing. And who can say if one is capable of reaching the top?'

Pantaleone also joined in this debate. As he had served them for many years and was an old man, he was even permitted to sit in the presence of his employers: the Italians in general are not strict in matters of etiquette.

Naturally the old man was resolutely on the side of art. To tell the truth, his arguments were a little weak. He was mainly concerned to insist that the first requirement for the artist was *un certo estro d'ispirazione*, a certain dash of inspiration. Frau Lenore observed that he certainly had possessed this *estro* and yet ...

'I had enemies,' remarked Pantaleone gloomily.

'And how do you know,' (she addressed him in the familiar *tu* since Italians use this form very readily), 'that Emil will not have enemies, even if some of this *estro* should become apparent in him?'

'All right,' said Pantaleone angrily, 'make a tradesman of the boy – but Giovan' Battista would not have done it, even though he was a pastry-cook himself.'

'My husband, Giovan' Battista, was a very sensible man . . . and if he *did* get carried away in his youth . . .'

But the old man did not wish to hear any more and went off muttering once again reproachfully, 'Ah! Giovan' Battista . . .!'

Then Gemma declared that if Emil turned out to be a patriot, and wished to devote all his energies to the liberation of Italy, that would be another matter: it was right to sacrifice one's future security to such a noble and sacred cause – but not for the theatre! At this Frau Lenore became excited and began to implore her daughter at least to refrain from putting dangerous ideas into her brother's head. Wasn't it enough for her that she was a desperate republican herself? With these words, Frau Lenore began to groan and to complain of her aching head which was 'ready to burst' (Frau Lenore, out of consideration for their guest, spoke French with her daughter).

Gemma immediately began to minister to her mother. She moistened her forehead with eau de Cologne, and then blew on it very gently. She kissed her lightly on the cheeks, arranged her head on a pillow, ordered her to keep quiet and began kissing her again. She then turned to Sanin and began to tell him, in a voice which showed both humour and emotion, what an excellent mother she had, and what a beauty she had been. 'What am I saying? *Was* a beauty! She is one now, an absolute delight! Look at her eyes, just look at her eyes!'

Gemma whipped a white handkerchief out of her pocket and covered her mother's face. Then, very slowly, she lowered the top hem of the handkerchief, gradually disclosing Frau Lenore's forehead, eyebrows and eyes. She waited a little and then demanded that Frau Lenore should open her eyes. Her mother obeyed. Gemma exclaimed with delight (Frau Lenore's eyes really were very beautiful), then quickly drew the handkerchief right down to reveal the lower and less regular features of her mother's face, and once again began covering her with kisses. Frau Lenore laughed, turned aside slightly, and pretended to push her daughter away. The girl also made some pretence of struggle with her mother, and kissed and fondled her – not like a cat, in the French manner, but with that Italian grace which always makes one feel the presence of vigour.

At last Frau Lenore declared that she was tired . . . Gemma at once advised her to sleep for a little, here in the chair, 'while I and the Russian gentleman, *le Monsieur Russe*, will be as quiet . . . as quiet as little mice, *comme des petites souris* . . .' Frau Lenore smiled by way of an answer, closed her eyes, sighed once or twice and dozed off.

Gemma sat down on a stool by her side and stayed there without moving – except that occasionally she raised a finger of one hand to her lips (the other hand was supporting the pillow under her mother's head) and quietly shushed at Sanin, looking askance at him when he permitted himself to make the slightest movement. It ended with Sanin as motionless as if he were frozen in his seat, spellbound, totally absorbed in admiring the picture before his eyes: the half-darkened room, in which bunches of magnificent fresh roses standing in antique vases of green glass glowed here and there like bright points of light; the sleeping woman, her hands folded simply before her and her tired, kindly face framed in the snow-white pillow; and this young creature, alert and also kindly, clever and pure, and beautiful beyond description, the black depths of her eyes suffused with shadows and yet luminous at the same time . . . What was it all? A dream? A fairy-tale? And how did *he* come to be there?

## XI

The bell on the entrance door to the shop suddenly jangled. A young peasant lad in a fur cap and a red waistcoat came into the patisserie from the street. Not a single customer had entered the shop throughout the entire morning ... 'This is the kind of business we do,' Frau Lenore had remarked to Sanin during breakfast. Now she continued to doze, and Gemma, who was afraid of removing her arm from under the pillow, whispered to Sanin: 'You go and deal with the shop for me.' Sanin immediately tiptoed into the shop. The lad was asking for a quarter of a pound of mint lozenges.

'How much is it? 'Sanin whispered to Gemma through the door.

'Six kreutzers,' she replied, again in a whisper.

Sanin weighed out a quarter of a pound, found a piece of paper, screwed it into a poke, wrapped up the sweets, spilled them, wrapped them up again, spilled them again, then at last delivered them to the customer and received the money. The lad was meanwhile staring at him with amazement, fumbling with his cap against his stomach, while Gemma next door, her hand held to her mouth, was dying of laughter. This customer had hardly had time to depart before another appeared, and then a third ... 'I seem to be bringing them luck,' Sanin thought. The second customer called for a glass of *orgeade*, and the third for half a pound of sweets. Sanin served them, enthusiastically rattling spoons, moving the saucers around and delving deftly into tins and drawers. In the final reckoning, it was discovered that he had undercharged for the *orgeade*, and had collected two kreutzers too many for the sweets. Gemma continued to laugh quietly to herself. As for Sanin, he felt unusually gay, and some special mood of happiness was upon him. He felt as if he was ready to stand behind the counter for all time dealing in sweets and *orgeade* under the friendly and slightly mocking eyes of that charming creature, while the midsummer sun beat down through the massive foliage of the chestnut trees which rose in front of the windows. He would stand for all time while the whole room was filled with the green and gold of the sun's mid-day rays and mid-day shadows, and his heart overflowed with the sweet languor of idleness and of carefree youth – carefree first youth.

The fourth customer demanded a cup of coffee, so Pantaleone's help had to be invoked. (Emil had still not returned from Herr Klueber's store.) Sanin once again sat down at Gemma's side. Frau Lenore continued to doze, to the great delight of her daughter.

'Mother's migraine always passes when she sleeps,' she observed.

Sanin began to talk – still in whispers, of course – about his transactions in the shop. He enquired gravely about the prices of various commodities on sale in the patisserie. Gemma answered in the same grave tones, reciting the prices. At the same time, both of them were inwardly consumed with companionable laughter, as if aware that they were enacting an amusing farce. Suddenly a street organ in the road outside broke into the strains of the 'Freischütz' aria *Durch die Felder, durch die Auen* . . . Its whimpering notes, tremulous and with an occasional whistle, came wailing through the still air. Gemma started . . . 'He will wake Mother!'

Sanin promptly dashed into the street, thrust a few kreutzers into the organ-grinder's hand and persuaded him to stop and to move on elsewhere. When Sanin returned Gemma thanked him with a slight nod, and, with a meditative smile, began to hum, almost inaudibly, under her breath, Weber's beautiful air in which Max expresses all the perplexities of first love. She then asked Sanin if he knew the 'Freischütz', if he liked Weber, and added that, although she was Italian, this was the kind of music she loved above all. From the subject of Weber, the conversation slipped to poetry and romanticism, and to Hoffmann, whom at that date everyone was still reading.

Meanwhile Frau Lenore slept on, even snoring just a little, while all the time the rays of sunlight, breaking through the shutters, in little narrow strips, imperceptibly but ceaselessly travelled across the floor, the furniture Gemma's clothes and over the leaves and petals of the flowers.

## XII

It appeared that Gemma was not too well disposed towards Hoffmann, and even found him – of all things – rather dull. The northern world of fantasy and mist in his tales meant little to her southern and luminous temperament. 'He writes nothing but fairy-tales, nothing but children's stories,' she kept on asserting with slight contempt. She was also dimly aware of the lack of poetry in Hoffmann – but there was one of his tales, of which she had incidentally forgotten the title, which she liked very much. At least, to be exact, she only liked the beginning of the story – she had either not read the end of it, or else had also forgotten it. It was about a young man who meets a girl of astonishing beauty, a Greek girl, somewhere or other – it might have been in a tea-room. The girl is in the company of a strange and mysterious, evil old man. The young man falls in love with the girl at first sight. She looks at him most piteously, as if imploring him to rescue her. He leaves the shop for a moment – and on his return neither the girl nor the old man is there. He hastens off in search of them, repeatedly lights upon the most recent traces of them, flies off in hot pursuit – and never at any time succeeds in finding them anywhere. The beauty vanishes from him for ever – and he is unable to forget her imploring look, and is tortured by the thought that perhaps all his life's happiness has slipped from his grasp.

This is hardly the way Hoffmann ends his tale. But this was the form in which it had remained imprinted on Gemma's memory.

'It seems to me,' she said softly, 'that such meetings and partings happen in the world more often than we think.'

Sanin did not reply. Then, after a pause, he began to speak

– of Herr Klueber. It was the first time that he had mentioned him. Until that moment he had not once remembered the man's existence.

It was Gemma's turn to remain silent. She was plunged in thought, her eyes were averted and she was biting at the nail of her forefinger. Then she praised her husband-to-be, mentioned the excursion which he had arranged for the following day, threw a quick glance at Sanin, and fell silent once more.

Sanin could not think of a subject for conversation.

Emil came running in noisily, and woke Frau Lenore. Sanin was glad that he had come. Frau Lenore rose from her armchair. Pantaleone appeared and announced that lunch was ready. The friend of the household, the retired singer and the servant also carried out the duties of cook.

## XIII

Sanin stayed on after lunch, too. They would not let him go on the same pretext – the terrible heat – and when it became cooler, they suggested taking coffee in the garden in the shade of the acacias. Sanin agreed. His sense of well-being was complete. There are great delights hidden in the uneventful, still and placid stream of life, and he abandoned himself to them with rapture – demanding nothing specific of this day and neither thinking of the morrow nor recalling yesterday. How he treasured the very proximity of a creature such as Gemma! He would soon part from her, probably for ever. But for the moment, they were drifting together in the same barque along the safe and gentle course of life's river, just like the travellers in Uhland's poem. Rejoice, wanderer! Be happy! And everything seemed agreeable and dear to our lucky traveller! Frau Lenore suggested that he should join her and Pantaleone in a game of *tresette*. She instructed him in this uncomplicated Italian card game, won a few kreutzers off him – and he was most delighted.

At Emil's request, Pantaleone made the poodle Tartaglia go through all his tricks – and Tartaglia jumped over a stick, 'spoke' – that is to say barked – sneezed, shut the door with his nose, dragged along his master's well-worn slipper and at last, with an old cuirass on his head, enacted the part of Marshal Bernadotte being subjected to a severe reprimand from the Emperor Napoleon for treason. Napoleon was naturally portrayed by Pantaleone, and very faithfully portrayed. With his arms crossed on his chest, and a three-cornered hat pushed down over his eyes, he spoke coarsely and very sharply in French – and, heavens, what French! Tartaglia sat all huddled up before his sovereign, his tail between his legs, blinking from shame, and screwing up his eyes under the peak of the cuirass which sat askew on his head. From time to time, as Napoleon raised his voice, Bernadotte would stand on his hind legs. '*Fuori, traditore!*' exclaimed Napoleon at last, having quite forgotten, in his excessive fury, that he should maintain his part of a Frenchman to the very end. Bernadotte dashed headlong under the divan, and immediately jumped out again, barking delightedly, as if to indicate that the performance was over. The spectators laughed a great deal, and Sanin more than anyone.

Gemma had a very special and lovable way of laughing. It was a quiet laugh which hardly stopped, but was punctuated by the most amusing little squeals. Sanin was completely captivated by her laughter – he wanted to cover her with kisses for those little squeals!

Night fell at last. Now it really was time to go, and so Sanin said goodbye to everyone several times over, repeatedly saying, 'Till tomorrow,' to each of them (Emil he actually embraced), and went on his way. The image of the young girl went with him – now laughing, now pensive, sometimes calm, even indifferent, yet always attractive. And all the time he seemed to see her eyes before him – sometimes open wide, luminous and full of joy like the light of day, and then half-shaded by their lashes, and deep and dark as night. These eyes penetrated all other images and perceptions in his mind, and suffused them with a strange sweetness.

Not once did he think of Herr Klueber, of the reason which had induced him to stay on in Frankfurt – in short, of all the things which had perturbed him the day before.


# XIV


However, we must devote a few words to Sanin himself. In the first place he was very far from bad-looking – very far indeed. He was well built and tall, his features, if somewhat formless, were agreeable. His eyes, small and of a faded blue, were kindly, his hair was fair with some gold in it, his complexion was all pink and white. But the chief thing about him was his expression of unsophisticated gaiety – trusting, open, and at first impact slightly silly. In the old days, one could immediately spot the sons of the sedate provincial gentry by this expression – those 'father's boys', the 'good young masters', born and fattened up in those wide and open parts of our country which are half steppe. He had a mincing, slightly hesitant way of walking, a trace of a lisp in his voice, a smile like a child's, which appeared as soon as he caught your glance, and finally freshness and good health – yes, and softness, softness, softness – there was all Sanin for you.

And secondly he was no fool, having picked up a bit of experience. But he had remained fresh in outlook, in spite of his travels abroad: he knew little of the disturbing emotions which had raised a storm in the breasts of the best of the younger generation of that epoch.

It has become fashionable of late in our literature, after long and vain attempts to discover 'new men', to portray youths who have determined, come what may, to be fresh – as fresh as the oysters which are imported into St Petersburg from Flensburg ... Sanin was not a bit like these youths. If comparisons are necessary, he was rather like a young, newly grafted, curly-headed apple tree in one of Russia's southern orchards in the black earth country ... or better still, one of those sleek, well-groomed, tender and fat-legged three-year-olds that one used to see on the master's studfarm, just beginning to be broken in ... Those who came across Sanin in later years, when life had buffeted him around, and after he had long shed his youthful puppy-fat, saw quite a different kind of man.

On the following day, Sanin was still in bed when Emil, wearing his Sunday best, carrying a cane and with his hair heavily pomaded, burst into the room and announced that Herr Klueber would be arriving at any moment with the carriage, that the weather promised to be wonderful, that they had everything ready, but that Mother would not be joining them because her headache had come on again.

He began to hurry Sanin, assuring him that there was not a minute to lose ... and indeed, Herr Klueber arrived to find Sanin still at his toilet. He knocked on the door, entered, delivered a bow from the waist, expressed his willingness to wait for any length of time that was desired – and then sat down, resting his hat elegantly upon his knee.

The exquisite shop walker had dressed himself up to the eyes and was drenched in scent: his every movement was accompanied by great waves of the most delicate fragrance. He arrived in a commodious open carriage of the kind known as a landau, drawn by two strong and well-developed, if rather ugly, horses. A quarter of an hour later, Sanin, Klueber and Emil, seated in this carriage, ceremoniously drew up at the porch of the patisserie. Signora Roselli definitely refused to take any part in the excursion; Gemma wanted to stay behind with her mother, but the latter drove her out, as the saying goes.

'I need no one,' she said. 'I am going to sleep. I would send Pantaleone with you as well, but someone must look after the customers.'

'May we take Tartaglia?' Emil asked.

'Of course.'

Tartaglia immediately, with some effort, but with obvious delight, clambered up on to the box. He sat there licking his chops – it was plain that all this was customary procedure for him.

Gemma had put on a large straw hat with brown ribbons. The brim of the hat dipped down in front and shielded almost all her face from the sun. The shadow line stopped just short of her lips, which glowed soft and virginal like the petals of a Provence rose. Her teeth glistened almost stealthily and with the innocence of a child. Gemma sat down on the back seat next to Sanin: Klueber and Emil sat opposite. The pale figure of Frau Lenore appeared at the window. Gemma waved to her with her handkerchief, and the horses started.

## XV

Soden is a small town about half an hour's distance from Frankfurt. It lies in pretty countryside on a spur of the Taunus mountains and is well known among us in Russia for its waters, which are reputed to be beneficial for weak chests. The inhabitants of Frankfurt mostly visit it for recreation, since Soden contains a magnificent park and a number of *Wirtschaften* where one can drink beer or coffee in the shade of tall lime or maple trees.

The road from Frankfurt to Soden follows the right bank of the Main and is lined with fruit trees. While the carriage rolled quietly along the excellent metalled road, Sanin was unobtrusively observing how Gemma conducted herself in the company of her betrothed: it was the first time that he had seen the two of them together. *She* remained calm and unaffected, although somewhat more restrained and serious than usual. *He* presented the appearance of a condescending tutor who was conferring both upon himself and his charges modest and polite enjoyment. Sanin did not observe that he paid Gemma any of the particular attentions which the French call *empressement*. It was evident that Herr Klueber considered the business as settled, and therefore had no occasion to put himself out or to fuss. Condescension never left him for a moment – not even during the long walk before lunch over the wooded hills and dales beyond Soden. Even while he was enjoying the countryside, his attitude to natural beauty remained one of patronage, occasionally marked by his usual stern tones of the man in authority. Thus, for example, he remarked on the subject of a certain stream that it flowed in too straight a line along the vale, instead of forming a few picturesque curves. He was also disapproving on the subject of a bird – a chaffinch – which had failed to display sufficient variety in the notes of its song.

Gemma was not bored and even seemed to be enjoying herself. But Sanin could not recognize the former Gemma. It was not that her beauty was dimmed – never, indeed, had it been so radiant – but her spirit had withdrawn. She had opened her parasol and, without unbuttoning her gloves, she walked in a staid and unhurried manner, like a well brought-up young lady, and spoke little. Emil did not feel at ease either, and Sanin even less. He was, incidentally, somewhat put out by the fact that the conversation was all conducted in German. Tartaglia alone was in high spirits. He would dash off in pursuit of any blackbird he encountered, barking like mad, jump over ditches, tree-stumps and puddles, throw himself into the water, hurriedly lap up a few mouthfuls, shake himself and then, with a yelp, make off again like an arrow, his red tongue curling round almost to his shoulder.

Herr Klueber for his part did everything that he considered necessary for entertaining the company. He requested everyone to be seated in the shade of a spreading oak tree, produced from his side pocket a small volume entitled *Knallerbsen oder Du Sollst und Wirst Lachen* (Merry Quips or You Must and Will Laugh) and proceeded to read aloud the mirth-provoking anecdotes which the work contained. He read about a dozen without, however, provoking very much merriment. Only Sanin bared his teeth politely and Herr

Klueber himself after every anecdote executed a short, businesslike and, at the same time, condescending laugh. Around noon the whole company returned to Soden to the best inn that the town could offer.

It was necessary to make arrangements for luncheon.

Herr Klueber proposed that luncheon should be partaken in a summer house which was enclosed on all sides, '*im Gartensalon*'; but at this point Gemma suddenly rebelled and declared that she refused to eat anywhere but in the open air, in the garden, at one of the small tables that stood in front of the inn. She announced that she was bored with seeing the same faces all the time, and wanted to see some new ones. There were already groups of newly-arrived patrons seated at some of the tables.

While Herr Klueber, who had graciously yielded to the 'caprice of my fiancée', departed to consult the head waiter, Gemma stood motionless, her eyes lowered, her lips firmly pursed. She sensed that Sanin was looking at her fixedly and a little interrogatively, and this seemed to make her angry. At last Herr Klueber returned, announced that luncheon would be ready in half an hour and proposed to pass the time with a game of skittles, adding that this was very good for the appetite, hee, hee, hee! He was a masterly skittles player. When he bowled, he adopted a number of remarkably energetic stances, made great play with his muscles and executed the most elegant motions in the air with his leg. In his own way, he was an athlete, and superbly well-built. And his hands were so white and beautiful, and he kept on wiping them with such a luxurious Indian foulard handkerchief, rich in gold and bright colours.

The moment for luncheon arrived, and the company sat down at the table.

## XVI

Who is not acquainted with a German meal? A watery soup with bullet-like dumplings flavoured with cinnamon, boiled

beef, dry as cork, with some white fat adhering to it,
garnished with soapy potatoes, puffy beetroot and some
chewed-up looking horse-radish, followed by a bluish eel,
with capers and vinegar, a roast of meat with some jam, and
the inevitable '*Mehlspeise*' – a sort of pudding with a sourish
red sauce. However, the wine and beer are excellent. This was
exactly the kind of meal that the Soden innkeeper now
provided for his patrons. Actually the luncheon went off quite
successfully. True, it was not marked by any special gaiety –
not even when Herr Klueber proposed a toast to 'whatever we
love' (*was wir lieben*). Everything was most decorous and most
refined. Coffee was served after luncheon – weak and amber-
coloured, real German coffee. Herr Klueber, always the
perfect gentleman, asked Gemma's permission to light a cigar
... And, at this point, something suddenly happened, something quite unforeseen and certainly most unpleasant – even
indecent.

A few officers from the Mainz garrison were ensconced at
one of the neighbouring tables. From their glances and
whispering, it was easy to guess that Gemma's looks had
made a great impression on them. One of them, who had
probably already had time to go into Frankfurt, kept eyeing
her, rather as if she were someone with whom he was well
acquainted. Evidently he knew who she was. All of a sudden,
he rose and, with his glass in his hand (the gallant officers had
consumed a fair amount of drink and the tablecloth in front of
them was crowded with bottles) approached the table at
which Gemma was sitting. He was a flaxen-haired and very
young man. His features were agreeable enough and not
unattractive, but the wine which he had taken had distorted
them. There was a tremor in his cheeks and his roving eyes
were swollen, and had assumed an expression of insolence.
His companions at first tried to restrain him, but then let him
go – 'Well, what's the odds? Let's see what happens.'

Swaying slightly, the officer halted in front of Gemma and
declaimed, in an artificially shrill voice which betrayed his
inner conflict, 'I drink the health of the most beautiful coffee-

house lady in all Frankfurt and in all the world' (at this point he drained his glass in a gulp), 'and, as a reward, I claim this flower, plucked by her own divine little fingers.' He picked up a rose which was lying by Gemma's place on the table.

She was at first startled and frightened, and went deathly pale. Then her fright gave way to indignation. She flushed to the roots of her hair and looked steadily at the man who had insulted her. Her eyes went dark and at the same time seemed to blaze, as a flame of uncontrollable fury burned through the deep shadows. The officer was apparently embarrassed by her look. He murmured something unintelligible, bowed and went back to his friends, who greeted him with laughter and some light applause.

Herr Klueber rose abruptly from the table, drew himself up to his full height, put on his hat and pronounced, with dignity but not too loudly, 'This is unheard of! Unheard-of insolence!' (*Unerhoert! Unerhoerte Frechheit!*) He then immediately summoned the waiter in a voice of great severity and demanded the bill without delay. More than that, he ordered the carriage to be made ready, and added that decent people could not be seen in this establishment in view of the fact that they were liable to be subjected to insults. At these words Gemma, who had remained motionless in her place, her breast heaving violently, transferred her look to Herr Klueber with a gaze of the same intensity and with exactly the same expression as she had bestowed on the officer. Emil was literally trembling with rage.

'Please rise, *mein Fraulein*,' Herr Klueber said in the same severe voice, 'this is no fit place for you to remain. We will accommodate ourselves there, inside the inn.'

Gemma rose silently. He offered her his arm, she took it, and he proceeded towards the inn, with a majestic gait which, like his whole bearing, became the more majestic and haughty the farther he retreated from the spot where luncheon had taken place. Poor Emil shuffled along behind them.

But while Herr Klueber was settling with the waiter, whom as a punishment he did not tip a single kreutzer, Sanin briskly walked up to the table at which the officers were sitting. Addressing himself to the one who had insulted Gemma (and who at that moment was inviting each of his friends in turn to sniff at her rose), he said in a clear voice and in French:

'Your conduct just now, sir, was unbecoming to a gentleman and unworthy of the uniform you wear, and I have come to tell you that you are an ill-bred bounder.'

The young man jumped to his feet, but another slightly older officer barred him with a motion of his arm, and made him sit down again. Turning to Sanin, he asked him, also in French:

'Are you related to this young lady – a brother, or engaged to be married to her?'

'I am a complete stranger to her!' exclaimed Sanin. 'I am a Russian, but I cannot be an indifferent witness to such insolence. Here, incidentally, is my card, with my address. This officer can find me there.'

With these words, Sanin flung his visiting card on the table and at the same time deftly seized Gemma's rose which one of the officers had dropped onto his plate. The young officer once more made as if to jump to his feet, but the older man stopped him with the words, 'Quiet, Doenhof!' (*Doenhof, sei still!*) He then rose to his feet himself, saluted and, with a certain degree of respect in his voice and manner, informed Sanin that an officer of their regiment would have the honour of waiting on him the following morning at his lodgings. Sanin replied with a curt bow and quickly returned to his party.

Herr Klueber made pretence that he had completely failed to notice either Sanin's absence or his conversation with the officers. He was engaged in urging on the coachman who was harnessing the horses, and was indignant with him for his dilatoriness. Gemma said nothing to Sanin either, and did not even glance at him. It was clear from her frown, from her pale, clenched lips, from her very stillness, that her heart was heavy. Only Emil was obviously longing to speak to Sanin and to question him. He had seen Sanin go up to the officers and had seen him hand them something white – a scrap of paper, a note, a card ... The poor boy's heart was thumping, his cheeks were burning; he was ready to throw his arms around Sanin, to burst into tears, or to set off with him straight away and beat the life out of all those odious officers! However, he restrained himself and contented himself with following attentively every movement of his noble Russian friend.

The carriage at last was got ready and the company took their seats. Emil clambered up on to the box after Tartaglia. He felt more at ease there. Besides, he did not have Klueber, whom he could not look at calmly, sticking up in front of him.

During the entire journey, Herr Klueber pontificated ... and pontificated on his own. No one disagreed with him, but then no one agreed with him either. He stressed with particular insistence how wrong everyone had been to reject his proposal that they should take luncheon in the enclosed summerhouse. There would have been no unpleasantness then! He then vouchsafed several quite sharp and even radical judgements on the subject of the Government's unpardonable policy of pandering to the officers, failing to pay adequate attention to their discipline and failing in its respect for the civilian element of society (*Das buergerliche Element in der Societaet*). Such a policy gave rise to feelings of dissatisfaction from which it was only a step to revolution – a fact regarding which France served as a sad example. At this point he gave a sigh of sympathy, but of sympathy tinged with censure. However, he immediately added the observation that he himself had a veneration for authority and would never ... no, never ... become a revolutionary. But he could not refrain from expressing his ... how should he put it? ... disapproval at the sight of such laxity! He then offered a few more observations on morality and on immorality, on decency and on the sense of dignity.

During all this 'pontification', Gemma quite obviously

began to be ashamed of her husband-to-be. She had already seemed a little unhappy about Herr Klueber during the morning walk – that was why she had kept some distance from Sanin and had appeared somewhat embarrassed by his presence. Towards the end of the drive, she was positively wretched, and although, as before, she did not say a word to Sanin she suddenly threw him a glance of entreaty ... as far as he was concerned, he felt much more pity for her than indignation towards Herr Klueber ... Secretly and half-unconsciously, he was even rejoicing at everything that had happened in the course of the day, although he could expect a challenge the following morning.

At last this painful *partie de plaisir* came to an end. When he handed Gemma out of the carriage in front of the patisserie, Sanin, without saying a word, placed in her hand the rose which he had recaptured. She coloured violently, pressed his hand and immediately hid the rose away. Although the evening was only just beginning, he did not wish to enter the house. She did not invite him in. Besides, Pantaleone, who had appeared at the porch, announced that Frau Lenore was resting. Emil said goodbye to Sanin in a state of some confusion. The boy seemed to shy away from him now – so much did the Russian astonish him. Klueber conveyed Sanin to his hotel and bowed a stiff farewell. For all his self-assurance, the well-regulated German was ill at ease. But indeed, everyone was ill at ease.

However, this unease soon disappeared so far as Sanin was concerned. It was replaced by another mood, difficult to define, though agreeable, even exalted. He strode up and down the room, did not want to think about anything, whistled from time to time – and felt very pleased with himself.

## XVII

Next morning as he was dressing, he said to himself, 'I will wait for this officer until ten o'clock, and after that I will leave

it to him to find me.' But the Germans are early risers. It had
not yet struck nine when the waiter came in to announce that
Second Lieutenant (*der Herr Seconde Lieutenant*) von Richter
wished to see him. Sanin quickly threw on his coat and told
the waiter to show him in. Contrary to Sanin's expectations,
Herr Richter turned out to be a very young man indeed, little
more than a boy. He did his best to give his beardless face an
expression of importance, but was extremely unsuccessful.
He could not even conceal his embarrassment – as he sat
down, he nearly fell over his sword which had got caught in
the chair. With much stumbling and stammering he declared
to Sanin, in atrocious French, that he had come at the
instance of his friend, Baron von Doenhof; that his mission
was to demand of Herr von Zanin an apology for the insulting
expressions which he had used the day before; and that in the
event of Herr von Zanin refusing such an apology, Baron von
Doenhof required satisfaction.

Sanin replied that he had no intention of apologizing, but
was prepared to give satisfaction. Thereupon, Herr von
Richter, still stammering, enquired the time when, and the
place where, and the person with whom the necessary
discussions could take place. Sanin replied that he could
return in about two hours' time, and that in the meantime,
he, Sanin, would endeavour to find a second. (Who the devil
shall I have as my second? he was thinking to himself
meanwhile.)

Herr von Richter rose and began to make his farewell bows
... but stopped as he reached the door, as if his conscience
had smitten him, and turning towards Sanin, muttered that
his friend, Baron von Doenhof, did not conceal from himself
... some degree of blame on his own part ... for what
occurred yesterday, and would therefore be satisfied with a
very mild apology – '*des exghizes léchères*'. To this, Sanin
replied he had no intention of making any apology whether
deep or mild, since he did not consider himself to be in the
wrong.

'In that case,' replied Herr von Richter, blushing even

more, 'it will be necessary to exchange some amicable pistol shots – *des goups de bisdolet à l'amiaple.*'

'I don't understand this at all,' remarked Sanin. 'Are we to fire in the air, or what?'

'Oh no, not at all,' babbled the subaltern, now in a state of complete confusion. 'I only thought that since this was an affair between gentlemen ... I will talk to your second,' he interrupted himself, and was gone.

As soon as von Richter had left the room, Sanin sank on to a chair and stared at the floor. 'What on earth is all this? How has life all of a sudden taken this turn? Everything past and future has vanished, is lost, and all that remains is that here I am in Frankfurt, about to have a fight with someone about something or other.' He remembered a mad aunt, who was in the habit of singing a little doggerel to herself, and dancing to it:

> Fiddle-de-dee,
> Fiddle-de-doh
> My subaltern, my boy – O
> Come dance with me
> Come prance with me
> My subaltern, my joy – O!

And he burst out laughing and sang like her:

> Come dance with me,
> Come prance with me,
> My subaltern, my joy – O!

All at once, he exclaimed aloud: 'However, I must act and not lose any time,' jumped up and saw Pantaleone in front of him with a note in his hand.

'I knocked several times, but you did not answer. I thought you were not in,' murmured the old man and handed him the note. 'From Signorina Gemma.'

Sanin took it – mechanically, as the saying goes – opened it and read it. Gemma wrote that she was very much perturbed on account of a certain matter of which he was aware, and would like to see him at once.

'The Signorina is worried,' remarked Pantaleone, who was evidently aware of the contents of the note. 'She told me to find out what you were doing and to bring you to her.'

Sanin glanced at the old Italian – and plunged into thought. An idea flashed through his mind. It seemed at first so strange as to be impossible. And yet – why not? he said to himself, and then out loud, 'Signor Pantaleone!'

The old man pulled himself together, tucked his chin into his cravat and fixed his eyes on Sanin.

'Do you know,' continued Sanin, 'what happened yesterday?'

Pantaleone went through some chewing motions and jerked his enormous mane.

'I do.' (Emil had told him everything as soon as he got back.)

'You do, do you? Then listen to me. An officer has just left this room. That bounder has challenged me to a duel. I have accepted his challenge. But I have no second. Would *you* like to be my second?'

Pantaleone gave a start and raised his eyebrows so high that they disappeared under the overhanging hair.

'It is absolutely necessary for you to fight?' he asked at last in Italian. Until then he had been expressing himself in French.

'Absolutely. To act otherwise would mean dishonour for the rest of my life.'

'Hm. If I do not agree to act as your second, will you then look for someone else?'

'Certainly. Of course I will.'

Pantaleone dropped his gaze.

'But may I ask you, Signor de Zannini, do you not think that your duel may cast a certain unfavourable shadow on the reputation of a certain personage?'

'I don't think so. But, in any case, there is nothing to be done about it.'

'Hm.' Pantaleone had by now completely disappeared into his cravat. 'Well, and that *ferroflucto* Kluberio, what about him?' he exclaimed, suddenly jerking his face upwards.

'He? Oh, nothing.'

'*Che!*'*

Pantaleone shrugged his shoulders contemptuously. 'In any event, I have to thank you,' he pronounced at length in an unsteady voice, 'for the fact that you are able to recognize a gentleman – *un galant'uomo* – even in my present degraded state. By acting in this manner, you have demonstrated that you are a real *galant'uomo*. But I must think over your proposal.'

'Time will not wait, dear Signor Ci . . . Cippa . . .'

'Tola,' prompted the old man. 'I am only asking for one hour's time for reflection. The daughter of my benefactors is involved in this, and therefore I must, I am in duty bound, to give the question some thought. In an hour's time, in three-quarters of an hour's time, you will learn my decision.'

'Very well. I will wait.'

'And now, what answer am I to give Signorina Gemma?'

Sanin took a sheet of paper and wrote: 'Do not worry, my dear friend, I will come to see you in about three hours' time and all will be explained. Thank you with all my heart for your concern.' He entrusted the note to Pantaleone, who put it carefully in a side pocket, repeated, 'In an hour's time', and made for the door. But suddenly he turned back sharply, ran up to Sanin, seized his hand, pressed it to his frilled shirt-front and, raising his eyes to Heaven, exclaimed, 'Noble youth! Great heart! (*Nobil giovanotto! Gran cuore!*) Suffer a feeble old man (*a un vechiotto*) to press your valiant hand! (*la vostra valorosa destra!*).' He then leapt back a little, waved both arms in the air . . . and was gone.

Sanin followed him with his eyes . . . then picked up a newspaper and began to read. But he scanned the printed lines in vain: he could take in nothing.

*An untranslatable Italian exclamation rather like our Russian *nu* (Oh, well! *Tr.*).

## XVIII

An hour later, the waiter came up once more and handed
Sanin an old and dirty visiting card on which the following
words were engraved: *Pantaleone Cippatola of Varese, Court
Singer (Cantante di Camera) to his Royal Highness the Duke of
Modena*. The waiter was closely followed by Pantaleone
himself. He had changed all his clothes from top to toe. He
was wearing a black frock-coat which had gone brown with
age, and a white piqué waistcoat, across which a pinchbeck
watch-chain was elaborately draped. A heavy cornelian seal
hung low over the flap of his narrow black breeches pocket. In
his right hand, he held a black hat made of hare's wool, and in
his left two thick chamois leather gloves. His cravat was tied
even wider and higher than usual, and a tiepin with a stone
which is called a 'cat's eye' (*oeil de chat*) was stuck in his
starched shirt-front. The index finger of his right hand was
embellished with a ring representing two clasped hands with a
flaming heart between them. A heavy smell of storage, of
mothballs and of musk came wafting across from the old man.
But the most indifferent spectator would have been struck by
his appearance of perplexed solemnity. Sanin rose to greet him.

'I am your second,' murmured Pantaleone in French, and
bowed with the whole of his trunk, at the same time placing
his heels together and his toes apart like a ballet dancer. 'I
have come for my instructions. Do you wish to fight without
mercy?'

'Why without mercy, dear Signor Cippatola? Nothing in
the world would make me withdraw the words which I used
yesterday – but I am not bloodthirsty! But wait, my opponent's second will be here any moment. I will go into the next
room, and you two can agree conditions. Believe me, I will
never forget your services to me, and I thank you with all my
heart.'

'Honour must come first,' replied Pantaleone, and sank
into an armchair without waiting for Sanin to invite him to be
seated.

'If this *ferroflucto spizzebubbio*,' he continued, mixing French and Italian, 'if this shop-walker Kluberio was incapable of perceiving where his plain duty lay, and was too cowardly – so much the worse for him! A tuppeny ha'penny good-for-nothing – and there's an end of it. As for the conditions of the duel, I am your second and your interests are to me sacred! When I lived in Padua, a regiment of White Dragoons was stationed there – and I was very close to many of the officers. I know their code intimately. Of course I also frequently discussed these matters with your Principe Tarbussky ... Is that second due here soon?'

'I expect him any minute – and indeed here he comes,' Sanin added, glancing into the street.

Pantaleone rose, looked at his watch, adjusted his great lock of hair and quickly pushed back into his shoe an errant tape which was dangling from under his breeches. The young subaltern came into the room, still as red-faced and confused as before.

Sanin presented the two seconds to each other.

'Monsieur Richter, *sous lieutenant* – Monsieur Cippatola, *artiste*.'

The subaltern was a little taken aback at the sight of the old man ... What would he have said if someone had whispered to him at this moment that the '*artiste*' who had just been introduced to him was also occupied in the culinary arts! But Pantaleone assumed the air of one for whom arranging duels was an everyday affair. He was helped on this occasion by the memories of his theatrical career, and he played the part of a second precisely as if it were a stage role. Both he and the young officer were silent for a few moments.

'Well, shall we begin?' Pantaleone, playing with his cornelian seal, was the first to speak.

'Yes, let us begin,' replied the subaltern. 'But ... the presence of one of the adversaries ...'

'I will leave you immediately, gentlemen,' Sanin exclaimed. He bowed and went into the bedroom, locking the door behind him.

He flung himself on the bed and began to think about Gemma ... but the conversation of the seconds reached him through the closed door. It was being conducted in French, and each was massacring that language mercilessly after his own fashion ... Pantaleone once again mentioned the Dragoons of Padua and the Principe Tarbussky, and the subaltern spoke of '*exghizes léchères!*' and of '*goups à l'amiaple*'. But the old man refused to listen to any talk of '*exghizes*'. To Sanin's horror, he suddenly launched into a lecture on the subject of a certain young and innocent maiden, whose little finger alone was worth more than all the officers in the world (*oune zeune damigella innoucenta qu'a ella sola dans soun peti doa vale più que toutt le zouffissié del mondo!* ), and repeated several times with heat, 'It is shameful, shameful (*E ouna onta, ouna onta!* ).'

The subaltern did not at first react, but before long a tremor of anger appeared in the young man's voice, and he remarked that he had not come for the purpose of listening to moral sermons.

'At your age, it is always salutary to listen to the truth,' exclaimed Pantaleone.

The argument between the two seconds grew stormy at several stages. It lasted for over an hour, and resulted at length in agreement on the following conditions: 'Baron von Doenhof and Monsieur de Sanin to duel with pistols on the following day at ten o' clock in the morning, in a small wood near Hanau, at twenty paces' distance. Each to have the right to fire twice on a signal to be given by the seconds. Pistols to have unrifled barrels and the triggers not to be fitted with hair-springs.'

Herr von Richter departed, and Pantaleone ceremoniously opened the bedroom door, announced the result of the conference and once again exclaimed, '*Bravo Russo! Bravo giovanotto!* Thou wilt be victorious!'

A few minutes later, the two of them set off for the Roselli patisserie. Before setting out, Sanin had exacted a promise from Pantaleone to keep the whole matter of the duel a deep secret. In reply, the old man merely raised a finger, screwed up one eye, and whispered twice '*Segredezza!*' He was visibly younger and even seemed to walk more jauntily. All these extraordinary, if unpleasant, events vividly transported him to that epoch when he himself had issued and accepted challenges – on the stage, it is true. Baritones, as is well known, are very full of sound and fury in their stage roles.

## XIX

Emil ran out to meet Sanin – he had been keeping a look-out for over an hour – and hurriedly whispered in his ear that his mother knew nothing about the unpleasant incident of the day before, and that it must not even be hinted at, that he was once again being sent off to Herr Klueber's store, but that he would not go, and would hide somewhere. Having imparted all this information in a few seconds, the boy suddenly fell on Sanin's shoulder, kissed him impetuously and dashed off down the street.

Gemma met Sanin in the shop, tried to say something – and could not do so. Her lips were trembling slightly and her eyes were half-closed and restless. He hastened to calm her, and to assure her that the whole matter had ended in a mere trifle.

'Did anyone call to see you today?' she asked.

'Yes, a certain person called on me, we had a discussion and we came to a most satisfactory conclusion.'

Gemma withdrew behind the counter.

'She didn't believe me,' he thought to himself . . . However, he went into the adjoining room and there found Frau Lenore. Her migraine had passed, but she was in a mood of melancholy. She welcomed him with a friendly smile, but at the same time warned him that he would be bored by her today, she was in no state to entertain him. He sat down beside her, and noticed that her eyelids were red and swollen.

'What is the matter, Frau Lenore? Surely you haven't been crying?'

'Sh ... sh ...' she whispered and motioned with her head towards the room where her daughter was. 'Don't say that so loudly.'

'But what have you been crying about?'

'Ah, Monsieur Sanin, I don't know myself.'

'Has someone caused you distress?'

'Oh, no. I suddenly grew very lonely. I also remembered Giovan' Battista ... my youth ... then I thought how quickly it had all passed. I am getting old, my friend, and I cannot reconcile myself to that. It seems to me as if I were the same as I was before ... but old age ... here it is, here it is!'

Traces of tears appeared in Frau Lenore's eyes.

'I can see that you are looking at me with astonishment – but you too will grow old, my friend, and you will discover how bitter it is!'

Sanin began to comfort her, mentioned her children in whom her own youth was resurrected, even tried to tease her a little by assuring her that she was fishing for compliments. But she earnestly begged him to stop, and he realized for the first time that such despondency, the despondency that comes with the awareness of growing old, cannot ever be comforted or dispelled. One can but wait until it passes of its own accord. He suggested a game of *tresette*, and could have thought of nothing better. She immediately agreed, and seemed to grow more cheerful.

Sanin played cards with her before and after luncheon. Pantaleone also took part in the game. Never had his locks fallen so low upon his forehead, never had his chin sunk so deeply into his cravat. His every movement breathed such concentrated self-importance that merely to look at him gave rise to the involuntary thought: 'What is the secret that this man is guarding with such firm determination?'

But – *segredezza, segredezza!*

During that entire day, he tried in every way to show the deepest respect for Sanin. At table, he passed over the ladies and ceremoniously and firmly handed Sanin the dishes. During the game, he let Sanin take cards first and did not have the effrontery to claim any penalties. From time to time, without rhyme or reason, he would declare to all and sundry that the Russians are the most magnanimous, the bravest, and the most determined people in the world!

Oh, you old mummer! Sanin thought to himself.

But what amazed him more than the sudden change in Signora Roselli's mood was the way in which her daughter behaved towards him. It was not that she avoided him – rather the contrary: she kept on settling down a little away from him, listening to what he said, looking at him. But she decidedly did not wish to enter into conversation with him, and every time that he spoke to her, she would quietly rise from her seat and quietly disappear for a few moments. She would then reappear, and sit down again somewhere in a corner and there she remained motionless, as if meditating and wondering – wondering above all. Frau Lenore at last noticed her extraordinary behaviour and enquired once or twice what the matter was.

'Nothing,' replied Gemma. 'You know I am like this sometimes.'

'Yes, that is so,' her mother agreed.

And so passed the whole of that long day – neither gay nor dull – neither amusing nor boring. Who knows? Maybe if Gemma had behaved otherwise, Sanin would have been unable to resist the temptation to show off a little, or would simply have surrendered to the feeling of sadness at parting from her, possibly for ever ...

But since he did not even have an opportunity of speaking to Gemma, he had perforce to content himself with sitting at the pianoforte picking out minor chords for a quarter of an hour, before evening coffee.

Emil returned late, and in order to avoid enquiries about Herr Klueber, withdrew to bed very shortly afterwards. The time came for Sanin, too, to take his leave.

He said goodbye to Gemma. For some reason, he remembered Lensky's parting from Olga in Pushkin's *Evgeniy Onegin*. He pressed her hand firmly, and attempted to look her

in the eyes ... but she turned aside slightly and released her
fingers from his grasp.


## XX


The stars were out when he emerged on to the porch. And
what an array of stars was scattered in the heavens. Large and
small, yellow and red, and blue and white, they glowed in
clusters, their rays dancing in the darkness. There was no
moon in the sky, but even without moonlight each object was
clearly visible in the shadowless, half-illuminated dusk. Sanin
walked the length of the street ... He did not want to return
home at once; he felt the need to wander in the fresh air. He
retraced his steps, and had hardly drawn level with the
Rosellis' house, when one of the windows facing on to the
street suddenly opened with a knock. On the black square
surface of the opening (there was no light in the room), there
appeared the figure of a woman and he heard his name called:
'Monsieur Dmitry!'

He rushed headlong to the window ... Gemma!

She leaned forwards with her elbows on the sill.

'Monsieur Dmitry,' she began in a hesitant voice, 'all day
long I have wanted to give you a certain thing ... but could
not summon up the courage. But now, suddenly seeing you
again, I thought evidently this is something that is fated ...'
Gemma stopped involuntarily at this word. She could not go
on: at that instant something quite extraordinary happened.

Suddenly, in the midst of the deep silence, in a completely
cloudless sky, there arose such a rush of wind that the very
earth seemed to quake beneath their feet. The thin light of the
stars shuddered and scattered, and the very air was whirling
around them. The onrush of wind, which was not cold but
warm and even torrid, struck at the trees, at the roof of the
house, at its walls, at the street. In an instant, it had whipped
Sanin's hat from his head, and blown the black strands of
Gemma's hair into disorder. Sanin's head was level with the

windowsill. He leaned against it involuntarily, while Gemma gripped his shoulders with both hands and pressed her breast against his head. The noise, the ringing and the rattling lasted about a minute ... The whirlwind sped away, as fast as it had risen, like a flock of enormous birds ... Once again there was deep silence.

Sanin raised his head and saw above him such a wonderful, frightened, excited face, such enormous, such terrifying, such marvellous eyes, he saw a creature of such beauty, that his heart seemed to stop. He sank his lips in the thin spray of hair that had fallen across his chest. 'Oh, Gemma ..'

'What was that? Was it lightning?' she asked, opening her eyes wide and keeping her bare arms on his shoulders.

'Gemma!' Sanin repeated.

She started, glanced behind her into the room, and then with a swift movement took from her bosom a rose that was already faded and threw it to Sanin.

'I wanted to give you this flower.'

He recognized the rose which he had won back the day before ...

But the window was already slammed to, and there was nothing to be seen, no sign of any pale reflection behind the dark pane.

Sanin returned to his hotel without his hat ... He had not even noticed that he had lost it.

## XXI

It was morning when he fell asleep, and no wonder! Under the impact of that sudden summer squall, he had realized almost as suddenly not that Gemma was a beautiful girl, not that she attracted him – he knew that before – but that he had ... very nearly fallen in love with her. Love had swept down upon him as suddenly as the squall, and now there was this idiotic duel! He began to be tortured by gloomy forebodings. Well, he might not be killed. But what could come out of his love for this girl, who was engaged to be married to another man? No doubt this other man was not a very serious rival, and suppose even that Gemma would come to love him, Sanin, or loved him already – what then? How would it end? And such a beauty . . .

He walked about the room, sat down at the table, took a sheet of paper, scribbled a few lines on it, and straight away scratched them out . . . Then he recalled the wonderful image of Gemma, all blown about by the warm rush of wind, in the dark window under the rays of the stars . . . He remembered her arms which were like marble, like the arms of the goddesses on Olympus; he could feel their living weight on his shoulders . . . then he picked up the rose which she had thrown him . . . and it seemed to him that its faded petals gave off a scent which was even more fragrant than the usual scent of roses . . .

'But suppose I am killed or maimed?'

He did not go to bed, but fell asleep fully dressed on the divan.


Someone was shaking him by the shoulder. He opened his eyes and saw Pantaleone.

'Asleep, like Alexander of Macedon on the eve of the Babylonian battle,' exclaimed the old man.

'But what is the time?' Sanin enquired.

'A quarter to seven. It is two hours' drive to Hanau, and we must be first on the scene. The Russians always forestall their enemies. I have engaged the best carriage in Frankfurt.'

Sanin began to wash.

'And where are the pistols?'

'They will be brought by that *ferroflucto tedesco*. He will bring the doctor, as well.'

Pantaleone was evidently putting on a show of courage, as he had done the day before. But when he sat down beside Sanin in the carriage and the coachman had cracked his whip and the horses had set off at a brisk trot, the former singer and friend of the Padua Dragoons suffered a change. He became confused, and a bit frightened. It was as if something within him had crashed to the ground, like a badly aligned wall.

'What are we doing, dear God, *Santissima Madonna?*' he exclaimed, in a voice which had suddenly become plaintive, and clutched at his hair. 'What am I doing, old fool that I am, old madman, *frenetico?*'

Sanin was surprised and laughed, and putting his arm lightly around Pantaleone's waist, reminded him of the French saying: '*Le vin est tiré – il faut le boire*' (or, as the Russians say, 'If you put your hand to the cart, you can't draw back').

'Yes, yes,' replied the old man, 'we will drain this cup together. But even so, I am off my head. Off my head! Everything was so quiet, so pleasant ... and now suddenly: ta-ta-ta, tra-ta-ta.'

'Just like the passages for *tutti* in the orchestra,' Sanin remarked with a forced smile, 'but it is not your fault, after all.'

'I know it isn't – what next? Even so, this is such an impetuous action. *Diavolo, diavolo,*' Pantaleone kept repeating, shaking his mop of hair and sighing.

And the carriage rolled on and on.

It was a beautiful morning. The streets of Frankfurt, which had scarcely begun to stir, seemed so clean and comfortable. The window-panes on the houses sparkled like silver foil, as the sun played on them. And no sooner had the carriage left the town boundary than the shrill song of the larks came cascading down from the blue, but not as yet bright sky. Suddenly, at a turning in the main road, a familiar figure appeared from behind a tall poplar tree, took a few steps forward and stopped. Sanin looked at it more closely. Dear God, it was Emil!

He turned to Pantaleone. 'Does he know anything?'

'Didn't I tell you that I am a madman?' the poor Italian almost shouted in his despair. 'This wretched boy gave me no peace all night, and at last, this morning, I told him everything.'

'There's your *segredezza* for you,' thought Sanin. The carriage drew level with Emil. Sanin told the coachman to stop and called the 'wretched boy' to him. Emil came towards him with uncertain, faltering steps, as pale as pale could be, as on the day of his fainting fit. He could hardly stand up.

'What are you doing here?' Sanin asked severely. 'Why are you not at home?'

'Please, please, allow me to drive with you,' Emil babbled in a trembling voice, his hands folded in entreaty. His teeth were chattering, as in a fever. 'I won't be in the way, only please take me with you.'

'If you feel the slightest affection or respect for me,' Sanin replied, 'you will return home or to Herr Klueber's shop immediately, will not say a single word to anyone and will wait for my return.'

Emil moaned, 'Your return . . .' and his voice rang out and then broke. 'And what if you. . .'

'Emil,' Sanin interrupted, motioning with his eyes at the coachman, 'remember yourself! Emil, please go home! Please listen to me, my friend. You assure me that you are fond of me. Please, do as I ask.'

He put out his hand to the boy, who lurched forward with a sob, pressed the hand to his lips, and then jumped off the road and ran back across a field in the direction of Frankfurt.

'There's another noble heart for you,' murmured Pantaleone, but Sanin glared at him. The old man sat huddled into his corner of the carriage. He knew he had done wrong. Besides, his amazement grew with every moment. Was it really possible that *he* had agreed to act as second in a duel, that *he* had procured the horses and made all the arrangements and had left his peaceful abode at six o'clock in the morning? On top of everything, his legs were aching painfully.

Sanin thought it necessary to put some heart into him, and found the right chord to strike, found the very word.

'Where is your former spirit, my worthy Signor Cippatola, where is *il antico valor*?'

Signor Cippatola sat up straight and frowned. '*Il antico valor?*' he repeated in a deep bass voice, '*Non è ancora spento il antico valor* (The ancient valour is not yet all spent).'

He preened himself, began to talk about his career, about the opera, and the great tenor Garcia, and arrived in Hanau full of vitality. When you come to think of it, there is nothing in the world more powerful – or more impotent – than a word.

# XXII

The little wood in which the battle was destined to take place was about a quarter of a mile from Hanau. As Pantaleone had foretold, he and Sanin were the first to arrive. They ordered the carriage to wait at the edge of the wood and walked deeper into the shade of the thickly grown and close-set trees. They had about an hour to wait.

The time spent waiting did not weigh too heavily on Sanin. He strolled up and down the little path, listened to the song of the birds, watched the dragonflies as they flew past and, like the majority of Russians in similar circumstances, tried not to think. He was only once plunged into melancholy reflections, and that was when he came upon a young lime tree, which had to all appearances been felled by yesterday's squall. The tree was actually dying, all its leaves were withering. What is this? An omen? flashed through his mind. But he immediately started to whistle, jumped over the very same lime tree and went striding along the path. As for Pantaleone, he grumbled away, abused the Germans, groaned and kept rubbing either his back or his knees. He even kept yawning from excitement, which gave his tiny, pinched and drawn face a most comical expression. Sanin nearly burst out laughing when he looked at him.

At last the sound of carriage wheels was heard on the soft road. 'It is they,' muttered Pantaleone, alert now and straightening himself. He did shiver nervously for a moment,

but proceeded to camouflage this with a 'brrr', and a remark
that it was a fresh morning. The leaves and the grass were
drenched with dew, but the heat of the day penetrated right
into the wood.

The two officers soon appeared, framed at the edge of the
forest. They were accompanied by a short, stoutish man with
a phlegmatic, almost sleepy expression – the military doctor.
He was carrying in one hand an earthenware jug of water,
ready for any emergency. A satchel, containing surgical
instruments and bandages, was dangling from his left
shoulder. It was evident that he was more than used to
expeditions of this nature. They formed one of the sources of
his income: every duel was worth eight sovereigns to him,
four from each combatant. Herr von Richter was carrying a
box containing the pistols, Herr von Doenhof was twirling a
small riding switch, probably in order to show off.

'Pantaleone,' Sanin whispered to the old man, 'if ... if I am
killed – after all anything can happen – get a paper from my
side pocket – there is a flower wrapped in it, and give the
paper to Signorina Gemma. Do you hear me? Do you
promise?'

The old man looked at him dejectedly – and nodded his
head ... but goodness knows if he had understood Sanin's
request.

The adversaries and their seconds exchanged bows, as is
customary. The doctor alone did not move an eyebrow, but
sat down on the grass with a yawn, as if to say, 'I have no time
for these manifestations of knightly courtesies.' Herr von
Richter proposed to Signor 'Cibbadola' that he should select
the spot; Signor 'Cibbadola' replied, with his tongue hardly
moving in his palate (the 'wall' in him had once again
collapsed), 'You take the necessary action, my dear sir, and I
will observe.'

And so Herr von Richter took the necessary action. He
found there in the wood a very pretty clearing, all decked with
flowers. He measured the paces and marked out the limits
with two small twigs which he had hastily peeled, got the

pistols out of the box, sat down on his heels and packed in the bullets. In a word, he made himself uncommonly busy, constantly mopping the sweat from off his face with a white handkerchief. Pantaleone, who accompanied him, looked more like a man shivering with cold. While all these preparations were going on, the two adversaries stood some distance apart, like two schoolboys who had been punished and who were showing resentment against their masters.

The moment of decision was come ...

'Each took his pistol in his hand ...'

But at this point, Herr von Richter remarked to Pantaleone that as the senior second it was his duty, according to the rules of duelling, before pronouncing the fatal, 'One, two, three,' to address to the adversaries words of last-minute advice and to make a proposal for reconciliation; that while such proposals had never been known to lead to any results, and were in fact nothing more than an empty formality, nevertheless by going through with the formality, Signor Cippatola would divest himself of a certain degree of responsibility for the consequences; that while it was true that an allocution of this nature was the direct responsibility of the so-called impartial witness, *unparteiicher Zeuge*, nevertheless, since none such was present, he, Herr von Richter, would willingly yield this privilege to his respected confrère.

Meanwhile Pantaleone had had time to disappear so completely behind a bush as to be unable to see the officer who had been guilty of the insulting behaviour. At first, he understood nothing of Herr von Richter's oration, particularly since it had been delivered through the nose. But suddenly he sprang into action, stepped forward nimbly and, feverishly beating his chest, bellowed in his hoarse voice, in his comic mixture of languages, '*A, la la la ... Che bestialità! Deux zeun' ommes come ça qué si battono – perchè? Che diavolo! Andate a casa!*'

'I am not willing to be reconciled,' Sanin said hurriedly.

'And I also am not willing,' his adversary repeated after him.

'Well then, call out, "One, two, three",' said von Richter, addressing himself to Pantaleone, who by now had completely lost his head.

Pantaleone instantly dived back into his bush, where he huddled, and with his eyes shut and his head averted yelled at the top of his voice:

'*Una ... due ... e tre!*'

Sanin fired first – and missed. The bullet struck a tree with a thud. Baron Doenhof fired immediately after him – deliberately to the side and into the air.

There followed a strained silence ... no one moved. Pantaleone uttered a weak 'Oh –'

'Do you wish to continue?' said Doenhof.

'Why did you fire into the air?' Sanin asked.

'That is not your business.'

'Does it mean that you will fire the second shot into the air as well?' Sanin asked him again.

'Perhaps. I don't know.'

'Please, gentlemen, please,' began von Richter. 'Adversaries in a duel have no right to converse with each other. That is quite out of order.'

'I renounce my right to fire,' said Sanin, and threw his pistol to the ground.

'And I, too, have no intention of going on with this duel,' exclaimed Doenhof and also threw down his pistol, 'and besides, I am now prepared to admit that I was in the wrong the day before yesterday.'

He took a few hesitant steps and stretched out his hand. Sanin quickly walked towards him and grasped the hand. Both young men looked at each other with a smile, and each of them blushed.

'*Bravi, bravi!*' Pantaleone suddenly bellowed like a madman, and, clapping his hands, ran out from the bush like a tumbler pigeon. The doctor, who had seated himself on a tree-stump a little way off, promptly rose to his feet, emptied the water from the jug and ambled lazily towards the edge of the wood.

'Honour is satisfied and the duel is concluded,' von Richter declared in a loud voice.

'*Fuori!*' Pantaleone barked from force of habit.

Having exchanged bows with the officers and taken his seat in the carriage, Sanin was certainly conscious in his whole being of a sensation, if not of pleasure then of relief, like that which follows a successful operation. But another feeling stirred within him as well, something akin to shame ... The duel in which he had just enacted his part now began to take on the appearance of something false, a pre-arranged regimental ceremonial, an ordinary piece of officer and student nonsense. He remembered the phlegmatic doctor and recalled how he had smiled – or rather wrinkled his nose – at the sight of his emerging from the wood practically arm-in-arm with Baron Doenhof. And then, while Pantaleone was paying over to that same doctor the four sovereigns which were his due ... Oh dear ... it was not very agreeable.

Yes, Sanin felt a little remorseful and ashamed ... and yet, when he thought about it, what should he have done? Surely not have left the insolence of the young officer unpunished, and behaved like Herr Klueber? He had intervened on Gemma's behalf, he had defended her ... That was so, but for all that, he was uneasy in his mind, and felt pangs of remorse and even of shame.

Pantaleone, on the other hand, was nothing less than triumphant. He was overwhelmed with pride. No general returning victorious from the field of battle could have looked around him with greater self-satisfaction. Sanin's behaviour during the duel had fired him with enthusiasm. He kept calling him a hero, and would not listen to protestations or to requests to desist. He compared him to a monument of marble, or of bronze, to the statue of the Commendatore in 'Don Giovanni'. As for himself, he admitted he had suffered a certain loss of nerve. 'But, after all, I am an artiste,' he remarked. 'I am highly-strung by nature, while you – you are a child of the snows and of the granite cliffs.'

Sanin simply did not know how to restrain the ardour of the old singer, who was now in full spate.

At about the same spot on the road where they had overtaken Emil a couple of hours before, the boy once again jumped out from behind a tree. With cries of joy, waving his cap above his head and jumping up and down with excitement, he rushed straight at the carriage, nearly falling under the wheels in the process. Then, without waiting for the horses to stop, he clambered over the closed carriage doors – and hurled himself on Sanin.

'You are alive, not wounded!' he kept exclaiming. 'Forgive me, I disobeyed you. I didn't return to Frankfurt ... I couldn't do it... I waited for you here ... Tell me all about it. Did ... did you kill him?'

Sanin had considerable difficulty in calming him and settling him down in his seat.

Pantaleone, with much rhetoric and evident pleasure, related all the details of the duel and of course did not omit to mention the bronze monument and the statue of the Commendatore. He even rose from his seat, stood legs apart to keep his balance, folded his arms across his chest, squinted haughtily over his shoulder, and gave a life-like impersonation of Commendatore Sanin! Emil listened reverently, occasionally interrupting the recital with an exclamation, or else rising swiftly to implant an equally swift kiss on his heroic friend.

The carriage wheels rattled on the paved roads of Frankfurt, and eventually stopped before Sanin's hotel.

Sanin was ascending the stairs to the second floor with his two companions, when suddenly a woman stepped briskly from a small, dark corridor. Her face was covered with a veil. She paused in front of Sanin, swayed slightly, heaved an agitated sigh, ran immediately down to the street, and disappeared – to the great surprise of the waiter who announced that, 'This lady has been waiting for the foreign gentleman to return for over an hour.' Although her appearance had been only momentary, Sanin had had time to recognize Gemma. He recognized her eyes under the thick silk of her brown veil.

'Was Fräulein Gemma then aware. . .?' he asked in German, slowly and with annoyance in his voice, turning to Emil and Pantaleone who were following closely on his heels.

Emil blushed and looked embarrassed.

'I was forced to tell her everything,' he mumbled. 'She guessed what was going on, and there was nothing I could . . . But it doesn't matter at all now,' he went on brightly, 'everything has ended so splendidly, and she has seen you well and unharmed!'

Sanin turned away.

'What a pair of gossips you are, the two of you,' he said crossly, as he went into his room and sat down on a chair.

'Oh, please don't be angry,' begged Emil.

'All right, I won't be angry' (Sanin was not, in fact, angry – he could indeed have hardly wished that Gemma would discover nothing). 'All right, that's enough embracing. You had better go now. I want to be alone. I am tired and will go to sleep.'

'An excellent thought,' exclaimed Pantaleone. 'You need repose, and you have fully earned it, most noble Signore. Come, Emilio. On tiptoes, on tiptoes . . . sh . . . sh . . . !'

Sanin had only said that he wanted to sleep in order to be rid of his companions. But when he was alone, he did indeed feel a considerable weariness in all his limbs. He had scarcely closed his eyes during the whole of the previous night. He threw himself down on to the bed and immediately fell into a deep sleep.


## XXIII

He slept for several hours without waking. Then he began to dream that he was once again fighting a duel, that the adversary before him was Herr Klueber, while on a pine tree sat a parrot, which was, in fact, Pantaleone, and which kept snapping its beak and saying, 'One, one, one! One, one, one!'

'One, one, one.' He was now awake. He opened his eyes and raised his head ... Someone was knocking at the door.

'Come in!' Sanin called out.

A waiter appeared and announced that a lady was very anxious to see him.

Gemma flashed through his mind ... but the lady turned out to be her mother, Frau Lenore.

As soon as she had entered the room, she sank down on a chair and began to weep.

'What is the matter, dear, good Signora Roselli?' Sanin began, sitting down beside her and touching her hand with a gentle caress. 'What has happened? Please calm yourself, I beg of you ...'

'Oh, Herr Dmitry, I am very, very unhappy.'

'Unhappy? You?'

'Oh, desperately. How was I to expect this? Suddenly like a clap of thunder from a clear sky ...' She was drawing breath with difficulty.

'But what is happening? Won't you explain? Would you like a glass of water?'

'No, thank you.' Frau Lenore wiped her eyes with her handkerchief, then burst out weeping with renewed abandon. 'You see, I know everything, everything...'

'What do you mean by everything?'

'Everything that happened today, and the reason ... I know about that, too ... You behaved like an honourable man. But what a miserable chain of circumstances! I never liked the idea of the trip to Soden, and I was right – quite right.' (Frau Lenore had implied nothing of the kind on the day of the trip, but had now convinced herself that she had had a 'premonition'.) 'It is because you are an honourable man and a friend that I have come to you, though I only first set eyes on you some five days ago ... But I am a widow, a lonely widow ... my daughter ... !' Tears drowned Frau Lenore's words. Sanin did not know what to think.

'Your daughter?' he repeated.

'My daughter, Gemma,' Frau Lenore's words burst out with something like a groan, from under the tear-soaked handkerchief, 'declared to me today that she does not wish to marry Herr Klueber, and that I must break off the engagement.'

Sanin actually backed away from her slightly. He had not expected this.

'I say nothing of the disgrace,' Frau Lenore went on. 'This is something that has never happened before in the history of the world, for a girl to break off an engagement. This means ruin for us, Herr Dmitry!' She carefully and methodically rolled up her handkerchief into a tight little ball, exactly as if she wished to roll up her grief in it. 'It is no longer possible for us to live on the income from the shop, Herr Dmitry, and Herr Klueber is very rich and will in time be even richer. And why should the engagement be broken, just because he did not stand up for his fiancée? Well, perhaps that wasn't quite right of him, but after all he is a civilian, he hasn't been to a university and it was only right for a solid businessman like him to treat a light-hearted prank of an unknown little officer with contempt. And in any case, what *was* there insulting about it, Herr Dmitry?'

'Forgive me, Frau Lenore, you seem to be condemning my own behaviour.'

'No, indeed not, indeed I don't condemn you for what you did. It is quite a different matter for you. You are a military man, like all Russians ...'

'But forgive me, I am not ...'

'You are a foreigner, passing through the town. I am grateful to you.' Frau Lenore went on, not listening to Sanin. She was quite breathless, gesticulating, and then once again unrolling the handkerchief and blowing her nose. It was evident, if only from the way in which she gave expression to her grief, that she had not been born under northern skies.

'And how is Herr Klueber to do business in his shop if he spends his time fighting with his customers? It makes no

sense at all. And now I am to break off the engagement! And
what are we going to live on? Formerly, we were the only shop
to make maiden-skin and nougat with pistachio nuts, and we
had special customers for these things, but now everyone
makes maiden-skin. Just think: even as it is, everyone in town
will be talking about your duel ... How can these things be
kept secret? And suddenly, the wedding is off! But it will
mean a scandal, a real scandal! Gemma is an excellent girl and
she is very fond of me, but she is a stubborn republican and
quite defiant about what others think. You alone can persuade
her to change her mind.'

Sanin was even more amazed now.

'I, Frau Lenore?'

'Yes, you and only you. Only you. That is why I have come
to you – I was at my wits' end! You are such a learned, such a
good, man and you stood up for her, she will listen to you.
She *must* listen to you – after all, you risked your own life! You
will prove to her – I can't do anything more with her. You will
prove to her that if she persists she will ruin both herself and
all of us. You saved my son – now save my daughter! You
were sent to us by God Himself ... I am ready to go down on
my knees to beg you to do it!'

And Frau Lenore half rose from the chair, as if with the
intention of throwing herself at Sanin's feet. He restrained
her.

'Frau Lenore! For Heaven's sake! What are you doing?'

She seized his hands. She was trembling all over.

'Do you promise?'

'But think, Frau Lenore, why should I ... ?'

'Do you promise? Or do you wish me to die, here in front
of you, this very moment?'

Sanin lost his head. This was the first time in his life that
he had had to deal with a case of hot Italian blood.

'I will do everything you wish!' he cried. 'I will speak to
Fräulein Gemma.'

Frau Lenore gave a cry of joy.

'Only I really do not know what the outcome will be.'

'Oh please, don't refuse again, don't refuse!' Frau Lenore entreated. 'You have already agreed. And I am sure the outcome will be excellent. In any case, there is nothing more that I can do. She will certainly not listen to *me*.'

'And she was very definite about her refusal to marry Herr Klueber?' Sanin asked after a short silence.

'Like a cut from a knife. She is the image of her father, Giovann' Battista. A real madcap!'

'A madcap? She?' Sanin sounded incredulous.

'Yes ... yes ... but she is an angel too. She will listen to you. You will come, and come soon? Oh, my dear Russian friend!' Frau Lenore rose impulsively from her chair, and just as impulsively seized the head of Sanin who was sitting before her. 'Receive a mother's blessing – and give me some water.'

Sanin brought Signora Roselli a glass of water, promised faithfully that he would come without delay and escorted her downstairs into the street. When he got back to his room, he was in such a state of confusion that he wrung his hands and his eyes were staring.

There, he thought, now life really is spinning round and spinning so fast that it makes me giddy. He did not even attempt to try to fathom what was happening inside him – bedlam, and there's an end on it! 'What a day, what a day,' he whispered involuntarily... 'A madcap, according to her mother. And I am supposed to advise her – her! And what advice am I to give?'

Sanin's head was spinning now and above all this whirligig of sensations, impressions and unuttered thoughts he could see the image of Gemma – the image which had been so indelibly stamped on his mind on that warm, electrically charged night, framed in that dark window, beneath the light of the clustering stars.

## XXIV

As Sanin approached Signora Roselli's house his steps were
hesitant. His heart was beating wildly: he could distinctly feel
and even hear it thumping against his ribs. What was he going
to say to Gemma? How would he start the conversation? He
did not enter the house through the shop, but by the back
porch. In the small front room he met Frau Lenore. She was
pleased to see him and at the same time alarmed.

'I was waiting for you, waiting for you,' she whispered,
shaking his hand with each of her own in turn. 'Go into the
garden, she's there. And remember: all my hopes are on you!'

Sanin set off into the garden. Gemma was sitting on a
bench near the path, engaged in selecting the ripest fruit from
a large basket filled with cherries, and putting them on to a
plate. The sun was low in the sky – it was already after six –
and there was more red than gold in the broad, slanting beams
with which it was warming the whole of Signora Roselli's
little garden. From time to time the leaves exchanged a
scarcely audible, leisurely whisper. Some belated bees
occasionally uttered a sharp buzz as they navigated from one
flower to the next. Somewhere a dove was cooing mono-
tonously and interminably.

Gemma was wearing the same big hat which she had worn
for the expedition to Soden. She glanced at Sanin from under
its down-turned brim, and once more bent over her basket.

Sanin approached Gemma, involuntarily taking shorter
and shorter steps as he did so and ... and ... and he could
think of nothing better to say than to ask her why she was
picking over the cherries.

Gemma did not reply immediately.

'These riper ones,' she said softly at last, 'are for jam; the
others are for the filling of tarts. You know those round tarts
that we sell, with sugar on them?'

Having said these words, she bent her head even deeper.
Her right hand, which held two cherries, paused in the air
between the basket and the plate.

'May I sit beside you?' Sanin asked.

'You may.' Gemma moved slightly along the bench. Sanin sat down beside her, thinking, 'How am I to begin?' But she helped him out of his difficulty.

'You fought a duel today,' she began in a spirited manner, turning her face full towards him, her lovely features aflame with a modest blush. And oh, the profound gratitude that shone in her eyes! 'And you are so calm! Does that mean that danger simply does not exist for you?'

'For Heaven's sake! I was in no danger of any kind. Everything went off very successfully and quite harmlessly.'

Gemma moved a finger to the right and to the left in front of her eyes. Another Italian gesture.

'No, no, you must not say that. You can't deceive me. Pantaleone told me everything.'

'That's a fine source of information! I expect he compared me with the statue of the Commendatore?'

'His way of putting things may be comic, but there is nothing comic either about his feelings or about what you did today. And it was all because of me ... for me ... I will never forget this.'

'But Fräulein Gemma, I assure you ...'

'I will never forget this,' she repeated, stressing each word, then looked at him intently and turned away.

He could now see her slender, clear profile. It seemed to him that he had never seen the like before, and had never in his life experienced what he felt at that moment. He was all aflame.

'And what about my promise?' flashed through his thoughts.

'Fräulein Gemma ...' he began, after a moment's hesitation.

'Yes?'

She did not turn towards him, she went on picking over the cherries, carefully holding the tips of the little stalks in her fingers, attentively lifting the leaves ... but what trust and warmth were to be heard in that one word, 'Yes'.

'Has your mother not told you anything . . . concerning . . .?'

'Concerning what?'

'Concerning me?'

Gemma quite suddenly let the cherries in her hand fall back into the basket.

'Did she have a talk with you?' she asked in turn.

'Yes.'

'And what did she tell you?'

'She told me that you . . . that you suddenly decided to change . . . your former intentions.'

Gemma's head dropped again. She disappeared entirely under her hat: all that was visible was her neck, supple and delicate like the stem of a large flower.

'What intentions?'

'Your intentions – concerning . . . the future arrangement of your life.'

'Do you mean . . . ? Are you referring to Herr Klueber?'

'Yes.'

'And Mother has told you that I do not wish to become the wife of Herr Klueber?'

'Yes.'

Gemma moved. The basket tipped over and fell . . . several cherries went rolling along the path . . . A minute passed – then another. At last her voice could be heard saying:

'Why did she tell you this?'

Sanin could still only see Gemma's neck. Her breast rose and fell more rapidly than before.

'Why? Your mother thought that since you and I have, as it were, become friends in this short time, and you have acquired some slight confidence in my judgement, that I might be in a position to give you some helpful advice . . . and that you would follow it.'

Gemma's hands quietly slipped to her knees. She began fingering the folds of her dress.

'And what advice will you give me, Monsieur Dmitry?' she asked, after a short pause.

Sanin could see that Gemma's fingers were trembling on

her knees. In fact, she was only playing with the folds of her dress to conceal the trembling. Very quietly, he laid his hand on those pale, quivering fingers.

'Gemma,' he murmured, 'why are you not looking at me?'

Instantly, she threw her hat back over her shoulder and fixed her eyes on him – they were full of trust and gratitude as before. She waited for him to speak ... but the sight of her face confused him and seemed to blind him. The warm rays of the evening sun lighted up her youthful head – and the radiance of this head was lighter and brighter than the sunlight.

'I will do what you tell me, Monsieur Dmitry ...' she began, with a very faint smile and a very slight lift of the eyebrows. 'What is your advice to me going to be?'

'My advice?' Sanin repeated. 'Well now, you know that your mother thinks that to break off your engagement to Herr Klueber just because he did not show particular bravery the day before yesterday ...'

'Just because?' Gemma echoed, bending down to pick up the basket which she placed beside her on the bench.

'That ... generally speaking ... it is imprudent for you to break off the engagement; that this is a step of such gravity that it is necessary to weigh all the consequences carefully; and finally, that the very state of your business affairs imposes a certain obligation on each and every member of your family ...'

Gemma interrupted him.

'These are all my mother's opinions; these are her words. I know them. But what is your opinion?'

'My opinion?' Sanin was silent. He felt as if a lump had come up into his throat and stopped him breathing. 'I also am of the opinion ...' he began with some effort.

Gemma stiffened.

'Also? You also?'

'Yes – at least ... that is to say ...' Sanin could not, definitely could not, add a single word.

'Very well,' said Gemma, 'if you, as a friend, advise me to change my decision ... I mean, not to change my former decision, I will think the matter over.' Without noticing what she was doing, she began putting the cherries back from the plate into the basket. 'Mother hopes that I will listen to your advice. Well, perhaps I really will listen to your advice.'

'But, Fräulein Gemma, I should first like to know what the reasons were which compelled you ...'

'I will take your advice,' Gemma repeated, but as she spoke, she kept frowning, her cheeks went pale, and she bit at her lower lip. 'You have done so much for me that it is my duty to do what you wish me to do. I am under an obligation to fulfil your wishes. I will tell Mother ... I will think it over. Here she comes, as it happens.'

So it was indeed: Frau Lenore appeared on the threshold of the door leading from the house into the garden. She was consumed with impatience: she could not keep still. By her reckoning, Sanin ought to have completed his discussion with Gemma ages ago, although his conversation with her had not lasted so long as a quarter of an hour.

'No, no no! For God's sake, don't say anything to her yet!' Sanin exclaimed quickly, in alarm. 'Wait a little. I will tell you. I will write to you, and meanwhile take no decision of any kind ... Wait!'

He squeezed Gemma's hand tightly, jumped up from the bench, and, to the great amazement of Frau Lenore, rushed past her, raised his hat, muttered something quite incomprehensible, and vanished. She went up to her daughter.

'Gemma, please tell me ...'

The girl rose abruptly and embraced her.

'Mother dear, can you wait just a little while, just a tiny little while ... till tomorrow? Can you? And not a word about it all until tomorrow? Oh!'

She suddenly burst into a flood of radiant, and for her quite unexpected, tears. This astonished Frau Lenore all the more because the expression on Gemma's face far from being sad in fact looked joyful.

'What's the matter with you? You, who never weep, and now suddenly ...'

'It's nothing, Mother, nothing. Just you wait. We must both wait. Don't ask me about anything until tomorrow – and let us sort out the cherries before the sun goes down.'

'But you are going to be sensible?'

'Oh, I am always sensible.' Gemma nodded her head wisely. She began tying the cherries into little bunches, holding them up high in front of her face which was blushing faintly. She did not wipe away the tears; they dried of their own accord.

## XXV

Sanin almost ran back to his lodgings. He felt, he knew, that only here, alone with himself, would illumination come and he would discover what was happening to him. And so it was. He had hardly entered the room, had barely had time to sit down at the writing desk before he exclaimed, in a dull and mournful voice, his elbows on the desk and with both palms pressed to his face: 'I love her, I love her madly.' At that moment, everything within him burst into a glow, like coal from which the layer of dead ashes has suddenly been blown away. Only one instant ... and he was no longer capable of understanding how it had been possible that he had been sitting next to her – to her! and talking to her, without feeling that he worshipped the hem of her dress, that he was ready, as the young men put it, 'to die at her feet'.

That last meeting in the garden had decided everything. When he thought of it now, he no longer pictured her with her hair all blown about under the light of the stars. He saw her seated on the bench. He saw her throw back her hat with a sudden movement and look at him so trustingly – and the fever and the longing of love coursed through all his veins. He remembered the rose which he had been carrying in his pocket since the day before. He pulled it out and pressed it to his lips with such feverish strength that he involuntarily flinched with pain. He was no longer debating anything inwardly, no longer reflecting, calculating, looking ahead. He had left the past entirely behind him, he had taken a leap forward: he had plunged headlong off the dreary shores of his solitary bachelor life into a gay, bubbling and mighty flood. Never mind what grief it might bring, never a thought for where the flood would carry him or indeed for the possibility that it would dash him to pieces against a cliff! Here were no longer the quiet streams of the Uhland Romanze which had lulled him not so long ago. Here were mighty waves which could not be restrained; they were flying, racing forward, and he along with them.

He took a sheet of paper and, without making a single blot, scarcely lifting the pen from the paper, he wrote the following:

Dear Gemma,

You know what advice I undertook to urge upon you, you know what your mother wants, and what she asked me to do. What you do not know, and what I am now in duty bound to tell you, is that I love you, love you with all the passion of a heart that has felt love for the first time. This fire has flared up within me suddenly, but with such force, that I cannot find words! When your mother came to me and made her request, the fire was only just smouldering within me – otherwise, as an honest man, I would certainly have refused to carry out her wishes ... the admission which I am now making to you is the admission of an honest man. It is essential for you to know with whom you are dealing – there must be no misunderstanding between us. You see now that I can give you no advice of any kind ... I love you, I love you, I love you – and there is nothing else in me, in my mind or in my heart.

D. Sanin

Having folded and sealed this note, Sanin at first thought of ringing for the waiter and sending it by him ... but no, that seemed a little embarrassing. Send it with Emil? But to go to the store and search for him among the other shop assistants was also embarrassing. Besides, it was already dark and Emil would probably have left. For all these reflections, Sanin nevertheless put on his hat and went out into the street. He turned one corner and then another and – to his boundless delight – saw Emil in front of him. A satchel under his arm and a roll of paper in his hand, the young enthusiast was hurrying homewards.

'It is not for nothing that they say that every lover has his lucky star,' thought Sanin and called out to Emil.

The boy turned and immediately rushed at Sanin.

Sanin cut short his raptures, gave him the note, and explained to whom and in what manner it was to be delivered. Emil listened attentively.

'You want no one to see me deliver it?' he asked, assuming a purposeful and mysterious expression, as if to say, We understand all about this affair!

'Yes, my dear boy,' said Sanin, who was beginning to feel slightly awkward, but nonetheless patted Emil's cheek ... 'and if there should be an answer ... you will bring me the answer, won't you? I will stay in.'

'Oh, you need not worry about that,' Emil whispered gaily and ran off, nodding to him once again as he ran.

Sanin returned to his room, threw himself on the divan without lighting the candles, put his arms above his head, and abandoned himself to those sensations of newly apprehended love which it is pointless to describe. He who has experienced them knows their languor and sweetness; there is no way of explaining them to one who has not.

The door opened and Emil's head appeared.

'I've brought it,' he said in a whisper. 'Here it is, the answer.' He raised a folded paper above his head and showed it to Sanin.

Sanin leapt from the divan, and snatched the note from Emil's hand. His ardour was by now deeply aroused and he had no time for concealment or keeping up the politenesses, even in front of this boy, her brother. Had he but been in a state to observe such proprieties, his conscience would have pricked him, and he would have forced himself to be more

restrained. He went to the window, and by the light of the
street lamp, which stood immediately in front of the building,
he read the following lines:

I ask you, I beg of you – *not to come to us the whole of
tomorrow, not to make an appearance*. This is necessary to me,
absolutely necessary, everything will be decided then. I know
you will not refuse me this request, because ...

                                                    Gemma


Sanin read the note through twice – how touching, sweet
and beautiful her handwriting seemed to him. Then he
thought for a moment, turned to Emil (who, in order to
convey what a tactful young man he was, was standing with
his face to the wall and excavating it with his fingernail) and
called his name loudly.

Emil immediately ran up to him.

'Sir?'

'Listen, my friend ...'

'Monsieur Dmitry,' Emil interrupted in a piteous voice,
'why do you not say *tu* to me?'

Sanin laughed.

'Oh, very well. Listen, my friend.' (Emil gave a little jump
of joy at the sound of the word *écoute*.) 'Listen to me. Over
*there*, you understand, you are to say that everything will be
carried out to the letter.' (Emil pursed his lips and nodded
importantly.) 'As for yourself – what are you doing
tomorrow?'

'I? What am I doing? What do you wish me to do?'

'If you are allowed to, come here in the morning early, and
we shall go for a walk in the neighbourhood of Frankfurt until
evening. Would you like that?'

Emil gave another jump.

'Good gracious, as if there could be anything better in the
world! To go walking with you – but that will be simply
marvellous! I will certainly come.'

'And what if they don't let you?'

'They'll let me all right!'

'Listen. Don't say anything *there* about the fact that I have asked you to go for a whole day's walk.'

'Why should I say anything? I'll simply slip away. I don't care!'

Emil imprinted a great kiss on Sanin and ran off.

As for Sanin, he walked about the room for a long time and went to bed late. He abandoned himself to the same sensations as before, in which apprehension was mingled with sweetness, and to the same joyful trepidation in the face of a new life. Sanin was very pleased that he had thought of asking Emil to spend the following day with him: the boy was like his sister to look at. He will remind me of her, he thought.

But what surprised him more than anything was to think that he could have felt differently yesterday from the way he felt today. It seemed to him that he had loved Gemma since the beginning of time – and had loved her exactly in the way in which he loved her now.

## XXVI

The following morning, at eight o'clock, Emil reported to Sanin with Tartaglia on a lead. He could not have carried out his instructions more meticulously had he been a born German. He had lied at home. He had said that he was going for a walk with Sanin before breakfast and would then go on to the shop. While Sanin was dressing, Emil touched on the subject of Gemma and of the broken engagement to Herr Klueber – though he did so rather hesitantly. Sanin met this with grim silence and Emil, having indicated by his expression that he understood the reason why so important a topic should not be broached in so light a fashion, returned to it no more. But from time to time he assumed a look of concentration, even of severity.

Having finished their coffee, the two friends set off – on foot, of course – for Hausen, a little village surrounded by woods not very far from Frankfurt. The whole Taunus mountain range is visible from there, as if spread out on the palm of one's hand. The weather was superb: the sun was bright and warming, but not oppressive. A fresh breeze rustled vigorously among the green leaves. The shadows of little round clouds high up in the sky glided swiftly and gracefully across the ground, forming small dark patches. The young men soon left the town behind them and stepped out gaily and energetically along the well-swept road.

They went into a wood and spent a long time wandering around in it. Then they ate a very solid breakfast in a village inn; then they climbed up hills, admired the views, rolled stones and clapped their hands at the amusing and strange way in which the stones bobbed about like rabbits – until a passer-by down below, whom they had not seen, abused them roundly in a ringing voice. Then they lay outstretched on some dry, short moss of a yellowish-violet colour; then they drank beer at another inn, then they raced and made bets on who could jump farthest. They discovered an echo, and had a conversation with it, they sang, they yodelled, they wrestled; they broke off branches, they decorated their hats with ferns, and they even danced. Tartaglia participated in all these activities to the best of his ability. It is true that he did not throw any stones, but he dashed down headlong after them, howled when the young men sang, and even drank beer, though with evident disgust. (He had been taught this art by a student to whom he had once belonged.) He was not, incidentally, very obedient to Emil – it was very different when his master Pantaleone gave the orders. When Emil ordered him to 'talk' or to 'sneeze' all he did was wag his tail and stick his tongue out in a little roll.

The young people also talked. At the beginning of the walk, Sanin, as the older of the two and the better informed, started a conversation on such subjects as Fate and predetermined Destiny and the meaning of a man's Calling and in what it consisted. But the discussion soon took a less serious turn. Emil began questioning his friend and protector about Russia, about the way they fought duels there, and whether the women were beautiful, and whether the Russian language could be learned quickly, and what Sanin felt when the officer was aiming his pistol at him.

Sanin in turn questioned Emil about his father, his mother and their family affairs, trying in every way not to mention Gemma's name and thinking of nothing but her. Strictly speaking, he was not really thinking about her, but about the following day, that mysterious morrow that was to bring him undreamed-of happiness, such as had never been known before. It was as if a curtain, a thin, light, slightly swaying curtain, was suspended before his mind's eye – and beyond the curtain he sensed ... he sensed the presence of a young, quite motionless, divine image with a gentle smile on its lips, the lashes lowered severely, but with mocking severity. And this image was not Gemma's face – it was the face of happiness itself – and now at last *his* hour has struck, the curtain sweeps upwards, the lips open, the eyelashes are raised – and his divinity has seen him and there is light like the light of the sun, and delight and ecstasy without end! He thinks of this morrow – and once again his soul is still with joy and elation – waiting and longing, waiting and longing!

And this waiting and longing is in no wise disturbing. It is with him all the time – and makes no difference of any kind. It does not stop him from enjoying an excellent lunch with Emil in yet a third inn. Just occasionally, like a brief flash of lightning, the thought would strike him: just suppose that anyone in the whole world knew about it all? His longing does not stop him from playing leap-frog with Emil after luncheon. The game takes place in a small, open green field ... Imagine Sanin's astonishment and confusion when, to the accompaniment of Tartaglia's shrill bark, he has just taken a flying leap with his legs apart, over the crouching Emil, and suddenly sees in front of him, at the very edge of the green field, two officers whom he immediately recognizes as yesterday's adversary and his second – Herr von Doenhof and Herr von Richter! Each officer fixes a piece of glass in his eye and grins ... Sanin falls on his feet, turns away, quickly puts on his topcoat which he had cast aside, and utters a curt word to Emil. Emil also puts on his jacket, and the two of them immediately make themselves scarce.

They returned to Frankfurt very late.

'They will scold me,' Emil told Sanin as they parted, 'but what does it matter? I have spent such a wonderful, wonderful day!'

When he returned to his hotel, Sanin found a note from Gemma. In it she appointed a meeting for the following day, at seven o'clock in the morning, in one of the many public parks with which Frankfurt is surrounded.

Oh, how his heart jumped! How glad he was that he had obeyed her so implicitly. And, dear God, what was in store for him ...? what was in store for him on this morrow, this unprecedented, unique and impossible – and never-to-be doubted morrow?

His eyes devoured Gemma's note. The long and eloquent tail of the letter G, the initial of her name, which was at the bottom of the sheet of paper, reminded him of her lovely fingers, of her hand. The thought crossed his mind that he had not once touched this hand with his lips ...

Italian women, he thought, in spite of their reputation, are modest and strictly behaved ... And Gemma above all! An Empress – a goddess – marble, pure and virginal – but the day will come – and it is not far off ...

There was one happy man that night in Frankfurt. He slept, but he could have said of himself in the words of the poet:

'I sleep ... but ever wakes my sentient heart!'

And his heart beat as gently as the wings of a moth which is clinging to a flower and is drenched with the rays of the summer sun.

## XXVII

Sanin woke at five and was dressed by six. At half past six, he was already walking in the public garden within sight of the small summerhouse which Gemma had mentioned in her note.

It was a quiet, warm, grey morning. Sometimes it seemed as if it was going to rain any moment, but if one stretched out a hand one could feel nothing, and it was only when one looked at one's sleeve that one noticed traces of tiny drops like the smallest of beads; but that stopped very soon. As for wind – it was as if there had never been any wind in the whole world. Sounds did not so much fly through the air as flow in enveloping waves. In the distance, white mist was forming, and there was the scent of mignonette and white acacia flowers all around.

The shops in the street were still closed, but a few people had already appeared. Occasionally the sounds of a solitary carriage could be heard ... There were no visitors in the park. A gardener was scraping the path in a desultory manner with a spade, and a decrepit old woman in a black cloak hobbled across an alley. Not for a moment could Sanin have mistaken this poor creature for Gemma, but for all that his heart jumped, and his eyes followed with close attention the black shape disappearing into the distance.

Seven o'clock. The hours boomed from a near-by tower.

Sanin stopped in his tracks. Was she not coming then? A cold shiver suddenly ran through him. A few moments later he felt the same cold shiver, but for another reason. He heard a light footstep behind him, and the soft rustle of a woman's clothes ... He turned – it was she!

Gemma was walking along the path behind him. She was wearing a light grey mantle and a small dark hat. She glanced at Sanin and averted her head – and, as she drew level with him, walked briskly past him.

'Gemma,' he murmured, almost inaudibly. She gave him a slight nod, and continued walking. He followed her.

He was breathing in gasps. His legs did not obey him very well.

Gemma passed the summerhouse, turned right, walked past a small shallow pond where a sparrow was busily preening itself, stepped behind a clump of tall lilacs, and sat down on a bench. It was a comfortable and well-sheltered spot. Sanin sat down beside her.

A minute went by – and neither spoke a word. She did not even look at him, and he did not look at her face, but at her folded hands in which she held a small umbrella. What was there to say? What words could be uttered which were not totally meaningless compared to the fact that they were here, alone, so early in the morning, so close together?

'You ... are not angry with me?' Sanin murmured at last.

It would have been difficult for Sanin to have said anything more stupid – he realized that himself – but at least the silence had been broken.

'I?' she replied. 'Why should I be? No.'

'And you believe me?' he continued.

'You mean what you wrote to me?'

'Yes.'

Gemma dropped her head and said nothing. The umbrella slipped from her hands. She hurriedly retrieved it before it fell.

'Oh, believe me, believe what I wrote to you!' Sanin exclaimed. His timidity had suddenly vanished and he spoke with passion. 'If there is any truth on this earth, any sacred truth which cannot be doubted, it is that I love you, love you passionately, Gemma!'

She threw him a brief sidelong glance, and once again nearly dropped her umbrella.

'Believe me, believe me,' he urged – he was imploring her, stretching out his hands towards her, not daring to touch her. 'What do you want me to do to convince you?'

She glanced at him again.

'Tell me, Monsieur Dmitry,' she began, 'the day before yesterday, when you came in order to persuade me, you did not know then ... did not feel ...?'

'Yes, I did feel it,' Sanin interrupted, 'but I did not know it. I loved you from the very first moment, but did not at once realize what you had come to mean to me. And besides, I learned that you were engaged to be married. As for carrying out your mother's request – well, in the first place, how could I refuse? And secondly, I think I passed on her message in such a manner that you could guess ...'

There came the sound of heavy footsteps, and a stout man, evidently a foreigner, with a travelling bag slung on his shoulder, appeared from behind the lilac bushes. With the lack of ceremony which revealed the visiting stranger, he eyed the couple on the bench, coughed loudly and went on his way.

'Your mother,' said Sanin, as soon as the sound of heavy feet was gone, 'told me that your breaking your engagement would cause a scandal' (Gemma frowned slightly), 'that it was I who had in some measure given cause for the unseemly gossip and that ... consequently ... to some extent ... it was my duty to persuade you not to break your engagement to marry ... Herr Klueber.'

'Monsieur Dmitry,' said Gemma, passing her hand over her hair on the side closest to Sanin, 'please do not refer to my engagement to marry Herr Klueber. I will never be his wife. I have refused him.'

'You have refused him? When?'

'Yesterday.'

'You told him this to his face?'

'Yes. At our house. He called.'

'Gemma! That means you love me?'

She turned towards him.

'Otherwise ... would I have come here?' she whispered, and let both her hands fall on the bench.

Sanin seized those listless hands as they lay, palms upwards, and pressed them to his eyes, to his lips ... This was the moment when the curtain, which he had kept seeing the day before, swept up. Here it is, here is happiness with its radiant countenance!

He raised his head and looked at Gemma boldly, straight in the eyes. She was looking at him, too – with a slightly downward glance. There was scarcely any lustre in her half-closed eyes: they were flooded with shining tears of joy. But her face was not smiling ... No! It was laughing, with soundless laughter that was also the laughter of bliss.

He wanted to draw her to his breast, but she resisted him, and, still laughing silently, shook her head. 'Wait,' her happy eyes seemed to be saying.

'Gemma!' Sanin exclaimed. 'Could I have ever imagined that you' (his heart vibrated like a string when his lips first formed the word *tu*), 'that you would love me!'

'I did not expect it myself,' Gemma said quietly.

'How could I ever have thought,' Sanin went on, 'how could I ever have thought, as I drove into Frankfurt, where I only intended to stay for a few hours, that I should find happiness here for the whole of my life!'

'For the whole of your life? Is that really true?'

'Yes, for the whole of my life, for ever and for all time!' cried Sanin with a new burst of emotion.

The gardener's spade could suddenly be heard scraping a few paces away from the bench where they sat.

'Let us go home,' Gemma whispered, 'let us go together. *Veux tu?*'

If at that moment she had said to him, 'Throw yourself into the sea – *veux tu?*' she would hardly have had time to complete the second syllable before he would have been flying headlong into the depths of the ocean.

They left the garden together and set off for the house, not by the town streets but through the outskirts.


## XXVIII

Sanin sometimes walked by Gemma's side, sometimes a little behind her. He never once took his eyes off her, and never stopped smiling. As for her – at times she seemed to be hurrying, at times about to stop. Truth to tell, both of them – he all pale, she all pink with excitement – moved forward as in a trance. What they had done together a few moments before, this mutual surrender of one soul to another, was so shattering, so novel, so disturbing. Everything in their lives had changed and had been re-ordered so suddenly that neither had yet regained composure. They were only conscious of the sudden rush of wind which had swept them away, like the powerful gust which a few nights ago had all but hurled them into each other's arms. As Sanin walked, he felt that he was even looking at Gemma in a different manner: he instantly noted certain characteristics of her gait, her way of moving, and oh, dear God, how infinitely precious and delectable they seemed to him! And she in turn sensed that he was looking at her 'like that'.

Sanin and Gemma were in love for the first time, and all the miracles of first love were happening for them. First love is exactly like a revolution: the regular and established order of life is in an instant smashed to fragments; youth stands at the barricade, its bright banner raised high in the air, and sends its ecstatic greetings to the future, whatever it may hold – death or a new life, no matter.

'Look – surely that is our old man?' said Sanin, pointing at a muffled-up figure which was quickly edging its way along, as if trying to remain unnoticed. In his state of overflowing bliss, Sanin felt the need to talk to Gemma about something other than love – love was a settled and holy matter.

'Yes, that is Pantaleone,' Gemma replied gaily and happily. 'I expect he left the house with the intention of following me. He was already watching every step I took yesterday. He has guessed!'

'He has guessed!' repeated the enraptured Sanin. Was there anything that Gemma could have said that would not have sent him into raptures?

Then he asked her to tell him in detail everything that had occurred the day before.

She immediately began her account, hurriedly and in some confusion, smiling, periodically uttering brief little sighs, and exchanging quick, radiant glances with Sanin. She told him that after their conversation of the day before yesterday, her mother had persistently tried to elicit something definite from

her, Gemma, and she had avoided the importunities of Frau
Lenore by promising to reveal her decision within twenty-
four hours; how she had begged for this delay and how
difficult it had been to get her mother to agree to it; how Herr
Klueber had appeared quite unexpectedly, looking more
pompous and starched than ever; how he had declared his
indignation over the puerile, and unforgivable and for him,
Klueber, deeply insulting (this was his actual expression)
escapade of the Russian stranger ('he meant *ton duel*') and how
he demanded that the door of the house should be *te défendu*.
'Because,' added Herr Klueber – and at this moment Gemma
gave a slight imitation of his voice and manner – 'this casts a
reflection on my honour. As if I could not have intervened to
protect my fiancée had I considered this course necessary or
desirable! The whole of Frankfurt will know tomorrow that
some stranger fought a duel with an officer over my fiancée –
what a state of affairs! It is a stain on my honour!'

'Mother was agreeing with him – just imagine! But at this
point I suddenly declared that he was wasting his efforts in
worrying about his honour and his position in the matter, that
he had no reason to be affronted by any gossip about his
fiancée, since I was no longer engaged to be married to him
and would never be his wife! I confess that I had wanted to
have a talk *avec vous ... avec toi* – before finally breaking off
the engagement; but he came ... and I just could not restrain
myself... Mother was so frightened that she even began to
shout, and I went into the other room and fetched his ring –
you did not notice that I stopped wearing this ring two days
ago – and gave it to him. He was terribly offended. But he is
so vain and so self-opinionated that he did not want to discuss
the matter any further and left. As you can imagine, I had a
very difficult time with Mother, and it distressed me greatly
to see her so upset. I even thought that I had been somewhat
hasty, but I already had your note – and in any case, I knew
without it ...'

'That I love you,' Sanin interrupted.

'Yes – that you had fallen in love with me.'

Such was Gemma's account, told with a good deal of confusion. She smiled as she talked, and lowered her voice or became completely silent every time anyone came towards her or passed her on the way. And Sanin listened in a state of euphoria, delighting in the sound of her voice, much as he had doted on her handwriting the day before.

'Mother is extraordinarily upset,' Gemma began again, her words tumbling out one after another with great rapidity. 'She simply will not even consider that Herr Klueber could have become repugnant to me, that in any case I was not marrying him for love, but because of her persistent pleas ... She suspects ... *vous ... toi* ... to put it plainly, she is certain that I have fallen in love with you. This is all the more painful to her because the day before yesterday this possibility had not even occurred to her, and she had even commissioned you to persuade me. It was rather a strange commission, was it not? Now she has honoured *toi ... vous* ... with the title of a man of cunning, of a deceiver, and says that you betrayed her trust and warns me that you will deceive me ...'

'But Gemma,' Sanin exclaimed, 'surely you told her ... ?'

'I told her nothing. What right had I to tell her anything before I had discussed it *avec vous?*'

Sanin actually wrung his hands with agitation.

'Gemma, I hope that now at any rate you will admit everything to her, that you will take me to her. I want to prove to your mother that I am not a deceiver.'

Sanin's breast was literally heaving from the onrush of noble, fiery emotions.

Gemma looked him full in the face.

'You (*vous*) really want to go and see Mother with me now? Mother, who keeps saying that all that kind of thing is impossible between us ... and can never take place?'

There was one word which Gemma could not bring herself to utter ... it scorched her lips; but Sanin pronounced the word all the more readily.

'To marry you, Gemma, to become your husband – I can imagine no greater happiness.'

He could now no longer conceive of any limits to his love, to his magnanimity, or to his resolution!

When she heard these words, Gemma who had almost stopped for a moment, now walked on faster ... it was as if she wished to run away from this too great and too unexpected happiness.

Suddenly her legs swayed beneath her. From round the corner of a side street, a few steps in front of her, attired in a new hat and short overcoat, straight as a ramrod and curled like a poodle, there appeared the figure of Herr Klueber. He saw Gemma and he saw Sanin – and then gave a kind of inward smirk. With a backward bend of his elegant trunk, he walked towards them with an air of bravura. Sanin was momentarily disconcerted. But then he glanced at the Klueber face to which its owner was trying, within the limits of his ability, to give an expression of contemptuous surprise and even condolence, and the sight of this pink, common face suddenly threw him into a rage. Sanin stepped forward.

Gemma seized his arm, put her arm through it with quiet determination, and looked her former betrothed straight in the face. Klueber narrowed his eyes, hunched his shoulders, stepped quickly aside, muttered through his teeth, 'That's the way the song usually ends' (*Das alte Ende vom Liede*), and went on his way with the same air of bravura and with a slight spring in his gait.

'What did the scoundrel say?' asked Sanin and was about to rush after him. But Gemma stopped him and they walked on. She did not remove her arm from his.

The Roselli establishment appeared in front of them. Gemma stopped once again.

'Dmitry, Monsieur Dmitry,' she said, 'we have not yet entered the house, we have not yet seen Mother ... If you (*vous*) want to think it over, if ... you are still free, Dmitry.'

Instead of replying, Sanin pressed her hand very tightly to his breast and drew her onwards.

'Mother,' said Gemma as they entered the room where Frau Lenore was sitting, 'I have brought the real one!'

# XXIX

Had Gemma announced that she had brought along the cholera or even death itself, Frau Lenore could not conceivably have received the news with greater despair. She immediately sat down in a corner with her face to the wall, burst into a flood of tears and almost began to keen, for all the world like a Russian peasant woman at the side of her husband's or son's coffin. To begin with Gemma was so much put out that she did not even go up to her mother, but stood as still as a statue in the centre of the room. Sanin was completely at a loss and very nearly ready to burst into tears himself. This disconsolate weeping went on for a whole hour, for a whole, entire hour!

Pantaleone thought it wise to lock the outer door of the patisserie in case some stranger should come in, although happily it was still early morning. The old man was himself a bit put out. He did not approve of the haste with which Gemma and Sanin had acted, but he was reluctant to condemn them and was ready, in case of need, to give them his support – his dislike for Klueber was so strong. Emil saw himself as the intermediary between his sister and Sanin, and was really rather proud of the fact that everything had succeeded so magnificently. He simply could not understand Frau Lenore's desolation, and decided there and then that women, even the best of them, suffer from the lack of capacity for rational judgement. Sanin was the worst off of all. As soon as he approached Frau Lenore, she raised a great outcry and waved him away with her arms. His efforts on several occasions to pronounce in a loud voice, stationed at a distance, 'I ask for the hand of your daughter,' were completely in vain. Frau Lenore particularly could not forgive herself for the fact that she 'had been so blind', that she 'had seen nothing'. 'If only my Giovan' Battista had been alive,' she kept repeating through her tears, 'nothing of the kind could have happened!' Heavens! What is all this about? Sanin thought to himself.

This is absolutely preposterous! He dared not look at
Gemma, nor did she have the courage to raise her eyes to
glance at him. She contented herself with patiently looking
after her mother, who at first pushed even her aside.

At long last, the storm began to abate. Frau Lenore
stopped weeping, allowed Gemma to ease her out of the
corner in which she had immured herself, to settle her in an
armchair near the window, and to give her a drink of water
flavoured with orange blossom. She suffered Sanin – not to
approach her, oh no – but at least to remain in the room (up
till then, she had kept on demanding that he should leave) and
did not interrupt him.

Sanin immediately made the most of the calm which had
descended, and displayed amazing eloquence: he would
hardly have been capable of expounding his intentions and his
feelings to Gemma herself with such fervour and with such
conviction. These feelings were of the most sincere quality
and the intentions of the very purest – like those of Almaviva
in the 'Barber of Seville'. He did not conceal either from Frau
Lenore or from himself the disadvantageous aspects of these
intentions; but these disadvantages were more apparent than
real! True, he was a foreigner, one with whom they had only
recently become acquainted, and of whose person and property they had no certain information. But he was prepared to
adduce all the necessary proof that he was of respectable
character, and not without means: he would call in aid the
most incontrovertible evidence of his compatriots. He hoped
that Gemma would be happy with him, and that he would
find a way of making the separation from her family less
painful. The mention of separation – the very word
'separation' – nearly spoiled the whole business. Frau Lenore
was thrown into a tremble of agitation. Sanin hastened to
point out that the separation would only be a temporary one –
and indeed that perhaps, in the end, there would be no need
for any separation at all!

His eloquence was not in vain. Frau Lenore began to cast
glances at him which, although still full of grief and reproach,

were no longer charged with rage and repugnance. Then she allowed him to approach her, and even to sit down at her side. (Gemma was sitting on the other side.) Then she began to reproach him – not with looks alone, but in words, which clearly indicated a certain softening in her attitude. She began to complain, and her complaints became quieter and gentler. They were interspersed with questions addressed now to Sanin, now to her daughter. Then she allowed him to take her hand, and did not immediately snatch it away ... Then she burst into tears again, but they were tears of quite a different kind ... Then she smiled sadly and expressed regret at the absence of Giovan' Battista, but already in quite a different sense from before ... Another instant passed – and both criminals, Sanin and Gemma, were kneeling at her feet, and she was placing her hands on the head of each in turn. Then, after another moment, they were embracing and kissing her, and Emil, his face radiant with delight, came running into the room and threw himself at this closely united family group.

Pantaleone glanced into the room, gave a combined smirk and frown, then went into the patisserie and unlocked the street door.

## XXX

Frau Lenore's transition from despair to sadness, and from sadness to quiet resignation, took place fairly rapidly. But before long the quiet resignation was swiftly transformed into secret satisfaction. However, for the sake of decency, this was concealed and restrained in every way. Frau Lenore had very much taken to Sanin from the first day of their acquaintance. Having once got used to the idea that he was to be her son-in-law, she no longer found the prospect altogether unpleasing, though she considered it her duty to preserve an expression of affront – or perhaps rather of concern – on her face. Besides, everything that had happened in the last few days had been so extraordinary ... One thing led to another!

As a practical woman and as a mother, Frau Lenore also

considered it her duty to submit Sanin to all kinds of questions. Sanin, who had had no thought of marriage in his mind when he had set out that morning to meet Gemma – truth to tell, he had thought of nothing at all at the time, and simply surrendered himself to the driving force of passion – very readily, and indeed enthusiastically, entered into the part of the future husband. He willingly answered the interrogation to which he was submitted, with full and circumstantial details. Frau Lenore first satisfied herself that he was a genuine member of the nobility by right of birth, and even expressed some slight surprise that he was not a prince. She then put on a serious mien and gave him 'fair warning' that she would speak frankly and without ceremony, since she was bound to do so by her sacred duty as a mother. To this, Sanin replied that he had indeed expected nothing else from her, and most earnestly requested her not to spare him.

Thereupon Frau Lenore remarked that Herr Klueber (at the mention of the name she gave a slight sigh, pursed her lips and hesitated for a moment), that Herr Klueber, Gemma's *former* fiancé, was already in possession of an income of eight thousand guldens, and that this income would increase rapidly year by year. And what might Monsieur Sanin's income be?

'Eight thousand guldens,' Sanin repeated the words meditatively, 'in our money that is around fifteen thousand paper roubles ... My income is considerably less. I have a small estate in Tula province ... if properly run, it can yield ... indeed, it certainly must yield, five or six thousand ... And then if I take an appointment in the public service, I can easily earn a salary of about two thousand.'

'Service in Russia?' exclaimed Frau Lenore. 'That means I shall be parted from Gemma!'

'It will be possible for me to arrange to enter the diplomatic service,' Sanin interjected quickly. 'I have certain connections ... It will then be possible for me to serve abroad. And here is another idea – and that is far and away the best plan: sell my estate and invest the capital in some lucrative undertaking.

For instance, we could use it to make a going concern of your patisserie.'

Sanin knew that he was talking nonsense, but he was possessed by an incomprehensible foolhardiness. One glance at Gemma (who, as soon as the 'practical' discussion began, kept on rising from her chair, walking about the room and sitting down again) – one glance at Gemma, and all difficulties vanished. He was ready to arrange everything straight away in the best possible manner, to do anything to stop her worrying.

'Herr Klueber also wished to give me a small sum for the improvement of the patisserie,' said Frau Lenore after a moment's hesitation.

'Mother! For God's sake! Mother!' Gemma cried in Italian.

'It is necessary that these things should be discussed in good time, my daughter,' replied Frau Lenore in the same language. She turned once again to Sanin, and began questioning him about the law relating to marriage in Russia, and in particular whether there were any difficulties in the way of a Russian marrying a Catholic, as there were in Prussia. (At that date, in 1840, the whole of Germany still remembered the quarrel between the Prussian Government and the Archbishop of Cologne on the subject of mixed marriages.) But when Frau Lenore learned that, by marrying a Russian nobleman, her daughter would herself become a member of the nobility, she showed some signs of pleasure.

'But surely it will be necessary for you first to return to Russia?'

'Why?'

'Surely, to obtain permission from your Emperor?'

Sanin explained that this was quite unnecessary. He went on to say that he might indeed have to pay a very brief visit to Russia before the wedding. (Even as he spoke the words, his heart was wrenched with grief, and Gemma, who was watching him, guessed what he felt, blushed and became pensive.) He would try to use his time in Russia to sell his estate ... but in any case he would obtain the money that was necessary.

'I should be grateful if you would bring me back some good Astrakhan lambskins for a cape,' said Frau Lenore. 'According to what I hear, they are remarkably good there, and remarkably cheap.'

'Certainly, with the greatest of pleasure, I will bring some for you and for Gemma,' exclaimed Sanin.

'And I would like a Morocco leather cap, embroidered with silver,' Emil interrupted, putting his head through the door from the next room.

'All right, you shall have one – and Pantaleone shall have some slippers.'

'Now, now what *is* all this about?' Frau Lenore remarked. 'We are discussing serious things now. But there is another matter,' added this practical lady, 'you say: sell your estate. But how will you do this? Do you mean that you will sell your peasants as well?'

Sanin felt as if he had been struck. He remembered that in the course of conversation with Signora Roselli and her daughter on the subject of serfdom in Russia, which, as he had told them, aroused in him feelings of the deepest indignation, he had assured them more than once that he would never contemplate selling his peasants for any consideration whatever, because he regarded such sales as immoral. He now spoke with some hesitation.

'I will try to sell my estate to someone whom I know to be a decent person, or perhaps the peasants will wish to redeem themselves.'

'That would be best of all,' Frau Lenore agreed, 'because really, the sale of live human beings ...'

'*Barbari!*' growled Pantaleone, who had made an appearance at the door after Emil, then shook his mane and disappeared.

This is a nasty business, Sanin thought to himself, and stole a glance at Gemma. She did not appear to have heard his last words. Well, that's all right! he thought again.

The practical conversation continued in this manner until it was almost lunchtime. In the end, Frau Lenore was quite softened. She was already calling Sanin 'Dmitry', shaking her finger at him affectionately, and promising to revenge herself on him for his treacheries. She asked him many detailed questions about his family, because 'this is also a very important matter'. She also made him describe to her the marriage ceremony according to the rites of the Russian Orthodox Church, and was delighted at the thought of Gemma in a white dress with a golden crown on her head.

'You know, she is as beautiful as a queen,' Signora Roselli spoke with a mother's pride, 'and indeed there is no queen in the world like her.'

'There is no other Gemma in the whole world!' Sanin cried out.

'Yes, that is the reason why she is Gemma.' (In Italian, of course, 'Gemma' means a precious stone.)

Gemma rushed to kiss her mother ... it was only now that she felt herself again, as if a crushing weight had been lifted from her heart.

As for Sanin, he suddenly felt overwhelmed with happiness. His heart was filled with childlike joy. To think that the dream in which he had indulged so short a while ago in these very rooms had come true, had actually come true! He was in such transports of rapture that he went straight to the shop: he was determined, whatever happened, to do some selling behind the counter, as he had done a few days before ... 'After all, I now have every right to do so! I am now one of the family!'

He actually took his place behind the counter, and actually did some selling – that is to say, he sold a pound of sweets to two girls who came in, giving them fully two pounds in weight and charging them only half the price.

At lunch, he sat next to Gemma by right of his status as her betrothed. Frau Lenore continued with her practical reflections. Emil kept on laughing, and pestered Sanin to take him with him to Russia. It was decided that Sanin would leave for Russia in two weeks' time. Only Pantaleone looked gloomy, so much so that even Frau Lenore said to him reproachfully, 'And to think that he even acted as second!' Pantaleone glared at her from under his thick eyebrows.

Gemma was silent most of the time, but her face had never been more radiant or beautiful. After lunch she called Sanin into the garden for a moment and, stopping at the same bench where she had sat picking over the cherries two days before, said:

'Dmitry, do not be angry with me, but I want to remind you again that you must not regard yourself as bound ...'

He would not let her finish.

Gemma turned her face aside.

'And about what Mother mentioned, the difference in our faith, do you remember? Well, look' – she seized a small garnet cross which hung on a thin cord about her neck, and pulled at it sharply. The cord broke, and she handed him the little cross.

'If I am yours, then your faith is my faith.'

Sanin's eyes were still moist when he returned with Gemma to the house.

By the evening everything was normal again. They even played a few hands of *tresette*.


## XXXI

Sanin awoke very early next day. He was at the very pinnacle of human well-being, but it was not for this reason that he had been unable to sleep longer. One question had disturbed his rest – a question of life and destiny: how was he to sell his estate for the best possible price, and at the earliest possible moment? All kinds of plans kept forming in his mind, but so far he could not see his way clearly. He went out of the hotel into the street to clear his brain and for a breath of air. He wanted to appear before Gemma with a cut-and-dried plan – nothing else would do.

*

Now whose is this thick-legged solid figure walking in front of him, actually quite well dressed, rolling from side to side as it hobbles along? Where had he seen the back of that head, thickly thatched with flaxen-coloured hair? Where had he seen that head which looked as if it had been set straight on to the shoulders, and that soft, fat back, and those puffy hands, dangling limply? Could it be – could it be Polozov, his schoolmate of long ago, whom he had completely lost sight of for five years? Sanin overtook the figure in front of him and turned to look back ... He saw a broad, yellowish face with small pig's eyes and white eyebrows and lashes, a short, flat nose, thick lips which looked as if they had been stuck together, a round, hairless chin, and that expression on the face, a bit sour, lazy and suspicious – there was no doubt, it was he, Ippolit Polozov. 'Perhaps my lucky star is at work again!' flashed through Sanin's mind.

'Polozov! Ippolit Sidorych! Is that really you?'

The figure stopped in its tracks, raised its tiny eyes, waited a little – and then, at last, having unstuck its lips, spoke in a hoarse falsetto.

'Dmitry Sanin?'

'None other,' exclaimed Sanin, and wrung one of Polozov's hands. Encased in ash-coloured smooth-fitting kid gloves, they hung as before, lifelessly against his rotund thighs. 'Have you been here long? Where have you come from? Where are you staying?'

'I arrived yesterday from Wiesbaden,' Polozov replied unhurriedly, 'to do some shopping for my wife, and I am returning to Wiesbaden this very day.'

'Oh, of course, you are married – and they say to a great beauty.'

Polozov made a sideward movement with his eyes.

'Yes, so they say.'

Sanin laughed. 'I see you are still the same – as phlegmatic as you were at school.'

'Why should I change?'

'And they say,' Sanin added, placing a special emphasis on the word 'say', 'that your wife is very rich.'

'Yes, they say that too.'

'But surely you know all about this yourself, Ippolit Sidorych?'

'My friend Dmitry ... Pavlovich – yes, it is Pavlovich – I don't meddle in my wife's affairs.'

'You don't meddle? Not in any of her affairs?'

Polozov made the same movement with his eyes.

'None at all, my friend. She goes her way, and – well – I go mine.'

'And where are you going now?' Sanin asked.

'I am going nowhere at the moment: I am standing in the street talking to you. But when we have finished our conversation, I shall go to my hotel and have luncheon.'

'Would you like to have me as a companion?'

'Do you mean as a companion for luncheon?'

'Yes.'

'By all means, it is much more convivial to eat *à deux*. You are not a chatterbox, I take it?'

'I don't think so.'

'Well, all right then.'

Polozov moved forward. Sanin followed at his side. Polozov's lips were stuck together again; he kept silent and rolled along, wheezing. Meanwhile Sanin was thinking to himself. How on earth had this oaf succeeded in landing a beautiful and rich wife? He was neither rich nor famous nor clever. At school he had been considered a dull and dreary boy, sleepy and gluttonous. His nickname had been 'Dribbler'. Wonders would never cease!

'But if his wife is really very rich – they say her father owned state concessions – maybe she will buy my estate? Although he says that he does not interfere in any of his wife's affairs, one can scarcely believe that. Besides, I will ask an attractive price which will give her some profit. Why shouldn't I try? Perhaps this is my lucky star again ... So be it! I will try.'

Polozov led Sanin towards one of the best hotels in Frankfurt, in which, of course, he had taken the best room.

On the tables and chairs there were heaped boxes, parcels and cartons ... 'These are all purchases for Maria Nikolaevna, my friend.' (That was the name of Polozov's wife.) Polozov sank into an easy chair, groaned, 'Oh, this heat,' and unknotted his neck-tie. Then he rang for the head waiter and ordered an elaborate luncheon with many detailed instructions. 'And my carriage is to be ready at one o'clock. Do you hear, at one o'clock sharp!'

The head waiter bowed obsequiously, and vanished like the perfect slave. Polozov unbuttoned his waistcoat. From the very way in which he raised his eyebrows, puffed and wrinkled his nose, it was evident that all conversation was going to be a great effort to him, and that he was somewhat anxious to discover whether Sanin would force him to set his tongue in motion, or would take upon himself the whole burden of conducting the conversation.

Sanin sensed his companion's mood, and therefore did not tax him with too many questions. He restricted himself to discovering the necessary minimum: that Polozov had been in military service for two years (in the Light Cavalry, of all things – he must have been a pretty sight in a short tunic!), that he had married three years ago, and that he was already spending a second year abroad with his wife, 'who is now taking a cure for something or other in Wiesbaden', and was then going on to Paris. Sanin, for his part, was also not very communicative, either about his past life or his plans. He went straight to the point – that is to say he broached the question of his intention to sell his estate. Polozov listened silently, only now and again casting a glance at the door through which luncheon was due to appear. It arrived at last. The head waiter, accompanied by two other servants, brought in a few dishes, surmounted by silver covers.

'Is that your estate in Tula province?' Polozov asked, sitting down at the table and tucking a napkin into the collar of his shirt.

'Yes.'

'In the Efremov district ... I know it.'

'You mean you know my Alekseevka?' asked Sanin, also sitting down at the table.

'Yes, of course I know it.' Polozov stuffed a piece of truffle omelette into his mouth. 'Maria Nikolaevna, my wife, has an estate next to it. Waiter, open this bottle! It is quite a decent piece of land – only the peasants have cut down your forest. Why are you selling?'

'I need money, my friend, I am prepared to sell quite cheaply. Why don't you buy it, it is an opportunity ...'

Polozov swallowed a glass of wine, wiped his mouth with his napkin and once again resumed chewing – slowly and noisily.

'Hm – yes,' he said at last. 'I don't buy estates: I haven't any capital. Pass the butter, will you? My wife might buy it. You talk to her about it. If you don't ask too much, she likes that kind of thing ... But what asses these Germans are. They don't know how to boil fish. You would think it was the simplest thing in the world. And these are the people, if you please, who talk about the need to unite the *Vaterland*. Waiter, take this revolting stuff away.'

'But do you mean that your wife deals with these business matters herself?'

'Oh, yes. Now these cutlets are good. I recommend them ... I have told you, Sanin, that I don't meddle in any of my wife's affairs and I am telling you so again.'

Polozov continued to chew noisily.

'Hm ... But how can I discuss the matter with her?'

'Very simply. Go to Wiesbaden. It isn't far. Waiter, have you any English mustard? No? Animals! Only don't delay. We are leaving there the day after tomorrow. Let me pour you a glass of wine: it has bouquet, it isn't the usual vinegar.'

Polozov's face became animated and flushed: it only came to life when he was eating or drinking.

'Well, but ... I really don't know if I can do that ...' muttered Sanin.

'Anyway, what has suddenly happened to make you so desperate for money?'

'That's the whole point, I am desperate, my friend.'

'Do you need a large sum?'

'Yes – I – how should I say? I have it in mind to get married.'

Polozov put down the wine glass which he had been about to raise to his lips. 'Married!' he said in a hoarse voice, a voice which had turned hoarse from surprise, and folded his puffy hands on his stomach. 'And so precipitously?'

'Yes, quite soon.'

'The girl is in Russia, of course?'

'No, not in Russia.'

'Where then ?'

'Here, in Frankfurt ...'

'And who is she?'

'A German – that is to say not a German, an Italian, she lives here.'

'With capital?'

'No, without capital.'

'So it must be a case of being very seriously in love?'

'How odd you are! Yes, very seriously.'

'And that's what you need the money for?'

'Well, yes ... yes ...'

Polozov swallowed some wine, rinsed out his mouth, washed his hands and dried them carefully on his napkin, selected a cigar and lit it. Sanin watched him in silence.

'There is only one remedy,' Polozov boomed at last, throwing back his head and blowing out the smoke in a thin stream. 'Go and see my wife. If she is so inclined, she can resolve all your troubles with a wave of her hand.'

'But where am I to see your wife? You say that you are leaving the day after tomorrow?'

Polozov closed his eyes.

'Listen, do you know what I am going to suggest?' he said at last, turning his cigar around with his lips and sighing. 'You run off home, get yourself ready as quickly as you can, and then come back here. I leave at one o'clock, there is plenty of room in my carriage, and I will take you with me. That will be the best way. And now I am going to sleep. That is how it is, my friend: as soon as I have eaten, I must sleep without fail. Nature demands it, and indeed I don't resist her. And don't you disturb me.'

Sanin considered the matter for a while. Suddenly, he raised his head: he had made up his mind.

'All right, I agree. And thank you. I shall be back here at half past twelve, and we shall set off for Wiesbaden together. I hope that your wife will not be annoyed ...'

But Polozov was already wheezing. He murmured, 'Don't disturb me,' made a few movements with his legs and fell asleep like a baby.

Sanin threw another glance at the heavy figure, the head and neck, and the chin, raised high in the air and round as an apple. He then left the hotel and walked briskly towards the Roselli patisserie. Gemma had to be warned.


# XXXII

He found her with her mother in the front shop. Frau Lenore was bending down measuring the distance between the two windows with a small folding footrule. When she saw Sanin, she straightened up and greeted him gaily, but not without some slight hesitation.

'After what you said yesterday,' she began, 'I keep on turning over in my mind ideas for improving our shop. Here, for example, I think we should have two small cupboards with mirror shelves. You know, they are very fashionable now. And then ...'

'Splendid, splendid ...' Sanin interrupted. 'We must think about all that ... but come in here now, I have something to tell you.'

He took Frau Lenore and Gemma by the arm and led them into the next room. Frau Lenore was alarmed, and dropped the footrule. Gemma was also alarmed at first, but a closer look at Sanin reassured her. His face appeared worried, it was true, but at the same time it showed animation, confidence and resolution. He asked both ladies to be seated, and took up a position in front of them. Waving his arms in the air and ruffling his hair, he told them everything: his meeting with Polozov, his imminent visit to Wiesbaden, and the possibility of selling his estate.

'Just imagine my good fortune!' he exclaimed at last. 'Things have so turned out that it may well prove unnecessary for me to go to Russia. And we shall be able to arrange the wedding much sooner than I expected!'

'When do you have to leave?' asked Gemma.

'This very day, in an hour's time. My friend has hired a carriage, and will take me with him.'

'Will you write to us?'

'Immediately. As soon as I have had a talk with this lady, I will write at once.'

'This lady, you say, is very rich?' asked the practical Frau Lenore.

'Exceedingly rich. Her father was a millionaire, and left her everything.'

'Everything? To her? Well, that is your good luck. Only be careful that you do not ask too little for your estate. Be sensible and firm. Do not let yourself be carried away! I can understand your desire to become Gemma's husband as soon as possible, but ... caution before all else! Don't forget: the higher the price you get for the sale of the estate, the more there will be left for the two of you – and for your children.'

Gemma turned away, and Sanin began waving his arms again.

'You can have absolute confidence in my prudence, Frau Lenore! I am not even going to bargain! I will name the proper price. If she accepts, well and good; if not, then let her be!'

'Do you know her ... this lady?' Gemma asked.

'I have never set eyes on her.'

'And when will you be back?'

'If nothing comes of the business, the day after tomorrow. But if things appear to be going well, it may be necessary to stay a day, or even two days, longer. In any event, I will not delay a moment longer than is necessary. You know that I am leaving my soul behind! But I must not go on talking – I still have to rush back to my lodgings before leaving ... Give me your hand for luck, Frau Lenore – that is our custom in Russia.'

'The right hand or the left?'

'The left, nearest the heart. I will be back the day after tomorrow – bearing my shield, or borne upon my shield! Something tells me I shall return victorious! Goodbye, my dear, good friends!'

He embraced and kissed Frau Lenore, and asked Gemma to go into her room with him for a moment, since he had something very important to tell her. He only wanted to say goodbye to her alone. Frau Lenore realized this, and therefore showed no curiosity about the very important matter ... Sanin had never before been in Gemma's room. No sooner had he crossed the hallowed threshold than all the love which possessed him, its fire, its rapture and its sweet terrors, overwhelmed his whole being and burned within him ... He glanced around him with tender adoration, fell at the feet of his beloved, and pressed his face to her body ...

'*Tu es mien?*' she whispered. 'You will come back soon?'

'I am yours ... I will come back.' His breath came in gasps as he murmured his assurance.

'I shall be waiting for you, my darling.'

A few moments later, Sanin was running down the street towards his lodgings. He never noticed that a bedraggled Pantaleone had leapt out after him from the door of the patisserie and shouted something at him, holding his arm high in the air and shaking it wildly in what looked like a menacing gesture.

At exactly a quarter to one, Sanin reported to Polozov. A four-horse carriage stood ready at the gates of the hotel.

When he saw Sanin, Polozov only muttered, 'Ah, so you've made up your mind,' and then, having put on his hat, greatcoat and galoshes, and stuffed his ears with cotton wool, although it was summertime, came out on to the porch. Under his directions, the waiters disposed his numerous articles of shopping in the interior of the carriage, lined a place for him to sit on with little silk-covered cushions, bags and bundles, placed a basket of provisions at his feet, and lashed his trunk to the coachman's box. Polozov distributed generous largesse and climbed into the carriage, grunting and supported, from behind it is true, but respectfully, by the obsequious porter. It was only after thoroughly pressing down everything around him to make himself comfortable, and after selecting and lighting a cigar, that he signed to Sanin, as if to say, all right, you can get in too. Sanin sat down beside him. Polozov, through the porter, ordered the postillion to drive carefully if he wished to be tipped. There was a rattle of steps and a banging of doors, and the carriage rolled off.

## XXXIII

Nowadays it takes less than an hour by railway from Frankfurt to Wiesbaden. In those days, the journey by express post horses took about three hours. The horses were changed some five times. Polozov either dozed or else just sat swaying, holding his cigar in his teeth and talking very little. He did not once look out of the window. He was not interested in picturesque views, and even declared that 'Nature was death to him'. Sanin also kept silent, and did not admire the scenery: he had other things to think about. He was completely sunk in his thoughts and memories. At every stage, Polozov paid what was due, checked the time on his watch, and rewarded the postillions – generously or less generously, according to their efforts. When they were about halfway to their destination, Polozov extracted two oranges from the provisions basket, selected the better of the two, and offered

the other to Sanin. Sanin looked closely at his companion –
and suddenly burst out laughing.

'What's all this about?' asked the other, carefully peeling
the orange with his short white nails.

'What's it about?' Sanin repeated. 'Why, about this journey
of ours.'

'What of it?' asked Polozov again, inserting into his mouth
one of the long segments into which an orange divides.

'It is a very strange business. Yesterday, truth to tell, I had
as little thought of you as of the Emperor of China, and here I
am today, driving with you in order to sell my estate to your
wife, about whom I know absolutely nothing.'

'All kinds of things happen,' Polozov replied. 'If you live
long enough, you will see everything in your time. For
example, can you imagine me, mounted as an orderly officer?
But I was. And the Grand Duke Michael shouted: 'At the
canter! That fat subaltern there, at the canter! Faster, at the
full canter!'

Sanin scratched his ear.

'Now tell me please, Polozov, what is your wife like? What
kind of a woman is she? After all, I must know.'

'It's all very well for him to give the order, at the canter,'
Polozov went on, with sudden heat, 'but what about me, I ask
you, what about me? And I thought to myself: "Take all your
ranks and your epaulettes, you can keep them." Oh yes ...
you were asking about my wife. Well – what is she like?
Human like everyone else. Don't trust her too far – she
doesn't like it. The main thing is, talk as much as possible so
as to give her something to laugh about. Tell her about your
love affair, perhaps, but you know, make it amusing.'

'How do you mean, amusing?'

'Just that. You tell me that you are in love and want to get
married. Well, just describe all that to her.'

Sanin was offended.

'And what do you find so funny about that?'

Polozov merely made a movement with his eyes. The juice
from the orange was running down his chin.

'Was it your wife who sent you into Frankfurt to do the shopping?' Sanin enquired after a while.

'It was.'

'And what have you been buying?'

'Toys, obviously.'

'Toys? Have you got children?'

Polozov actually moved away from Sanin.

'What next! Why on earth should I have children? I mean women's playthings ... Trimmings. For their dressing-up.'

'But do you know anything about such things?'

'Certainly.'

'Then how is it that you told me that you don't meddle in any of your wife's affairs?'

'This is the only affair of hers in which I do interfere. This ... is not so bad. It relieves boredom a bit. Besides, my wife trusts my taste. And I am extremely good at beating down the tradesmen.'

Polozov had begun to speak in jerks. He was already exhausted.

'And is your wife very, very rich?'

'Oh yes, she's rich enough. Only mostly for herself.'

'Still, it looks as if you don't have much to complain about!'

'Well, after all, I am her husband. It would be a fine thing if I did not benefit from it. And I am pretty useful to her. She's got quite a good bargain in me. I am a convenient husband!'

Polozov wiped his face with a silk handkerchief and puffed heavily, as if to say, 'Have mercy on me, don't force me to utter another word. You can see what a strain I find it.'

Sanin left him in peace, and once again sank into his own reflections.

The hotel in Wiesbaden, in front of which the carriage stopped, looked like a real palace. A ringing of bells resounded immediately from its depths, and a flurrying and scurrying began. Distinguished-looking persons in black frock-coats sprang about at the main entrance. A doorman, covered with gold, flung open the carriage door with a flourish.

Polozov dismounted like an emperor in triumph, and began to ascend the well-carpeted and sweet-smelling staircase. A man, also very well-dressed, but with a Russian face, hurried up to him – it was his valet. Polozov remarked to the servant that in future be must take him with him, since the evening before, in Frankfurt, he, Polozov, had been abandoned for the whole night without any warm water. The valet's face expressed due horror, and he bent down briskly to remove his master's galoshes.

'Is Maria Nikolaevna at home?' asked Polozov.

'Yes, sir, she is dressing, sir. She is going to dine with Countess Lasunskaia.'

'Ah, with that ... Wait, there are some things in the carriage, get them all out and bring them in. And you, Sanin – get yourself a room and come along in three-quarters of an hour. We will have dinner.'

Polozov swam on his way, and Sanin asked for a modest room. He changed and had a short rest, and then set off for the enormous suite occupied by His Serene Highness (*Durchlaucht*) Prince von Polosoff.

He found the 'Prince' enthroned on a luxurious, velvet-covered armchair in the middle of a most magnificent drawing-room. Sanin's phlegmatic school-fellow had already had time to take a bath and to envelop himself in a dressing-gown of the richest satin. He wore a crimson fez on his head. Sanin approached him and stood for some time examining him. Polozov sat motionless like an idol: he did not even turn his face towards Sanin, nor move an eyebrow, nor emit any sound. It was, in truth, a majestic spectacle! Having admired the scene for almost two minutes, Sanin was about to speak and to shatter the hieratic silence, when suddenly the door from a neighbouring room opened: there appeared on the threshold a young and beautiful woman in a white silk dress trimmed with black lace, her hands and neck decked with diamonds. It was herself – Maria Nikolaevna Polozova. Her

thick fair hair, which had not yet been dressed, hung in two
heavy plaits.

## XXXIV

'Oh, do forgive me,' she said with a smile, in which confusion
and mockery were equally blended, immediately seizing the
end of one of her plaits with her hand, and fixing her large,
bright grey eyes on Sanin, 'I had no idea that you had already
arrived.'

'Dmitry Pavlovich Sanin, a childhood friend,' murmured
Polozov, still without turning round or rising from his chair,
but pointing a finger at him.

'Yes ... I know. You told me already. Very glad to make his
acquaintance. But I wanted to ask you to do something for
me, Ippolit Sidorych ... my maid seems unable to do
anything right today ...'

'You want me to do your hair?'

'Yes, yes, please. Forgive me,' Madame Polozov repeated
with her former smile. She gave Sanin a quick nod, and
turning swiftly, disappeared through the door, leaving behind
her a fleeting but elegant impression of a beautiful neck,
wonderful shoulders, and a wonderful figure.

Polozov rose, and lumbered heavily after her. Sanin never
had a moment's doubt that his presence in 'Prince Polozov's'
drawing-room was perfectly well known to the lady of the
house: the whole object of the incident had been to display
her hair, which was indeed very fine. In his heart Sanin
was even rather pleased by Madame Polozov's performance:
if, he thought, her ladyship wanted to impress me, to cut
a fine figure in front of me, then perhaps – who can tell? –
she will show less resistance when it comes to the price of
my estate. He was so wholly absorbed by Gemma that other
women no longer had any significance for him. Indeed,
he scarcely noticed them, and on this occasion only went so
far as to think, Yes, what they say is true, this fine lady is not
bad looking.'

However, had he not been in this exceptional state of mind, he would probably have expressed himself differently: Maria Nikolaevna Polozova, born Kolyshkina, was a very remarkable personality. Not that her beauty was beyond challenge: in fact the traces of her plebeian origins were evident enough. Her forehead was low, her nose somewhat fleshy and upturned. She could boast neither a delicate skin nor elegant hands and feet – but what did this matter? It was not the 'hallowed shrine of beauty', to use Pushkin's phrase, that would have made any man who met her stand and stare. It was the overwhelming presence of a Russian, or perhaps gipsy, woman's powerful body in full flower. Yes, any man would have been willing enough to stop and admire her.

But Gemma's image protected Sanin, like that triple armour of which the poets sing.

Some ten minutes later Madame Polozov reappeared with her husband. She came up to Sanin ... and how she walked! In fact, some extraordinary fellows in those, alas! far distant days, would go out of their minds just from seeing her walk. 'When this woman walks towards you, it is as if she is bringing you all your life's happiness' – as one of them used to put it. She came up to Sanin, offered him her hand and said, in Russian, in her gentle and strangely withdrawn voice: 'You will wait up for me, won't you? I will be back soon.'

Sanin bowed respectfully while Maria Nikolaevna was already disappearing behind the heavy curtain which hung before the outer door. As she vanished, she once more turned, looked over her shoulder and smiled, and once again left behind her the former impression of elegance. When she smiled, not one, not two, but three dimples appeared in each cheek and her eyes smiled more than her lips – her long, scarlet, tempting lips with two tiny birthmarks on the left.

Polozov lumbered into the room, and once again ensconced himself in the armchair. He was as silent as before. But from time to time a slight smile puffed out his colourless and prematurely wrinkled cheeks.

He looked old, although only three years senior to Sanin.

The dinner with which he entertained his guest would
certainly have satisfied the most exacting gourmet, but to
Sanin it seemed endless and insufferable. Polozov ate slowly,
'with feeling, sense and measure', bending attentively over his
plate, and sniffing at almost every morsel. He would first swill
the wine round his mouth and only then swallow it, and
smack his lips. But when the roast was served, he suddenly
burst into conversation – and on what a subject! He spoke of
pedigree Merino sheep, of which he intended to import a
whole flock, describing everything in the greatest detail, with
tender affection, using diminutives throughout.

Having drunk a cup of coffee which was almost at boiling
point (he had several times reminded the waiter in lachrymose
tones of irritation that the other day he had been served coffee
which was quite cold, cold as ice) and having inserted a
Havana cigar between his crooked yellow teeth, he dozed off
in his customary manner. This delighted Sanin, who began to
walk slowly and noiselessly up and down the deep-piled
carpet, and abandoned himself to daydreams of life with
Gemma, and of the news which he would bring back to her.
However, Polozov woke up earlier than usual, as he himself
remarked, since he had only slept an hour and a half. He
drank a glass of iced soda water and swallowed about eight
spoonfuls of jam, Russian jam, which his valet brought him in
a genuine dark green Kiev jar. He could not live without it –
to quote his own words. He then fixed his puffed eyes on
Sanin, and enquired if he would like a game of Old Maid.
Sanin readily agreed. He was afraid that Polozov might once
again begin to talk about Merino rams, ewe lambs and fat-tail
sheep.

Host and guest went into the drawing-room, a waiter
brought cards and the game began – not for money, of course.

They were engaged in this innocent pastime when Maria
Nikolaevna returned from her visit to Countess Lasunskaia.
She burst out laughing as soon as she entered the room and
saw the cards and the open card table. Sanin jumped up from
his seat, but she exclaimed: 'Please go on with your game. I

will go and change and return at once' – and again she
vanished with a rustle of skirts, pulling off her gloves as she
went.

She did indeed return very soon. She had changed her fine
dress for a voluminous lilac-coloured silk robe with loose,
wide sleeves. A thick plaited cord was knotted about her
waist. She sat down by her husband, waited until he had lost
the hand, and then said to him: 'Well, Fatty, that's enough'
(at the word 'Fatty' Sanin looked at her with amazement, and
she smiled gaily in answer to his look, displaying all the
dimples in her cheeks). 'That's enough. I can see that you are
sleepy. Kiss my hand and take yourself off, while Monsieur
Sanin and I have a talk on our own.'

'I am not sleepy,' Polozov murmured, rising heavily from
the chair, 'but I will take myself off, and I will kiss your
hand.'

She extended the palm of her hand, but continued to smile
and kept her eyes on Sanin.

Polozov also glanced at him, and left without saying
goodnight.

'Well, come on now, tell me everything,' Maria Nikolaevna
said eagerly, placing her bare elbows on the table and
impatiently tapping her nails together. 'Is it true that you are
getting married?'

Having said these words, Madame Polozov even inclined
her head a little so as to look Sanin in the eyes the more
attentively and the more searchingly.


## XXXV


Madame Polozov's easy manner would probably have put
Sanin off from the start – although he was no novice in
society, and had rubbed along a good deal in the world – had
he not once again interpreted this ease and familiarity of
manner as a good omen for his enterprise. Let us indulge the
caprices of this rich lady, he decided inwardly, and answered

her with the same informality of manner as she employed for her questions.

'Yes, I am getting married.'

'To whom? To a foreigner?'

'Yes.'

'Did you meet her recently? In Frankfurt?'

'Just so.'

'And who is she? May one enquire?'

'Certainly. She is the daughter of a pastry-cook.'

Maria Nikolaevna opened her eyes wide and raised her eyebrows.

'But how perfectly delightful!' she said, drawing out the words. 'This is wonderful! And I thought that there were no longer any young men like you left in the world. The daughter of a pastry-cook!'

'I can see that this surprises you,' Sanin observed, not without some show of dignity. 'But in the first place, I am entirely free of those prejudices ...'

'In the *first place* I am not in the least surprised,' interrupted Madame Polozov, 'and I have no prejudices either. I am a peasant's daughter myself. So we're quits. What surprises and delights me is the fact that here is a man who is not afraid of loving. You do love her, don't you?'

'Yes.'

'And is she very good-looking?'

Sanin was slightly put out by the last question. However, it was too late to retreat.

'As you know, Maria Nikolaevna,' he began, 'every man thinks that his beloved is better looking than anyone else. But my future wife is indeed a very beautiful girl.'

'Really? And in what style? The Italian? The antique?'

'Yes. She has very regular features.'

'Have you her portrait with you?'

'No.' (In those days no one had thought of photographs. Even daguerreotypes were hardly known.)

'What is her name?'

'She is called Gemma.'

'And what are you called?'

'Dmitry.'

'And your patronymic?'

'Pavlovich.'

'Do you know what?' said Madame Polozov, still in the same deliberate drawl, 'I like you very much, Dmitry Pavlovich. I am sure you are a very good man. Give me your hand. Let us be good friends.'

She gripped his hand firmly with her beautiful, white, strong fingers. Her hand was slightly smaller than his, but much warmer and smoother, softer and more vital.

'But do you know what has occurred to me?'

'What?'

'Are you sure you won't be angry? Sure? You say you are engaged to be married to this girl. But was it ... was it really absolutely necessary?'

Sanin frowned.

'I don't understand you, Maria Nikolaevna.'

She laughed quietly and shook her head so as to throw back the hair that was falling on her cheeks.

'There is no doubt about it – he is a delight!' she said in a half-meditative, half-absent way, 'a knight in armour – and now, after this, just try to believe those who insist that there are no more idealists left!'

Maria Nikolaevna spoke all the time in Russian, in a remarkably pure Moscow form of speech, but as spoken by the lower classes, not the gentry.

'You were presumably educated at home in a patriarchal, god-fearing family?' she enquired. 'In what province?'

'In Tula province.'

'Well, then we were fed at the same trough. My father ... But you must know who my father was?'

'Yes, I know.'

'He was born in Tula ... a Tula man ... Well, all right.' (Maria Nikolaevna pronounced the Russian word *khorosho*' deliberately now in a plebeian manner – *khersho .. oo.*) 'Well, let us get down to business.'

'What do you mean – get down to business? What do you mean by that?'

Madame Polozov narrowed her eyes.

'What then have you come here for?'

(When she narrowed her eyes, their expression became very gentle and a little mocking: but when she opened them to their full extent something cruel, something threatening showed through their clear and chilly brilliance. Her thick and slightly close-set eyebrows, which were in truth like sable, lent a special beauty to her eyes.)

'You want me to buy your estate, don't you? You need money for the celebration of your marriage? Is that not so?'

'Yes, that is so.'

'And do you need a great deal of money?'

'I should be content with a few thousand francs to start with. Your husband knows my estate. You can ask his advice. I am prepared to accept a low price.'

Madame Polozov shook her head.

'In the *first place*,' she began, stressing each word, tapping the tips of her fingers on the cuff of Sanin's coat, 'I am not in the habit of asking my husband's advice – except, perhaps, in the matter of dress, on which he is a great expert. And *secondly*, why are you telling me that you are asking a low price? I do not wish to take advantage of the fact that you are now in love and ready for all sacrifices ... I am not going to accept any sacrifice from you. Are you suggesting that, instead of encouraging ... how can I best put it? – encouraging your noble feelings – is that right? I am to skin you like a rabbit? I am not in the habit of doing that. I can sometimes be quite ruthless with people – but certainly not in this way.'

Sanin was at a complete loss to make out whether she was laughing at him or speaking seriously, but he kept thinking to himself, 'You have to keep your wits about you with this one.'

A servant came in with a Russian samovar, a teaset, cream, rusks and the like on a large tray, distributed all this bounty on the table between Sanin and Madame Polozov, and withdrew.

She poured a cup of tea.

'Do you mind?' she asked, putting sugar in his cup with her fingers – and the sugar tongs were lying in front of her.

'For Heaven's sake! From such a fair hand ...'

He did not finish the phrase, and nearly choked over his mouthful of tea, while she observed him attentively and serenely.

'The reason I mentioned a low price for my estate,' he continued, 'is because I could not assume, since you are now abroad, that you would have much free capital at your disposal, and, in a word, I myself feel that the sale ... or the purchase of an estate in such circumstances is something unusual and that I must take all this into account.'

Sanin talked confusedly and with hesitation, while Madame Polozov leaned quietly against the back of the chair with her arms crossed, and kept looking at him in the same attentive and serene manner. At last he stopped.

'That's all right, go on, go on,' she said, as if coming to his rescue. 'I am listening to you, I like listening to you. Go on talking.'

Sanin started to describe his estate, its acreage, its position, its assets and the profit that it could be made to yield ... He also mentioned the picturesque situation of the house; meanwhile, Maria Nikolaevna kept on looking at him, even more fixedly and openly. Her lips were moving slightly, but without a smile, and she kept biting at them a little. At last he began to feel awkward, and fell silent once again.

'Dmitry Pavlovich,' began Madame Polozov, and then paused to think. 'Dmitry Pavlovich,' she repeated, 'do you know what? I am certain that the purchase of your estate is a very profitable business for me, and that we shall agree on a price. But you must give me two days, yes, two days' time. You are surely capable of parting for two days from your beloved? I will not keep you here any longer against your will – I give you my word of honour. But if you are now in need of five or six thousand francs it would give me great pleasure to offer to lend you the money – we can settle up later.'

Sanin rose.

'I have to thank you, Maria Nikolaevna, for your open-hearted and courteous readiness to help a man who is almost a complete stranger to you ... But if it is your wish, I should prefer to await your decision about the estate, and I will stay for two days.'

'Yes, it is my wish, Dmitry Pavlovich. And will it be very difficult for you? Very? Tell me.'

'I love Gemma, Maria Nikolaevna, and it is not easy for me to be parted from her.'

'Oh, you are a man with a heart of gold,' Maria Nikolaevna said with a sigh. 'I promise not to torment you too much. Are you going?'

'It is late,' observed Sanin.

'And you must rest after your journey, and after your game of Old Maid with my husband. Tell me, are you a great friend of my husband?'

'We went to the same boarding school.'

'Was he already like that – in those days?'

'How do you mean, "Like that"?'

Madame Polozov suddenly burst out laughing, and laughed until her whole face was scarlet. She put a handkerchief to her lips, rose from her chair, and, swaying as if from fatigue, went up to Sanin and held out her hand.

He took his leave and walked towards the door.

'Be here as early as possible tomorrow, will you? Do you hear?' she called after him.

As he left the room, he glanced back and saw that she had once again sunk into her armchair and had thrown her arms above her head. The wide sleeves of her robe had dropped almost to her shoulders. No one could deny that the pose of those arms, and the whole of that figure were of fascinating beauty.

## XXXVI

The lamp in Sanin's room burned far into the night. He sat at the desk and wrote to 'his Gemma'. He told her everything. He described the Polozovs, husband and wife – though incidentally, he enlarged mainly on the subject of his own feelings – and ended with making an appointment in three days' time!!! (with three exclamation marks). Early next morning, he took the letter to the post, and went for a walk in the gardens of the Kurhaus, where the music was already playing. There were as yet few people about. He paused in front of the bandstand, listening to a potpourri from 'Roberto Diavolo' and, after drinking some coffee, went down a secluded side alley, sat down on a small bench, and plunged into thought.

A parasol handle tapped him briskly and quite sharply on the shoulder. He came to with a start ... before him, attired in a light grey-green dress of *barège* silk, a white tulle hat and suède gloves, stood Maria Nikolaevna, rosy and fresh as a summer morning. Her glance and her movements were still soft with the glow of untroubled sleep.

'Good morning,' she said. 'I sent for you this morning, but you had already gone out. I have just finished my second tumbler – you know they make me drink the waters here, God knows why. If I am not perfectly well, then who is? And now I have to walk for a whole hour. Would you like to come with me? And after that we will drink coffee.'

'I have already had my coffee,' said Sanin, rising to his feet, 'but I should be delighted to walk with you.'

'Then give me your arm ... don't be afraid, your intended is not here – she will not see you.'

Sanin gave a forced smile. He had a disagreeable feeling every time Madame Polozov referred to Gemma. However, he quickly and obediently offered his arm – Maria Nikolaevna's arm sank slowly and softly on to his, glided along, and clung as if welded to it.

'Come along, this way,' she said, tossing her open parasol

over her shoulder. 'I am at home in this park and will take you
to the prettiest spots. And, do you know' (she often used these
three words) 'we shan't talk any business now – we will have a
good discussion about that after breakfast. But you must now
tell me about yourself so that I know what kind of man I am
dealing with. And after that, if you like, I will tell you
something about myself. Agreed?'

'But, Maria Nikolaevna, what possible interest can you
have ... ?'

'Stop, stop! You have misunderstood me, I have no wish to
flirt with you.' Maria Nikolaevna shrugged her shoulders.
'The man is engaged to a girl who looks like a classical statue,
and I should flirt with him! But you have something to sell,
and I am a business woman. So I want to know all about your
goods. Well, show me – what are they like? I want to know not
only what I am buying, but from whom I am buying. That
was my father's rule. So begin ... Well, not from childhood,
perhaps – but, have you been abroad long, for instance? And
where have you been up till now? Only don't walk so fast – we
are in no hurry.'

'I came here from Italy, where I spent a few months.'

'It seems as if you are drawn towards everything Italian.
How strange that you did not find your particular object *there*.
Do you like art? Paintings? Or do you prefer music?'

'I love art ... I love everything that is beautiful.'

'Music, too?'

'Yes, music as well.'

'And I don't like it at all. All I like is Russian songs, and
then only in the country and in spring – songs and dances,
you know ... the red cotton of the peasants' clothes, the girls'
bead headdresses, young grass on the common pasture land,
the smell of smoke in the air – marvellous! But we are not
talking about me. Go on with your story. Go on, go on with
your story.'

Madame Polozov walked on and kept glancing at Sanin as
she walked. She was tall – her face was very nearly level with
his.

He began his account, reluctantly at first and not very skilfully, but then he got into his stride and even became talkative. Madame Polozov was a very good listener. Besides, she seemed so frank herself that she had the effect of inducing frankness in others, however unwilling. She possessed the great gift of putting a man at his ease, *le terrible don de la familiarité*, which is mentioned by Cardinal de Retz. Sanin spoke of his travels, of his life in St Petersburg, of his youth ... Had Maria Nikolaevna been a society woman, with refined manners, he would never have let himself go in this way. But she referred to herself as a 'good fellow' who could not bear any ceremony: it was in these very terms that she had described herself for Sanin's benefit. And at the same time, here was the 'good fellow' walking beside him softly like a cat and leaning slightly against him, looking up at him. What is more, the 'good fellow' was cast in the image of a young female creature who simply radiated that destructive, tormenting, quietly inflammatory temptation with which Slav natures alone – and then only some of them, and sometimes not pure Slav at that, but with a dash of something else – know how to drive us poor men, us sinful, weak men, out of our minds.

So Sanin walked in the company of Madame Polozov, and his conversation with her lasted for over an hour. And they did not stop once, but kept on walking along the interminable avenues, now going uphill, admiring the view on the way, now down into the valley, into the cover of dense shadows – and all the time arm in arm. There were moments when Sanin felt a certain irritation: never had he walked so long with Gemma, his darling Gemma – and here this grand lady had taken possession of him, and that was that!

'Are you not tired?' he enquired on several occasions.

'I am never tired, she replied.

Occasionally, other walkers would cross their path. Nearly all of them bowed to her – some respectfully, some even obsequiously. To one of them, an extremely good-looking and very well-dressed man with dark hair, she called out from some distance in the best Paris accent: '*Comte, vous savez il ne faut pas venir me voir – ni aujourd'hui, ni demain.*' The man raised his hat without saying a word, and gave a deep bow.

'Who was that?' asked Sanin, betraying the bad habit of idle curiosity with which all Russians are afflicted.

'That? That's a little Frenchman – there are many of them running around here. He's one of those dancing attendance on me. But it's time for coffee. Let's go home: I imagine you must be hungry. I expect my old man has got his eyes unstuck by now.'

' "Old man". "Got his eyes unstuck," ' repeated Sanin to himself. And she speaks such excellent French ... what a curious character ...

Maria Nikolaevna was not mistaken. When she and Sanin returned to the hotel, the 'old man', or 'Fatty', was sitting, with the inevitable fez on his head, at a table laid for breakfast.

'I got tired of waiting for you,' he exclaimed, screwing up his face in a sour grimace. 'I was about to have coffee without you.'

'That's all right, that's all right,' replied his wife gaily. 'Were you angry? That's good for you, otherwise you will become completely ossified. Here, I have brought a guest. Go on, ring! Let us drink coffee, the very best coffee, in Dresden china cups on a snow-white tablecloth!'

She threw off her hat and her gloves, and clapped her hands. Polozov peered at her from under his eyebrows.

'What has made you go off at the gallop today, Maria Nikolaevna?' he asked in a low voice.

'That's not your business, Ippolit Sidorych. You ring the bell. Dmitry Pavlovich, sit down and drink coffee for the second time. Oh, what fun it is to give orders! There is no greater pleasure in the world!'

'When people obey them,' grunted her husband.

'Just so, when people obey me. That is why I enjoy myself. Especially with you. Isn't that so, Fatty? And here is the coffee.'

Lying on the enormous tray brought in by the waiter there was also a theatre playbill. Madame Polozov immediately seized it.

'Tragedy!' she cried indignantly. 'German tragedy! Never mind, that's better than German comedy. Will you tell them to reserve a box for me in the pit tier – no, better take the *Fremden Loge*,' she said, turning to the waiter. 'Do you hear, the *Fremden Loge* without fail!'

'But what if the *Fremden Loge* is already taken by His Excellency, the Town Director (*Seine Excellenz der Herr Stadt-Direktor*)?' the waiter ventured to object.

'Then you give His Excellency ten thalers – and see that I get the box. Do you hear?'

The waiter inclined his head, submissively and sadly.

'Dmitry Pavlovich, you will come to the theatre with me, will you not? German actors are terrible, but you will come, won't you? Yes? Yes? Oh, how polite you are. And you, Fatty, will you come?'

'Just as you say,' Polozov said into his cup, which he had lifted to his mouth.

'Do you know what, stay at home. You always sleep at the theatre, and in any case you know practically no German. I will tell you what you can do. You can write an answer to the estate manager about our mill – do you remember? About the peasants' milling. Tell him that I won't do it, that I won't do it, and again that I won't do it. That will provide you with an occupation for the whole evening.'

'Very well,' Polozov agreed.

'That's excellent. You're my clever boy. And now, gentlemen, this talk of the estate manager reminds me that we must discuss our principal business. And so, as soon as the waiter has cleared the table, you, Dmitry Pavlovich, will tell us all about your estate – how, and why, and how much you want, and what deposit you require – everything.'

At last, thought Sanin, thank goodness!

'You did tell me a little about it, and I think I remember that you gave a wonderful description of the garden, but Fatty wasn't there at the time ... Let him hear it all. I expect he may even contribute a relevant grunt. It is very agreeable for me to think that I can help you to get married, and besides I promised that after breakfast I would devote myself to your affairs. I always keep my promises – is that not so, Ippolit Sidorych?'

Polozov rubbed his face with the palm of his hand.

'Yes, that is true, and it is only right to say so. You never deceive anyone.'

'Never. And I never *will* deceive anyone. Now Dmitry Pavlovich, please state your case, as we say in the Senate.'

## XXXVII

Sanin began to state his case, that is, for the second time, to describe his estate, but omitting from this recital references to natural beauty, and occasionally seeking confirmation from Polozov of some fact or figure. But Polozov only muttered 'Hm ... m', and shook his head – and whether this was a sign of assent or of dissent, the devil himself would probably have been unable to determine. In any case, Maria Nikolaevna was in no need of his assistance. She revealed such extraordinary commercial and administrative talents as to leave one amazed. She had complete mastery of every minute detail of the estate. She questioned Sanin closely and exactly about everything and explored every aspect. Each time she used a word she hit the mark, and dotted the I's. Sanin did not expect such an examination and was unprepared for it. It lasted for all of an hour and a half. He experienced all the sensations of a prisoner on trial, seated on a very narrow bench, before a severe and searching judge. 'Why, this is a cross-examination,' he whispered to himself unhappily. Madame Polozov was laughing a little all the time, as if she were making a joke of the whole affair, but this did not improve matters for Sanin. He even broke out in a cold sweat in the course of the 'cross-examination' when it became evident that he was not certain of the exact meaning of the words used in peasant households for land re-allocation, or for plough lands.

'All right,' Maria Nikolaevna decided at last. 'Now I know your estate . . . as well as you do. What price are you asking for a soul?' (In those days, it will be recalled, the price of estates was determined by the number of souls, that is to say peasants.)

'Yes . . . Well . . . I think . . . that it would hardly be possible to take less than five hundred roubles,' Sanin managed to say with difficulty. (Oh, Pantaleone, Pantaleone, where are you? This would have made you say once more: *Barbari*!)

Madame Polozov raised her eyes to the heavens as if making her calculations.

'Well,' she said at last, 'this price seems inoffensive to me. But I obtained two days' grace for myself – and you must wait until tomorrow. I expect that we shall agree, and you will then tell me what deposit you require. And now, *basta così*!' she added, having noticed that Sanin was about to make some objection, 'we have spent enough time on filthy lucre – *à demain les affaires*! Do you know what, I am now releasing you' (she glanced at the small enamelled watch which she kept tucked into her waist-band) 'until three o'clock . . . I must, after all, let you have a rest. Go and have a game of roulette.'

'I never gamble,' remarked Sanin.

'Really? Why, you are perfection itself! As a matter of fact, I don't gamble either. It is stupid to throw one's money to the winds – and that is what it certainly means. But go to the gaming room, and have a look at the characters. There can be some very amusing ones. There is an old woman with a moustache and a lapdog – wonderful! There is also one of our Princes, he is pretty good too. A majestic figure, an aquiline nose, and every time he stakes a taler, he crosses himself secretly under his waistcoat. Read the journals, go for a walk – in short, do what you like. But I expect you at three o'clock . . . *de pied ferme*. We must dine early. These comic Germans start their theatre performances at half past six.' She stretched out her hand. '*Sans rancune, n'est-ce pas?*'

'Good gracious, Maria Nikolaevna, and why should I have any ill feelings towards you?'

'Because I have been tormenting you. You wait, I have something else in store for you,' she added, half-closing her eyes, so that all her dimples appeared at once in her cheeks, which were flushed. '*Au revoir!*'

Sanin bowed and turned to leave the room. There was a burst of merry laughter behind him – and the following scene was reflected in a looking-glass as he passed it: Madame Polozov had pushed her husband's fez down over his eyes, and he was struggling helplessly, with his arms waving about in the air.


# XXXVIII

Oh, what a deep sigh of relief and joy Sanin breathed as soon as he found himself alone in his room! Maria Nikolaevna had spoken truly – he needed a rest, a rest from these new acquaintances, impacts and conversations. He needed time to dispel the fumes which this unexpected and unasked-for intimacy with a woman so alien to him had generated in his heart and head. And think when it was happening – almost the day after he had discovered that Gemma loved him and he had become engaged to her! Why, it was blasphemy! In his thoughts he sought forgiveness a thousand times from his innocent dove, although truth to tell there was nothing for which he could blame himself; he pressed a thousand kisses on the little cross which she had given him. Had he not had every hope of concluding quickly and successfully the business which had brought him to Wiesbaden, he would have rushed back headlong to dear Frankfurt, to that house which he loved, and which had now become a part of his life, to the feet of his beloved . . . But there was nothing to be done. The cup had to be drained, he must dress, go to dinner . . . then on to the theatre. If only she would let him go as early as possible tomorrow!

There was another matter which dismayed and angered him. He kept thinking of Gemma, with love akin to worship, with rapture, with gratitude, thinking of the life which the two of them would share, of the happiness which lay before him – and all the time this strange woman, this Madame Polozov, incessantly appeared – no, hung around – as Sanin expressed it, with a feeling of especially malicious pleasure – hung around in front of his eyes, and he could not get rid of her image, could not shut out the sound of her voice or put the things she had said out of his mind. He could not even free himself of the memory of that particular delicate, fresh and penetrating scent, like the scent of yellow lilies, which came from her clothing. This woman was obviously making a fool of him, and making every kind of overture. Why? Why did she do it? Was it really just the whim of a spoiled, rich, almost immoral woman? And that husband? What sort of a creature was he? What was his relationship with her? And why did these questions bedevil him, Sanin, who in truth had no concern with either Polozov or his wife ? Why could he not dismiss this persistent image, even at a time when his soul was wholly turned towards the vision of another, clear and serene as God's daylight? How dare *those* features even show themselves against the vision of *hers*, which were almost divine? Show themselves – why, they leered at him provocatively. Those grey eyes, like those of a bird of prey, those dimples, those plaits which looked like snakes – was it really possible that they had so possessed him that he could not shake himself free? Did he lack the will to do it?

Nonsense, nonsense! Tomorrow all this would vanish without trace. Ah, but would she let him go tomorrow? Yes ... he asked himself all these questions, and meanwhile three o'clock was drawing near. So he put on a black evening coat and, after a short walk in the park, set off for the Polozovs.

In their drawing-room he found an Embassy secretary of German origin, a long, thin individual with a horse's profile, fair hair, and a parting at the back of his head (this was just coming into fashion in those days). But, wonder of wonders, whom else? None other than von Doenhof, the officer with whom he had fought a duel a few days before. Sanin had never expected to meet him here and could not help being put out, although he exchanged bows with him.

'You know each other?' asked Maria Nikolaevna. Sanin's confusion had not escaped her.

'Yes ... I have had the honour,' murmured Doenhof, with a slight bow towards Madame Polozov, and added softly with a smile, 'It is the same one ... your compatriot ... a Russian.'

'Impossible!' she exclaimed, also in an undertone. She shook her finger at him and immediately began to make her farewells both to him and to the long secretary, who was obviously head over heels in love with her, since he stood gaping every time she looked at him. Doenhof left at once, politely submissive, like a friend of the house who only needs a hint to know what is expected. The secretary tried to stall, but Madame Polozov saw him off without ceremony.

'You go along to your high-powered personage,' she told him. (A certain Principessa di Monaco was then living in Wiesbaden, who looked remarkably like a somewhat low-grade cocotte.) 'Why should you waste your time on a plebeian like me?'

'For heaven's sake, Madame,' the unhappy secretary began to assure her, 'all the princesses in the world ...'

But Madame Polozov was quite merciless – and the secretary took himself off, parting and all.

Maria Nikolaevna had dressed herself up very much to her '*avantage*', as our grandmothers used to say. She was wearing a rose-coloured dress of watered silk, with sleeves in the fashion of the Comtesse de Fontanges, and a large diamond in each ear. Her eyes shone no less brilliantly than the diamonds, and she seemed to be in a good mood and on the top of her form.

She placed Sanin beside her and began to talk about Paris, where she intended going in a few days' time. She told him how bored she was with the Germans, who were stupid

whenever they tried to be clever, and suddenly inappropria-
tely clever when they were being stupid; then, quite suddenly,
out of the blue – as they say, *à brule pourpoint* – she asked him
if it was true that he had fought a duel on account of some
lady a few days ago with the very same officer who had been
sitting there a short while back?

'But how do you know about this?' muttered the startled
Sanin.

'The world is full of rumours, Dmitry Pavlovich. But I
know, by the way, that you were in the right, a thousand times
in the right, and behaved like a man of honour. Tell me, was
this lady your betrothed?'

Sanin frowned slightly.

'All right, all right, I won't ask,' Madame Polozov said
hurriedly, 'since you find it unpleasant to talk about it.
Forgive me, I won't say any more; don't be angry!' Polozov
appeared from the room next door with a newspaper in his
hand. 'What are you up to? Or is dinner ready?'

'Dinner will be served in a minute; you have a look at what
I have read in "The Northern Bee" – Prince Gromoboy has
died.'

Maria Nikolaevna raised her head.

'Oh well, God rest his soul! Do you know,' turning to
Sanin, 'every year in February, for my birthday, he used to fill
all my rooms with camellias, but this still does not make it
worth spending the winter in St Petersburg. I suppose he was
over seventy?' she asked her husband.

'Yes. There is a description of his funeral in the paper. The
whole court was there. And there is a poem by Prince
Kovrizhkin for the occasion.'

'Splendid!'

'Would you like me to read it to you? The Prince calls him
a man of counsel.'

'No , thank you. Some man of counsel! He was simply his
wife's, Tatiana Yurievna's, man. Let us go to dinner. Life is
for the living. Dmitry Pavlovich, your arm.'

*

The dinner was superb – like that of the day before, and passed with much animation. Maria Nikolaevna knew how to tell a story – a rare gift among women, and Russian women at that! She had no reticence in choosing her words: her female compatriots were particular targets for her wit. Sanin was more than once forced to burst out laughing at the aptness and vividness of her characterizations. Above all, Maria Nikolaevna could not bear hypocrisy, the empty phrase or the lie . . . She found all these about her everywhere. She seemed actually to parade and to boast of the humble surroundings in which her life had begun, told a number of rather odd stories about her relations from the time of her childhood, and described herself as a peasant girl, not a whit worse than Natalia Kirillovna Naryshkina. It became evident to Sanin that she had, in her time, lived through far more than the great majority of women of her own age.

Meanwhile, Polozov ate with concentration, drank attentively, and only occasionally threw, now at Sanin, now at his wife, a glance from his colourless eyes, which looked blind, but were, in fact, extremely keen.

'What a clever boy you are!' exclaimed his wife, turning to him. 'How well you carried out all those errands for me in Frankfurt! I would give you a little kiss on your forehead, only you don't care for that sort of thing very much.'

'No, I don't,' replied Polozov, and cut open a pineapple with a silver knife.

Maria Nikolaevna looked at him, and drummed on the table with her fingers.

'So our bet is on,' she said in a meaningful manner.

'Yes.'

'Very well. You will lose.'

Polozov stuck out his chin.

'This time, you had better not be too confident, Maria Nikolaevna: my opinion is that you are going to lose.'

'What is the bet about? May I know?' asked Sanin.

'No . . . not now,' replied Maria Nikolaevna, and laughed.

Seven o'clock struck. A waiter announced that the carriage

was ready. Polozov accompanied his wife to the door, and
then immediately waddled back to his armchair.

'Now, remember! Don't forget the letter to the manager!'
she called to him from the hall.

'Don't worry, I will write. I am a methodical man.'


## XXXIX

In 1840 the Wiesbaden Theatre was not only ugly to look at,
but bad. Its pathetic company was distinguished for its
ranting mediocrity, and its productions for their plodding
vulgarity. In fact it did not rise one whit above the standard
which can be considered normal to this day for all German
theatres. (The most perfect example of German theatre has in
latter days been offered us by the company at Karlsruhe,
under the 'celebrated' direction of Herr Devrient.)

Behind the box which had been reserved for 'Her Serene
Highness, Frau von Polosoff' (Goodness only knows how the
waiter had contrived to secure it – could he really have bribed
the *Stadt Direktor?*) there was a small room furnished with
little settees. Before entering, Maria Nikolaevna asked Sanin
to close the shutters which screened the box from the
auditorium.

'I don't want to be seen,' she said, 'otherwise they'll start
coming in here.'

She also made him sit beside her, with his back to the
auditorium, so that the box should look empty.

The orchestra played the overture to the 'Marriage of
Figaro', the curtain rose and the play began.

It was one of those innumerable home-grown products in
which well-read but talentless authors, using stilted, lifeless
language, bring before the audience some 'profound' or
'palpitating' thought. They portray a so-called tragic conflict,
diligently but clumsily, and induce boredom – Asiatic boredom, much the same as there is Asiatic cholera.

Maria Nikolaevna patiently listened through the first half

of the first act. But when the First Lover, having learned that
his beloved had been false to him, stuck both his fists on his
chest, pushed his elbows out at acute angles and howled for all
the world like a dog, she could stand it no more. (The First
Lover, incidentally, was dressed in a long white coat, with
puffed sleeves and a plush collar, a striped waistcoat and
mother-of-pearl buttons, green pantaloons braided with
patent leather, and white chamois leather gloves.)

'The very last French actor in the very last provincial town
acts better and more naturally than the greatest German
celebrity,' she declared indignantly, and moved into the back
room.

'Come here,' she said to Sanin, tapping the space beside
her on the settee. 'Let us talk.'

Sanin obeyed.

Maria Nikolaevna threw him a glance.

'Ah, I can see you are as soft as silk. Your wife will have an
easy time with you. This clown,' she continued, pointing with
the end of her fan at the actor who had started howling (he
was playing the part of a domestic tutor), 'has reminded me of
my youth. I was also in love with a tutor. That was my first . . .
no, my second passion. I fell in love for the first time with a
young lay brother in the Don monastery in Moscow. I was
twelve. I only saw him on Sundays, he wore a velvet cassock,
sprayed himself with lavender water, and, as he made his way
through the crowd with the censer, would say to the ladies in
French "*Pardon, excusez*". He never raised his eyes, but his
lashes were that length' – she marked off a whole half of her
little finger with her thumbnail and showed Sanin. 'My tutor
was called Monsieur Gaston. I must tell you that he was
terribly learned and extremely strict, a Swiss – and what a
dynamic face he had! He had side whiskers as black as tar, a
Greek profile, and his lips looked as if they had been cast in
iron. I was terrified of him! He was in fact the only man I have
ever been afraid of in my life. He was also my brother's tutor
– that was my brother who died later . . . He was drowned . . .
A gipsy once foretold that I too would die a violent death, but

that's nonsense. I don't believe it. Just imagine my husband with a dagger in his hand!'

'There are other ways of dying than by a dagger,' remarked Sanin.

'All that kind of thing is nonsense. Are you superstitious? I am not a bit. But what is to be, will be. Monsieur Gaston lived in our house, and his room was over mine. I used to wake up sometimes at night and hear his footsteps – he went to bed very late – and my heart would miss a beat from sheer veneration ... or some other feeling. My father could scarcely read or write, but he gave us a good education. Do you know that I can understand Latin?'

'You? Latin?'

'Yes – I. Monsieur Gaston taught me. We read the *Aeneid* together. It's a dull thing, but there are some good parts in it. Do you remember when Dido and Aeneas are in the forest ... ?'

'Yes, I remember,' Sanin said hurriedly. He had forgotten all his Latin long ago, and had only the faintest notion about the *Aeneid*.

Maria Nikolaevna glanced at him in her characteristic manner – with a sidelong look from under lowered lids.

'But you mustn't imagine that I am very well-educated. Oh, good gracious me, no, I am not educated at all, and I have no accomplishments. I can scarcely write – truly, and I can't read aloud. I can't play the piano or draw or sew – nothing. That's what I'm like – all here!'

She flung her arms wide.

'I am telling you all this,' she went on, 'first, in order not to have to listen to those dolts' (she pointed to the stage: at that moment instead of an actor, an actress was setting up a howl, and she too had thrust her elbows forward); 'and secondly, because I am in your debt: you told me about yourself yesterday.'

'It was your pleasure to ask me to tell you about myself,' remarked Sanin.

Maria Nikolaevna suddenly span round at him.

'And is it not "your pleasure" to know what kind of a woman I really am? However, I am not surprised,' she added, leaning back once again on the cushions of the settee. 'Here is a man, about to get married, and moreover for love, and on top of that after a duel ... how would you expect him to think of anything else?'

She became pensive, and began to bite the handle of her fan with her large, regular teeth, which were as white as milk.

But to Sanin it seemed that the fumes which he had been unable to drive away for two days, were once again beginning to rise to his head.

He and Maria Nikolaevna were talking in low voices, almost in whispers – and this only increased his irritation and his excitement ...

When, oh when, would all this come to an end? Weak people never make an end themselves – but keep waiting for the end.

Someone was sneezing on the stage. The sneeze had been introduced by the author as a comic 'moment' or 'element'. Certainly, the play had no other element of comedy, and the spectators had to be satisfied with this tiny crumb of light relief, and were laughing.

This laughter also irritated Sanin. There were moments when he simply did not know – was he angry or pleased? Bored or entertained? Oh, if only Gemma could see him!

'You know, it really is strange,' Maria Nikolaevna suddenly spoke again, 'a man announces in the calmest manner, "I intend to get married, don't you know?" And yet no one will ever say calmly, "I intend to jump into the water." But, when you come to think of it, what is the difference? It really is strange.'

Sanin was now really annoyed.

'There's a very big difference, Maria Nikolaevna. For some people, there is nothing very frightening about jumping into water – there are those who can swim. Besides ... so far as strange marriages are concerned ... if that is what we ...'

He stopped suddenly, and bit his tongue. Maria Nikolaevna struck her fan against the palm of her hand.

'Finish what you were saying, Dmitry Pavlovich, finish
what you were saying! I know what you meant to say: "If that
is what we are discussing, my most respected Maria Nikolaevna Polozova" – you wanted to say – "It would be difficult
to imagine a stranger marriage than yours. After all, I have
known your husband since childhood." That is what you
wanted to say – you expert swimmer!'

'But, really . . .' Sanin tried to interpose.

'Isn't that right? Am I not right?' she persisted. 'Now, look
me in the eyes and tell me that what I have said is untrue.'

Sanin did not know where to look.

'All right, as you please, it is true, if you insist on knowing,'
he said at last.

Maria Nikolaevna nodded her head.

'That's right, that's right . . . Well – but have you, who
know how to swim, ever asked yourself what the reason might
be for such strange conduct by a woman who is not poor . . .
and not stupid . . . and not plain? Perhaps you are not
interested – but never mind. I will tell you the reason, but not
now – as soon as the interval is over. I keep on worrying in
case someone should come in . . .'

She had indeed hardly had time to finish her sentence
before the outer door was half opened. A head was thrust into
the box: it was red, oily and sweating, young but already
toothless, with flat, long hair, a long pendant nose, enormous
ears like a bat's, with golden spectacles in front of its
inquisitive and dull little eyes, and a pince-nez on top of the
spectacles. The head took in the scene, noticed Madame
Polozov, broke into a mean grin, started to nod . . . a scraggy
outstretched neck was visible behind the head . . .

Maria Nikolaevna waved her handkerchief at the appari-
tion. 'I am not at home! *Ich bin nicht zu Hause, Herr P.! Ich bin
nicht zu Hause* . . . Shoo . . . Shoo . . .'

The head showed signs of astonishment, emitted a forced
laugh and said, with something like a sob, in imitation of Liszt

at whose feet he had once grovelled, '*Sehr gut, sehr gut*,' and disappeared.

'Who is that character?' asked Sanin.

'That? The Wiesbaden critic. "*Litterat* – or *Lohn Lakai*", as you prefer. He is in the pay of the local concessionaire, and is therefore obliged to praise everything and to enthuse about everything, while at the same time he is overflowing with spiteful bile, which he does not even dare to discharge. But I am afraid: he is a terrible gossip, and will immediately run off and tell everyone that I am in the theatre. Well, never mind.'

The orchestra played a waltz, the curtain soared again ... the grimacing and the simpering began once more upon the stage.

'Well, now,' began Maria Nikolaevna, sinking back on to the settee, 'since you are trapped and have to sit with me, instead of enjoying the bliss of being near your beloved – now, don't roll your eyes and don't get angry, I understand your predicament and I have already promised to let you go free as the wind – now listen to my confession. Do you want to know what I love more than anything else in the world?'

'Freedom,' Sanin prompted.

She placed her hand on his.

'Yes, Dmitry Pavlovich,' she said, and there was a special note in her voice, a note which suggested solemnity and absolute sincerity. 'Freedom more than anything else, and before everything else. And don't imagine that I am boasting about this – there is nothing very praiseworthy about it, but *that's* how it is, and that's how it will be for me to the end of my days. I suppose I saw a great deal of slavery in my childhood, and suffered from it. And of course, Monsieur Gaston, my tutor, opened my eyes. Perhaps you understand now why I married Polozov: with him I am free, completely free, as free as the air, as the wind ... and I knew all that before the wedding, I knew I should be as free as a bird with him.'

Maria Nikolaevna fell silent and threw aside her fan.

'I will tell you something else. I am quite a reflective

woman, it's amusing, and that's what our minds are for. But I never reflect about the consequences of anything I do myself, and when something goes wrong I don't indulge in self-pity – not *that much*: it's not worth it. I have a favourite saying – *Cela ne tire pas à conséquence* – I don't know how to put it in Russian. And just so – what does *tire à conséquence*? No one is going to demand an account from me *here* on this earth; as for there' (she lifted a finger in the air), 'well, they can do what they think best up there. When the time comes for them to judge me *there*, I shall no longer be *I*. Are you listening to me? Are you bored?'

Sanin was sitting with his head bowed. He raised his head.

'I am not at all bored, Maria Nikolaevna, and I am listening to you with great interest. But I ... I confess, I am asking myself why you are telling me all this.'

Maria Nikolaevna made a slight movement on the settee.

'You are asking yourself? ... Are you so bad at guessing? Or so modest?'

Sanin raised his head even higher.

'I am telling you all this,' she continued in a calm voice, which did not, however, match the expression on her face, 'because I like you very much; yes, don't be surprised, I am not joking; because, having met you, it would be unpleasant for me to think that you might remember me in a bad light ... or perhaps not so much in a bad light – I don't care about that – but simply a wrong light. That is why I have inveigled you in here, and am remaining alone with you, and that is why I am talking so frankly. Yes, yes, frankly – I don't lie. And, please note this, Dmitry Pavlovich, I know that you are in love with someone else, that you plan to marry her ... at least give me credit for my disinterestedness ... but, by the way, here is the chance for you to say in your turn "*Cela ne tire pas à conséquence*".'

She laughed, but the laughter stopped abruptly, and she sat motionless, as if amazed by her own words; her eyes, usually so gay and so bold, showed for a moment a hint of shyness, even grief.

Oh, she's a snake, Sanin thought meanwhile, but what a beautiful snake!

'Give me my lorgnette,' Maria Nikolaevna said suddenly. 'I want to see if the leading lady is in fact as plain as she seems. Really, one might think that the authorities had selected her with a moral purpose – to prevent young men from being too much carried away!'

Sanin handed her the lorgnette: as she took it from him she quickly, but almost imperceptibly, placed both her hands on his.

'None of this solemnity, if you please,' she whispered with a smile. 'Do you know what? No one can put chains on me, but then I don't put chains on others. I love freedom and recognize no ties – and that goes not only for me. And now move up a little, and let us listen to the play.'

Maria Nikolaevna directed her lorgnette at the stage. Sanin began to look at the stage too, sitting by her side in the half-darkened box, and breathing in, however unwillingly, the warmth and the fragrance of her magnificent body, and equally unwillingly turning over in his mind everything she had said to him in the course of the evening – and especially during the last few minutes.

## XL

The play continued for another hour or more, but Maria Nikolaevna and Sanin soon stopped looking at the stage. Before long they started to talk again, and their conversation followed the same course as before: only this time Sanin was less silent. In his heart he was angry both with himself and with Maria Nikolaevna: he tried to prove to her how much her 'theory' lacked foundation – as if she was interested in theories! He began arguing with her, at which she was secretly very pleased: once he has started arguing, she thought, it means that he is giving in, or will give in. He is beginning to eat out of my hand, he is coming on, he no longer shies away!

She argued back, laughed, agreed with him, reflected, attacked him ... and meanwhile their faces came closer, his eyes no longer evaded her gaze ... her eyes, as it were, wandered over, circled around his features, and he smiled back – politely, but still, he smiled. It suited her book very well that he should be indulging in abstractions: discussing honesty in mutual relationships, duty, the sanctity of love and marriage ... It is a well-known fact, after all, that these abstractions are exceedingly useful as a start, as a point of departure ...

Those who knew Madame Polozov well used to insist that whenever her powerful and vital personality suddenly showed signs of something like tenderness or modesty, something almost like virginal pudicity – though, when one thinks of it, where *did* these qualities come from? – then, why then, things were taking a dangerous turn!

It seems that things were taking just such a dangerous turn for Sanin ... Had he been able to concentrate even for a moment, he would have despised himself. But he had no time for either concentration or for self-contempt.

She certainly lost no time – and all this was happening because he was not bad looking! One is indeed forced to say: 'Take heed you find not that you did not seek!'

The play came to an end. Maria Nikolaevna asked Sanin to throw her shawl about her, and stood motionless while he wrapped the soft fabric around her truly regal shoulders. Then she took his arm, went out into the corridor – and nearly screamed: right by the door of the box, like some kind of ghost, Doenhof was hovering. Behind his back was visible the odious figure of the Wiesbaden critic. The oily face of this '*Littérateur*' was positively radiant with malicious pleasure.

'Will you allow me, Madame, to find your carriage for you?' the young officer asked Maria Nikolaevna, his voice trembling with ill-concealed rage.

'No, thank you most kindly,' she replied, 'my servant will find it. Stay here,' she added in a whispered tone of command, and quickly made off, taking Sanin with her.

'Go to the devil! Why are you pestering me?' Doenhof suddenly barked at the '*Littérateur*'. He had to vent his rage on someone.

'*Sehr gut, sehr gut,*' murmured the literary gentleman, and made himself scarce.

Madame Polozov's servant was waiting in the foyer, and immediately found her carriage. She jumped lightly into it; Sanin followed. The doors were briskly shut – and Maria Nikolaevna burst out laughing.

'Why are you laughing?' Sanin was curious to know.

'Oh, forgive me, please, but it has just occurred to me, suppose Doenhof should fight another duel with you ... about me, this time ...? Wouldn't that be fun?'

'Do you know him very well?' asked Sanin.

'Him? That boy? He's just my errand boy. You needn't worry.'

'Oh, I'm not at all worried.'

Maria Nikolaevna sighed.

'Ah, I know that you are not worried. But listen, you are such a dear boy, you must not refuse me a last request. Don't forget, in three days' time I am leaving for Paris, and you are returning to Frankfurt ... When shall we ever meet again?'

'What is the request?'

'You ride, of course?'

'Yes.'

'Well, then. Tomorrow morning I will take you with me and we will ride out of town. We shall have excellent horses. Then we shall come back, finish our business, and amen! Don't be surprised, don't tell me that I am capricious or mad – all of which is quite possible – just say: "I agree." '

She turned her face towards him. It was dark in the carriage, but her eyes shone even in the darkness.

'As you please, I agree,' murmured Sanin with a sigh.

'Ah, you sighed!' Maria Nikolaevna mocked him. 'That means – "I have put my hand to the plough, I can't draw back." But no ... no, no. You're delightful, you're a good man – and I will keep my promise. Here is my hand, my right hand, my business hand, with no glove on it. Take it and trust this handshake. I don't know what kind of a woman I am, but I am an honest human being ... and you can trust me in business matters.'

Only half aware of what he was doing, Sanin put her hand to his lips. She quietly withdrew it, and suddenly fell silent, and remained silent until the carriage stopped.

She began to dismount ... What was that? Did Sanin imagine it, or did he really feel a swift and burning touch on his cheek?

'Until tomorrow,' Maria Nikolaevna whispered to him, as they stood on the stairs which were all illuminated by the four candles of a candelabra which a gold-bedecked porter had grasped as soon as she appeared. She kept her eyes lowered. 'Until tomorrow.'

When he returned to his room, Sanin found a letter from Gemma on the table. For a moment he took fright ... and then immediately was overjoyed, the more quickly to hide his alarm from himself. The letter consisted of a few lines. She was pleased about the successful start of the 'business', counselled him to be patient, and added that all were well at home, and were looking forward to his return. Sanin found the tone of the letter a little dry. However, he picked up pen and paper – and then threw them aside. 'What's the point of writing? I shall be back tomorrow ... It's high time, high time.'

He went to bed immediately, and tried to get to sleep as soon as possible. Had he stayed up and awake he would certainly have started thinking about Gemma – and for some reason he felt too ashamed to think of her. His conscience was troubling him. But he comforted himself with the thought that tomorrow everything would be over for all time, and then he would say goodbye for ever to this crazy woman, and forget all this nonsense! When weak people talk to themselves, they are fond of using forceful turns of speech. *Et puis ... Cela ne tire pas à conséquence!*

## XLI

That is what Sanin thought as he went to bed. But history does not relate what he thought on the following day when Maria Nikolaevna knocked impatiently at his door with the coral handle of her riding switch; when he saw her on the threshold of his room, holding the train of her dark blue riding habit over her arm, a small, masculine hat on her thick, plaited hair, a veil thrown over her shoulder, and with a provocative smile on her lips, in her eyes, on her whole face – this history does not relate.

'Well, are you ready?' her voice rang out gaily.

Sanin quickly buttoned his coat, and picked up his hat, without saying a word. Maria Nikolaevna threw him a radiant glance, nodded and ran quickly down the stairs. And he ran after her. The horses were already standing in front of the porch. There were three of them. For Madame Polozov, a pure-bred golden chestnut mare, somewhat lean, but beautiful, and as spirited as fire. She had delicate legs like those of a deer, a spare, fine-boned muzzle, showing the teeth a little, and black, slightly prominent eyes. For Sanin a powerful, broad, rather heavy black steed without markings; the third horse was intended for the groom.

Maria Nikolaevna sprang lightly on to her mare ... the animal pawed the ground and began to circle, raising its tail and pressing up its haunches, but Maria Nikolaevna (who was an excellent horsewoman) kept her collected.

It was necessary to take leave of Polozov, who, with his fez, from which he was never parted, and with his dressing-gown thrown open, appeared on the balcony, waving a lawn handkerchief. He was not smiling, however, but almost frowning. Sanin also mounted. Maria Nikolaevna waved to her husband with her switch, and then struck the flat, arched neck of her mare. The mare reared, leapt forward and then began to step out in tiny, short, collected paces, trembling all over and mouthing at the bit, snatching at the air and snorting violently. Sanin rode behind, observing Maria Nikolaevna:

her elegant, supple figure, closely corseted but unconstrained, swayed gracefully, effortlessly and confidently as she rode. She turned her head and signed to him with a look. He drew level with her.

'Well, there you are, you see how wonderful it is,' she said. 'Let me tell you this, now that the party is coming to an end, and before we finally separate: you are delightful – and you won't regret this.'

As she spoke, she nodded her head several times, as if in confirmation of her words and to make him feel their significance.

She seemed so utterly happy that Sanin was amazed. Her face even showed that placid expression that can sometimes be seen on the faces of children, when they are very, very pleased. They walked their horses to the town limit, which was not far away, and then broke into a brisk canter along the highway. The weather was superb, a real summer's day: the wind rushed at them as they rode, and roared and whistled agreeably in their ears. Life was good. Both were possessed by a sense of young and healthy vitality and of the bounding freedom of the ride. Their sense of well-being increased with every instant.

Maria Nikolaevna reined in her horse, and once again set off at a walk. Sanin followed her example.

'There,' she began with a deep and blissful sigh, 'this is the only thing that makes life worth living. If you have succeeded in doing something you wanted to do, something that seemed impossible – well, then, make the most of it, with all your heart, to the very brim.' She drew her hand across her throat. 'And how kind one feels when it happens! Now take me – how kind I am at this moment. I feel I could embrace the whole world! Well, no, not the whole world ... I don't think I could embrace him' – she pointed with her whip at an old beggar, who was making his way along the side of the road. 'But I am ready to make him happy! Here, take this!' she called out loudly in German, and threw a purse at his feet. The heavy little bag (in those days, no one had even thought of the modern form of purse), fell on the road with a thud. The passer-by was astonished and stopped, while Maria Niko-laevna burst into a roar of laughter, and set her horse off at a gallop.

'Do you find riding so amusing?' asked Sanin, when he had overtaken her.

Maria Nikolaevna once again reined in her mare with a sharp movement, as she always did when she wished to stop her.

'All I wanted to do was to get away from gratitude. As soon as someone starts thanking me all the pleasure is gone. After all, I didn't do it for him, but for myself. So how dare he thank me? I didn't catch what you said, what were you asking me?'

'I was asking ... I wanted to know why you are so gay today.'

'Do you know what?' said Maria Nikolaevna, who had either not heard what Sanin had asked her, or else did not think it necessary to answer his question. 'I am very bored with the groom hanging around; I expect that all he's thinking of is when the gentry will decide to go home. How can we get rid of him?' She swiftly produced a note-book from her pocket. 'Shall we send him back to town with a letter? No ... that will not do. Ah? I've got it. What is that over there? An inn?' Sanin glanced in the direction she had indicated.

'Yes, it looks like an inn.'

'Splendid! I shall tell him to stay at this inn and drink beer until we return.'

'But what will he think?'

'What's that to do with us? In any case, he won't even think: he will just drink beer.

'Well, Sanin' (it was the first time that she had addressed him by his surname alone), 'forward, at the canter!'

When they had drawn up at the inn, Maria Nikolaevna called the groom over and gave him his orders. The groom, a man of English origin and English temperament, said nothing, raised his hand to his cap, jumped off his horse and took hold of the reins.

'Well, now we are as free as the birds!' Maria Nikolaevna exclaimed. 'Where shall we make for? The north, the south, the east or the west? Look – I am like the King of Hungary at his coronation ceremony' (she pointed with the end of her whip at the four corners of the earth). 'It's all ours! No, do you know what? Do you see these wonderful hills, and what wonderful hills they are, and what woods! Let us ride up there to the hills, to the hills! *In die Berge, wo die Freiheit thront!*'

She turned off the road and galloped along the narrow, uneven path, which seemed indeed to lead up to the mountains. Sanin galloped after her.


# XLII

The path soon turned into a track and eventually disappeared completely, barred by a ditch. Sanin advised turning back, but Maria Nikolaevna said 'No! I want to go to the mountains. Let's go straight on, as the birds do!' and put her horse over the ditch. Sanin also jumped. Beyond the ditch was a meadow, which was dry at first, then became rather wet, and finally completely marshy. Water was welling up everywhere, forming big puddles. Maria Nikolaevna purposely put her horse at the puddles, laughing heartily and saying repeatedly: 'Let's go mad!'

'Do you know,' she asked Sanin, 'what splash-hunting means?'

'Yes,' Sanin replied.

'My uncle used to splash-hunt with dogs,' she continued. 'I used to go out with him, on horseback, in the spring. Wonderful! Now you and I will go splash-hunting – the only thing is that here are you, a Russian, but you want to marry an Italian. Well, what of it – that's your funeral! What's this, another ditch? Up!'

The horse jumped the ditch, but Maria Nikolaevna's hat fell off and her hair tumbled all over her shoulders. Sanin was about to dismount to retrieve the hat, but she called out to him: 'Don't move, I'll get it myself', bent low from the saddle, caught the veil with the handle of her whip, and did indeed seize the hat. She put it on, but did not gather up her hair, and was off again at the gallop, even uttering a shout as she went.

Sanin sped along beside her, jumped at her side over ditches, fences and streams, tumbled through them and scrambled up again, flying around the hills, into the hills, and looking at her face all the time.

And what a face it is! It is all, as it were, open, the eyes are open, predatory, bright and wild; the lips and nostrils are open too, breathing avidly. She keeps her eyes steadily fixed in front of her, and it seems as if this creature wishes to be mistress of everything she sees before her – the earth, the sky, the sun and the very air – and regrets one thing only, that there are not enough dangers – she would surmount them all. 'Sanin!' she shouts. 'Why, this is just like Buerger's *Lenore*, only you're not dead, or are you? Not dead? Not dead ...? *I* am alive!'

Wild forces are now in play. Here is no Amazon putting her steed to the gallop – a young female Centaur gallops along, half-beast and half-goddess. The placid and well-bred German countryside lies amazed at the trample of her wild Russian Bacchanalia.

At last Maria Nikolaevna drew in her horse: it was covered with foam and sweat, and swayed under her. Sanin's powerful but heavy pony was also breathing hard.

'Well, is it good?' whispered Maria Nikolaevna with some kind of magic in her voice.

'It is good,' the elated Sanin rejoined. His blood was also aflame.

'You wait, you don't know what's coming.' She stretched out her hand. The glove was torn.

'I said I would bring you to the forest, to the mountains. There they are, the mountains!' She was right. Some two hundred paces beyond the point where these bold riders had emerged rose the mountains. They were covered with tall trees. 'Look, there is the path, let us collect ourselves, and go on. But at a walk, we must let the horses recover their breath.'

They set off. Maria Nikolaevna threw back her hair with one strong sweep of her hand. Then she looked at her gloves and drew them off.

'My hands will smell of leather. But you don't mind, do you?'

She was smiling and Sanin was smiling too. This mad gallop seemed finally to have brought them together and made them friends.

'How old are you?' she asked suddenly.

'Twenty-two.'

'No! I am also twenty-two. A good age! Add our years together and it's still a long way from old age. But it's hot! I suppose my face is all red?'

'As red as a poppy.'

She wiped her face with a handkerchief.

'Once we get into the forest we shall be cool. What an old forest it is – like an old friend. Have you any friends?'

Sanin thought for a moment.

'Yes ... But not very many. No real friends.'

'Well, I have some real friends – but not very old ones. This mare – she's a friend, too. How carefully she carries me. Oh, how wonderful it is here. Am I really going to Paris the day after tomorrow?'

'Yes, is it possible?'

'And you will be going to Frankfurt?'

'Yes, I am certainly going to Frankfurt.'

'Well, good luck to you! But this day is ours ... ours ...'

The horses reached a glade and entered. The shadow of the forest closed in on them from every side, soft and expansive.

'Oh, but this is paradise!' Maria Nikolaevna exclaimed. 'Come on, Sanin, deeper, farther into the shade!'

The horses moved quietly 'deeper into the shade', swaying and blowing a little. The path along which they were moving suddenly turned, and led into a narrow gully. A powerful, soporific scent of heather, ferns, pine resin and of last year's decaying leaves pervaded the place. From the crevasses between the brown rocks, a strong sense of dampness assailed them. On each side of the little path rose round mounds covered with green moss.

'Stop!' exclaimed Maria Nikolaevna. 'I want to sit down and rest on this velvet. Help me down!'

Sanin jumped off his horse and ran towards her. She leaned on his shoulders, jumped swiftly to the ground and sat down on one of the mossy clumps. He stood in front of her, holding the reins of both horses.

She looked up at him.

'Sanin, do you know how to forget?'

Sanin remembered what had happened the night before in the carriage.

'What is this – a question or a reproach?'

'I have never reproached anyone in all my life. Do you believe in love charms?'

'What do you mean?'

'Love charms. You know, the kind that they talk about in our folk-songs, in the Russian peasant songs.'

'Oh, that's what you mean,' Sanin said slowly.

'Yes, that. I believe in them, and so will you.'

'Love charms? That's a kind of folk magic,' repeated Sanin. 'Everything in life is possible. I never believed in them, but now I do. I don't recognize myself.'

Maria Nikolaevna was thoughtful for a while, and then looked about her.

'Do you know, I have the impression that I know this spot. Have a look, Sanin, is there a red wooden cross behind that broad oak tree – or am I wrong?'

Sanin took a few paces to the side.

'Yes, yes, there is.'

Maria Nikolaevna grinned.

'Ah, good, very good. I know where we are, we are not lost so far. What is that knocking? A wood-cutter?'

Sanin looked into the woods.

'Yes, there's a man chopping down the dry branches.'

'I must put my hair in order,' said Maria Nikolaevna. 'He might see me and think the worst of me.' She removed her hat and began to plait her long hair, silently, solemnly. Sanin stood in front of her ... the contours of her handsome limbs were clearly apparent to him under the dark folds of the cloth to which some strands of moss were clinging.

Suddenly one of the horses gave a shudder behind Sanin's back. Sanin too trembled involuntarily from head to foot. Everything was confounded inside him – his senses were as tense as strings. He had been right when he said he could not recognize himself. He was, in fact, bewitched. His whole being was filled with ... one thought and one desire. Maria Nikolaevna glanced at him searchingly.

'Well, everything is now as it should be,' she said, putting on her hat. 'Won't you sit down? Here. No, wait ... don't sit down. What is that?'

A dull, quaking sound rolled over the tops of the trees and through the forest air.

'Can that be thunder?'

'It sounds like thunder,' said Sanin.

'Well, well, what could be better, this is a real holiday! That's the only thing that was missing.'

The dull boom sounded again. It rose through the air, then fell, scattering itself in full force.

'Bravo! *Bis!* Do you remember I was telling you yesterday about the *Aeneid*? They were also overtaken by a storm in the woods. However, we must get away.' She jumped to her feet. 'Bring my horse up, will you ... Give me a leg-up – that's right ... I'm not heavy ...' She swung into the saddle like a bird. Sanin also mounted his horse.

'Are you going home?' he asked in a faltering voice.

'Home!!' she replied, dwelling on the word, and then gathered up the reins. 'Follow me!' she ordered, almost brutally. She moved out on to the path, avoiding the red cross, rode down a hollow, reached an intersection, turned right, and then uphill once again ... Evidently she knew where she was going ... and the way she took led farther and farther into the depths of the forest. She did not say a word, and did not look round; she moved forward imperiously, and he followed, obedient and submissive, drained of every spark of will and with his heart in his mouth. A few drops of rain began to fall. She quickened the pace of her horse, he kept close behind her. At last, through the dark greenery of the pine brush, he caught a glimpse of a woodman's humble shelter, with a low door in its wattle wall, set under an overhanging grey rock. Maria Nikolaevna forced her horse through the brush, jumped to the ground and found herself by the entrance to the hut. Turning to Sanin she whispered: 'Aeneas!'

Four hours later Maria Nikolaevna and Sanin, accompanied by the groom, who was nodding in the saddle, returned to Wiesbaden to the hotel.

Polozov came forward to greet his wife, holding in his hand the letter to the estate manager. However, having taken a closer look at her, he showed a certain displeasure in his expression – and even muttered:

'Surely I haven't lost my bet?'

Maria Nikolaevna merely shrugged her shoulders.

And on the same day, two hours later, Sanin stood before her in his room, like a lost man, a man destroyed.

'So where are you going?' she was asking him. 'To Paris, or to Frankfurt?'

'I am going wherever you are, and I will be with you until you drive me away,' he replied in despair, and pressed himself against the hands of his sovereign mistress. She released her hands, placed them on his head and seized his hair with all ten fingers. Slowly she handled and twisted his unresponsive hair ... She drew herself up, quite straight. Her lips curled in triumph. Her eyes, so wide and shining that they looked almost white, showed only the pitiless torpor of one sated with victory. A hawk clawing at a bird caught in its talons sometimes has this look in its eyes.

## XLIII

This is what Dmitry Sanin remembered when, on going
through his old papers in the quiet of his study, he found the
little garnet cross among them. The events which I have
related appeared clearly and in their proper order before his
mind's eye. But, when he came to the moment when he had
turned imploringly to Madame Polozov, when he had so far
abased himself, when he had thrown himself at her feet, when
his enslavement had begun – then he turned aside from the
images which he had conjured up; he did not wish to
remember more. Not that his recollection was unclear – oh
no! He knew, he knew all too well everything that had
happened after that moment, but shame stifled him, even
then, so many years later. He was afraid of the feeling of self-
contempt which he knew he could not conquer, and which he
knew beyond doubt would wash over him, and, like a tidal
wave, drown all other sensations, as soon as he allowed his
memory to speak. But try as he might to turn away from the
mental images which welled up inside him, he was powerless
to obliterate them all.

He remembered the wretched, lachrymose, lying, miserable letter which he had sent to Gemma and which remained
unanswered ... To appear before her, to return to her, after
such deceit, after so great a betrayal – no, no, no! He had had
enough conscience and honour left not to do that. Besides, he
had lost all confidence in himself and all self-respect, he
would no longer have been responsible for anything that
might have happened. Sanin also recalled how later – oh,
shame, shame! – he had dispatched the Polozovs' servant to
Frankfurt to fetch his things, how afraid he had been, with
only one thought in his mind: to Paris, to Paris, to get to Paris
as soon as possible! Then, how, on Madame Polozov's orders,
he had made himself agreeable to her husband and tried to
adapt to his ways – and had exchanged politenesses with
Doenhof, on whose finger he observed an iron ring, identical
with the one that Maria Nikolaevna had presented to him!

There followed recollections which were even worse, even more shaming . . .

A waiter hands him a visiting card – and on it is engraved the name of Pantaleone Cippatola, Court Singer to His Royal Highness, the Duke of Modena. He tries to hide from the old man, but cannot escape a meeting in the passage. And now there rises before him an indignant face beneath a mane of upstanding grey hair: the old eyes burn like coals of fire, and the air resounds with terrible admonitions and maledictions – *maledizione!* There are some frightening words, too: *Cobardo! Infame tradittore!* Sanin closes his eyes and shakes his head, trying again and again to shut out the memories. And yet, now he sees himself seated in a travelling *dormeuse*, on the narrow front seat. On the rear and comfortable seat recline Polozov and his wife. Four well-matched horses are bearing them at the canter along the Wiesbaden road – to Paris! To Paris! Ippolit Sidorych Polozov is eating a pear which he, Sanin, has just peeled for him, while Maria Nikolaevna gazes at him and mocks him with a smile which, as a bondsman or serf, he already knows so well – the smile of the serf owner, of the sovereign lord and master . . .

And, oh God! Is that not Pantaleone again, standing at the corner of the street, not far from the limits of the town? And who is that with him? Can it be Emilio? Yes, it is he, that boy who was so full of enthusiasm and devotion. Why, only the other day his young heart was ready to worship his hero, his ideal – and now? His pale and beautiful face – so beautiful a face that Maria Nikolaevna notices it and leans out of the carriage window – this noble face is now ablaze with anger and contempt; his eyes – so like *those* eyes – are riveted on Sanin and his lips are tight – and then open suddenly to utter an insult . . .

And Pantaleone extends his arm and points out Sanin – to whom? – why, to Tartaglia, who is standing at his side, and Tartaglia barks at Sanin: the very bark of this honest dog sounds like the hardest insult of all to bear . . . Oh, terrible, terrible!

And then, life in Paris, all the degradations and vile sufferings of a slave, who is not permitted either to be jealous or to complain, and who is discarded in the end like a worn-out garment ... Then, the return to Russia, the poisoned life, emptied of all meaning, the petty flurries and the petty worries, the bitter and fruitless contrition, and the equally fruitless and bitter oblivion – the punishment, although it was not evident, was constant, every minute of the day, like some insignificant but incurable pain, a repayment in farthings of a debt which cannot even be calculated ...

The cup is overflowing – enough!

What strange chance had preserved the little cross which Gemma gave to Sanin? Why had he not returned it? How had it happened that he had not discovered it until today? He sat for a long, long, time, plunged in thought and, for all that experience had taught him over so many years, was still quite unable to understand how he had been capable of abandoning Gemma, whom he had loved so tenderly and passionately, for a woman whom he had never loved at all? The next day he surprised all his friends and acquaintances: he announced that he was leaving for abroad.

Society was at a complete loss. Sanin was leaving Petersburg, right in the middle of winter, having only just rented and furnished excellent chambers, and having even taken a season ticket for the performances of Italian opera, in which Madame Patti herself – her very self – Madame Patti in person, was going to appear. His friends and acquaintances were at a loss – but people are not generally given to concerning themselves for long with the affairs of others. And so, when Sanin departed for abroad, there was no one to see him off at the railway station except for a French tailor – and he had only come in the hope of being paid for a little unsettled account '*pour un saut-en-barque en velours noir, tout à fait chic*'.

# XLIV

Sanin told his friends that he was going abroad, but did not tell them precisely where he was going. My readers will easily guess that he made his way straight to Frankfurt. Thanks to the widespread expansion of the railway system, he was already there on the fourth day after leaving St Petersburg. He had not visited the town since that very year of 1840. The white Swan Hotel was still in the same spot, and flourishing, but was no longer considered first class. Frankfurt's main street, the Zeile, had changed very little. But there was no trace left of Signora Roselli's house, nor indeed of the street where her patisserie had once stood. Sanin wandered in a daze through places that had once been so familiar, and could recognize nothing. The buildings that had been there had disappeared, and their place had been taken by new streets, flanked by enormous houses, one adjacent to the other, and by elegant villas. Even the public park, the scene of the avowals of mutual love between him and Gemma, had grown so large and was so changed, that Sanin had to ask himself whether it really was the same place. What was he to do? How, and where was he to make enquiries? After all, thirty years had passed since those days ... it was no easy matter. No one of whom he enquired had ever heard the name Roselli. The owner of his hotel advised him to ask at the public library where they would have the old newspapers. But what use they might be, the hotel owner was unable to explain.

In despair, Sanin enquired after Herr Klueber. This name was well known to his host – but once again, the search was no further advanced. The elegant shop-walker, after resounding success in commerce which raised him to the status of a capitalist, had over-reached himself, gone bankrupt, and died in prison ... This information, incidentally, did not cause Sanin the least distress. He was beginning to think that his journey might have been somewhat precipitous ... and then one day, while he was idly turning over the pages of a

Frankfurt street directory, he happened upon the name von Doenhof, Major, retired (*Major a.D.*). He immediately took a carriage, and drove to the address – though why should *this* Doenhof necessarily be *that* Doenhof? And in any case why should that Doenhof be able to give him any information about the Roselli family? But, no matter. A drowning man clutches at a straw.

Sanin found Major von Doenhof (retired) at home, and immediately recognized his former duelling opponent in the grey-haired man who received him. Doenhof likewise recognized Sanin, and was even pleased to see him: he brought back memories of his youth and of its follies. Sanin learned from him that the Roselli family had long, long ago moved to America, to New York; that Gemma had married a businessman; that, incidentally, he, Doenhof, had an acquaintance, also a businessman, who would probably know the address of Gemma's husband, since he had many commercial dealings with America. Sanin persuaded Doenhof to go round to see his acquaintance and – oh joy! – Doenhof brought him the address of Gemma's husband, Mr Jeremiah Slocum: Mr J. Slocum, New York, Broadway, No. 501. Unfortunately, the address dated from 1863.

'Let us hope,' exclaimed Doenhof, 'that our one-time Frankfurt beauty is still alive and has not left New York! Incidentally,' he added, dropping his voice, 'what about that Russian lady? The one who was then, you remember, on a visit to Wiesbaden – Frau von Bo . . . von Bozoloff – is she still alive?'

'No,' replied Sanin, 'she died years ago.'

Doenhof looked up, but noticing that Sanin had turned away with a frown, did not say another word and withdrew.

That same day, Sanin sent a letter to Mrs Gemma Slocum in New York. He told her that he was writing from Frankfurt, having come there for the sole purpose of discovering some trace of her; that he was only too conscious of the degree to which he had lost the slightest right to expect any answer from her, that he had done nothing to deserve her forgiveness; and that his only hope was that in the midst of the happiness with which she was surrounded, she had long forgotten his very existence. He added that he had plucked up the courage to remind her of himself as a result of a chance circumstance which had only too vividly brought back to him the image of past events; he told her about his life, his solitary life, without family and without joy; implored her to understand the reasons which had moved him to write, and not to let him carry with him to his grave the bitter sense of his guilt – long paid for in suffering, yet not forgiven; and asked her to bring him some happiness by sending him even the briefest account of her life in the new distant world to which she had removed. 'If you write me even one word,' so Sanin concluded his letter, 'you will be doing a good deed, worthy of your fine and generous spirit, and I will thank you for it until I draw my last breath. I am staying here, in the *White Swan Hotel* (he underlined the name) and I will wait – I will wait until the spring for your answer.'

He dispatched the letter and began his vigil. He lived for six whole weeks in the hotel, hardly leaving his room, and seeing absolutely no one. No one could possibly write to him, from Russia or from anywhere else. This was just what he wanted: if a letter should arrive addressed to him, he would know at once that it was *the* letter, the one he was waiting for. He read from morning till night – not the journals, but serious books, works of history. This long period of reading, the silence, the hermit life of the snail in its shell, were all exactly what best suited his state of mind – for that alone he was grateful to Gemma. But was she alive? Would she answer his letter?

It arrived at last: a letter with an American postage stamp, addressed to him from New York. The handwriting on the envelope was English in style. He did not recognize it, and his heart sank … It was some time before he could summon up courage to open the letter. He glanced at the signature: Gemma! Tears started from his eyes: the very fact that she had signed her Christian name alone without surname meant for him an earnest of forgiveness and reconciliation. He unfolded the thin blue sheet of writing paper, and as he did so a photograph slipped out. He quickly picked it up – and was rooted to the spot with amazement. It was Gemma, Gemma to the life, and young as he had known her thirty years before. The eyes, the lips were the same, it was the same face. The back of the photograph was inscribed with the words, 'My daughter Marianna'.

The whole letter was friendly and simple. Gemma thanked Sanin for not hesitating to turn to her, for showing trust in her; she did not conceal from him that, after his flight, she had lived through some painful moments, but added at once that, for all that, she regarded and had always regarded her meeting with him as a source of happiness, since it had prevented her from becoming the wife of Herr Klueber, and thus, if only indirectly, had been the cause of her marriage; that she had lived for over twenty-seven years with her husband in complete happiness, contentment and prosperity: their house was known all over New York. Gemma informed Sanin that she had five children, four sons and an eighteen-year-old daughter, engaged to be married: she enclosed her photograph because, by general consent, they were very much alike. Sad news was reserved for the end. Frau Lenore had died in New York, where she had moved to join her daughter and son-in-law, but she had lived long enough to derive pleasure from the happiness of her children and to enjoy her grandchildren. Pantaleone had also made plans to move to New York, but had died just before he was due to leave Frankfurt. 'And Emilio, our darling, incomparable Emilio, died a hero's death for the freedom of his country in Sicily, where he had been numbered among that thousand who were led by the great Garibaldi. We shed many tears at the death of our brother, who was very dear to us; but even as we wept, we felt proud of him, and we will be eternally proud of him, and we keep his memory sacred. His noble, selfless spirit was worthy of a martyr's crown.' Then Gemma expressed her regret that

Sanin's life seemed to have unfolded so unhappily, wished him, above all, consolation and peace of spirit, and said that she would be glad to meet him again, although she realized that such a meeting was most unlikely to prove possible ...

I cannot attempt to describe what Sanin felt when he read this letter. There are no phrases adequate for such feelings: they are deeper and stronger than any words, and cannot be defined. Music alone could convey them.

Sanin replied at once. As a present for the young bride, he sent 'Marianna Slocum, from an unknown friend' the little garnet cross set in a magnificent pearl necklace. This present, although very costly, did not ruin him: in the course of the thirty years which had passed since his first stay in Frankfurt, he had had time to amass a considerable fortune. In the early days of May he returned to St Petersburg – but hardly for long. They say that he is selling all his estates and is planning to move to America.

# A FIRE AT SEA

TRANSLATED FROM THE FRENCH
BY ISAIAH BERLIN

# Translator's Note

\* \* \*

On May 27, 1838, Ivan Sergeyevich Turgenev, having shortly before graduated at the University of St Petersburg at the age of nineteen, went abroad for the first time. He had some difficulty in persuading his mother, a savage and unbalanced woman who ruled her son like an oriental despot and alternately spoiled and tormented him, to let him continue his studies in philosophy at the University of Berlin. After a special Cathedral service for those about to set out on a voyage, she accompanied him to the boat, the *Nicholas I*, and parted from him in a violent flood of tears, ending, as so often, in hysteria and a fainting fit.

On the third day out the steamer, then about a mile away from Travemünde, caught fire, and was completely destroyed. The great majority of the passengers escaped without injury. Turgenev's behaviour during the fire excited a great deal of talk. According to stories that circulated in Moscow and St Petersburg he had completely lost his head, loudly lamented his approaching end, tried to push his way into the lifeboat, brutally shoving aside women and children, and finally, in full sight of the entire company, seized a sailor by the arm and offered him ten thousand roubles in his mother's name if he would save him, saying that he was the only son of a rich widow and could not bear to die so young. Some nine months after he had safely reached Germany he received a very characteristic letter from his mother. She had no intention of sparing him. 'Why were only your lamentations

noticed on the boat?' she wrote, 'everyone is talking about it
... a great many people speak – it is not very agreeable for me
– about *ce gros Monsieur Tourguéneff qui se lamentoit tant, qui
disoit mourir si jeune* ... there was a Madame Tolstoy there ...
and a Madame Golitsyn ... and many, many others ... ladies,
mothers of families.... Why are all the stories only about
you? That you are a *gros monsieur* is not your fault, but that
you behaved with such cowardice that other people noticed it
in spite of all the panic – this has left a stain on you, if not of
dishonour, certainly of ridicule.' What had really occurred,
and what, if anything, Turgenev said in reply to his mother,
we do not know. What is certain is that he was never again
allowed to forget the incident. His mother had not exaggerated the rumours. Avdotya Panaeva, the wife of a friend and
literary associate of Turgenev in the forties and fifties, and
herself a prominent literary hostess in St Petersburg, tells the
story with immense relish.[1]

Panaeva disliked Turgenev, was fond of gossip and uncon-
trollably malicious; her memoirs, entertaining and often
brilliantly written, are not a repository of objective truth. But
the story had, in any case, gone far beyond her drawing-room.
A very different figure, one of the most celebrated beauties of
her day in Russian society, the half-French Alexandra Smir-

---

1 In her memoirs (A. Panaeva, *Vospominaniya*, Moscow, 1929,
pp. 127–128) she says that shortly after meeting Turgenev in 1842, he told
her about the incident, but described himself as the one man who kept his
head, kept up the spirits of his panic-stricken companions, calmed the
nerves of their hysterical wives and generally displayed great serenity and
courage. She goes on to say that she had first heard about the shipwreck
from a friend of hers who had given her an eyewitness account of it and had
spoken of the peculiar behaviour of a young man who tried to get to the
lifeboat ahead of all the women and children, and then bitterly complained
to all and sundry that the captain had stopped him, exclaiming from time to
time in a heartrending voice, '*Mourir si jeune!*' ... 'One day,' Panaeva
continues, 'I showed my friend – he had come up from the country –
various celebrities at a concert, among them ... Turgenev. "Good gracious!
But this is the very man who kept on screaming *mourir si jeune!*" I was
quite sure that he must be mistaken, but was astonished when he added:
"He has a high, thin voice, very unexpected in that huge, thick frame."'

nova, née de Rosset, the adored friend of Pushkin and of Gogol and a favourite of the Emperor Nicholas, in her readable (and equally unreliable) memoirs gives a slightly different version of the story,[1], which she was probably sedulous in spreading. A good many years later Turgenev avenged himself by using her as the model for his unflattering portrait of the hard-hearted, worldly, cynical mother of the heroine in his novel *Rudin*. Our best authority on literary life in Russia at this time – Pavel Annenkov – tells the same tale.[2] The story of Turgenev's moment of craven fear, variously embroidered and embellished, gained him wide notoriety in the aristocratic-artistic world of the capital.

At first Turgenev did not, or (perhaps from fear of appearing ridiculous) did not wish to seem to, take this too much to heart. In 1855, when he was staying at his estate, Spasskoye, with four or five of his literary friends from St Petersburg, the company wrote and acted a farcical comedy before an audience of country neighbours invited for the occasion. The farce fell flat except for a scene in which a fire broke out and Turgenev himself came running out with the by now celebrated words, 'Save me! save me! I am the only son of my mother!' According to the novelist Grigorovich who described the scene, this caused loud laughter. It is scarcely possible to imagine, say, Tolstoy or Flaubert, caricaturing themselves in this way. Turgenev's behaviour was characteristic of his incurably ironical sense of his own person

---

1 Smirnova (in a letter to her daughter, *vide Zapiski A. O. Smirnovoi*, pt. II, p. 54, St Petersburg, 1895) quotes Prince P. A. Vyazemsky's vivid and malicious eyewitness account to her of how Turgenev ran to and fro on board the burning ship, crying like Schiller's Don Carlos 'To die so young – and nothing achieved!' while Vyazemsky himself displayed sangfroid and courage. Perhaps Vyazemsky, who was an excellent *raconteur*, is the 'witty prince' to whom Turgenev attributes the invention of the unfortunate phrase quoted by Dolgorukov (i.e. 'Save me, save me . . .'). But this can be no more than a conjecture. Vyazemsky, who died in 1878, did not, so far as is known, make any direct mention of the incident.

2 P. V. Annenkov, *Literaturnye vospominaniya*, p. 472 (St Petersburg, 1909).

and conduct, which he often used as a defensive weapon to
blunt the edge of the hostility and mockery which he
constantly excited in his native land.

Nothing was heard of the story for another twelve years,
when a Russian émigré, Prince Peter Dolgorukov, revived it
in his reminiscences which appeared in Geneva in 1867. Peter
Dolgorukov was a queer and unattractive character – a
political exile who suffered for his convictions, and at the
same time a professional mischief maker specializing in
libellous genealogies of noble families of the Russian Empire.
He was almost certainly the author of the notorious anonymous letter that directly led to the death of Pushkin in the
duel (which Dolgorukov has been suspected of trying to
instigate) and he wrote, in addition to his political pamphlets
and blackmailing letters, a series of fascinating memoirs. The
publication abroad of an old and familiar story might perhaps
not have done Turgenev much damage, if a reviewer in Russia
had not, in the course of a generally hostile account of
Dolgorukov's book, quoted the account of Turgenev's cowardice, ostensibly as an example of the author's characteristic
love of malignant invention. Turgenev felt obliged to reply.
In a letter to the editor,[1] he said among other things that 'the
presence of death might well have perturbed a boy of
nineteen, and I have no wish to tell the reader that I looked on
death with indifference, but the words in question, which a
witty prince (not Dolgorukov) had made up on the very next
day, had not been spoken by me. Evidently Prince Dolgorukov, in his wish to insult me, could not find anything better
to say about me than to produce this ancient and absurd piece
of malicious gossip that he has resurrected.'

Dostoevsky, as might have been expected, did not fail to
allude to the incident in his caricature of Turgenev as the
writer Karmazinov in *The Possessed*. All this gave new life to
the story. Melchior de Vogüé, who knew Turgenev well
towards the end of his life, says that his friends often

---

1  *Sankt-Peterburgskiye Vyedomosti*, no. 186, 1868.

entreated him to write something on the subject, but that 'he refused because of a superstitious feeling about his first triumph over death. Only when he saw that she was determined to take her revenge, did he decide to hurl this ancient challenge at her.' This may be so; or perhaps he was simply suffering from a lingering feeling of shame. Be that as it may, in the last year of his life he composed his own account of the incident. He had been ill for over a year, and although the great Charcot had diagnosed his disease incorrectly, Turgenev knew that he was dying. He was dying of cancer of the spine; the pain became progressively more agonizing, and he was able to work only during increasingly rare intervals. By the summer he was no longer able to write and dictated his last stories to his friend Pauline Viardot. *Un Incendie en Mer* was finished in June, and translated into Russian by a writer called A. V. Lukanina soon after. She brought the translation to him in August, about three weeks before his death. 'As to the translation,' she later wrote, 'Turgenev looked through it, and remarked that it had a few gallicisms in it, but on the whole he approved.'[1] This was generous, for the translation is in places gratuitously free.[2] At last the memory of a moment's weakness that must (if my hypothesis is correct) have preyed on him for more than forty years was exorcized, turned into literature, rendered innocuous and even delightful. He represents his own conduct as that of an innocent, confused, romantically inclined young man, neither a hero nor a coward, slightly cynical, slightly absurd, but above all amiable, sympathetic and human. The incident of the panic-stricken appeal to the sailor and the offer of a sum of money is

1 *Severny Vestnik*, 1887, No. 3, p. 87. (Quoted in Vol. 10, p. 645, of Turgenev's collected works, ed. B. M. Eikhenbaum, Moscow, 1956.)

2 The translation here provided is from the French original, published in Paris in 1883 (I. Tourguéneff, *Oeuvres Dernières*, J. Hetzel) with an introduction by the Vicomte E.-M. De Vogüé from which the above quotations are taken. Lukanina's translation, reproduced in all the standard Russian editions of Turgenev, has been excellently edited and annotated in *I. Turgenev, Literaturnye i zhiteiskive vospominaniya* (Leningrad, 1934, ed. A. Ostrovsky), a work of scholarship to which I am greatly indebted.

told in so light and ironical a fashion, and is tucked away so inconspicuously in the rich mass of beautifully described, amusing detail out of which the story is constructed, that his own conduct appears neither craven nor ridiculous. Whatever the facts, and however his own attitude towards them may be interpreted (and we may be sure that both were distorted and exaggerated by his friends and enemies, for, like all great writers, he found that the possession of genius is something that people find it difficult to forgive), the writing itself, despite the conditions in which he was working, shows no falling off in Turgenev's powers. He meant to incude *A Fire at Sea* in a collection of autobiographical fragments, and, like some of the other sketches designed for this purpose, *Monsieur François* (also written in French, and translated into Russian as *The Man in the Grey Spectacles*) and *The Execution of Tropmann*, its value is independent of its considerable biographical or psychological interest, for it is a masterpiece in its own right.

# A Fire at Sea

* * *

It happened in May 1838. With a great many others I was a passenger on board the steamer *Nicholas I*, of the regular Petersburg-Lübeck service. Since, at that time, railways were still in their infancy, everyone travelled by sea. For the same reason many travellers took their own carriages with them, to continue their journey in Germany, France and so on. We had, I remember, no fewer than twenty-eight carriages on our ship. There were about two hundred and eighty passengers on board, including some twenty children. I was then very young, and being a good sailor was able to enjoy all these new impressions. There were several remarkably beautiful or pretty ladies on board – the majority no longer alive, alas!

This was the first time that I was allowed by my mother to travel alone, and I had to promise her to behave sensibly, and above all not to touch cards ... and it was precisely this last promise that was the first to be broken.

One evening there was a large gathering in the main saloon, and there happened to be present several well-known gamblers from St Petersburg. They made up a bank (the game was a kind of *lansquenet*) every evening, and the ring of gold pieces, which in those days were more frequently seen than now, produced a tremendous din. One of these gentlemen, observing that I kept apart, and not knowing the reason for it, suddenly invited me to join his game; when I, with all the naïveté of my eighteen years,[1] told him why I preferred to

1 He was in fact nearer twenty (translator's note).

abstain, he burst out laughing and, turning to his friends, exclaimed that he had found a real treasure: a young man who had never touched cards, and was consequently destined to have the most fabulous, the most unheard of luck, real beginner's luck. ... I don't know how it happened, but ten minutes later, I was at the card table, my hands full of cards, firmly installed – and playing, playing like mad.

I must admit that the ancient proverb turned out to be true enough. Money flowed towards me in streams: two little heaps of gold rose higher and higher on either side of my trembling, sweating hands. The gambler who had inveigled me into the game kept working me up, and ceaselessly egged me on. I really did believe that my fortune was made!

Suddenly, the door of the saloon was flung wide open, a lady rushed in, crying in a despairing, strangled voice, 'The ship is on fire!' and fell in a dead faint on the sofa. This produced the most violent commotion. Everybody leaped from their seats: gold, silver, banknotes, rolled and scattered in every direction, and we all hurled ourselves through the doors. How we had failed before this to notice the smoke which, by now, was pouring in upon us from all sides, I simply cannot conceive! The stairs were full of it. A reddish glow, as of burning coal, flared up here and there. In an instant everyone was on deck. Two vast swirling pillars of smoke rose on either side of the funnel and along the masts, and a most terrible uproar began, which from then on never ceased. The chaos was unbelievable: one felt that each one of these human beings was in the violent grip of the most desperate instinct of self-preservation, among them not least myself. I remember that I grasped a sailor by the arm and promised him ten thousand roubles in my mother's name if he managed to save me. The sailor naturally could not take these words seriously, and prised himself loose from me; nor indeed did I myself insist, realizing that what I was saying made little sense; but, then, what I saw round me did not make any better sense. Nothing, it has been truly observed, can equal the tragedy of a shipwreck, save only its comedy.

For example, a rich country squire, beside himself with terror, was crawling on his hands and knees along the floor, prostrating himself from time to time in an absolute frenzy; but when the water, which was being poured in vast quantities into the coal-holes, for a moment checked the fury of the flames, he rose to his full height, and shouted in a voice of thunder: 'Men of little faith! Did you really think that our God, the God of Russia, would abandon us?' At this very moment the flame suddenly leaped higher, and the unfortunate man of much faith again went down on all fours, and began to kiss the floorboards once more. A general, with a fixed, haggard stare kept bellowing: 'We must send a courier to the Emperor! When there was a mutiny of the military settlements, a courier was sent, I was there, I was there myself, and this did save at any rate some of us!' Another gentleman, who had an umbrella in his hands, suddenly began to stab ferociously at a poor little portrait in oils, tied to an easel, that stood near him among the luggage; with the tip of his umbrella he pierced five holes through its eyes, nose, mouth and ears. He accompanied this act of destruction with cries of 'What is the use of all this now?' And the picture did not even belong to him! A plump man, bathed in tears, who looked like a German brewer, kept on moaning 'Captain! Captain!' ... And when the captain, who finally lost patience, seized him by the scruff of his neck and shouted at him, 'Well? I am the captain! What do you want?' the fat man looked at him in a dazed way, and again began moaning 'Captain!'

It was actually this captain who saved all our lives. First, because at the very last moment, when it was still possible to get to the machine-room, he altered our course. If our ship had continued on straight to Lübeck, instead of turning sharply towards the shore, she would have been burnt out before she reached harbour. And secondly, because he ordered the sailors to draw their dirks and show no mercy to anyone who tried to touch one of the two remaining lifeboats – the others had capsized owing to the inexperience of

passengers who had themselves tried to lower them into the
sea. The sailors, for the most part Danes, with their cold,
energetic faces, the reflected light of the flames giving an
almost blood-stained glint to the blades of their knives,
inspired instinctive terror. There was a fairly strong squall; it
was made stronger still by the fire roaring through a good
third of the ship. I must admit, unflattering though this may
be to my own sex, that on this occasion the women showed
more spirit than most of the men. Pale, white-faced, the night
found them in their beds (instead of clothes they had blankets
thrown over them), and unbeliever as I already was, they
seemed to me like angels descended from heaven to shame us
and give us more courage. However, there were men, too,
who showed daring. I remember one particularly, Monsieur
D-V, our former Russian ambassador in Copenhagen: he had
taken off his shoes, tie, and coat which he tied by the sleeves
round his chest, and sitting on a thick taut cable, and
swinging his legs, he quietly smoked his cigar and surveyed us
each in turn with an expression of mocking pity. As for me, I
found a refuge on an outside stair and sat down on one of the
lower steps. I gazed with stupefaction on the crimson foam
boiling below, the spray of which I felt on my face, and kept
saying to myself: 'So this is where one must die at the age of
eighteen!' for I had firmly resolved to be drowned rather than
fried. The flame rose above me in an arch, and I quite clearly
distinguished its roar from that of the waves.

Near me, on the same steps, sat a little old woman,
probably a cook who belonged to one of the families travelling
to Europe. Her head hidden in her hands, she seemed to be
whispering prayers – suddenly she threw a quick glance
towards me, and, whether because she imagined that she saw
some fatal resolution upon my face, or for some other reason,
anyway she seized my arm and in an imploring tone said to
me with great earnestness: 'No, Sir, nobody may do as he will
with his life – you no more than anyone else. We must accept
what Providence sends us – otherwise it would mean taking
your own life, and you would pay for that in the next world.'

I had not felt the least inclination to suicide, but now, out
of some kind of bravado quite inexplicable in my position, I
once or twice pretended to be about to carry out the intention
she attributed to me – and each time the poor old woman
would rush towards me to prevent what in her eyes would
have been a crime. In the end I felt a sort of shame, and
stopped. And really, why this comedy in the presence of death
which, at that moment, genuinely seemed to me imminent
and inevitable? However, there was no time either to meditate
about the strangeness of these feelings, or to admire the
absence of egoism (to-day it would be called 'altruism') of the
poor woman, for at this moment the roaring of the flames
above our heads redoubled in fury; when, suddenly, a voice
that rang like bronze (this was the voice of our rescuer)
sounded above us: 'What are you doing down there, you poor
wretches? You will never escape, follow me!' And at once,
knowing neither who was calling, nor where we had to go, the
old woman and I jumped up as if propelled by a spring, and
threw ourselves through the smoke behind a sailor in a blue
jacket who was climbing up a rope ladder. Not knowing why,
I too climbed the ladder behind him; I think that if at this
moment he had flung himself into the water, or had done
anything else, however extraordinary, I should have followed
him blindly. Having hoisted himself up two or three rungs,
the sailor jumped heavily down on to the roof of one of the
carriages, the lower part of which was already in flames. I
jumped after him and heard the old woman jump behind me;
then, from the first carriage, the sailor jumped on to a second
carriage and then on to a third, with me always behind him; in
this way we presently reached the bow of the ship.

Nearly all the passengers were gathered there. The sailors,
under the eye of the captain, were lowering one of our two
lifeboats into the sea – fortunately the largest. Across the
other side of the ship, I saw the steep line of cliffs that stretch
along the shore towards Lübeck lit up vividly by the fire. It
was well over a mile to the foot of the cliff. I could not swim –
the shoal on which we were grounded (without even noticing

it) was probably shallow enough, but the waves were very high. Nevertheless, as soon as I saw the rocks, I was overwhelmed by the feeling that I was saved; to the astonishment of my companions, I jumped into the air several times and cried 'Hip, Hip, Hurrah!'. I had no wish to go towards the place where the crowd was swarming thickest in order to reach the ladder which led to the big boat – there were too many women, old men and children there. Besides, ever since I had seen the rocks, I was no longer in a hurry: I was certain that I was saved. I noticed with surprise that almost none of the children showed any fear; several of them even fell asleep against their mother's shoulder. Not a single child perished.

I noticed among a group of passengers a tall general, his clothes streaming with water; he was quite motionless, leaning on a bench which he had just pulled out of the wall and stood upright. I learned that in the first moment of terror he had brutally pushed aside a woman who wanted to get in front of him in order to jump into one of the lifeboats that later capsized. One of the stewards threw him back on to the ship. The old soldier, ashamed of his moment of cowardice, swore he would be the last to leave the ship, after the captain. Stately, pale, bleeding from a wound in the forehead, he stared with a crushed, resigned look upon his face, as if asking for forgiveness.

In the meantime I made my way towards the port side of the ship, and I saw our little lifeboat dancing on the waves like a toy; two sailors were making signs from it inviting the passengers to jump, but this was perilous and by no means easy. The *Nicholas I* was a high-decked steamer, and one had to drop with extreme skill not to upset the lifeboat. Finally I decided to do it. I began by placing myself on the anchor chain which was stretched alongside the ship, and was just about to leap, when a soft, heavy mass fell on me. A woman clutched me round the neck and hung like a dead weight on me. I must admit that my first impulse was to force the hand off my neck and get rid of the mass by flinging it over my head; most fortunately, I did not yield to it. The initial shock nearly threw us both into the sea, but luckily, just in front of me, suspended from I don't know where, a piece of rope was waving in the air; I seized it with one hand so violently that it bled . . . then, glancing down I saw that my burden and I were just over the lifeboat, and . . . praise be to God! I slid down . . . the boat cracked in all its seams . . . 'Hurrah!' cried the sailors.

I laid down my companion, who had in the meanwhile fainted, on the floor of the boat, and at once turned to look at the ship; I saw a multitude of heads, especially female ones, feverishly pressing alongside. 'Jump!' I cried, stretching out my arms. At this moment the success of my bold attempt and my conviction that the flames could not reach me, filled me with unbelievable strength and courage: and I caught the only three women who ventured to jump into my boat as easily as apples tossed at one in an orchard. All these ladies, I may add, always uttered a piercing scream as they jumped, and invariably fainted on arrival. One fellow, probably from sheer panic, nearly killed one of these unfortunate women by throwing a heavy travelling chest which broke to pieces as it fell into our boat, revealing a valuable dressing case. Without asking myself whether I had a right to dispose of it I instantly presented it to two sailors, who, just as unhesitatingly, accepted it.

We at once started to row with all our might towards the shore, followed by cries of 'Come back quickly! Send us back the boat!' When the water was no more than about three feet deep, we therefore had to climb out. A fine, cold drizzle had set in more than an hour before; it had had not the slightest effect on the fire, but it drenched us to the bone.

Finally we reached the happy shore which turned out to be nothing but a gigantic pool of liquid, sticky mud into which we sank up to the knees. Our boat left rapidly and, like the bigger lifeboat, began to shuttle to and fro from ship to shore. Only a few passengers perished, eight in all: one fell into the coal-hole, another was drowned because he insisted in taking all his money with him – this last, whose name I hardly knew, had been playing chess with me during most of the day with

such fanaticism that Prince W ...,[1] who had been watching
our game, could not help exclaiming: 'You look as if your lives
were at stake!' As for the baggage, it was nearly all lost,
including the carriages.

Among the ladies rescued from the shipwreck, there was a
Madame T ...,[2] very pretty and charming, but encumbered
by her four little girls and their nurses. Consequently she was
left deserted on the shore, barefoot, her shoulders scarcely
covered. I felt called upon to behave gallantly; this cost me
my coat which, until then, I had managed to preserve, my
cravat and even my boots. Furthermore, the peasant with a
cart drawn by a couple of horses, whom I had gone to find on
the top of the cliff and duly sent on to meet the ladies, did not
consider it necessary to wait for me, and drove off to Lübeck
with all my companions, so that I found myself alone, half-
naked, soaked to the skin, in sight of the sea where our ship
was slowly burning itself out. I say 'burning itself out'
deliberately, because I should never have believed that such a
huge contraption could be destroyed so quickly. It was now
no more than a large patch of flame, motionless on the surface
of the sea, furrowed with the black silhouettes of funnels and
masts, while seagulls, in their heavy, impassive flight, circled
about it – and soon after, a vast clump of ash strewn with tiny
sparks falling in large curves upon the by now more tranquil
waves. 'And is this all?' I thought, 'is our whole life, then,
only a handful of ashes scattered by the wind?'

Fortunately for the philosopher whose teeth had begun to
chatter violently, another carter picked me up. For this the
good man made me pay two ducats, but he did wrap me in his
thick cloak and sang two or three Mecklenburg songs for my
benefit, which I thought quite pretty. I reached Lübeck at
dawn. Here I met my fellow victims, and we went to
Hamburg together.

1 Probably Prince Vyazemsky, see footnote 1 (p. 241) of Translator's
Note.
2 Almost certainly the wife of the famous poet Tyutchev who was a
Russian diplomat in Munich at this date (translator's note).

There we found twenty thousand silver roubles which the Emperor Nicholas, who at that very moment happened to be passing through Berlin, had sent us by one of his equerries. The gentlemen unanimously agreed to offer his money to the ladies. It was all the easier for us to do this since in those days any Russian traveller in Germany enjoyed unlimited credit. Now this is no longer so!

The sailor to whom I had offered a fantastic sum of money in my mother's name if he saved me, appeared to demand the fulfilment of my promise. But as I was not quite sure whether he was really the very same sailor, and since, moreover, he had done absolutely nothing to rescue me, I offered him a thaler which he was only too glad to accept.

As for the poor old cook who had been so concerned to save my soul, I never saw her again, but I feel quite happy about her. Whether she was roasted or drowned, she had a place reserved in paradise.

BOUGIVAL June 17, 1883

## ABOUT THE INTRODUCER

SIR VICTOR PRITCHETT was born in England in 1900. A novelist, critic and short story writer, he has also written two celebrated volumes of autobiography and literary lives of Chekhov, Balzac and Turgenev.

## ABOUT THE TRANSLATORS

Formerly President of the British Academy (1974–1978) and Professor of Social and Political Theory in Oxford (1957–1967), SIR ISAIAH BERLIN, O.M., was the first President of Wolfson College, Oxford. Among many other volumes, he is the author of *Karl Marx*, *Four Essays on Liberty* and *Vico and Herder*.

LEONARD SCHAPIRO was a distinguished historian of the Soviet Communist Party, and the author of a biography of Turgenev (*Turgenev: His Life and Times*, 1978). He died in 1983.

# TITLES IN EVERYMAN'S LIBRARY